DOMINO EFFECT

Kristin Mayer

Domino Effect
Book Two of The Effect Series

Cover Designer: Lisa Jay
(http://lisajaystudio.com/)
Interior Designer: JT Formatting
(http://www.facebook.com/JTFormatting)
Editor: Nichole Strauss with Perfectly Publishable
(https://www.facebook.com/perfectlypublishable)

Domino Effect / Kristin Mayer – 2nd ed.
Library of Congress Cataloging-in-Publication Data
ISBN-13: 978-0-9899913-9-1

VISIT MY WEBSITE AT
http://www.authorkristinmayer.com

Dedication

I dedicate this book to my *Aunt Pam* –

The *warrior* of our family.
I wish everyone could have
someone like *you* in their lives.

Brandt

I ROLLED OVER and looked at the clock. It was five in the morning, and I hadn't slept worth a shit. My head throbbed and my throat felt dry. Throwing the sheet aside, I sat up and placed my feet on the floor. *Hell, it's cold*! I leaned my head to the side to crack my neck. For a few seconds after the pop, my head felt pressure-free. The relief was short-lived, as the suffocating throb started again. At least it was obvious from the throbbing pain that I was alive. I pushed myself off the bed and threw on some sweatpants.

My head was a fucking mess after seeing Nikola last night. I was still in love with her, even after having not seen her for almost a year. *Shit.* Last night had been a disaster from the get-go. I rehashed what had happened for the millionth time.

Adam, my business partner and best friend since childhood, and I were the only ones at Club Envy. We always closed on New Year's Eve so we could go out and have some fun. The club lost a shit-ton of money, but our employees appreciated it, so what the hell? I hated having the bar closed since losing Nikola. It meant I had to find something to fill the hours. For the fifth time, I made sure all the cameras were working before I headed to Adam's office. Since it reminded me of the girl I'd lost in a bout of stupidity, I rarely used my office. Instead, I'd taken over the security station within the club. I peered through the open door and saw Adam focused on his computer.

I knocked. "Hey, man, you need anything?"

Adam hit a few more keys then closed his laptop. "Nah, I got it done. I'm about to leave. You still going with Trigger tonight?"

Adam and Ainsley had invited me to hang out with them. But hell, that was like salt in the wound. I was happy for my friend, but there was also a tinge of jealously. I'd had that happiness once but had thrown it away. New Year's Eve was not a good time to be around a newly engaged couple. They'd be involved in a complete shag-fest tonight.

I cracked my neck. "Yeah, he's convinced we'll get more ass by teaming up. I figure I'll see if anything catches my fancy. May get a quick fuck in. Who knows?"

*Adam gave me that look, so I headed it off before he could bring up...*her. *"I know you think I should contact Nikola, but after what I put her through with my addiction, she deserves to be happy."*

Adam stood to leave. "I know. I'm not going to say anything about it. You know what I think, but you're your own man. It's your life. I think you need to take your own advice—

you know, what you told me about Ainsley. That's all."

Adam knew I wasn't going to respond to that statement. We'd been friends for too damn long.

We were in the bar area turning off all the lights when Adam asked, "Where are you going tonight with Trigger? Is it that girl bar he prowls when there isn't anything here he wants to tap?"

I chuckled. "Yeah, Coyote Ugly. He says it's the best place to get a piece. You still taking Ainsley into the city tonight?"

We walked out of the club and I locked up, rechecking everything as we went. Outside, it was cold enough to see our breath in the night air.

"Yeah, after all the family time we had over Christmas, I wanted us to have some uninterrupted us *time. She's with our moms, baking."*

Ainsley's mom had come back for Christmas and was leaving tomorrow to go back to Arizona to be with her aunt for a little while longer. The past week had been nothing but celebration after Adam and Ainsley announced their engagement. I was happy for them, I really was, but it hurt—I wanted that, too.

We walked a few steps as Adam added, "I think we've about figured out a date. Sometime this summer after she's done with school, before she starts working."

Adam had asked me to be his best man the moment he told me he'd asked Ainsley to marry him. Of course I'd agreed. I was honored. "Sounds good. I'm happy for you, man. You deserve it."

I veered off to my SUV and ended the conversation. "Have fun, Happy New Year. Are you guys still coming over tomorrow for the traditional collards and black-eyed peas at my mum's?"

"Of course we are! Ainsley talked to your mom and is bringing some sort of dessert she's baking. Happy New Year to you, too, Brandt. See ya tomorrow."

As I closed the door I said, "See ya."

I put the key in the car and cranked it, cursing to myself. I hadn't used my automatic car starter. I hated the cold, but I hated wearing a coat even more.

Trigger texted me.

Trigger: You ready? I'll meet you there. I'm about two minutes away. My buddy texted and said there's gonna be pussy a-plenty.

Me: I'm on my way.

As I pulled out of the parking lot, I tried to tell myself that I'd be fucking someone senseless tonight. Maybe that would get this restless feeling out of my system. I made a mental note to call my sponsor this week. I needed to talk to him. He helped keep it real and understood me in a way that you can't unless you're a recovering addict.

A few minutes later, I pulled up to the bar. In pink neon letters was the name of the bar.

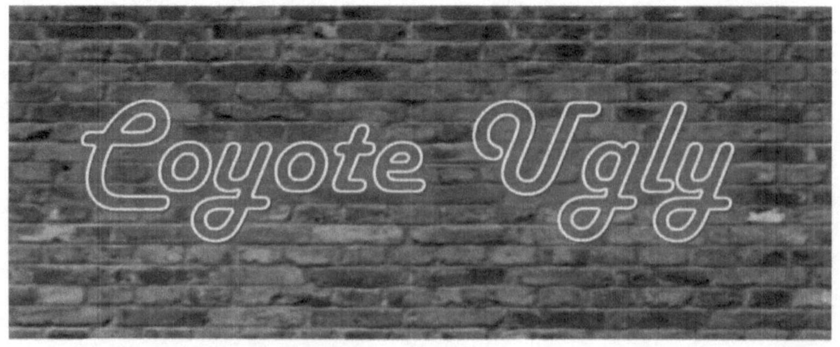

I opened my car door and headed inside. Rock music blared and there were girls dancing up on the bar. I saw potential ass in here, but every time I tried to think about fucking someone, Nikola's face flashed in my mind. That was always the problem that kept me from pursuing anyone else. I couldn't go through with it. The one time I had, guilt had plagued my thoughts for days. I spotted Trigger across the bar at a table with two ladies.

Obviously, everyone was on the prowl tonight, looking for hookups. Lust filled the air as bodies ground against one another. Some rubbed against me. Nothing happened in response; I wasn't interested. Hell, I felt like a pansy.

I went over to the table. "Hey, man."

Trigger looked like as if he'd already been hitting the booze pretty hard. I drank in moderation these days. I'd learned the hard way that anything in excess led to trouble.

"Hey, Brandt. This is Amy and Lucy."

They were both gorgeous. I tried to force my mind to get in the game. Nikola wasn't an option, so I needed to make the most of what was left of my life: empty meaningless sex. Amy licked her lips, and I decided to go for her since Lucy already had her hand on Trigger. Amy had blonde hair and vivid blue eyes. She wore a tight, black mini skirt with a sparkly blue halter top. The outline of her nipples showed through the top. She'd be a good distraction—I hoped.

"What's your poison, Amy?"

Amy leaned in closer to me. "Cranberry and Vodka."

"You got it."

I signaled and the waitress came to the table. "Guinness for me, cranberry and vodka for the lady."

The waitress nodded and took off toward the bar.

Amy put her lips to my ear. "How about you and I go somewhere and start the night right before our drinks come back—there's not room for two of us under the table. I want to take turns getting each other off all night while we ring in the New Year."

Well, she was forward. Trigger gave me a wink and took a swig of his beer. I leaned over slightly to see that Lucy was under the table giving him head. Fuck. The girls were horny tonight, that was for damn sure.

I looked at Amy and decided some space was needed while I tried to push Nikola to the far recesses of my mind. "Give me a minute. I'll be back."

I pushed away from the table and headed to the bar to intercept my beer. She called after me, "Hurry back."

Without bothering to reply, I kept walking. There was a very good chance I would not be coming back to the table. I might leave. I was messed up. I'd definitely be setting up a meeting next week with my sponsor. Decision made, I started toward the bar. I'd take a shot, pay for the drinks, then leave. The music rocked around me, but I wanted to be home. Making it to the bar, I laid my hand on the cool counter.

When the bartender came over, I said, "Shot of tequila."

"You got it." She went to work, barely speaking as the throng of people kept moving toward the bar. The place was packed.

I pulled out a twenty and handed it to her. "Keep the change."

"Thanks." She stuffed it in her pocket and went to the next customer.

Someone pushed past me as I was about to down the shot.

"I'm so sorry. It's packed."

I froze. That voice. I turned and the auburn-haired, green-eyed goddess I'd only dreamed about seeing again stared back at me. She had on leather pants and a low-cut red shirt. I remembered how good those breasts felt in my hands. My cock was fully erect now at the sight of her. I still wanted her. I still loved her.

"Nikola—"

"Brandt—"

Her eyes searched mine, and I saw it—the flicker of emotion between us that I'd thought was dead. She still had some sort of feelings for me. But to what extent?

I set my shot back on the counter. "How have you been?"

"Good, how about you?" She swallowed hard, and I could feel something crackling between us.

Before I had a chance to respond, hands came around my waist. "I was missing you at our table. I think it's time we found ourselves some privacy. I want you."

Fucking hell.

Nikola walked backward. "I can't do this. I need to go."

She turned and rushed into the sea of people. I called after her. "It's not what you think."

Fuck.

I took Amy's hands off me. "It's not going to happen."

She pouted, but I turned away, searching for Nikola. I needed to find her and explain what she'd seen. A new determination to fight for her— for us—filled me. I hoped she'd listen to me.

Pushing through the crowd, I saw the top of her auburn hair at the side door. Not caring about anyone else, I pushed harder to get through. If she'd give me a chance to apologize, to make things right, we could take it slow. The metal door was heavy as I shoved it open. Nikola stood there, waiting on the curb.

"Nikola...wait. It's not what you think."

She turned, an alarmed look in her eyes. "That's what you always used to say when I'd catch you with drugs."

Her words knocked the breath out of me. Nikola was the one who'd been the most affected by my drug addiction. "Nikola, I don't know what to say... I've changed. Can we talk?"

Her lip trembled and it looked as if she was about to capitulate when a black sports car pulled up beside her. Some dark-haired, built asshole got out of the car. He looked me up and down, sizing me up. A possessive rage boiled within me as he put his hands around Nikola's waist. It was an instinct that had been ingrained in me—she'd been mine for so long before I'd lost her. I reminded myself she wasn't mine now. Whoever this guy was, he leaned down and whispered something in her ear.

I gave it one last shot. "Nikola, two minutes of your time."

She looked at me with tears in her eyes as the guy brought her closer. She shook her head. "I can't, Brandt. Not right now. I hope you're better, but I...I...I need to go."

The asshole opened her door and said something else. She shook her head, and he shut the door. He glared my way. "Brandt, I think you've caused her enough grief. Leave her the hell alone. She doesn't need someone who can't be depended on."

I was stunned, not knowing what to say after that low blow. I deserved it, but it still felt like shit. I had *changed and* was *clean. The guy looked at me like he had Nikola's best interest at heart. I wondered if she'd moved on with him. If I was too late.* Am I too late? *The Nikola I remembered was full of life, happy. In the past, she'd have run into my arms and I would have kissed the life from her. We'd been each other's everything. The Nikola that I'd seen had looked broken and sad. All I wanted to do was chase her and explain that I was better. She'd been changed by my decision to use. This was all my fault. The red lights faded as the car drove away with the love of my life in the passenger seat.*

I forced myself to think of something other than last night. Making my way to the kitchen, I put a pod in the coffee machine and pushed the blue button that would give me my beloved cup of java. Finally taking a sip of black coffee, I looked around my house. It looked as if I hadn't been here long. Only the essentials occupied the space, no decorations. In the last place I'd owned, Nikola had lived there with me. She'd taken care of making the place feel like a home. *Our home.* Our home was where all hell had broken loose, ending us. After rehab, I couldn't live with the guilt of what I'd done, so I'd sold the house and bought a smaller place. This place.

Needing to talk to my sponsor, Quentin, ASAP, I picked up my phone from the counter where it had been tossed last night, and sent a text.

Me: Hey, can you meet today? I need to talk. Saw Nikola last night.

Quentin: Sure thing. Can we meet at Dave's Diner in fifteen minutes?

Me: Thanks, man. Works for me.

The diner was only five minutes away. I made my way back to the bedroom to change into jeans and a long-sleeved shirt. Hopefully, Quentin could help me sort through all this shit. Even though I loved Nikola, I had to wonder if it harmed me to hold onto the memory of us. Maybe she was better off without me. Would she be better off if I let her go…forever? I hoped Quentin could help—somehow.

Nikola

THE AROMA OF sausage and biscuits caused me to open my eyes. Grandmama was up and cooking breakfast. My body was so tired—I hadn't slept very well last night. Every time I closed my eyes, I saw Brandt at the club last night. His blue eyes pierced me in my dreams. I longed to run my hands through the blond hair that fell to his shoulders. I wanted his strong arms wrapped around my body. Last night, Brandt had looked healthy—not sick like the last time I'd seen him right before he entered rehab. Instead of going to another bar after seeing him, I decided to spend some time with Grandmama in the comforts of her home. She'd always helped to ground me while I sorted through tough stuff. Even though I had my own place, I had a room here. Grandmama's home was the place that gave me solace and peace.

I got out of bed and glanced up at the kitten puzzle we'd put in a picture frame. Three kittens in a sewing basket looked back at me. Putting the puzzle together was a project Grandmama and I had done on a rainy day. A perfect memory for a perfect day. I headed toward the kitchen. I imagined seeing my Grandaddy at the end of the long bar on the last of its five barstools. He'd always greeted me with, *Morning, monkey, your apple juice is in the refrigerator—chilled like you like it.* But he'd died three years ago from lung cancer. I pushed the memory aside. Losing a grandparent was hard.

"Morning, Grandmama. Breakfast smells delicious."

Grandmama turned and gave me a sweet smile. Her blonde hair was short and perfectly styled. Her blue eyes sparkled—she didn't look a day more than fifty, even though she was in her seventies. She was beautiful. I hoped I would age well like she had.

Grandmama put the gravy into a dish and set it on a trivet next the plate of sausage and biscuits on the bar. Giving me a hug, she said, "Morning. How'd you sleep?"

I sat on the barstool and fixed myself a plate. "Horrible. I'm sorry I came here so late without calling. I needed to be here, where it feels like home."

My parents had lived in China for the past five years. Dad had gotten a huge promotion to run the Asian branch of the sales company he'd been with for twenty years. The decision for them had been swift and, within weeks, my childhood home and everything I'd ever known had been gone. That's when I'd moved from Arkansas to Georgia to be closer to Grandmama. When he had time, I talked to my dad about once a month. Our conversations usually lasted only a few minutes before we were interrupted and my father had to leave for business.

Interaction with my mom was even rarer. I tried to feel fortunate that I still got to see them twice a year, usually for a couple of days before they'd take off on a small vacation for themselves. Whether they were plugged into my life or not, it was hard being away from my family.

One nice thing about being self-employed as a Strategic Analyst was that it allowed me to work from home. Companies would hire me to review their sales numbers, trends, and problematic areas—I'd then help them develop a strategy to increase productivity for items trending down. My business was growing, and I was pleased at the success I'd achieved on my own. Since *the* break-up, I'd thrown myself into my work. If I worked, I could almost ignore my loneliness. I missed Brandt, though. I missed us.

Grandmama sat on a little stool in front of me. That side of the bar had cabinets, but Grandmama liked us to look at each other when we talked. She'd always done that, even when the kitchen was filled with the entire family. "This is your place too. You come here anytime you want. You know I love having you."

I pushed a piece of sausage around on my plate. "I saw Brandt last night. He was at the same bar as me."

That got Grandmama's attention. She stopped eating. "Are you okay? Did he go back to drugs?"

Of course, Grandmama knew everything that had happened with Brandt and me.

"I'm okay. Brandt looked good. He looked like he did the first time I saw him, actually, at that concert where we met. Seeing him last night, though—it awoke so many emotions in me. Wesley arrived right when this happened, so I left without giving Brandt a chance to speak."

"Did he know you were there?" Concern was evident in

my grandmother's voice.

I shook my head. "I don't think so. He looked as startled as I felt. I was about to ask how he was doing when a girl came up and draped herself all over him. Seeing that gutted me." I took a breath and wiped a tear from my eye.

Grandmama took a sip of her orange juice. The New Year had started with a bang. I wished there was a redo button. "Do you think he's with someone else?"

The thought of him dating someone else bothered me. After seeing him last night, there was a part of me that still felt as if I had a claim on him. I was too scared to face the reality that he'd moved on. A part of me hoped that he'd reach out to me when he got healthy and clean, but he hadn't.

"He said it wasn't what it seemed. But I've heard that line so many times—and it was usually a lie. I honestly can't be sure. I'm so confused." I took a deep breath as all the confusion bubbled to the surface. "Maybe talking to him would give me closure. But I don't think I want it to be over. What should I do?"

She scrunched her brow and took another sip of juice. "I don't know, Nikola. Only you can decide which path you should be on. Sometimes we want what's bad for us and we should stay away. But sometimes, it's truly the path we were meant to be on. It can take work to pull all the weeds to see what's beneath the surface."

This conversation wasn't helping much. "He may not even have feelings for me."

"Will you contact him?" I loved the soothing tone in her voice.

I wanted to call him, but I feared what I'd find behind that door. "I haven't decided."

We ate for a few minutes, and I tried to single out just one thought from the mess running through my mind.

"What if he comes and seeks you out?"

Excitement lit inside of me at the thought of being near him again, but thinking I might hurt his recovery dampened that feeling. I always wondered if I was part of the trigger that had sent Brandt toward drugs. Deep down, I knew this was one of the reasons I'd never tried to reconnect. Brandt's wellbeing came first—before my broken heart.

"There's still a lot of unanswered questions. I want to talk, but I'll have to see."

"I think that's a wise decision. Are you still up for cooking our traditional black-eyed peas and collards dinner today?"

Grateful for the subject change, I got up and kissed her on the cheek. She smelled like the skin cream she used religiously, night and day. It was subtle and sweet.

"Of course I am. I wouldn't miss it for the world! I'm going to take a shower-bath, then I'll be ready."

Shower-bath was a term my dad had coined when I was a kid before work had consumed him and he became uninvolved in my life. He would announce it every time before he went to get ready. The whole thing was silly since it was a contradictory term, but it had become part of our family's vocabulary.

Grandmama chuckled, then coughed heavily. She'd been doing that a lot lately. I went to her side.

"Maybe you should have that checked out. It seems it's getting worse."

She patted my hand as she stopped coughing. "It's just a winter cold."

"I'll make you an appointment."

"Okay, Nikola."

Grandmama hated going to the doctors since Granddaddy had passed. I kissed her cheek, then headed for the shower.

In the bathroom across the hall from my bedroom, I turned on the shower. I stared in the mirror as steam formed a cloudy layer on the surface. Brandt was in the forefront of my mind. My hair lay tumbled around my face while I stared at my reflection. My eyes looked tired, and I sighed wearily. As though it had clouded out the present, when the last of the steam covered the mirror, I thought back to the last night we'd spent at our home before I'd left him.

A client had flown in from New York to go over my plan to market their new microfiber cloth. I had a major rebranding strategy to share that would hopefully solve their problems. However, the meeting had gone later than I intended.

Walking up to our front door, I took a deep breath. I opened the door not knowing what was going to be on the other side. Brandt and I had been together for three years. Almost a year ago, we'd decided to move in together. And until three months ago, we'd been madly in love. He was my soul mate. My heart. My world. But he'd been changing, distancing himself from me.

At first, the change in Brandt had been sporadic—like every other week. From there, the frequency of the mood swings increased. Most times, it'd be early morning and I'd be dead asleep. Brandt would come in noisily, hours after leaving his club, feeling like a million bucks and ready to conquer the world. He'd be vivacious and ready to go on crazy adventures that didn't even make sense. In Brandt's mind, he was invincible.

In the last two or three weeks, irritation and paranoia had replaced his chemically-induced highs. He was a Ping-Pong ball of emotions. I never knew what to expect, and the man I'd fallen in love with had become a shadow.

I knew that something was off the moment he snorted his first line. It took me two months to find the proof of the white powder. One morning, I was doing the laundry and I found a little white bag of cocaine in his pants pocket. When confronted, Brandt told me that it wasn't what I thought. He'd found it on some guy at the club and planned to flush it. I offered to do it, but Brandt snatched it from me and went to the bathroom himself. The toilet sounded, but when he came out he was high, acting like nothing was wrong.

I thought my love for him was strong enough to see him through this phase.

I was wrong.

When Brandt was high and we slept together, he never cared if I had an orgasm or not. That wasn't the Brandt I knew. The Brandt I knew always put me first. Honestly, I wasn't sure who the real Brandt was anymore. Pots and pans clanked around in the kitchen as I quietly shut the door behind me. I thought maybe I should turn and leave, go see Grandmama for the night instead. Lately, I'd been staying at her house eighty percent of the time.

"Damn it all to hell! Where is it?" Brandt yelled from the kitchen. I stopped in my tracks. He was agitated. "Where's the fucking cash? I know it's here somewhere. Fucking Adam and his...salary...all corporate bullshit...bastard...I need the money."

At least now I knew why Brandt had been running low on money lately; Adam had changed the way they were paid. I turned back toward the front door when he came barreling across the house. Brandt stopped when he saw me. "Hey, how was your day? Did the lawyer meeting with your Grandmama go well?"

My smile faded. That meeting had been two days ago.

Brandt looked as if he hadn't slept in three days. That's how long it had been since I'd been home. It was best not to contradict him. "Yeah, it went well. I'm going to grab a couple of things and go see her. Do you want me to order you some dinner before I go?"

Glancing at his palms, I confirmed his coke craving. His fingers were scratching at his palms and his arms were twitching, as if he wasn't comfortable in his skin. Thanks to the Internet, I'd gotten an education on drug addiction. Specifically, cocaine addiction.

"I left my wallet at the club. Can you spot me a hundred or so? I'll order it myself. That way you don't have to keep Grandmama waiting." His tongue raked across his gums—another sign he needed a hit.

Glancing at the coffee table, I saw his wallet sprawled open, a couple of twenties peeking out. I needed to get out of here. Even though he'd never raised a hand to me, I knew he lost touch with reality.

"Okay, let me see what I've got."

Brandt came toward me as car lights flashed in our driveway. "Fuck. I told them I'd meet them across town."

The stress in his voice made my mind race. "Brandt, who's here?"

"Just stay cool, baby. Give me the cash in your wallet. It's not what you think."

He grabbed my purse from my shoulder, and I let him take it. He took out about four hundred dollars that I had left from my business trip two weeks ago and tossed my purse behind us on the couch. Our house was a mess. I stood behind Brandt as three guys came in, not bothering to knock. They were in leather, shades, do rags on their heads, and covered in tats.

The leader spoke with a forced fake accent. "Hey, buddy, where's our money? You said you'd meet us an hour ago. You're late. You trying to skip town on us?"

When he looked around the room, I realized that it did look as if we were in a rush to leave—clothes and miscellaneous items were everywhere.

Brandt took the money from his wallet on the table and added it to mine. "Nah, man. I was on my way. I fell asleep."

The leader took the money. "You're about a thousand short, pal. You said you'd have fifteen hundred dollars as payment for your debt. That was the agreement when we gave you drugs in advance. Bossman is getting anxious for his fifteen grand you owe him."

"I'll to get it for you when the bank opens on Monday." Brandt sounded calm.

They laughed, and my heart broke amid all the anxiety I felt. "Asshole, it's Thursday. Has the blow fried you that much? The bossman is gonna have to start collecting from you in advance—before you're a junkie who can't pay his debts."

The silver shades cut to me. Looking me over, the drug dealer gave me an appreciative smile. "I'd be willing to cover your debt, if you'd let me have a round or two with your bitch."

This was not good. Not good at all. My mouth went dry, and I wished like hell I had my purse with my mace in it. I looked at Brandt, expecting him to tell them to fuck off. But he didn't. He looked at me and then back at the guy. I was stunned. This was not the Brandt I knew. The man I loved was gone.

I was about to speak when Brandt said, "I can't man. She's not part of the deal."

I couldn't believe that Brandt had even paused to consid-

er it.

The dealer popped his knuckles. "Then, my friend, it's time you learn your lesson. We've been lenient since you were a rich boy, but it seems those glory days are over."

The thought of Brandt getting beaten slew me. Before I could even think, I blurted, "You'll have the money tomorrow."

The dealer pointed at me. "This is on you now. If you don't pay, your body will pay for you."

I shivered at the thought of him touching me. I'd kill him before it got that far.

Brandt's voice lacked any authority as he spoke again. "This isn't on her. You'll have it." He was barely keeping it together, scratching his palms.

The dealer and his two thugs pointed at me. "Tomorrow. Have the money by six, or you and I are gonna have ourselves a date, bitch."

I stood firm, though my insides were shaking.

Brandt shook his head. "Leave her out of this, man."

The dealer obviously saw the same thing that I did—Brandt wasn't fully there. Without another word, the assholes left the house and a sob escaped me. My body shook as I moved to the couch. Our life, our love had been ruined by cocaine. I was not going to live like this. I was not going to be one of those girls who got sucked into a life of lies.

"Nikola, it's not what you think."

My head snapped up and I glared. I hated that line with every fiber of my being. "Brandt, it is *what I think. You need help. I'll get you the money, but then I'm gone."*

"Don't say that, baby. I've got this under control." He searched through the clothes on the floor.

I pulled my phone out of my purse and dialed his best

friend. There was no way I could handle this on my own. Brandt was going to need someone to help him pick up the pieces. Our love hadn't stopped him from using. Perhaps I was even the reason he was using. The thought hurt, but I needed to get Brandt help. I'd been talking to Adam about how we could help Brandt, and I needed his help now. On the second ring, Adam picked up. I headed back to what used to be our bedroom.

"Hey, Adam, it's Nikola. Can you come over? Brandt's dealer paid us a visit. He's on the hook for fifteen grand. Well, technically now I'm on the hook for it, too."

I heard a door slam on the other end.

Brandt mumbled something about everything being fine. Bullshit.

"Shit. Are you okay, Nikola? I'm on my way. I called an interventionist this afternoon, like we talked about. We're going to try to get Brandt into rehab." Adam sounded as anxious as I felt.

My heart jumped with hope, but then I heard Brandt curse, asking himself where he'd hidden his coke. Taking a deep breath, I said, "They wanted to trade the debt for sex with me. And Brandt hesitated! Adam, he paused! I can't do this and worry he's willing to trade me to get high. His mood is all over the place. I never know what I'm going to walk in on. I rarely even stay here anymore."

"Fuck. He's so messed up he that doesn't know which way is up. You know the Brandt we know would never do that. Hell, I put us on salary and limited his access to the accounts when I figured out why he was blowing through money so quickly."

I glanced back into the living room where Brandt had found his stash. He dumped the white powder out and began putting it in a line. Not what I think? *My heart hurt as he did a line, then sat back with a dumb smile on his face.*

"Nikola, are you there?"

I knew what I had to do. "I'll help you get him into rehab. I love him, Adam, but I can't do this anymore. I'm leaving once we get him somewhere. He just snorted coke in our living room. He knows I'm here. I can't allow this. I won't allow this."

"I'm almost there. He loves you, Nikola. You're his world."

Seeing him sit on the couch with two more lines of blow in front of him made my heart break for the millionth time. Tears streamed down my face as I watched the life I'd planned for Brandt and me shatter.

"No, Adam, he loves his drugs. I won't enable him."

"I understand."

"I'll see you in a few."

I went to the closet and packed. Whatever I didn't take tonight, I'd leave behind.

I blinked, bringing my world back into focus, and stepped under the scalding water. Adam had paid the drug dealers. He'd refused to let me do it. Adam had called me after Brandt had been admitted into rehab. I'd been at Grandmama's dining room table, crying my eyes out after packing Brandt's bags. The inexperienced interventionist had almost pushed Brandt out the door. Brandt refused help until Adam stood and said, '*The drugs cost you Nikola. She's gone. You'll never get her back if you make the choice to keep using.*'

Brandt hadn't believed him until Adam told him about that night with the drug dealer. Brandt had been coherent enough in that moment, with the interventionist there, to remember pieces of what had happened in our home. The realization of what he had done registered and he went into treatment.

When Brandt got out of rehab, he never contacted me. I thought that maybe I threatened his sobriety. Afraid that I wouldn't have the willpower to make choices that were good for us—for Brandt—I'd cut myself off from everyone who knew Brandt.

But seeing Brandt again opened a jagged scar that never healed properly.

Brandt

I PULLED UP to Dave's Diner. Since it was open twenty-four hours, Quentin and I always met there. Despite the fake chrome accents and the goofy retro feel, the diner's familiar setting seemed to help when I needed to sort through my shit. Quentin was already sitting in a red vinyl booth.

Quentin helped me filter through all the noise in my head when we talked. Deep down, I knew what my heart wanted when it came to Nikola, but I had to figure out what I should actually do. A warm gust hit me as I walked inside. Christmas music played, and it made me want to unplug the radio. I felt anything but jolly, and Christmas was over.

Quentin was in his mid-thirties. He hadn't shaved today and had a blue baseball cap on. I felt like shit for taking him away from his family on New Year's Day.

He nodded. "Hey, man. I ordered you a cup of coffee when I saw you pull up."

"Thanks. Sometimes I wonder whether coffee should be considered a drug."

Quentin chuckled. "I've had the same thought many a time."

The middle-aged dark-haired waitress, Donna, who looked like she'd been serving all night, put my coffee down in front of me. I wasn't sure who looked more tired, her or me. "Here you go, darlin'. Can I get you anything else? Or do you want me to keep the caffeine coming?"

"No, keep the coffee coming and I'll be good. Thanks, Donna."

"Sure thing." She walked away.

I took a sip, centering myself.

Quentin was in a button-up flannel, making him look kind of like a lumberjack. "So you saw Nikola last night? Where's your head this morning?"

Taking a tired breath, I said, "It's a fucking mess. I was at a club last night when I ran into her. I thought I saw that spark that I used to see when we were together. Then a chick came up, and Nikola got the wrong impression. She left and I followed. A guy picked her up."

Quentin took a sip of coffee as he watched me closely. "Any desire to use with all this going on?"

I rarely let myself remember the freedom of using drugs. My mind was stronger, but thinking about it at all wasn't worth the temptation.

"Not yet. Knowing what using cost me, keeps me away from those thoughts. Still, I wanted to make sure I talked it out, in case the thought crossed my mind. I told Nikola that the girl wasn't what she thought. It's what I used to say to Nikola when she asked about the drugs. It killed me to see that pain on her face again." I took a sip of coffee and shifted in my seat.

A loud couple walked through the door. They seemed to be still wired from New Year's Eve. I adjusted myself in the seat so that I could stretch a little and release the stifling feeling that washed over me.

"What do you think you're going to do?" Quentin asked.

That was the question of the day. "I have no clue. I know what I want to do. But I don't know if *that's* what I should do."

Quentin had been my sponsor since rehab. "What are you wanting to do, and why wouldn't it be the right thing?"

I looked down at the steam coming off of my coffee. It would evaporate and disappear. It's what I wish would happen with these painful memories. "You know I want to talk to Nikola. I know you think I should, that it might give me closure. But I don't want to interrupt her life. She might have happily moved on. She deserves that."

My sponsor rubbed his beard as he thought. "I think it's best to get it out in the open, talk it through, so that everyone can move on. If you haven't talked since you left for rehab, she may have the same thoughts you do. And, quite frankly, think about this—last night might have been fate stepping in."

I dragged my hand down my face. "What the hell do I say? She changed her number, anyway."

The door opened again and a man came strolling in, taking a corner booth. He was an older guy and, as he sat, he opened a newspaper and read. I was always aware of what was going on around me. My security side never shut off.

"Well, Brandt, you know where her grandmother lives and you were close with Anne. I know you didn't want to involve Anne, but I think it's a good idea to talk to her. At this point, that may be your only option. Speak from the heart. Even if your relationship with Nikola is finished, at least you'll know."

My heart physically hurt thinking about Nikola never being in my life again. It was one reason I hadn't reached out yet. "Quentin, I know what you say makes sense. It's what I *should* do. But I don't know if I can face us being over."

Quentin sipped his coffee. I knew what he was going to say before he said it. "Then it's what you should do. Don't let the fear get to you. Fear is what drives people to unhealthy coping mechanisms, like drugs. Before now, I understood your reservation. But I think you're strong enough, Brandt, to handle this—regardless of what happens."

As we sat in silence, I mulled over his words for a bit. "I'm going to speak with Anne. At least I'll know and can stop tormenting myself. Thanks for meeting me. Tell Beth I'm sorry for taking you away on New Year's."

Beth was Quentin's wife. They gave me hope with their functional marriage and two kids, despite Quentin's past heroin use.

"Nonsense. She said to tell you 'hello.' When do you plan on going to see Anne?"

I stood and Quentin followed. My body was jittery with nerves and excitement at the thought of having a chance to see Nikola again as I remembered their yearly tradition. "I know Nikola's at Anne's today. I'll probably head there now so I'm not late to my mum's dinner."

Quentin gave me a manly bear hug. "Sounds good. Keep me posted. If you get the urge, know I'm here, no matter what."

"Will do, man." Quentin went to grab some cash, but I stopped him. "I've got it. Get back to your family."

"Thanks." He nodded at the waitress. "Happy New Year, Donna."

She replied, her voice smoky, "Happy New Year's to you, too."

I left some bills on the table and gave her a friendly wave. As I got in my car, I leaned my head against the leather seat. I was less than a half hour from Anne's—Nikola's grandmother's—house. *What if that guy from last night was there?* Nikola had seemed to want to talk to me. Regardless of who he was, we needed to talk. Nikola deserved an apology at the very least.

I cranked the car and headed toward Anne's, mentally preparing myself for the worst. The streets were fairly empty as I made my way to the country house. I turned down a gravel road toward a red brick house with yellow trim. Nikola's car, a black CTS, sat in the driveway. The car that the guy had been driving last night was nowhere to be seen—a good sign. At least I'd be able to talk to her alone, without an audience. What I had to say was for Nikola only. If she chose to share it, that was her choice.

I debated whether I should go to the door off the carport or to the front door. No one used the front door if they knew the family, but using the carport door that led into the kitchen seemed too intimate. *Shit, I am terrible at this.* Taking a deep, fortifying breath, I opened my car door and the cold air hit me hard. I cursed as I took the walkway up to the front door.

Before I could turn chicken-shit and run away, I rang the doorbell. I could hear it echo through the house. Anne's voice rang from the other side. "Nikola, I've got it!"

The door opened, and Anne greeted me. She'd aged well and was as full of life as always with her blonde hair done up perfectly. A knowing look momentarily replaced her pleasant expression.

She stepped out onto the front porch and closed the door. "Brandt, it's good to see you. I figured you might stop by here today."

Anne always seemed to know things. It's one of the reasons I stopped coming by when I used. Before then, Nikola and I used to come over on Sundays for a roast dinner that Anne always started prior to going to church, where she was the choir director. My guilt had stopped me.

Shame coursed through my body as I looked back at this loving woman. "It's good to see you, too, Anne. I knew Nikola would be here, and I guess she's told you about last night. For what it's worth, I'm sorry for what I put you through."

A gentle smile spread across my face. It used to feel like Anne was my grandmother, too. Losing her because of my habit had been hard.

"What do you think you put me through?" Anne asked as a look of sadness quickly passed over her features.

This was the worst part of apologizing—saying what you had done to a person in one of the darkest times in your life. There was a cleansing feeling that followed, but it sucked ass admitting to your own flaws. I met her eyes. "You were like a grandmother to me, too. I shut you out, lied to you, and hurt your granddaughter in ways that make me cringe when I think about them. I was ashamed when I made wrong choices, and I didn't want you to see what I was doing. Sorry isn't an adequate word. I wish I could think of one. But I *am* sorry for everything."

To my surprise, Anne hugged me; the warm blanket of her embrace covering me. "Welcome back, Brandt. Everyone makes mistakes. What matters is that we recognize them and grow from them." She pulled back. "I can't speak for Nikola, and you're going to have a fight to win her back. You need to make sure that this is what you want before I let you in my house. I'm not the one who had to live with you and what you were doing. Are you clean?"

Relief washed over me—she'd at least let me try to win Nikola back. I needed Anne's approval. From the corner of my eye, I saw the blinds propped slightly open. Nikola was watching. I kept facing forward so Nikola didn't know I saw her eavesdropping.

"I'm clean and have been for over a year. I understand it's going to be a hard road with Nikola, but I have to try. She's the love of my life. There's no one else."

The conviction in my voice rang true, and I knew Anne believed me when an understanding smile slipped into place.

"Let me go talk to Nikola. Whether she wants to see you is her choice. I'll be right back."

The blinds closed as Anne disappeared behind the front door. Knowing Nikola, she ran back to wherever she'd been. It always made me laugh anytime I caught her doing that, back when we lived together. It hurt, thinking about how happy we were. I ran a hand down my face. Honestly, I wasn't sure what I would do if Nikola turned me away. Time moved slowly while I waited outside in the cold. Finally, the door opened.

"Why don't you come on in, Brandt? Nikola's in the kitchen making cornbread while the collards and black-eyed peas cook. I need to take care of a few things in the basement."

"Thanks, Anne."

She gave me a welcoming smile as I stepped through the door. Happy memories welcomed me. Past the entryway and to the right was a door that led down to the basement, which Anne headed toward. I walked a little into the living room and then headed left to the kitchen. Nikola cracked eggs into her cornbread batter.

She looked up at me, her green eyes boring straight through me. She was in a sweater and jeans. I'd never tire of her beauty. I had to stop myself from kissing her senseless, like I would have if we were together.

We stayed locked in a trance. I noticed her chewing the inside of her cheek—she was nervous. It was a small gesture and not everyone knew of her tell.

"Hey, Nikola. Thanks for agreeing to see me."

"Hey, Brandt."

Hearing her speak my name twice within twenty-four hours did something to me. I would do whatever I had to in order to get the woman of my dreams back in my arms.

She. Was. Mine.

Nikola

MY HEART WAS about to beat out of my chest as Brandt stood before me. After all this time, I'd given up hope he would come by Grandmama's. I know I left him, but I'd hoped he'd come back and fight for us when he got clean. Not reaching out to him had been a constant struggle. Brandt being happy and healthy was what mattered.

That said, watching him talk outside with Grandmama made my heart flutter like it used to. I hadn't hesitated when Grandmama asked if she should let Brandt in. Hearing him say my name brought familiar feelings back to the surface. As much as I'd longed to see Brandt again, I was terrified of the hurt it would bring.

We were standing, locked in each other's gazes, when I

realized I should probably say something. "Why don't you take a seat at the bar? I'm making cornbread; we can talk while I finish." Having a predefined distance from Brandt would hopefully keep me rational. Luckily, there were no signs that he was either high or in need of another hit.

"Okay. If you need help, let me know. We used to be pretty good in the kitchen together."

I didn't know what to say. His sapphire eyes seemed to penetrate me. We *had* cooked together all the time. I forced the memories that were trying to assail me to the side. Having him so close was hard enough to process. So I focused on Brandt. His hair was pulled back and a green thermal shirt covered his tattoos. I wasn't surprised that he didn't have a coat with him. He hated coats, even in this cold weather.

Instead of saying anything, I cracked the last egg into the cornbread batter and tossed the shells into the trashcan at the end of the bar.

Brandt moved to the seat directly across from me. "Last night wasn't what it loo—"

My eyes shot to his and he stopped. Hearing that phrase from him reminded me of all the shit we'd been through, pushing away the warm fuzzies I'd been feeling.

Brandt cleared his throat. "Sorry. What I should have said is that I'm not with the girl you saw approach me. I went to the club to meet Trigger. I ran into her, and she wanted something I didn't. I went to the bar for a shot and was going to leave right before I saw you, but then that girl—she tried to make something happen that wasn't in the cards."

Thinking of Brandt with another woman made little cracks form in my still-delicate heart. *How many women has he been with since me? Is he seeing anyone?* I wasn't his girlfriend, and I had no right to be jealous, but I couldn't help myself. Brandt sounded like he told the truth, though, and wasn't lying like he used to with the coke.

"Thanks for telling me. Is that why you came by today?"

As my phone buzzed on the counter, I stopped stirring the batter. I glanced and saw it was Lance, my ex from three months ago. We'd dated for a month and slept together once before I'd ended it. Sleeping with someone else felt wrong. My body only wanted Brandt. Still, Lance kept texting and randomly showing up at places where I hung out. It was borderline stalking, and he put me on edge. Lance had been at the bar last night, which was why I'd texted Wesley to pick me up. I'd decided to wait by the bar to be near a bartender, in case Lance kept harassing me.

"What's wrong, Nikola?" Brandt watched me closely, and his concern was evident.

"I'm good. Sorry, what were we talking about?"

I looked back at the bowl and stirred again. I wasn't ready to share my concerns with Brandt. Hopefully, he wouldn't push. I didn't want him to feel obligated to deal with my problems, and I needed to keep my heart safe. As I went to the stove, I could feel him looking at me. The cast-iron skillet was hot. I poured the batter and heard it sizzle as it touched the pan. Without looking at Brandt, I closed the oven and put the bowl in the sink before sitting in front of him, across the bar.

"I won't push, but I know something's wrong."

I looked him in the eyes. Brandt still made me feel safe. I loved how he protected me fiercely when he thought clearly. But I wasn't his to protect anymore.

After a few seconds, he realized I wasn't going to talk, and he continued. "I came here for two reasons. The first was to apologize for all I did to you—the lying, the using, the hurtful things I said. I threw away the best thing that ever happened to me. Every bad choice I made, I'm sorry for it, Nikola. I accept full responsibility. *I* ruined *us.*"

The sincerity in his voice struck true and stirred something in me. "Thank you, Brandt. That means a lot. More than you know."

He took a deep breath. "You deserve to know. The other reason I came here was to see if you're seeing anyone. I'm not, so if you're not, I want to win your heart back. I know I fucked..." He looked at the doorway, probably because he thought Grandmama could be there at any second. "I know I messed things up, but I'm not ready to give up on us. I've been clean for over a year and haven't come close to a relapse. We can start as friends. I want to show you I'm clean and different now. I won't go back to drugs."

I massaged my tired eyes. "Brandt, you put me through hell."

He held up his hands. "I know I did, Nikola. Hell, I regret it every damn day. I lied to you and put you behind the drugs. It's something that will haunt me for the rest of my days. But are you seeing anyone? That guy who picked you up at Coyote Ugly last night?"

I swallowed, teetering on the edge of the unknown. There were so many unanswered questions running through my head. Did I want to open the safe I'd put my heart in? Should I give him a chance to prove himself to me? Did I want to be with him again? I knew the answer was yes, but I wanted to proceed with caution.

All he'd asked was whether I was seeing anyone. That was easy to answer. "No, I'm not seeing anyone."

A smile spread across his face, and I couldn't help but return it. "So, the guy who picked you up last night is just a—"

His voice trailed off and I finished, "A friend. His name is

Wesley. Wesley and I met at a support group we used to attend."

"What kind of support group was it?"

I traced a design on the counter as I answered Brandt. "It's a support group for spouses of addicts. I know we weren't married, but I still felt like I lost my other half."

He lowered his voice, casting his eyes downward. "I'm glad you went to a support group. Only those who've been in your shoes know what it's like. But I hope you'll give me a chance."

This felt like the old Brandt, and as much as I wanted to go sit on his lap and kiss him, part of me pictured him hiding blow all over our house and sneaking hits.

"The group was good. It helped me piece things together I didn't understand. Made the dark storm not so bleak."

Brandt flinched, but the truth needed to be out there in the open. Pretending nothing was wrong was what let cocaine take over our lives.

"The groups are good. They help a lot. I know you probably have questions. Would you mind if I text you sometime, maybe for coffee? We can start slow. I want to prove to you that I'm worthy of your heart."

My breath caught at his words. Our first date started with Brandt texting me for a coffee date. He'd always been very forthcoming with his feelings. He'd made me feel precious and desired.

"Coffee sometime would be nice. I can't promise anything. I'll need to take this one day at a time."

He stood. "I need a chance. That's all I'm asking for. As long as you feel anything for me, I can work with that."

Loving Brandt was never the issue. My heart still beat for Brandt, and denying it would do both of us an injustice. We deserved to figure this out on our terms, rather than being at the mercy of drugs. I wrote my number on a piece of paper and slid it across the counter. Brandt took it and smiled before putting it in his pocket. He walked to my side, and I could smell his cologne. It was cologne I'd gotten him when we started dating. The scent was a perfect balance between bold and understated with an earthy fragrance. He kept a safe distance, and I was glad. I wasn't ready for anything more than coffee, but the familiar feeling was hard to keep at a distance. Brandt's pull became stronger.

The timer went off for the cornbread, breaking the connection between us. I removed the cornbread, placing it on a trivet on the counter. When I turned, Brandt pierced me with his blue eyes and a huge megawatt smile.

"Thanks for giving me a chance I don't deserve, Nikola. I'm going to make you mine again, even if it takes me the rest of my life to prove to you that I'm worthy. I never stopped loving you, even when I was messed up. The only reason I didn't come after you when I got out of rehab was that I was too scared I'd fuck up your life even more."

I didn't know what to say. My skin tingled at his words. In the time Brandt had been here, my body felt more alive than it had since I'd last been in his arms.

Looking at the floor, I responded, "I've thought about you, too. About what we had."

I still loved Brandt. At the end of the day, though, love wasn't always what mattered.

Brandt

MY MIND FORCED my body to remain planted after hearing Nikola agree to coffee with me. She'd thought about me, too. That was a good fucking thing. I wanted to take her in my arms and sink so deep inside her that she'd never forget what it felt like to be connected. Nikola seemed confused, like she wanted to come to me, but held herself back. The familiar spark of love was there, but I'd have to bide my time and earn her trust.

"I'll see myself out, Nikola. Happy New Year."

"Happy New Year, Brandt."

I headed for the door when Anne came up the stairs. "Can you stay for lunch?" Her Georgia hospitality was like none other.

I shook my head. "I don't want to push my luck. I've got

a coffee date."

Anne gave me a sweet wink. "Don't be a stranger. Thanks for stopping by."

"I promise. Happy New Year."

"Happy New Year, Brandt."

I gave Anne a quick wave before I hurried out to my SUV, jumping into the car and cranking the heat up. I pulled out of the driveway and headed east, back toward my place. At a four-way stop, I pulled into a deserted parking lot of a gas station and pulled out my phone. I'd give anything to have Nikola back.

Me: Are you free for coffee tomorrow?

A couple of minutes passed before I received a response.

Nikola: You didn't wait long. Reminds me of that first date we had.

Me: I have this girl's heart to win back. Not much time to waste.

Nikola: Do I know her? I hope I do. She sounds like a lucky girl.

I smiled. She made me work for it.

Me: I'd say the chances are pretty good.

Nikola: Hmm...maybe I should consult my Magic 8 Ball.

Me: That damn thing has to be on my side this time. I can feel it.

Nikola: Hold please. I'm asking the wisest of all balls.

Every damn time I asked the Magic 8 Ball, it gave me some fucked-up answer that worked against me. I hated that thing, and Nikola loved using it on me. We'd had some pretty spectacular bouts of fucking thanks to that thing. Sometimes, though, it seemed to give me a bad case of blue balls. It had all started when we saw the Magic 8 Ball in a store. We'd been debating where to go on vacation—the beach or the mountains. I'd agreed to go with whatever the Magic 8 Ball said. It voted for the mountains, Nikola's choice. From then on, that ball had been a pain in my ass.

Nikola: Looks like you're in luck. You got a "Yes."

Me: Finally, that damn thing gave me a break! Are you free tomorrow?

Nikola: Should I consult the 8 Ball again?

Me: No, let's not push my luck today.

I pictured her laughing in the kitchen.

Nikola: Yes, I'm free. Does nine a.m. work? Or is that too early? Where do you want to meet?

Smiling that she'd picked the same time as our first date, I typed a response.

Me: Nine works. How about we meet at our coffee place?

Nikola: I'd love that.

Before I could respond, another text came through.

Nikola: I'm scared, Brandt.

Seeing those words on my phone was a knife in the gut. I never wanted Nikola to be scared, though she had every right to be. I hoped our old coffee shop would help. Kennedy's was where I'd met up with Nikola after I got her number at the concert.

Me: I understand. I'll give you all the time you need, and I'll try to never push you. I'm not giving up on us.

Nikola: Thank you for coming for me.

Me: I always will. I'll be there tomorrow at nine.

Nikola: See you tomorrow.

Tomorrow. We had a chance to get to know each other again. I thought about that moment when she'd looked at her phone and seemed worried. Hopefully, it was only a matter of time before what bothered her was considered my business again.

I texted an update to my sponsor.

Me: Nikola agreed to meet me for coffee. Thanks again for everything.

Quentin: That was fast! I'm happy for you. Stay grounded and true to yourself. What is meant to be will be. If you need me, I'm here.

Me: I know. Thanks.

I put my phone away and drove toward my house. I needed another shower and to change into slacks and a dress shirt before going to my mum's. For now, I wasn't going to say anything to her. She loved Nikola, and I think it devastated Mum when I'd lost her. Mum thought we had the same love as she had.

My dad died when I was ten. He was British. My mum was American. We always laughed when he called her "Mum" and it stuck. My accent was extremely faint to the point of being nonexistent, but it comforted me to hear myself sounding like my dad. We boys had been my dad's world, and it had been heartbreaking when an officer came to our house to tell us he'd been killed in Iraq. The loss of my dad was still acute, nearly twenty years later.

Coffee was a huge step for Nikola and me. It had been as big of a step the first time she'd agreed to meet me at Kennedy's. An involuntary smile spread across my face as I thought about the night I first saw the woman who would change everything for me.

The concert had ended. I was with Adam and my brother, Logan. The air smelled of beer and sweat, and the heat of the day lingered in the humid night. We were out celebrating the success of the club. The crowd was like a herd of elephants, all trying to make it to the parking lot. It was a beautiful summer night, and stars shone brightly in the clear sky. We were approaching a chain-link fence.

I nodded to the guys. "Why don't we stand over here while the crowd clears out? No need to wait in our car, all cramped up."

"Sounds good," Logan replied. We leaned against the fence. He was a younger version of me with short hair and no tats.

I ran my fingers through my hair to get it out of my face.

Adam looked at e-mails on his phone. "Our new security system should be installed in two days. I want the club side locked up tight. No fuckups."

"Same here. We'll get it figured out."

Adam was a rule follower. He wanted everything followed to a T. He babbled about something when an auburn-haired goddess in a short, frayed skirt walked by. She had on cowboy boots and a tight-fitting tank. I normally didn't go for the cowgirl type, but I couldn't take my eyes off of her. I pushed off the fence and looked to Adam and Logan. "I'll be right back."

"We'll leave your ass," my brother called after me.

I flipped him the bird and heard them laughing.

I jogged up to the girl—she was with two friends. "Hey, there."

She looked over and smirked. "Well, hey there."

This mystery woman kept walking. Normally, girls flirted with me and it was easy to start a conversation. Whoever she was, she'd piqued my interest.

"Enjoy the concert?"

I saw a smile on her lips and couldn't help but smile back. "Sure did. You?"

"I did. But I know what would make it the best concert for both of us."

The girls with her giggled. She turned my way, an eyebrow arched as if expecting some lame line. "Oh yeah, what's that?"

"A coffee date."

She stopped, so I did, too. "Coffee?" Her voice sounded skeptical. "Is that code for something? That's a new one."

I knew where she was going with that, and I played dumb, trying to hide my smirk. "Besides a caffeine fix, I'm not sure what it would be code for. Care to enlighten me?"

I noticed her friends staring.

She gave me a smile. "If I have to enlighten you here, then I would say there's another problem that you should probably be concerned about."

She was a breath of fresh air. I chuckled. "I'm Brandt. Have coffee with me. Just coffee."

Her eyes sparkled, and we were momentarily lost in each other's gaze. Finally, someone bumped her and she fell forward. I caught her, loving how her waist felt in my hands. I wasn't letting go until she said, "Yes."

She looked up. I wanted nothing more than to push that wayward bit of hair behind her ear, but I left my hands on her hips.

"Just coffee?" she asked, suddenly shy.

"Just coffee...for now. We'll see where it goes." There was something strong between us—a hurricane force.

She didn't immediately shoot me down, which was a good thing. Still, my breath caught in my throat as I waited for her answer.

Finally, she spoke. "I'm Nikola, and I'll give you my number. If you remember it, text me, and I'll meet you for coffee. It's 555-555-5689." She stretched up on her toes and whispered, "I hope I get a text from you."

Her breath tickled my ear, and I wanted to turn my face and kiss her. Nikola backed out of my arms, turned, and sashayed away.

Shit. Shit. Shit. *I repeated the number in my head while I fumbled for my phone. Was it 5689 or 5698 or something else? Fuck. I decided to go with 5689.*

While she was still visible, I typed a quick text. If I had to, I'd chase her again. I didn't care what she thought. You'd have to be numb not to feel the energy between us.

Me: How about Kennedy's Coffee tomorrow at nine?

Nikola laughed with her friends. She reached for the front pocket of her skirt and pulled out her phone. After she read it, she turned and smiled at me as she typed.

Nikola: That was fast. I think you have yourself a date. See you then.

Me: Great. See you then.

We were both smiling. Nikola gave me a little wave, turned, and walked away with her friends. We had something special...I could feel it.

My mind focused again on tomorrow's coffee date. I hoped for the same result as the last time we met at Kennedy's. And, maybe, instead of a few years of happiness, it would be a lifetime this time around.

But I knew what came tomorrow. Tomorrow Nikola was going to want answers. She was going to get the truth.

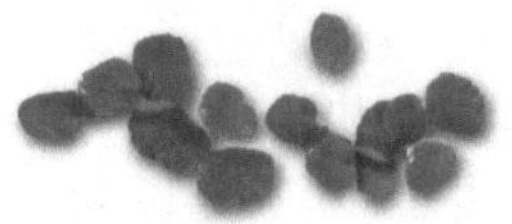

I pulled up to my mum's house, feeling fresh from a shower. Adam and Ainsley were already there, as was my brother, Logan. It had been a while since I'd seen him. When I got inside, everyone made fun of me for being stubborn and not wearing a coat. I shrugged.

My mum's laughter filled the room. She never remarried after losing my dad. Recently, I'd asked my mum why she hadn't dated since my dad had died. It was right after my one hookup, and I felt empty and guilty. Her response had been simple.

She'd said, "I had the ultimate when it came to love, and that's enough to last the rest of my life. When I'm lonely, I wrap myself in the memories of him. That's enough for me. Anything else would pale in comparison—I can't settle for second best."

It made sense. After that, I refused to settle for second best—even if that meant a lonely life. I used memories of Nikola and me to help soothe all the regret I felt each night.

The aroma of cooking ham and collards filled the room. Taking it all in, I salivated. My mum kept the house she and my dad bought together. It felt like home. Ainsley, wearing a red dress, stood at the bar arranging cookies on a platter. Mum stood at the counter, wearing a green apron, with her shoulder-length brown that she'd recently cut. My brother, Logan, tried to sneak bites from the food on the bar.

As I walked past my brother, I ruffled his hair. He ducked out of my reach.

"Hey, I'm going out later," he said. "Don't mess with perfection."

Logan slugged me in the shoulder as he stood. My mum smiled at our playful banter. Logan and I had always gotten along well.

I greeted everyone. "Where's your man-friend, Ainsley?"

Ainsley giggled as my mum walked up to me. Nora, our bartender at the club and Ainsley's best friend, had told me about the ridiculous term Ainsley had given Adam in a moment of panic at the grocery store.

"The man-friend is about head to the store to get some ice. I bet he'd like the company. Faith is teaching me the art of making the best collards."

Faith was my mum, and she'd always insisted on my

friends calling her by her first name. "Well, you've come to the right place. Mum knows her stuff."

My mum chuckled as she gave me a hug. "You might be a bit biased." She gave me a quick kiss on the cheek. "I love having my boys here."

I hugged her back. Logan had made his way to the stove and tried to sneak some ham while mum was distracted.

"Damn straight, I'm biased! You need help, or can I head out with Adam?"

"Logan, get your hands out of the ham," my mum scolded.

Logan shot away from the counter like it was on fire. We laughed. Mum had eyes in the back of her head. Now, she looked me over. She'd always said I looked like my dad. "You seem happier today. Anything good I should know about?"

"Just a good day, Mum. New year, new beginning."

She gave me a soft smile. "Good. I'm happy to hear that."

Logan's phone rang and he walked out of the kitchen, saying, "I need to take this. I'll be right back."

Adam walked in. I cocked my head to the side. "Hey, man-friend? You up for some company?"

He looked at Ainsley as she mashed her lips together, trying to stifle a laugh.

"This is your fault, you know, baby. It's one of the reasons I need to get you down that aisle sooner rather than later."

Adam's tone was full of love. It was amazing how much his outlook had changed so quickly. When you meet the right person, nothing else matters. He'd tried to keep her at a distance with his damn "rules," but love had won. I hoped that was in my future, too.

Ainsley blew him a kiss. "Deep down, you love your nickname. No matter when you get me down the aisle, you're stuck with it." She giggled as he gave her a kiss.

Now that I had another chance at love, my stomach didn't hurt when I saw them together. She pushed him away. "Go get ice. Take your MFS with you."

My mum laughed at the exchange and watched Adam with loving eyes. I knew she'd also thought he'd never find this kind of happiness.

I couldn't help but ask, "MFS?"

Adam walked toward me quickly. "You don't want to know. You're about to get tagged with a nickname. Walk away—fast."

"Oh, hell. Never mind. Don't answer, Ainsley."

We left the kitchen as Ainsley called out, "You're the man-friend's sidekick!"

Adam laughed as I muttered, "Fuck."

We headed to the gas station. Not even out of the neighborhood, I blurted, "I saw Nikola last night. She ran off when she saw me with this random girl. Long story short, I explained everything and Nikola has agreed to have coffee with me tomorrow."

Adam stopped the car in the middle of the road and looked at me. "Are you shitting me? Or did you grow a pair of balls and go after your woman?"

"I grew a pair, and I'm going to fight for her. It's going to take time, and she'll have to learn to trust me again, but she's at least giving me a shot." It felt good to get it out in the open. I needed someone to talk to that wouldn't push me and ask for constant updates, like my sponsor. Adam was always safe—I could trust him with anything.

The car moved again. "I'm glad, Brandt. Regardless of what happened, you still deserve to be happy. You and Nikola both deserve that."

"Thanks. I'm finally starting to believe it. Does Ainsley know what happened with the drugs yet?"

I figured she had an inkling, considering I'd helped find an interventionist when her mom had a breakdown, but I didn't know how much she knew. It was on my mind as we pulled into the gas station. The streets were empty and we were the only customers there.

Adam replied, "I think she has an idea, but we've never talked specifics. She won't push, either. I promised I'd never tell anyone."

I was probably the only secret between them. I didn't want that. "Tell her everything. You have my permission."

"Thanks, man. I'd never ask, but I appreciate that you're letting me tell her."

Ainsley had softened Adam in ways I'd never thought possible. He was becoming settled, and it suited him.

"I should have had you tell her a while ago, but I wasn't thinking. Sorry, man."

Adam opened the car door. "No apology needed," he said. "I'll go pay for two bags if you'll grab them from the cooler."

"Sounds good," I said. "It's fucking cold out here."

Adam called over his shoulder, "Your fault for not wearing a damn jacket!"

I laughed. *Bastard.* Slowly, things seemed to be falling into place. Patience and perseverance were going to be key in the coming days.

Nikola

IT TOOK ME nearly three hours to get ready for coffee. I wanted to look pretty without simultaneously screaming, "Take me to bed!" When I finally pulled into the parking lot, the place was fairly full with people getting their morning caffeine fix. This was where we had our first date after Brandt got my number at the concert. We'd talked for hours that morning. Brandt had asked me to dinner the following night, and from that point on, my heart had belonged to him. Taking the visor down, I checked my makeup one last time to make sure everything was still okay. My insides felt like I'd already had twelve cups of coffee when I hadn't had a drop yet.

In the passenger seat, my phone vibrated.

Brandt: I see you.

I flipped up the visor to find him standing at the front of my car. His hair was down, and he was still the most handsome guy I'd ever seen. In the winter, he always wore long-sleeved thermal shirts and jeans. Inside, I smiled. Maybe I still knew Brandt after all. I pushed my legs together in response to my natural impulses. Once, he'd been mine. I took a couple of settling breaths as we smiled at each other. They were nervous smiles, which calmed me—knowing he and I were probably feeling the same way. I got out of my car, pulling my jacket around me as I walked over to Brandt.

"Hey, stranger. Are you stalking me?" I couldn't help my flirtatious tone.

Brandt chuckled. "Honestly, I didn't want to miss a minute with you, so I got here twenty minutes early."

I blushed.

Someone brushed passed me in a hurry to get into the coffee shop.

An older gentlemen turned and said, "Sorry, ma'am. My apologies."

"It's okay, have a great day."

"You, too. My grandson is arriving today. I haven't seen him in ten years, and I want to greet him with his favorite coffee."

Total jubilation exuberated from the man, and my heart lightened seeing someone so happy.

I gave him a warm smile. "Have fun. That's so exciting!"

He was off through the door, whistling and hurrying to the counter.

Brandt took my hand, and I gasped at the sensation coursing through my veins. It was the first time we'd touched since the breakup.

Brandt stopped. "Is this okay?"

My initial response was to lean into him, to feel Brandt close to me. He felt like home, even though there were skeletons lurking in the dark corners of our past. My shoulder brushed his, and I pulled back, realizing what I was doing. My movement wasn't obvious, but I wanted Brandt to take the lead.

"Yes, I like it."

We stood on the sidewalk, smiling goofily at each other. I shivered in the breeze, and he said, "Let's get you inside, Nikola."

I nodded as he led me inside. The coffee shop smelled of freshly-ground beans and pastries, making me salivate. We were third in line, and there were still a few vacant tables. The man who had bumped into me received his order. He passed us and gave me another big grin. He was precious. I wondered what the story was behind him not seeing his grandkid for ten years. I'd never know, but I hoped they never lost touch again.

I looked up when Brandt squeezed my hand and said, "Do you want your usual?"

In this moment, it felt like we'd never been apart. "Yes. Thank you."

He winked. We moved up in line and Brandt moved his hand to the small of my back, bringing me a little closer. His scent enveloped me, and I leaned into him. We stood silently, but the vein in my neck pulsed quickly as excited, nervous energy took over.

At the front of the line, the barista greeted us. "Welcome to Kennedy's Coffee. What can I get for you today?"

"She'll have a blueberry muffin and a medium caramel macchiato. I'll have a large black coffee."

The barista punched in the order. She looked young, college-aged. “Is that all?”

“Yes.”

“Your total is nine eighteen.”

Brandt let go of my back, and I instantly missed the connection. He pulled out his wallet and handed her a ten and a few ones. “Keep the change.”

She smiled. “Thank you. Here’s your number. Place it on the table and we’ll bring your order to you when it’s ready.”

“Thank you,” I said with a smile.

As we made our way to the corner table, the memory of one of our last visits here came without warning.

It had been five days since I’d seen Brandt and I was anxious to be with him. An unexpected trip to New York, followed by endless problems, had delayed my return home. Adam was out of town, meeting with someone regarding a new security system for the members of Club Envy. Brandt had passed on the trip so he could see me since I’d been out of town, but that meant he had to work security. Otherwise, we’d have been at the club, having fun in our room. I loved being at the club with Brandt—the sex swing was one of my favorites. But at least we’d get to see each other for a bit tonight before he went back to work.

I pulled up to Kennedy’s Coffee, throwing my car in park as Brandt arrived. It was dark out, and I was desperate to have him. Brandt jumped out of his truck and met me at the front of my car.

He bent down, putting a hand on each side of my face. His tongue invaded my mouth as he kissed me with a passion that ignited the yearning I’d felt for the past five days. I bit his lower lip, and he growled at the sensation.

"Fuck. I missed you, Nikki."

I licked my lips. He only called me Nikki when he was about to take me.

"I missed you, too."

He looked around. The streets were fairly deserted as late evening approached.

Without saying a word, he took my hand and we walked to the dark alley. I knew what was coming. When he'd texted me before I took off, asking if we could meet for twenty minutes when I landed, I knew we'd end up being together—somewhere.

"Where are we going?" I asked.

"I can't wait. I need to come inside you. It's been too long."

After a year of dating, we'd stopped using condoms. Sex with no barriers was the way to go. There were a pile of pallets against the wall. A dim street light flickered across the way, leaving the area behind the pallets in a faint light.

Brandt looked back toward the street, then grabbed me before pushing me against the brick wall. "Take your panties off. I need your pussy bare."

Brandt was domineering in the bedroom. My independent personality faded when he took control. I loved giving myself to him. I trusted him explicitly.

"I'm not wearing any panties," I said. "I took them off on the plane, hoping you'd take me."

Leaning against the brick, I unzipped the front of my black, retro dress. It was stylish and out there, but made for great unplanned alley sex. The glow from the street light lit my body as the zipper made its way down the dress, showing my lack of undergarments.

"Fuck me. Nikki, you're about to have me in you." He

touched me and stuck two fingers in me, making sure I'd be able to take him without being primed.

"I needed you. I made sure I was ready."

The sound of his zipper had me breathing heavier. I jumped into Brandt's arms as my back slammed into the brick wall. His dick pushed in all the way as his mouth found my exposed nipple. My dress hung to the sides. The long-awaited sensation of Brandt pulsing within me was exquisite. Potentially being caught fueled the drive.

A moan escaped me as my head fell back. Brandt took a long stroke out, then slammed into me deep and hard, jarring my body against the brick.

"You drive me mad with want, Nikki."

"Don't stop."

The motions became faster, more desperate, rougher. I reveled in the sensation.

"Let go, Nikki. Let go."

My body complied as stars danced in my vision, and I spiraled into pleasure.

"I love you with all that I am, baby."

"I love you, too, Brandt. So much."

We kissed as Brandt stayed buried in me, releasing himself inside me.

Brandt's voice brought me out of my memory. "You're thinking about that time in the alley, aren't you? After you'd been gone for five days."

We were at the table, and he'd pulled the chair out for me. How long had I been standing here, lost in the past? I blushed as I took my seat. I'd been caught, and he knew it. Brandt's eyes danced over my body, and it ignited again. I looked away.

"It's hard not to remember those things when you touch

me." After a few seconds to gather my frazzled thoughts, I looked back into his eyes. "Regardless of how natural it feels between us, we have a lot to discuss."

He nodded. "I agree. I'm an open book, Nikola. The only way I think we can start building trust is with you asking anything that comes to your mind and me answering. If I share everything I think you want to know, you may settle for less than you want. I don't want that. I want something better than what we had."

Words of my Grandmama came to my mind, *Sometimes when something breaks and you fix it, the end result is twice as strong.*

"I want this to work, but I'm scared. What if we don't work together anymore?" My voice shook and the words made me want to cry.

His brow crinkled, as if the words I spoke were more unpleasant to hear than they were to speak. "I hope to hell that's not the case. I'll take this at a turtle's pace if needed. We'll cross that bridge when we get there. Let's focus on now and not all the what-if's."

"That's fair."

A waitress delivered our order, taking the number as she turned.

I took a small bite from my muffin, followed by a sip of coffee. Brandt drank his coffee and watched me closely.

"I can ask you whatever I want? Are there topics that are a no-go area?"

"None. Ask anything that comes to mind."

Brandt calmly sat back in his chair. I felt his leg intertwine with mine, and it was comforting. I pushed my leg against his, letting him know I was okay with the gesture.

"How many girls have you slept with since me?" Shocked

at my first question, I slapped a hand over my mouth. "I mean …you don't…oh, hell. I can't believe I asked that."

He put his hand over mine as he leaned forward. After a few moments, I glanced up into his searing blue eyes.

"You can ask anything." Brandt took a deep cleansing breath. "I slept with one person after we broke up. It was three months after getting out of rehab. She was a random person I met at a bar with Trigger. I thought having sex with someone else would help me get over you, since, at the time, I thought I'd never have a chance to get you back. I was wrought with guilt at what I had done to you and took the easy way out. But after that, I decided that if I couldn't have you, I didn't want anyone else."

Thinking of Brandt with someone else hurt, though he'd had every right to see other girls. But knowing Brandt couldn't sleep with anyone else warmed me. I'd felt the same way. *Maybe we have a shot.* As I processed his words, I decided to give him the same honesty.

"Thanks for telling me the truth. It stings thinking someone else had you, even though you weren't mine. Do you want to know about me? This can go both ways."

His voice lowered. Brandt looked down as he whispered, "Yes, I want to know."

"I slept with one person, one time. That was it. We dated for a month, and I slept with him in a moment of desperation, trying to force myself to forget you. Afterward, I felt dirty, like I'd betrayed you. We broke up the next day. That was three months ago."

I played with my muffin, squishing pieces of it on my napkin. There was so much hurt for both of us. The grip on my fingers slightly tightened, and I returned the squeeze.

Finally, he met my eyes. "Nikola, you're anything but

dirty. As you said, it stings, but at least there's only one fucker out there I have to be jealous of. Was it Wesley?"

I shook my head. "No. Since we met at the support group, we've strictly been friends. He had a girlfriend who used. She was released about four months ago, and they talked again about a month ago. He's afraid she might have relapsed last week, but isn't sure. Hopefully not. Wesley's working with her sponsor this week to see."

I felt his leg push against mine again as Brandt relaxed back into his seat and took another sip of coffee. A woman near us was blatantly staring at Brandt. He only had eyes for me. Without thinking, I raised an eyebrow at her—she turned away, blushing.

Brandt chuckled. "I like that you're still jealous. Gives me hope."

Taking another sip of coffee, I tried to hide my smile. Setting my cup back down, I took a serious tone. "Why'd you start using?" I asked. "I thought we were happy. I've replayed our time together over and over, and I can't figure out what drove you to start."

This was probably the question Brandt had thought I would start with. He cracked his neck. "I was at a party I'd heard about. You were out of town, and I figured why not. I went and realized that it was ultimately a drug fest. When I saw what was going on, I turned to leave when I overheard someone trying to convince someone else to try a line of blow. I wanted to hear the sales pitch and how ridiculous it was. They said it wasn't addictive if used in moderation. All the actors snorted a line from time to time. I was stupid enough to fall for it. I knew better. I fucking knew better, but I was tired and stressed out with all the success of the club."

He paused as if taking himself back to that day. "I went to

the guy and listened to the rest of his speech. He talked about how cocaine gave you endless energy and how you could conquer the world on it. I told myself that if I did it in moderation, and only used when you weren't in town, I could get twice as much done and have more time for you. My day had been beyond shitty, and I wanted to escape for a bit.

"Before I knew it, I'd convinced myself to snort a line. It did exactly what they said it would. I felt powerful and ready to take on anything. I went back to the club afterward and could get three days' worth of work done. From there, I craved that power, and I guess it took over my life before I realized it. I lied to everyone I knew and loved. The cravings happened more often and I'd developed a tolerance—I had to use more and more. It had nothing to do with our happiness at all. Before I knew it, I wasn't me anymore and I hurt everyone I loved. But the worst part was losing you."

His words cut right through me. As he spoke, memories played in my head: finding the coke, Brandt denying using, the end of our relationship.

"If we try this again, what will keep you from using again? I'm scared shitless that whatever triggered you last time could send you to drugs. I was part of that equation, and I don't think I could survive it again. It nearly killed me to lose you."

Without warning, Brandt scooted his chair next to mine and hugged me. I grabbed him as if he was the air I needed to breathe. My battered soul was soothed in his arms. I dug my nails into his back, trying to meld us together.

"Baby, I'll always be an addict. But I haven't used once since I left rehab, despite some pretty dark days. Knowing what the drugs cost me has kept me away from them. And it always will." He paused to take a deep breath. "Let's not put pressure on ourselves. I still love you, Nikola. You don't have to say it back, but I don't want you to doubt what I feel for you. I think losing you makes me love you even more now."

Tears spilled down my cheek, and I pulled away slightly. Brandt's thumbs came brushed them away, bringing me back to where I'd been. I was lost for words. He was right—I wasn't ready to say it back. Telling him I loved him at this point would leave me more vulnerable than I was ready to be.

He continued, "I don't expect us to pick up where we left off. We've changed and need to learn each other. I get you being scared. Just tell me when things are too much and we'll dial it down to where you're comfortable." He searched my eyes as a few more tears came down. "What do you think?"

Brandt's fingers grazed my cheek and said, "Even though we've changed, there are still things that are the same. Like you biting your cheek when you're nervous. We still know each other. Being with you feels better than anything, but you don't have to answer today, Nikola."

I wanted this, but we needed to set limits since our sexual chemistry was explosive. We had to make sure we weren't covering our problems with sex like we used to. Taking a deep breath, I replied, "I want to see where this goes." My voice trembled.

Brandt looked like he'd won the ultimate prize. He dropped his hands from my face and grabbed both of my hands. His thumbs stroked mine.

"I have one semi-condition, though."

"Name it. Anything." His voice was resolute.

That was powerful, knowing he wanted me bad.

"No sex until we're ready. Let's try to make it a month."

"Deal. Whatever it takes." I looked up a little surprised. "I told you, Nikola, whatever it takes to get us back to a healthy, happy spot."

We were both smiling when a devilish grin spread across Brandt's face. It was the smile from when he used to tease me. "What if you beg me for sex?"

I laughed, relieved that he wasn't physically driven to get me back. "We'll see." Truth was, when he touched me, I forgot everything else. More seriously, I added, "I want to make sure this isn't based on sex. It's obvious we still have chemistry, but I need to know we're still right for each other."

Brandt squeezed my hand.

"That works for me. So, as of February second, it's fair game to seduce you?"

"Yes, but I'm going to make you work for it."

The look of joy on Brandt's face warmed the places in my soul that I'd locked off, afraid of acute heartache.

"I'd expect nothing less from you. Just leave the damn 8 Ball out of it."

I giggled. I loved my Magic 8 Ball. From time to time, I'd bring it out and consult it. Whatever it said, I followed. The wise blue triangle knew all. Most of the time, the black ball of wisdom seemed to work against Brandt, which made me laugh. "We'll see. Depends on whether you misbehave."

The connection sizzled between us. We were going to fight for us. For love.

"Brandt?"

"Yes."

"Please take care of my heart. I'm entrusting it to you. It's broken and hasn't been the same since I lost you." My voice broke.

He put his forehead to mine. "I'll guard it with my life and do everything in my power to mend it."

Brandt

NIKOLA'S WORDS WERE like a wrecking ball. She deserved the best and showing her was the only way to convince her that I could be her guy again. It would be hard to keep from initiating sex with her for a month, but that was what she needed, and I was going to make it work. But I wanted to feel her wrapped around me.

We were still hugging, and after a long few minutes, I released her. She was glowing, but I could still sense her hesitation. To lighten the mood, I pulled out my phone.

"What are you doing?" Her voice was inquisitive.

Pulling up the app store, I found what I was looking for. "Downloading an app."

"What kind of app?"

I turned away as she leaned in to see my phone, but she

slapped my shoulder.

"You're keeping it away from me on purpose."

"That would be an affirmative."

She grunted, and I tried to suppress my amusement but failed. Quickly, before she had a chance to snatch the phone, I typed in February second and pressed *Start Timer*.

Proudly I held up the phone and she read it.

"Oh my gosh! You're terrible. This may last longer than a month."

Nikola scolded me, but she laughed. Nikola liked this quirky side. It was part of who we were together. We could bench the seriousness sometimes and be silly.

Life without laughter and fun wasn't living, only existing. Those were words my dad lived by. "We'll see if we make it a month." I gave her a wink. She blushed.

I took another sip of coffee, fighting the urge to kiss her as we settled back into our seats. "What's your schedule look like? I'm hoping I can take you on an actual first date in the next day or so."

Her face fell. *Shit. She's going out of town on business.*

"I fly out this afternoon to see a client in New Jersey. I've been working on a marketing proposal for them. Lately, I've been taking more out of town trips and expanding my client base. It's helped take my mind off things."

The regretful tone in her voice made me smile. Nikola wanted a first date. "How long are you gone?"

She pulled out her phone. "Three days. Each week for the next month I'm gone for three to four days."

Fuck. The selfish side of me wasn't ready to let her go, but it'd show her we could survive with time apart. Nikola would be able to see what I was like now as we got to know each other again. "That'll make you miss me more. It'll ensure my blue balls get relief in—" I checked my phone. "Thirty days, thirteen hours, and thirty-one minutes."

She giggled—a magical sound I thought I'd never hear again. "You may have a point there," she said. "However, I can't confirm or deny agreement."

This was us. As easy as breathing. A thought formed in the back of mind, and I wasn't sure how to feel about it. So much was the same, but what would be different?

How would that affect the balance we were used to?

I needed to ask Quentin what to expect.

In the end, it didn't matter. I'd crawl through fire for Nikola.

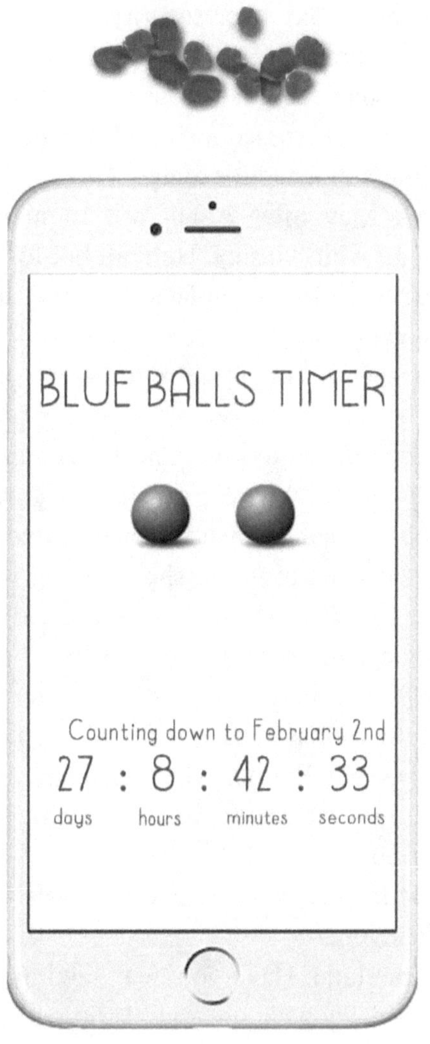

Nikola was flying home, and I was at Club Envy. She'd declined my offer to take her to the airport a couple of days ago, and I hoped she'd let me pick her up. But she hadn't. Honestly, it stung a little, but apparently, this flight had a history of delays and she didn't want to impose.

Adam knocked on the door to the security office. "Matt's coming in tonight to take over security. Are you going to let him do his job this time?"

I turned the chair around and threw my arm over the back of it. "The thought has crossed my mind. I might even hand the office over to him and leave for tonight."

We'd hired Matt after Adam had to man the security cameras one night with Ainsley. He'd all but forced me into it, and for the first time, I contemplated thanking the bastard for having the foresight.

Adam smirked. "I know you're thinking I'm the smartest man living."

"Asshole." I refused to give him the satisfaction, but Adam knew he was right. "Where's Ainsley tonight?"

Adam rubbed a hand down his face. "Ainsley's at home. Since I actually needed to work, she's having Emilyn over to watch *The Last Unicorn*. She's out of school for winter break, so they're doing a slumber party. I'll be here all night."

Emilyn was our bartender, Nora's, sister, and she and Ainsley had gotten close over the years. From time to time, Ainsley helped watch Emilyn when their mom had to work. What Nora had told me about Adam watching *The Last Unicorn* came to mind.

"You mind singing your Prince Lir parts for me? I hear you do a fantastic job."

"Fuck off, asshole. Have you been talking to Nora? That shit is private. Ainsley gave me a guilt trip with that big-eyed-puppy-dog crap." Adam was clearly getting worked up. It was rare that I could get under his skin.

To further agitate him, I smirked, rather than arguing verbally. I'd won this round, and there was no denying it. I made a mental note to see if I could buy the soundtrack and give it to Adam as a present.

"So, since you're not heading home to relive your role as Prince Lir, do you mind if I takeoff when Nikola lands?"

He flipped me the bird, and I laughed.

"Go have fun," he said. "Tell Nikola I said hi. No pressure, but when you're ready, maybe we could all go out together. Help pass the hours on your blue ball timer."

"How the fuck did you find out about that?"

No one knew about that timer except Nikola.

Adam smirked. *Bastard.* "Nora said you left your phone on the bar with the timer open. I guess the words 'blue balls' caught her attention." Adam walked toward the door. "I heard ice helps. Not that I'd know. Just be careful of frostbite."

"You're a dick sometimes, Adam."

Adam whistled down the hall. Nora loved to stir shit between Adam and me. This round seemed to have ended in a tie. I pulled out my phone and ordered *The Last Unicorn* CD. As I hit *Place My Order*, a text message came through from Nikola. We'd talked right before she'd boarded—her trip had been a success.

Nikola: Landed.

Me: You up for a date?

Nikola: I want to see you, but I don't want to go out and be social.

Me: Perfect. I know somewhere great. I'll pick you up in an hour. Wear comfy clothes.

Nikola: I'll be ready. Can't wait.
Me: Me either. I've missed you.
Nikola: I've missed you, too.

I cleared all my stuff from the desk, prepping the area for Matt. A few minutes later, Matt knocked on the door. He was ex-military and exuded the look with his crew cut and muscled stature. Many of our patrons had propositioned him, but so far, he hadn't found someone that suited his fancy.

"What do you want me to do tonight, Brandt?"

Standing, I gestured toward the seat. "I'm actually going to let you do what we hired you for. Sorry I've been a pain in the ass. Security is yours. We've sat together enough that you know the drill. I'm stepping back from security."

Without hesitation, he said, "Thanks, man. I'll keep you posted."

Nothing fazed Matt. It could be raining purple dinosaurs and he'd calmly assess the situation and then handle it. The control he possessed was like no other.

"Sounds good. I'll have my cell."

I ran by my house to pick up some essentials, and within an hour I pulled up to Nikola's. When my headlights hit in her windows, she walked out the door, locking it. She lived in a townhome complex, and the units all had the same gray siding. I bet the inside of her place was colorful and vibrant. Nikola loved weird-ass furniture.

I got out of my vehicle. "I would have come to the door."

She turned and ran into my arms, surprising me. Her missing me as much as I'd missed her reassured me since I still wasn't sure what all was going through her mind. I brought her to me. Her shampoo was still the same floral scent I remembered. Closing my eyes, I tried to memorize what it felt like to hold her like this.

"I guess you did miss me a lot."

Nikola nodded into my chest. "I did."

Something was off. I pulled back and searched her eyes. "Hey, is something wrong?"

"No, I'm glad you're here."

The light was dim and I couldn't see her face, but I was pretty sure she wasn't telling me everything. "If this is going to work, we're going to have to be honest with each other."

Her posture went rigid and I knew we were headed into rougher waters. It happened a little sooner than I wanted, but Quentin had said that the same thing had happened when he and his wife had gotten back together. The expectations they'd once had for each other had changed. Addicts needed honesty at all times.

"Brandt, please don't push me on this. Please. I want to leave."

I knew she was hiding something. "Nikola."

She looked away. I waited for her to look at me. Eventually, she'd have to. She knew I'd rather be silent than speak to her back or the side of her face.

Finally, her stubbornness gave in and her eyes met mine. "I'm not asking you for an explanation. I'm asking you to be truthful. If you don't want to talk about it, say that. Don't say it's nothing when I know that's a lie."

Nikola nodded. "You're right. I don't want to talk about it."

I couldn't remember whether we used to mask things, but I guess I wouldn't have been as sensitive to it as she. Maybe if I got her away from here, she'd open up.

"Are you ready to go, baby?"

She nodded and I guided her to the passenger side. When

I got in, I put the vehicle into reverse right as her phone rang.

She picked it up. "Yes. I'm good. I'm with Brandt. Yes, he just got here. I will. Thanks." She hung up, then looked out the window.

I wasn't sure what to make of the conversation, but she'd clearly called someone—presumably Wesley—about being scared.

Time. We need time. Wesley is safe. He's been her go-to person. Quentin warned me about this when Nikola was out of town.

I repeated this to myself over and over. It was hard as fuck to swallow that jagged pill—her going to another man first. But hell, I'd only been back in her life for five days.

Time. We need time.

Turning the radio on to break the silence, I pulled out of the driveway and resumed our course. After a few minutes, I felt a hand on mine. I'd left it on the console as an invitation.

"I'm sorry. I got spooked and called Wesley out of habit. I thought I heard something outside my apartment. It ended up being nothing."

And just like that, our waters smoothed without any urge to use. *Thank you.* One of the fears I'd expressed to Quentin was reading too much into the regular ups and downs of life and slipping back into old habits. I remembered his words: "Having a healthy respect for stress and not thinking you're invincible to the shit that happens in life will keep your mind on the right side of things."

"Do you get spooked often?" There was a fifty-fifty chance she'd answer me, and I wanted her to know that I wasn't giving up on hearing what had happened.

"Some. Where are you taking me?" Her breathing accelerated a little.

Obviously, we'd hit a subject that made Nikola uncomfortable. The soft blue light from the inside of the car cast a glow on her face. Her brows were slightly creased. At least she was honest. I let the subject change.

"To a place I like to go when I have a lot to think about."

She smiled. "I think that sounds like a perfect date tonight."

We lapsed back into silence. My mind sorted through clues as to what might be bothering her. I scrolled through all my recent interactions with Nikola when I remembered the text she'd received when I'd gone to Anne's on New Year's Day.

Eventually, Nikola's breathing returned to normal. Her posture relaxed, too.

I pulled up to one of my favorite places on Earth and turned the SUV around to park.

"We're at an airport?"

Looking over to meet Nikola's gaze, I answered, "Yes, we're at Peachtree DeKalb Airport. You'll see why I brought you here in a few minutes."

I pressed the button for the back hatch and it popped open. Without waiting for me, Nikola got out of the vehicle. The runway lights lit up the whole area.

She watched me inquisitively as I jumped in the back and slid the cooler over. Giving her a wink, I patted the space beside me. Nikola accepted the invitation and came to sit right next to me. Without saying a word, I opened the cooler and got out two bottles of water and two half-pints of Rocky Road ice cream.

"I hope this is still your favorite."

She beamed at me. "It is."

I handed her a spoon, and as we ate our ice cream, Nikola

asked, "Why'd you bring me here? I'm trying to piece this all together. I didn't know you liked planes."

The sound of an airplane engine accelerating sounded in the distance. It'd be less than a couple of minutes until we saw my favorite part.

"Watch the runway. It's a busy enough airport that you can see planes taking off and landing. The amount of control and precision it takes to fly is amazing. It may not make sense to you, but I wanted you to be part of this."

The one-prop plane sped up as it crossed in front of us on the runway. The front wheels barely lifted off the ground and, slowly, the rest of the plane followed. It was incredible to see each and every time.

Nikola was in awe. "Wow. I get it. Thank you."

I knew she would. We always got each other. She continued to speak. "You stay in control of yourself, as a pilot controls a plane, focused and determined not to go back to drugs."

"Yes. I never used drugs to escape anything bad. I did them because I thought I could control them and not become an addict. Control is something to be respected and not toyed with. I was humbled when I saw how wrong I was."

Another plane engine roared in the distance. There'd be another takeoff soon.

The wind blew and it was fucking cold. "Can we sit inside the car and lower the hatch? It's freezing."

"Sure thing."

We brought our knees in. I hit the button on the keychain to lower the back part of my vehicle. I hit the start button to get the heater going. Nikola curled into my side. I cracked the window so we could still hear the planes.

"Here's my ice cream. I'm too cold." Nikola's teeth were chattering as I grabbed her pint.

"I'll have to remember this next time I want you close to me." That got me a light slap on the stomach, where her hand stayed. I fucking loved her touching me like this. It's how we used to cuddle. I placed both half-pints back in the cooler before pulling her closer.

"I've always eaten ice cream when I came here. I don't know why, it just works." The car warmed up fast. We went to speak when our eyes connected. That familiar connection came back. Nikola's head slightly inclined to mine.

"I want to kiss you, Nikola."

She took a deep breath. So many emotions warred on her face. Her lips inched closer to mine. A tingling sensation hit my lips, knowing they were moments away from tasting the sweetest thing on Earth. An ambulance siren in the distance made Nikola pull back slightly, her eyes coming back into focus. Startled, she blinked rapidly as if to shake the connection.

"I'm not ready yet. I'm sorry." Her voice was filled with regret.

There were times that felt like we were together like we had been, and times like this with razor-sharp truth. I needed to work harder. I was a fucking moron for thinking it was going to be easy. I needed to earn the right to kiss her again.

Deep down, it hurt that I'd been denied. But she deserved to find total trust in the person she gave a piece of herself to. Hell, this was only our first date, and I'm sure she was scared shitless about dating an addict. She looked away when it took me a moment to respond. I tried to process everything on the fly.

I put a finger under her chin. "Hey, don't worry. It'll happen when it's meant to. I fucked up pretty bad. You deserve whatever time you need to see I've changed."

Another plane took off in the distance. "I like your plan

and the thought of having more time with you."

"I like that, too, baby."

Nikola wrapped her arms around me, and I took in her scent as I kissed the top of her head. An engine starting sounded in the distance. This was a perfect moment—I hadn't had one in a long time.

Nikola

FOR THE PAST few days I'd been in New York, and I was due to see Brandt tonight. We'd talked every day whenever I had spare time, which hadn't been much. There were parts of Brandt that had changed. He thought things through more, especially when it came to potential consequences. He had a regimented gym schedule. In the past year, it seemed like Brandt hadn't done much other than see his mom, work out, and work at the club. Before, he'd been a social creature—the life of the party.

But there was still a lot that was the same—his never-ending patience, the fun, silly side that made me laugh, and the ability to express what he felt.

My heels sounded against the concrete as I walked from my car to the door of my Grandmama's kitchen. As I entered, I called, “Hey, Grandmama, I’m here.”

She replied almost immediately. “Hey there! I’m in the back. I’ll be right there.”

After putting my coat and laptop bag on a barstool, I kicked off my heels. I was tired after four long days with a client. In the end, they’d disputed my suggestions, saying my ideas weren’t how they’d envisioned their brand. It was frustrating when they didn’t listen, but it was part of the game. I was only paid fifty percent for concept, rather than the full contract price, since they didn’t go with my plan. My expenses would be covered and I’d make a little in the end, but not as much as I had hoped.

A fresh chocolate pie sat on the bar, and the smell of cocoa had me salivating. Off to the side, flowers caught my eye. On second look, I noticed my name on the card.

Biting my lip, I opened the card. They were from Brandt.

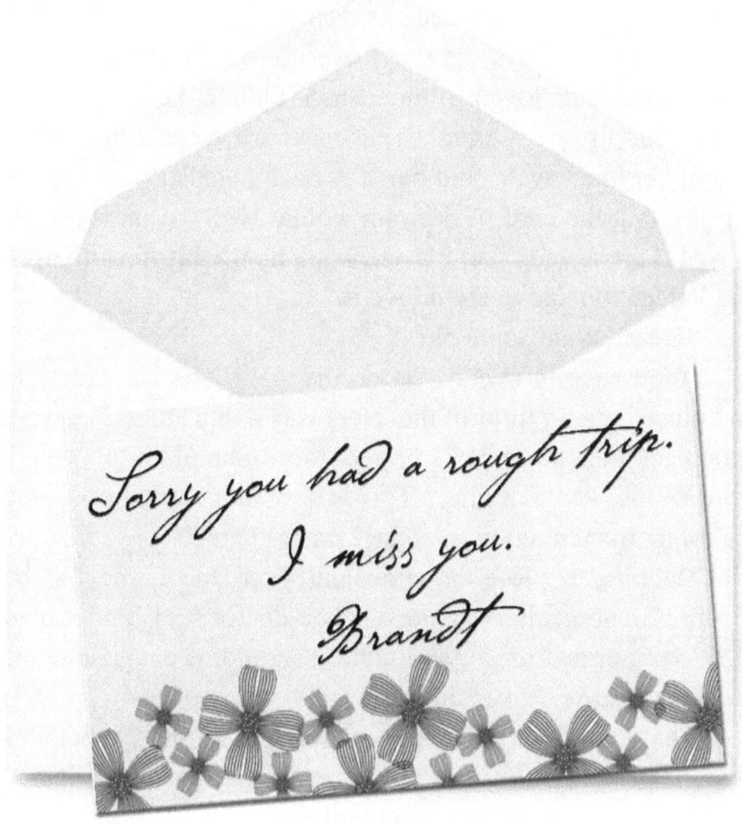

Sorry you had a rough trip.
I miss you.
Brandt

"Well, I guess the message from Brandt was good."

I glanced up and saw Grandmama in the doorway, a pleased look on her face.

Putting the card to my lips, I gave it a quick kiss before putting it back. "It was a very good note. He misses me."

She chuckled as she got plates and forks for us. "Of course, he does. Didn't he send you flowers daily while you were gone?"

"He did." Brandt had been lavishing me with attention. Late one night, on an especially long day, he'd arranged for an in-room massage. It had been heavenly.

"I hope you guys can come over for dinner soon."

Grandmama loved Brandt. She'd thought he was going to be my happily ever after. Even when we were broken up, a part of her knew we'd find our way back together.

Putting the card back in the holder with the message displayed, I answered, "Let me see when he has his next night off and I'll let you know. He'd love it."

"Good. Want some pie?"

"You have to ask?" I sat on the stool. She cut two slices and placed one in front of me. Hers was a thin slice. The warm chocolate melted out of its perfect form. She placed a piece in front of me. I took a bite. "This is so good. How'd your doctor's appointment go? I'm sorry I wasn't here."

Dabbing a piece of chocolate from the corner of her mouth, Grandmama responded, "The doctor said it's bronchitis. He prescribed me an antibiotic. I should be cough-free in a couple of weeks. It was fairly severe."

That was a relief. I always worried about Grandmama since she was getting older. I'd be lost without her. "Good, thank you for appeasing me and going."

She took her last bite of pie and stood. "I shouldn't have waited so long." She patted me. "I need to finish those vests for the school."

"Okay, I'll be back in a second. I'm going to thank Brandt for the flowers."

Grandmama winked and headed off to her sewing room. She was making little red vests for the kids at the local elementary school. They got badges for different things like math problems, spelling, good grades, friendship, and more. It was a neat program.

I pulled out my phone to text Brandt.

Me: Boy, someone sure does know how to make a girl feel special! I got these beautiful flowers and the sweetest note.

Brandt: It's just the beginning, baby.

Me: I love them. Thank you.

Brandt: You're welcome. How was Grandmama's appointment?

Me: She has bronchitis. So relieved. Should be clear in a few weeks. She invited you to dinner. Let me know when you can come next week.

Brandt: I'll be available whatever night works for her. When are you getting here? I miss you. I have a meeting in about thirty minutes.

Me: I miss you, too. I hope we can spend more time together soon. How about in two hours? Need to take a shower.

Brandt: Perfect. Tell me when you're here so I can meet you outside.

Me: Sounds good and I will.

Being back at the club was going to be a little intimidating—Brandt and I had an explosive history there. Tonight we'd only be on the bar side. I thought it was a good idea to ease back into the scene.

The sewing machine in the back room sounded like it was going ninety miles a minute. As a child, I'd lay on the daybed in there and let the hum of the machine lull me to sleep. Before I got ready, I wanted to spend some time with Grandmama, even if it was only watching her sew. Since Brandt had a meeting, I had time.

In the back room, a wallpaper boarder of needles and thread lined the top wall. Grandmama sat at her sewing table, effortlessly sewing the material. She'd given me sewing lessons as a kid, so I could sew some, but not like she could.

"Hey, Grandmama, mind if I keep you company before I get ready to head out?"

"Not at all. I'd love it."

She continued with her task as I took my spot on the daybed. I listened to the sound of the machine as I processed where Brandt and I stood. The other night, when Brandt had wanted to kiss me, I longed to feel his lips against mine. I ached to feel him, but I needed to tell him about Lance first. I didn't want any secrets between us.

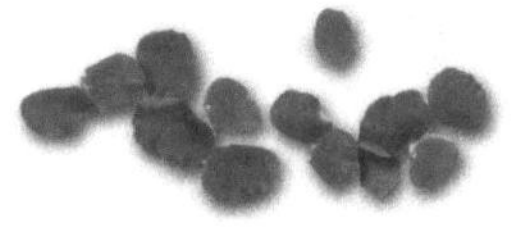

Pulling out of the driveway, I waved to Grandmama at the window. She was headed to bed early. The medicine took its toll on her, and she was tired. As I hopped onto the highway, my phone chirped. Figuring it was Brandt, I opened the text.

My body chilled when I saw Lance's name appear on the screen.

Lance: Why haven't you been home lately?

I pulled over. Lance and I lived in the same apartment complex. Since we'd broken up after sleeping together once, I rarely stayed there anymore. When Brandt had picked me up, Lance had spooked me by saying he knew I was home and was coming over to talk. Then there had been a tap on my window.

I felt bad that I'd only given Brandt half the truth. I needed to tell him everything.

Me: Lance, it's over between us. Please stop contacting me.

Lance: Have a good night, Nikola.

Pinching the bridge of my nose, I tried to push back the headache that formed. The lights from the dashboard cast a light glow within my car, calming me. An eighteen-wheeler sped by, making the car shake. With all the traffic, this had been a bad place to pull over. I put my blinker on and merged back into traffic.

My breathing was accelerated and I tried to slow it down. I needed to talk to someone. My first instinct was to call Brandt, but I didn't want to put this stress on him. Plus, he was in a meeting. Wesley came to mind next. He picked up on the third ring.

"Hey, Nikola. You make it back okay?"

I pushed the lump down in my throat and said, "I did, but Lance texted me. Asked me why I hadn't been home lately. I asked him to stop contacting me, and he wished me a good night. Do you think I'm overreacting?"

"If it makes you uncomfortable, then no. Have you talked to Brandt about it?" His voice was warm and soothing. He was like the brother I'd never had.

I should have told Brandt, and I felt guilty. There were several times at the airport as we sat in the back of his SUV that I'd wanted to tell him but hadn't. Part of me knew it would upset him that a guy was bothering me, and I wanted to avoid those triggers.

"Umm—no, I haven't," I confessed.

"Why not?" Wesley sounded as though he was driving, too, as his blinker sounded through the speaker.

"Umm—I don't know."

"Nikola, that's bullshit and you know it. What are you afraid of?"

I liked how Wesley always called it like it was. It reminded me of Brandt.

I blew out a big breath. "I'm afraid any extra stress could make us lose what we've got and even send him back to drugs. Why bother him with problems that may not even be problems? I want us to work so badly that I'm afraid I'll make us fall apart."

My lip trembled at the thought of losing Brandt again. I knew I needed to tell him everything.

"One second, Nikola." There was mumbling on the other end of the phone. "Give me a second and I'll be in." There was more talking. I couldn't make out who it was. "Sorry about that, Nikola. I'm over at Diane's parents' house. I'm going to talk to them about how I think Diane may be using again."

I felt like shit bothering him with my petty drama. He had a girlfriend that might be on heroin again. I would be devastated if Brandt did that. It's what terrified me.

"No, problem. We can talk later."

"Sounds good. I'll call you tomorrow. But, think about this: You *can't* spend your relationship walking on eggshells because that's not a relationship. I could pretend I don't think Diane is using and wring out the last few good days, but that doesn't help anyone. Hit it head on. Be honest with Brandt about everything."

In a whisper, I said, "I love him, Wesley. What if he only loves the old me?"

A car door opened on the other end. "Then it's better to

know now than five years from now. You can't stop living because you're scared. You'll either find middle ground, or you won't."

"Thanks, buddy."

"Anytime. Call me if you need me. I'm always here for you. I'll call you tomorrow to see how it went."

"Sounds good. Good luck, Wesley. I hope you're wrong about Diane."

"Me, too."

I hung up and drove, thinking about Wesley's advice. He'd been my rock after losing Brandt. We'd helped each other put the pieces back together after losing our partners. I'd never felt more than friendship with Wesley. I think he felt the same way. I was going to tell Brandt tonight about Lance. He needed to know. I had to trust our love.

You guys will last or you won't.

My insides knotted thinking the latter could actually happen. Hopefully, our love was strong enough. Hopefully. I would fight with everything I had to make it work.

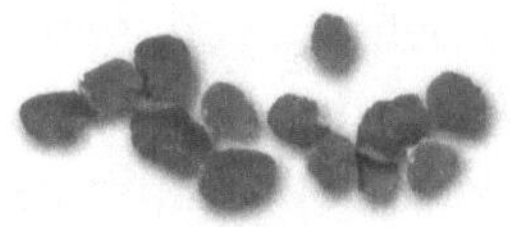

My mind was a jumbled mess as I pulled into the Club Envy parking lot. It was a busy night. The red sign lit up the club name as people stood in line, waiting to get in. On the marquee it said: THRILLHAMMERS: LIVE TONIGHT! The band always drew a crowd, and I loved their sound. I'd seen them at a few different venues after Brandt and I broke up. Remembering to tell Brandt I was in the parking lot, I texted him.

Me: I'm here.
Brandt: Okay, I'll be right out.

Brandt had always wanted to meet me at the car and bring me in the club. It made me feel special. Brandt came through the doors on the sex club side. He wore nice, dark-colored jeans with a thermal. His hair was loose, hitting his shoulders. He smiled as he jogged across the parking lot and I got out of my car.

"Hey there. I'm glad you're here. I missed you while you were in New York."

My smile spread wider across my face. "Missed you, too."

I leaned in for a hug. Brandt's strong arms came around me, and I loved how safe I felt. Pulling back, our eyes searched each other's. The atmosphere charged between us, and I involuntarily licked my lips. This had happened in the back of his car the other day. My pulse quickened and the palms of my hands felt slightly sweaty. Brandt watched me closely and leaned in. My body craved his lips. I wanted him. The moment our lips touched, need ignited within me. His lips were soft, yet firm, and I'd dreamed about them while we were apart. My memory had not done us justice.

The secret I'd been keeping came to mind as his tongue sought entrance. I needed to tell him about Lance first. I panicked and blurted, "I saw The Thrillhammers are playing tonight."

Brandt had a confused look on his face, along with a flash of disappointment. He cleared his throat and pulled back slightly. I felt like a bitch as he responded, but my rattled insides kept me from speaking.

"They are. Want to go see them?"

I nodded. My nerves were all over the place, being somewhere that screamed of our sexy former relationship. But once we were in the club, I'd find a way to bring up Lance—I had to before we left tonight.

The music vibrated in the pavement. Tonight, I'd gone with skinny jeans and an off-the-shoulder sweater—classy and sexy. We made our way inside, passing Jethro, the bouncer. He was a giant, bald teddy bear, and he'd always been kind to me.

"Hey, Nikola, long time no see. Welcome back."

I gave him a big hug. "Good to see you. How have you been?"

"Good! These fuckers keep me busy, but all's good. Have fun in there tonight. Good to see the two of you together."

I beamed and looked back at Brandt. "I couldn't agree more."

Brandt placed his hand on my lower back. I loved how possessive it felt.

Brandt smiled as he spoke. "I'm going to take Nikola inside."

"Sounds good."

"Matt has security if you need anything."

Jethro nodded. "It's all good."

Brandt nodded, and we went inside. The bar side of the club felt so familiar; I let it wash over me. Old street signs hung from rustic metal walls. Neon beer signs were lit up. The floor was packed with bodies dancing to The Thrillhammers. The band was in full swing, playing "Hippie House." Momentarily closing my eyes, I fortified myself, pushing away the craving for his hard length. My body wanted Brandt badly, especially after barely kissing him in the parking lot. I wanted to feel his tip graze the sensitive nerve endings of my inner walls. *Stop. I need to stop.* I brought myself back to the now, preparing to talk about Lance.

As we made our way through the crowd I asked, "So, you told everyone we're together?"

"I did. I said we'd started seeing each other. Are you okay with that?"

I smiled. "More than okay."

Our hands were intertwined as we approached the bar. Brandt pulled out his phone and showed me the app he'd downloaded.

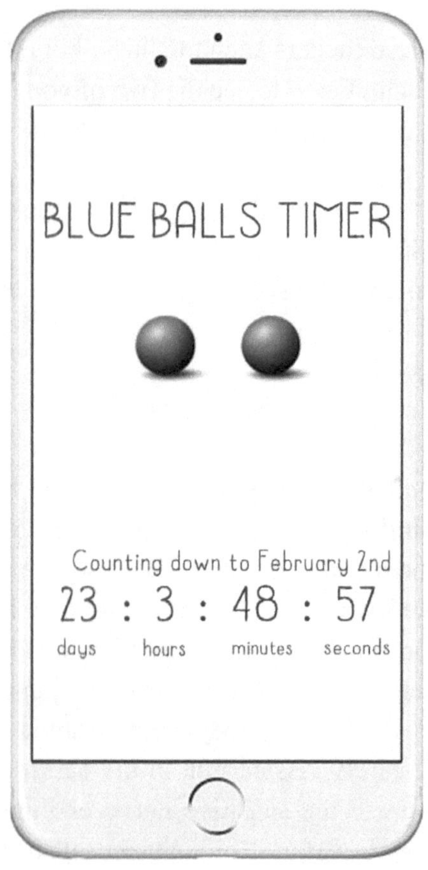

Brandt wiggled his eyebrows as I mock-slapped his chest.

"You're incorrigible."

His mouth came down to my ear; his hot breath tickling my skin. "I'll wait forever, but when I do sink myself into you, I'm going to make it last. I remember, like it was yesterday, just how incredible you feel."

His words made my face flush with passion. I remembered as if it were yesterday, too. His hand flexed against my waist. He knew what I was thinking. We'd always been able to sense each other's feelings. What made us perfect for each other hadn't changed. The thought made me smile—maybe our differences wouldn't be so hard to overcome.

We continued toward the bar and I took a deep breath. A heady mixture of sweat and alcohol filled the room, forcing memories to the forefront of my mind. When I touched the bar, an image had desire spiraling through me: Brandt, after closing the bar, bending me over the countertop and taking me from behind. A vibrator was going to be in order tonight. I needed to distract myself.

"Is Adam here?"

"Did someone say my name?"

I turned at the sound of the familiar voice.

Adam was behind me, arms open. I jumped to give him a sisterly bear hug. When I'd left Brandt after getting him to rehab, Adam had never judged my decision.

"Hey, now. She's my girl," Brandt called from over my shoulder.

Adam released me a bit. He looked the same with his warm, chocolate eyes and short, messy, brown hair. However, there was one difference—he looked happy. I glanced back at Brandt with a loving smile.

Adam said, "Payback's going to be hell with how much

you've hugged Ainsley."

Brandt cursed behind us, and I giggled. A beautiful chestnut-haired woman with the palest blue eyes came and stood behind Adam.

He hugged me again. "It's good having you around again. I missed you, Nikola."

The warm reception from Jethro and Adam further mended my broken heart. When I'd left Brandt, I'd left some dear friends. I thought it wouldn't be fair to Brandt, still doing things with people he'd need to lean on during his recovery.

"I've missed you too, Adam. Is this the lucky girl who's won your heart? I hear congratulations are in order."

The sound of Brandt tapping his hand twice on the bar top caused me to turn and look his way for a second. The waitress came and sat a beer down in front of Brandt.

Adam's voice took my attention away from Brandt. The woman, whom I'd assumed was Ainsley, stood beside Adam as he put his arm around her. Brandt had told me about her.

"This is Ainsley Pearson, soon to be Ryker. Ainsley, this is Nikola Kingston. Nikola owns her own company. She's a strategist."

Ainsley hugged me, and I could see how she'd been the person to sooth Adam's wounds and give him the unconditional love he deserved. "Nice to meet you, Ainsley."

We pulled back from the hug. Her features were warm, and I was glad she hadn't taken offense to me hugging Adam like I had.

"Nice to meet you, too. We have something in common. I'm going to school for business analysis. I graduate this semester."

"That's what my degree is in! Congrats. Maybe we can talk shop sometime."

Her eyes lit up. “Oh, I’d love that! Thank you.”

Brandt came from behind me and put his arm around my waist. I leaned into him, loving how this felt. He took a sip of beer and my nerves shot back up. Brandt used to drink when he did drugs. I tried to not overreact, but anything connected to the drugs had all my defenses up.

The Thrillhammers hit the chorus of their song and the crowd was going wild.

Adam leaned in between Brandt and me while speaking. “Ainsley and I are going to head back to the other side. Just wanted to say hey. You guys have a good time tonight.”

“Sounds good. Thanks, man.” Brandt nodded their way.

From the way Adam and Ainsley looked at each other, I knew exactly what waited on the other side of the wall separating the bar from the sex club side. I glanced over at Brandt and he winked. My thoughts were getting further jumbled. I hadn’t expected Brandt to be drinking. Memories of smelling alcohol on his breath when he would come home high and have sex with me hit hard. I tried to remember if Brandt had had any alcohol at Coyote Ugly when we’d first seen each other, but I couldn’t.

Adam nodded, then disappeared with Ainsley. We turned back around and I faced the bar while Brandt still held his beer. A strawberry-blonde bartender approached. “Can I get you anything?”

“Water, please.”

The bartender raised an eyebrow, but grabbed a cold bottle from underneath the counter. “Let me know if you need anything else.”

I nodded, watching Brandt sip his beer. This seemed like a normal routine with him. I wondered if it was every night. With his addiction, the alcohol had me on edge.

Chris, from The Thrillhammers, came on the microphone: "This next song goes out to all those who've had to pay a terrible price for love."

My heart physically hurt as I tried to keep all my painful memories with Brandt buried. We had a lot to overcome, and I needed to talk to him. That was how it had to be if we wanted a chance to make this last. Alcohol was a no-go for me with his history.

I had to be honest, like Wesley had suggested in the car.

The song started.

The Wages of Love have taken a toll on me
Embrace of emotion. A terrible hold on me
So what is it worth to lay down this burden
Shake off this curse, start a new life,
And draw back the curtain

And I can't ask why, and I don't know when
It was just a token, unspoken, now broken
Again and again

Once solid and whole now sand through my fingers
The ghosts are all gone, left from my home
But the memory lingers

And I can't ask how, it don't matter why
I'll set it aside all of these tears and these lies
And do what I can do

The wages of love
Is a terrible cost
And I've spent it all, and all of it's lost

Now I'm heart broke and destitute
But I ain't put on my funeral suit, I'll probably
Pay them again

The wages of love
A lesson I'm learning
The face of rejection
Still I stand yearning
And I can't ask why. And I don't know when
All that once mattered, was shattered,
And scattered along with the wind

I paid the boatman
Though I'm still not across
My heart ain't frozen yet
But I can feel the frost
Is it all lost

The song ended and Chris said, "We'll be back to rock it out after a twenty-minute break. Stick around, 'cause we're going to bring this house down."

The words from the song resonated within me. The crowd erupted. It was time to talk to Brandt. I hoped he hadn't been lying to me when he'd said he didn't want me to hide how I was feeling.

Brandt

I COULD SENSE something was on Nikola's mind. Her brow was creased with worry and she was chewing on her inner cheek. I'd been seconds from tasting her again in the parking lot and my dick ached at the thought. I needed more one-on-one time with her. Her traveling schedule made it hard as hell, but I'd figure out something.

The crowd died down after The Thrillhammers' last song. Nikola's sweater bared her shoulder, teasing my desire to touch her there. I knew that wasn't possible tonight, but fuck, I wanted her. I took another sip of beer.

Nikola's emerald eyes pierced mine. "Do you drink often?"

I cracked my neck, sensing she was about to drop a bomb on me. Obviously, it was alcohol-related. My rehab teachers had advised to stop using any addictive substance. Alcohol had never been a problem for me, so I kept drinking in moderation. Nikola's voice had the tone she took when she was about to scold me. It was rare, but it often resulted in a small fight. Whatever it was, I needed to stay calm. We used to work through these things quickly, but right now, our relationship was in rough seas.

I set the beer down. "I have a couple occasionally."

Nikola's tapped her fingers on the counter. "Do you think that's a good idea, considering your addiction?"

"Alcohol was never my problem. You *know* this. I've been sober for over a year now, without relapse."

I took another sip of beer out of habit because it was there. Her eyes widened. Nikola was my top priority, but I was still my own person. We needed to be real.

"You used to drink while you were high. I remember the smell of your breath when you'd come home, have sex with me, and then pass out."

She spoke in monotone and her lips pressed together tightly. This was not going well. The blank stare on Nikola's face had my nerves standing on edge. It felt like she wouldn't let this go.

"Nikola, I don't see why this is an issue. Alcohol is not my trigger. Yes, you know I drank while I was high, but we used to drink together. There were multiple times we had sex when we both had alcohol on our breath. I think you're making it out to be an issue when it's not. Can we talk about this later?"

Anger flashed in her eyes. "You want to push it aside, even though it's a big deal? I thought you said there wasn't a topic that was off-limits. We can go elsewhere to talk about this if you want, but it needs to be discussed now."

I went to take a sip of beer again then caught myself. Nikola's eyes followed my movement. "There isn't a topic we can't discuss. But you haven't been part of my life for the last year and seen how I'm handling things."

The air got heavy and our voices were rising. Nikola must have been feeling the same way. "I need some air. I'll be right back."

I was agitated at my addiction being used against me. She turned and I followed her out of Club Envy, leaving my beer on the counter. In the parking lot, she took deep breaths. She seemed panicked.

"Nikola, let's take a step back and look at this rationally. You're overreacting."

She stopped and turned toward me. It was cold outside, but the look on Nikola's face could burn me to the ground. "I'm overreacting? Are you fucking kidding me? I'm overreacting." She took a step closer and glanced around—people in the parking lot now staring.

With her voice lowered to a harsh whisper, she said, "So was I overreacting when you paused to consider the drug dealers' offer that time they wanted to rape me to settle your debt? Was I overreacting when you repeatedly lied to me? Was I overreacting when you were so drunk and high you didn't know what way was up or down? And now, because I'm concerned you're playing with something that could put *me* and *us* in danger, it's considered overacting? Tell me, Brandt, how the hell is that overreacting?"

"Are you going to throw this at me every time we disagree? That's bullshit, Nikola, and you know it. Yes, I fucked up, but you can't hold it over my head."

Nikola flinched. *Fuck. Here we go.*

She squared her shoulders and her eyes burned with emotion. I loved the fierceness in her, but it also pissed me off.

"We need a breather, before one of us says something we regret. You need to think about this, Brandt. You're asking me to go out on a limb and trust you while you play Russian roulette with alcohol. I'm going home. Call me when you're ready to be reasonable."

I loathed ultimatums. "You do the same. Think about *you* being unreasonable. I was at clubs, at restaurants, in cars, and who the fuck knows where else when I got high. Do you want me to sell my club and never go out to eat again?"

We were both fuming, and I knew we needed a time-out. Her chest heaved. It was best to let her go, even though I wanted her to stay. Nikola and I needed some distance to gain perspective.

"I'm going home. We're talking in circles."

Those words sobered me up. "Can I call you later?"

She stared at me for a minute. "Yes, I want to talk this out. This problem isn't going to go away. I hate this, Brandt, but either the alcohol goes or I go. I know you hate ultimatums, but I can't be stupid about what we're facing just because of how I feel."

"I love you, Nikola."

"Let your actions speak louder than your words, Brandt. I'm going home. We need some space." Her lip trembled. I went to take a step toward her, but she held up her hand. "I'll be okay. We'll talk later."

I nodded, wanting to hug her, but I stayed put as she turned and walked to her car. She paused and looked back. Part of me wanted to run and stop her. Nikola looked like she wanted to come to me; however, my pride won out, and I watched her taillights disappear.

Walking back toward the club, my insides shook with

turmoil. Laughter sounded at the other end of the lot as a group of people headed to their cars. I pulled out my phone and called the first person that came to mind.

"Brandt, what's up man?" Quentin's voice calmed me.

"Can we meet? I need to meet." My voice was strained.

"Yeah, meet me at Dave's Diner. I'll be there in fifteen."

Quentin never hesitated when I needed to talk. He got it.

"Thanks, man. I'll be there."

I turned and headed for my car. My mind raced as I thought about all the pressure I was suddenly under. Our fight had blown out of proportion before I'd had any chance to gain control. The being out of control feeling left me edgy. In the car, I revved the engine and drove as fast I could. The city was alive as I made my way to the familiar diner that brought me comfort and a mainline of caffeine.

Quentin was already there when I arrived. I sat at our regular booth, where Donna had poured two cups of coffee. She waved from behind the counter. She looked as if she'd recently started her shift with how fresh she looked.

"Let me know if you need anything else, Brandt," Donna called.

"Will do. Thanks, Donna."

The aroma of greasy meat filled the air. The diner was fairly empty since the dinner rush had ended hours ago. The red vinyl seat squeaked as I shifted my position, across from Quentin. I took a sip of the hot liquid, trying to calm my nerves. Reality set in: There was a chance I'd lost Nikola already. I felt like a fucking moron. I also felt torn between being a doormat and keeping my individuality.

Quentin was in his standard flannel shirt and ball cap. He watched me closely as I decided to lay it out there, skipping the standard pleasantries.

"Nikola got pissed that I was having a beer. She thinks I'm playing 'Russian roulette' with my sobriety. I want her like I've never wanted anything else, but she can't hold my addiction over my head every time I do something she doesn't agree with for the rest of my life. It'll never work. *And* she gave me an ultimatum."

Taking a slow sip of coffee, Quentin seemed to be trying to digest my words. "Nikola was hurt in this, too, Brandt. She's taking a gamble, as well, putting herself out there and hoping that you've actually recovered. I know she's seen you get high. We've touched on alcohol before and so far it hasn't been a problem. Your counselor urged you against drinking also. However, I'll ask the same thing I asked before: Was alcohol in your system when you got high?"

I ran a hand through my hair. Quentin knew the answer, but the images still popped into my head: snorting line after line of coke in various places. Each and every time, I'd been drinking. For some reason, I had ignored everyone's blatant warnings. I involuntarily raised my eyebrow as I answered. "You know it was there. But it was never the problem."

"So, if it were never the problem, why are you choosing it over the only girl you claim to have ever loved? Is it not worth giving up to give her security? She's not asking you to give up anything close to your heart. Nikola is asking you to give up something that went hand-in-hand with getting high. It doesn't matter if you think it did or not. Is alcohol worth it if there's even a small chance that it could lead to a relapse?"

Quentin's comment stunned me for a moment as I processed it. *I chose alcohol over Nikola. Fuck. I chose alcohol over Nikola.* I cradled my head in my hands, thinking about what an asshole I'd been, all because of a beer. Nikola had a right to be upset about *any* substance that was connected to the addiction that had put her through hell. And, yet, she was still willing to give me a chance.

Looking up at Quentin, I said, "I get it. Alcohol isn't worth losing her."

"I'd say you have your answer. You know, I made the same choice for Melody. She wasn't worth losing on the off-chance a beer led to something else. A beer doesn't keep my bed warm or give me unconditional love."

Quentin took another sip of coffee as I stood and laid some cash on the table.

As I backed away, I called, "Thanks, man. I owe you a dinner."

"What are you going to do?"

Right before I pushed through the door, I looked Quentin straight in the eyes and said, "I'm going to get my girl back."

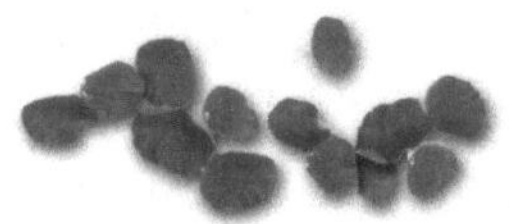

Pulling into Nikola's driveway, my fists tighten around the steering wheel. That same fucking black sports car from New Year's Eve was parked in her driveway. Nikola says they're friends, but hell, I want to still pummel Wesley's ass into next week. Even if it *was* my own stupid ass fault.

Taking a deep breath, I got out of the car. There was an eerie quiet that descended in the brisk temperatures as I walked to the front door. I tried to squelch my anger at the unlit front porch light. Was that asshole staying the night? *Fuck.* Trying to stay calm, I told myself not to jump to conclusions. That would only make more problems. Closing my eyes, I cracked my neck to release a bit of tension before I knocked.

There was a little noise on the other side of the door, and my mind went in a million different directions. *Stay calm. They're just friends.* The door creaked open and the dark-haired, built fucker answered.

"Can I help you?"

"Is Nikola here?" I asked, trying to sound friendly.

Wesley stepped out of the townhouse, closing the door behind him. I ran my hands through my hair as the wind blew a cold gust. He crossed his hands across his chest, trying to emphasize his size. This was clearly a pissing contest. I kept my hands to my side, but tensed ever so slightly. I was obviously bigger than he was.

He was equally friendly, but cold. "She's inside. I know what happened tonight."

"I think that's for her and me to discuss." I met his stare straight on, not wavering. For Nikola, I'd back down, but if this prick had intentions other than friendship, I was going to stop that shit in its tracks.

Nikola. Was. Mine.

Wesley eyed me then spoke. "Listen, I'm going to cut through all the shit and get right to the heart of it. Nikola and I are friends. She's been there for me and vice versa. She deserves the best—not someone making a half-assed attempt to stay clean. My girlfriend of several years got out about the same time you did from rehab but has relapsed twice. We're trying to get her readmitted, which is like living the damn nightmare again. So stop with the shit and think about what you want."

His voice turned to ice, but I could see the hurt in his eyes. It was terrible that she'd relapsed. From what I had seen, heroin was hard to bounce back from. Thank God I'd stuck to coke. That had been bad enough.

"I'm sorry to hear about your girlfriend. I've made my choice, and that's why I'm here rather than nursing a beer in spite."

For the first time, I saw that Wesley was in plaid sweatpants.

What. The. Fuck.

Wesley must have noticed what I'd seen. I met his eyes straight on and said, "Were you staying the night?"

"Yes," he said, matter-of-factly. "But before you jump to conclusions, she got scared and called me."

It fucking hurt that she hadn't called *me*. I waited for him to continue. He didn't.

"Why was she scared?"

Wesley replied, "I think that should come from her. Let me go inside real quick." As he reached for the door, he said, "There isn't anything between Nikola and me. I'm a friend with something in common. If you stay around and prove you deserve her, I hope we can be friends, too."

I nodded. "I appreciate it. Thanks for being there for her when I couldn't be."

"You're welcome."

He went inside, and I rubbed my eyes. Nikola had been nervous on New Year's Day and on the night I'd picked her up. Was this the same thing? I hoped she'd tell me what was up. Minutes passed like hours as I waited for the door to open again.

Finally, Nikola came to the door. She was in a sweatshirt and yoga pants. "I wasn't expecting to see you tonight," she said, her sad voice cutting through me.

"It didn't take me long to realize I'd fucked up. I'm sorry."

She looked down at her hands. "I'm sorry, too. I should

have talked to you instead of being aggressive. But, Brandt, I can't budge on the alcohol. I can't. The memory of alcohol is too raw for me. It takes me back to when you were using."

Without thinking, I reached out to touch her chin and raised her face to mine. "Nikola, I won't take another drink of alcohol. Whether I can handle it or not, it's not worth losing you. It's not worth the chance. I was a stupid prick back there. I don't deserve you now, but I want to."

I heard a few quick breaths before she threw herself in my arms. "You *do* deserve me, Brandt. I want you to keep fighting for us. I'm going to fight for us, too."

"I love you, baby."

She snuggled deeper into me. I knew she wasn't able to say it back yet, which was fine. I knew she loved me—I could feel it as she hugged me closer to her. She felt small and fragile in my arms, and I wanted to protect her. I kissed the top of her head.

"I'll never stop fighting for us. We're going to have our ups and downs, but the important thing is we work through it. Together."

She sniffled and nodded. "I agree."

Time passed as I held the love of my life in my arms. Nikola held me closer as an icy gust blew. She shivered. "Hey, baby, can we go inside? It's fucking cold out here."

She giggled. "Come on in."

I let her go as she turned. As she reached the door, she paused. "You know there's nothing between Wesley and me, right?"

"Yes. We can talk about that later."

She furrowed her brow, but we continued inside. Wesley walked to the door dressed in his jeans.

"I'm going to head out. My parents wanted to talk to me

about Diane. They may have found a longer-term facility."

"Keep me posted. I'm a phone call away if you need anything." She hugged him. They did seem to have that brotherly-sisterly friendship, though I was kind of raw at seeing her hug a man that I was still unsure about.

He let her go. "I will. Call me if you need anything again."

"Will do."

Wesley nodded at me as we exchanged goodnights. With Wesley gone, I walked in and looked around her place. It was tidy and modern. I knew everything was new since she'd left everything at our old house. A lime-green sofa sat on a white shag rug. Brightly colored modern art hung on the wall. The walls were a light, steel-gray. It suited Nikola.

"I like your place."

"Thanks. It's slowly becoming home."

The fact that it wasn't home yet was a good thing, for me. I walked toward her slowly, stopping when several feet still separated us. She took a deep breath, her eyes darting to my lips. I wanted nothing more than to kiss her, but we needed to talk. I needed answers. I hoped she'd tell me what was wrong as I sat on the couch next to her.

I touched her cheeks, and she closed her eyes. "Why were you scared, Nikola?"

Her eyes opened. Dark pupils darted back and forth between my eyes in distress.

"What did Wesley say?"

"He said to ask you. So I'm asking you. I know something is bothering you. I saw it on your face in Anne's kitchen and on the night we went to the airport. Please, tell me."

She swallowed hard. "It's not a big deal, but I'll tell you what's going on."

"It is a big deal to me if something is bothering you. We have to be honest with each other, like you were with me at the bar. It's the only way we're going to make it, and I want us to make it more than I've ever wanted anything. You calling Wesley to come stay the night tells me it's a big fucking deal."

My words seemed to soften Nikola even further and she nodded. "The guy I dated for a month won't leave me alone. He's been making me nervous."

"Is this the one you slept with?"

I saw the answer in her eyes. I couldn't be mad, but it hurt. If she felt like I had after sleeping with someone else, it was an acute torture that I wouldn't make worse.

Her voice was quiet. "Yes, he is. When I broke it off, he got a little crazy."

"What do you mean, he got crazy?"

I knew my voice grew harder as I thought about some asshole not only having Nikola but also scaring her. My blood simmered.

I repeated myself. "What do you mean he got crazy?"

Nikola looked tired as her shoulders drooped. "He texts me all the time, wanting me back. He sent one tonight asking why I hadn't been home when I was headed to the club. On my way back, I got spooked thinking about it, so I called Wesley. Grandmama had sent me a goodnight text, and I didn't want to wake her since she's been sick. I didn't know where you and I stood at the time, and I wasn't sure if it would stress you out too much, so I called Wesley. I'd planned to tell you everything tonight, but then..."

We'd address the rest of what she'd said in a minute. "What's his name?"

I was about to put an end to this prick. He needed to know Nikola was with someone who could beat his ass if he didn't stop his shit.

"Lance."

Lance was about to get a wake-up call.

Nikola

I SAT ON the couch, watching the protective side of Brandt emerge. A feeling of warmth came over my body. His blond hair hung loose as he ran his hands through it.

"Can I have your phone?"

Tentatively, I picked it up from the side table. Under Brandt's tight long-sleeved shirt, his muscles tensed. His presence filled the small room. I ran a hand over the soft suede of the couch as I tried to read Brandt's emotions.

"Are you going to call Lance?"

"Yes." His one-worded, no-arguments tone had me handing over my phone. "Do you have him under Lance?"

"Yes. But, Brandt, please don't do anything rash. I'll be okay." My voice cracked and I focused on the green splatter in the painting on the wall. My toes dug into the white shag rug as I attempted to stay calm.

He tapped a few numbers. "Nikola, don't bullshit me. Remember, I know you. And I know that if you called someone to come stay with you, you were more than spooked. This shit stops now. We'll talk about everything else later."

He punched the screen with his index finger then held up his phone. He walked to the big window and peeked out of the closed blinds. Brandt always had been one to take in all his surroundings. Lance must have picked up, because Brandt said, "Hello, is this Lance?" He paused. "Well, it's not Nikola. It's her boyfriend. You need to lose her fucking number or we're going to have problems. No, it's not a threat, asshole. It's a promise." He paused again and looked out the window. "I think I've said all I have to say. She won't be here for long."

Brandt hung up the phone and muttered a curse word under his breath before looking at me. The blue took on a sapphire hue as he penetrated me with his gaze. "He lives in your complex?"

Shit. I forgot to let Brandt know about Lance living here. "Yes, it's why I can't do anything about it. Wesley has had a friend look into it. There's nothing I can do until he crosses some arbitrary line. Sometimes I get spooked, but that's it."

The scowl on his face deepened. "I want you to pack a bag and come stay at my place."

I started to protest.

"Nikola, we'll stay in different rooms. Or I'll drive you to Anne's. You fly out tomorrow afternoon, and I want to spend as much time with you as possible. I don't want to make you feel uncomfortable, but this shit with you staying here and being scared isn't going to happen. You know I don't mess around with those I love. I know we're still figuring out what we are, but I don't want you scared."

I looked at the time. It was late. "I'll stay at your place tonight."

Part of me was relieved. I hated staying here. My lease wasn't up for another six months, and I couldn't afford two places with all the expenses that came with living in downtown Atlanta. I was a mess. Maybe more time together would be good for us.

Brandt was still staring at me, relief flooding his face. "Thanks for not arguing with me on this. I want you safe."

"I feel safe with you."

I stood, and Brandt pulled me into an embrace. His scent enveloped me and my nerves settled. *I am safe.* He kissed the top of my forehead.

"I know. Let's get you packed. Grab a few days' worth of clothes for after you get back from your trip, in case Lance is still a problem."

"Okay, I'll be right back."

He didn't follow me into my bedroom.

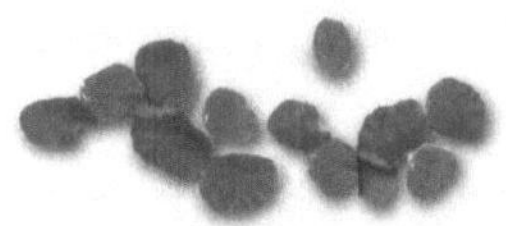

Following Brandt in my car, we pulled up to his place about twenty minutes later. My headlights flashed on the house. I could see the dark-bricked home with shutters on the windows. It was smaller than the place we'd shared. The two-car garage opened and Brandt pulled in on the left. The other spot housed his old, '63 split-window Corvette. The silver paint sparkled in the light. This was the car that Brandt had been restoring with his father before he passed away. After his dad's death, Brandt continued the work then drove it when he turned sixteen.

We had good memories in that car—happy memories. I grabbed my duffle bag and walked inside to meet Brandt standing at the hood of the car. Instinctively my hand touched the soft paint as a memory came without warning.

I was in the garage of our place looking through a box, trying to find my cookbooks. Brandt and I had moved in together, and this was the first meal we'd share in our new home. Over the past few months, we'd become inseparable, but our relationship had deepened when we'd made the leap and decided to move in together. We were in love, and he was going to be my happily ever after. Giving up my search in this box, I stood and noticed a box on the top shelf. It was my last hope to find the cookbook with all my favorite recipes. Grandmama and I had matching volumes that we continued to add to as we found new and exciting things to prepare.

Standing on my tiptoes, I felt fingers under my shirt, moving up my stomach toward my free breasts. I had gone braless after my shower. As his hands reached the cusps, I sank back onto the balls of my feet and leaned into a bare chest. His fingers continued to dance over my breasts, tickling them in pleasure. Softly he skimmed across my nipple. I moaned as the feathery light touches sent desire coursing through my body.

"You've been walking around in those tight-ass shorts and your tits have been free for an hour. It's time to fuck."

The sound of his voice, deep and commanding, got me every time. "Any place in particular?"

"Yeah, there is." We walked backward until he turned me around and pushed me down on the hood of his car. I complied, lying on the long, silver hood of the Corvette.

Brandt stood before me naked. His hands cupped my face

then trailed down my body until they reached the top of my shorts. The metal was cool against my ass as he peeled my shorts from my body, exposing my lower half.

He stood back and stroked his cock. "Touch yourself, Nikola."

My feet came up to the hood of the car and I opened my legs, letting my fingers begin to graze my clit. My abdomen contracted, making my back arch. Dipping into my core, I reveled in the feeling, knowing it was about to become more powerful. I brought my finger back up to my mouth, knowing what it did to Brandt when I tasted myself.

"Fuuuck!"

Brandt was on me in two seconds, penetrating deep inside me. My legs wrapped around his ass as they held on for one of Brandt's mind-blowing fucks. His large, thick cock was awakening every nerve ending in me. My body was on fire. He was a machine.

"Clench that pussy around me, hard." My body was a puppet to his command. I loved when he talked dirty. "That's right, Nikki."

His body glistened from the exertion. Brandt gave me a slight smirk, knowing, from the trembling walls of my core, that I was about to ignite.

I cried out incoherently as Brandt roared through his release, collapsing on me.

The light flickered, bringing me back to the present. I swallowed, wishing the memory would go away, too. As I glanced up at Brandt, his eyes burned with passion, and his breaths were short—like mine.

I took another step toward him as he whispered, "You were thinking about the time on the hood of the car when we fucked like animals."

Inside, my body begged for a release, but Brandt didn't move as I continued walking toward him. My voice was low as I said, "Yes."

We locked onto each other's eyes. Brandt's fingers came to trace my mouth as he said, "You've always had beautiful, pouty lips."

"Thank you."

My resolve faded as I felt Brandt's magnetic pull. My body wanted him—burned for him, even. And the stress of the day had left me needing him, like I used to. Wanting that feeling of being consumed, I closed my eyes and leaned forward.

Brandt pulled away. "I won't be a regret for you in the morning. It's taking every ounce of willpower not to fuck you again on the hood of my car."

"Brandt—"

He held up his hands as I looked down, shame coursing through me. I'd been weak when I was supposed to be strong. Our relationship couldn't be based on sex.

"Nikola." I moved my head back up to meet his eyes. "We've had a long day. There's nothing to feel ashamed of. The first time we're together again is not going to be in my garage. And it's not going to be when we are both on edge. Let's go inside."

The haze in my brain passed, and I realized what I'd tried to do. He was right—now was not the time. Without thinking, I grabbed his hand and squeezed. He looked back at me as I said, "You are wonderful. I'm glad you came for me tonight."

"I'll always try do what's right for us, baby."

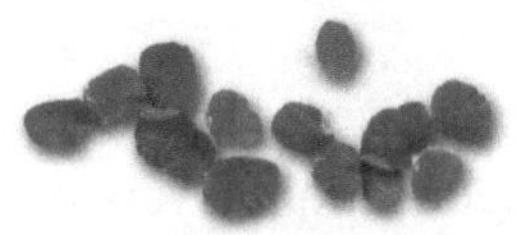

Startled, I sat up. *Where am I?* As my brain functioned, I remembered—I was at Brandt's. After showing me around his sparsely-furnished place, I'd elected for sleep over talking. At first, Brandt had wanted me to take his room, but sleeping while enveloped in his smell would not have been a good idea. I'd been exhausted and needed some time to myself to process. Stretching my legs, I prepared to get up.

The aroma of coffee permeated the air as I put my feet down on the floor. The hardwood's cold penetrated my socks. Taking my robe from the foot of the bed, I put it on, cinching the belt tight as I made my way to the kitchen.

Brandt was at the small breakfast table, reading the paper. It had been a habit of his for as long as I had known him.

"I got your caramel mocha creamer stuff you like, in case you want some coffee. And your favorite bagels with the strawberry cream cheese. If there's something else you want, let me know and we can get it."

He took another sip as he watched me. The way he phrased it made it seem like I was staying longer than one night.

I felt a little shy as I responded, "Thank you."

He set his coffee down and smiled. "You're welcome."

I went to the kitchen and made myself a cup of coffee, adding the creamer first. I could hear Brandt's paper rustling while I toasted my bagel and spread cream cheese on it. Picking up my mess, I made my way back to the breakfast table and sat next to Brandt.

He put down the paper and said, "You fly out at noon today, right?"

My travel was out of control. I'd already scaled my business trips back to twice a month versus weekly, starting next month.

"Yes. I wish I could cancel so we could spend more time together. I'm going to try to work on moving some meetings—I want to spend more time with you."

"I'd like that a lot."

"Me, too. I wanted to ask you something about last night."

Brandt put his hand on my knee. "Ask away."

"Last night you said we'd talk about everything else later. What did you mean?"

Brandt leaned back in his seat. His relaxed posture helped me relax some. Last night, I hadn't wanted to talk after our conversation in the garage.

"You can't withhold stuff from me because you're afraid it's going to stress me out. Life is stress, Nikola, and I have to learn to deal with it. If you're calling Wesley first because you're nervous about me using drugs again, well, don't. Call *me* first. If you're calling Wesley because you aren't comfortable enough with me yet, then that's an entirely different story that we need to address."

I took a sip of coffee. "I am comfortable with you. I was only scared of pushing you to drugs again. Do you care if I'm friends with Wesley?"

Brandt seemed pleased with my response as he looked at me. "If he looks at you truly as a friend, then yeah, I'm okay with it. If he starts looking at you with anything more than friendship, then I'll have a problem with it. I think you'd feel the same way." His tone wasn't threatening or jealous—just factual.

Over the months, I had asked myself several times if I felt anything for Wesley. Every time, I got the same internal answer: *No.* I knew Wesley felt the same way.

"I honestly don't think that would ever be the case. But if it was, I have more respect for what we have than to jeopardize it like that. When it comes to you and Wesley, you win every time."

"I like the sound of that…a lot." Brandt took a sip of his coffee. "Will you call me if you need something next time? Give me a chance to show you I can handle the stress."

"Yes, I promise."

"Good. I have some errands to run this morning. Do you want to ride with me? I'll drop you off at the airport so you don't have to worry about your car."

"I'd like that."

Brandt

SIX DAYS HAD passed since I'd dropped Nikola off at the airport. What started as a three-day trip had turned into a disaster. Nikola's business affairs ended up being extended by one day, then she got stuck in Arkansas for two days due to bad weather. She'd finally landed and was waiting at the baggage claim.

I was ready to see her and had been circling the airport for about forty-five minutes. It was drizzling and the forecast called for sleet, with temperatures hovering around thirty-two degrees. The sooner we got home, the faster we'd be out of the mess that was bound to ensue if the roads got icy. One thing Atlanta was not equipped for was bad weather. Plus, it was going to start getting dark within the hour.

My phone vibrated.

Nikola: Headed out.
Me: I'll be there.

As I came back around to the terminal, Nikola emerged from the sliding doors. I pulled up to the curb and hopped out of the car.

"Go ahead and hop in the car, I'll get your bags, baby."

It was good to see her again. I gave her a peck on the lips and felt her smiling. All I wanted to do was kiss her into oblivion, but I refrained. Nikola needed to control the pace of the relationship. I still had sixteen damn days before I could try to seduce her. If I kissed her like I wanted to, I'd be breaking my promise. If we were going to have sex prior to the blue balls timer going off, Nikola would have to instigate it.

She pulled the scarf back over her face and said, "Thank you."

As I winked, she scurried to the car. I put her shiny, red suitcase and her matching laptop bag in the back before getting in the vehicle myself. I had both seat heaters on high. Cars were lined up everywhere as people were scrambling to get to their loved ones before the weather set in.

"Glad you made it home. I missed you."

Nikola, still in her coat, said, "Me, too. I missed you. Seems like it took forever for me to get home. I'm *so* glad I drove to Memphis to catch that flight last night. They said we were one of the last flights to leave before they shut down the airport again."

"If I had to wait another day, I was coming to get you. I've done it before."

It was true, I would have driven this morning to get her.

I moved an inch forward and a police officer held up his hands for me to stop. I complied. Police were out to keep people for idling too long in front. The officer blew his whistle and signaled for us to keep going. I pressed the gas, but we were moving at a snail's pace due to the congestion.

Nikola pulled her scarf down; she smiled. "I remember. You came to get me during the last ice storm three years ago when I was stranded on Stone Mountain. I was at that conference and the company had put me up in a cabin. You ended up staying with me when they closed the roads for two days. Do you remember—" Abruptly, Nikola stopped and turned to face the window.

I finished her sentence with memories of my own. "I remember making love to you in front of the fireplace in that cabin. I remember what it felt like to be inside you. I remember having you as mine. I remember it was the first time we said, 'I love you' to each other. Is that what you were talking about?"

Every chance I got, I'd remind Nikola of how happy we were—even though she seemed to remember everything, too.

She turned my way as we continued to inch along in the baggage claim traffic.

"It would be impossible to forget."

"Yes, it would."

As I left the covered area, the sleet had started and the temperature was now below freezing. My house was about forty-five minutes away. Concerned about Nikola going to her place alone with that shithead living in her complex, I formulated a plan. I was either staying with her, or she would stay with me. Waiting for the right moment to try to convince her was important. I had a feeling the weather was going to work in my favor.

The sleet came down harder, tapping against the windshield. Ice accumulated on the wiper blades.

“Oh wow, Brandt, it’s starting to get bad out there. I’m going to call Grandmama to make sure she’s okay.”

“Good idea. I called her before I left to get you. She was going to call her neighbor to come and make sure the generator worked.”

“Thank you.”

Nikola gave me a gorgeous smile as she pulled out her phone, dialed some numbers, and then held it up to her ear. “Hey, Grandmama. Yes, I made it to Brandt. Are you okay? Good, I’m glad Steve is home and can help. Yes, he told me he called you. He is wonderful.” Nikola glanced my way before continuing. “I was going to either go home, I guess, or see if we could make it to you, but the weather is getting bad. Are you sure? Okay, let me know if you need anything. I’ll be glad when that cough goes away. Is it feeling like it’s breaking up at all? Good, that means the antibiotics are working. Okay, stay warm and keep your phone charged. I will. Love you, too.”

Nikola hung up the phone. “Grandmama is good. Steve, her neighbor, has already made sure the generator would start. He’s getting gas now. So you can take me home, I guess.” She sounded a bit disappointed.

We were stopped at a light when I saw a text flash across my screen.

Anne: I believe you have changed. Here’s your chance to show Nikola and be with her alone for a few days.

Anne was like family to me, and it warmed my heart she was rooting for me, for us to be together.

I responded quickly before the light turned green.

Me: Thank you, I will.

Here goes nothing. "Why don't we go to my place until the ice storm passes? That way I'll know you're safe, and we can spend some time together."

Relief washed over her face. Raising an eyebrow, she said, "Will you be good?"

"The question is, will *you* be good?" I rebutted.

A car in front of us slid as Nikola grabbed the handle over the door. The driver righted himself before an accident could happen, but the roads were slicking up fast.

"Oh, Brandt, this is getting bad. Let's go to your house."

"I think that's a good idea."

Finally, things were going my way. I was going to have Nikola alone for a few days. I turned the defroster on high as the inside of the windshield fogged up.

Nikola pulled up her messages and said, "I need to check on Wesley. He was on his way back from taking Diane to a new rehab facility they found in Florida."

Diane had agreed to check in to a better facility that specialized in heroin addiction. I'd suggested a place in Arizona, but Wesley and her parents had wanted Diane within driving distance. I thought it was better to leave the area and wipe the slate clean. My rehab had been in New Mexico. Sometimes, it's best to leave the area permanently. I was glad relocating wasn't a decision I'd needed to make—it had been easy to cut myself off from anyone I'd been involved with when I used. Luckily, I'd had the wherewithal to not use in our club.

Nikola and Wesley still talked often. I wanted to be okay with it, but I also wanted *me* to be her focus. My feelings were selfish, and I knew I was a prick, but there was still a lot about us that seemed up in the air. Once things settled, maybe I'd feel better.

She held the phone up to her ear. "Hey. Did you make it home? Oh, good. Yeah, I finally made it back. I'm with Brandt—I'll be staying with him until the ice clears. I will. I'm sorry. I know it was tough, but this time will be better." She paused to listen. "Don't lose hope, Wesley. Call me if you need anything. You too. Night." Nikola's voice was somber as she ended the call.

Nikola took a deep breath and leaned against the seat. "Diane freaked out right before they got to the treatment center, begging for one more hit. They still talked her into going, but she cried and apologized for ruining his life, talking about the baby they'd lost and how she would've been a good mother. It was heartbreaking to hear."

"Wait, she was pregnant?" I blurted, feeling even more like a selfish ass.

From the corner of my eye, I saw Nikola nod, sighing.

"Yes, she was. She miscarried two weeks before their wedding, at two and a half months. She canceled the wedding, gave Wesley back the ring, and turned to drugs to get numb. That's why he calls her his girlfriend now, instead of his fiancé—they aren't engaged anymore. All of Diane's life, doctors had said it would be a miracle if she ever got pregnant. And if she did conceive, they thought it would impossible to carry to term."

I imagined Nikola pregnant with our child then losing the baby. That would be so fucking hard. The amount of pain Wesley endured was unimaginable. When they lost their baby, he lost the love of his life to drugs.

Even though I'd royally fucked up, I had a lot to be thankful for. I had the love of my life back, and I was clean. Sometimes knowing what others were going through made me realize how lucky I was.

It had taken more than four hours to get home. I pulled up in the garage and parked next to my Corvette and couldn't help thinking that there had been some incredible sex on the hood of that car. But this was not the time to be thinking about sex. I was exhausted and it was pitch black out, and the thermometer read six degrees. Nikola was asleep in the passenger seat. My phone had been vibrating like crazy, and I was finally able to look at my texts. They were from Adam and my mum.

Adam: Closing Club Envy. Going to get Ainsley from school.

Adam: We made it. All employees checked in and made it home. Let me know when you guys make it.

Mum: Hey, sweetie, let me know when you make it home. Adam said you were headed to the airport to get Nikola. Glad she made it home. Didn't want to call in case you were driving on all this ice. Be careful. There's no rush, but I'd like to have you both over for dinner.

I typed back a response to Adam first.

Me: Made it! Glad to hear everyone got home. Nikola's staying with me.

Adam: Glad to hear it. That cock-block-timer you have is going to fucking suck.

Me: Tell me about it. But if I get her in the end, it's worth it.

Adam: I'd feel the same way about Ainsley.

I texted my mum. She'd been over the moon when I'd told her last week that Nikola and I were dating again.

Me: I have Nikola. We made it home. She's staying with me while the weather is bad. Let me know if you need anything and I'll be there. We'll do dinner sometime soon. We need a little time to work on us, if that makes sense. How about when you get back from your cruise?

Mum: It does make sense. After the cruise sounds perfect. I'm glad you guys are working it out. I always thought you'd be each other's forever. Your brother is here at the house and hunkering down with me. I'll be fine. Love you.

Me: Good. I'm glad Logan will be there. Love you, too, Mum.

Nikola stirred and sat up. "We made it. I'm sorry I fell asleep. Have you checked on your mom?"

I stroked her cheek. "Yeah, she's fine. Logan is with her. Want anything to eat?"

She yawned. Nikola had been on standby, which meant endless hours at the airport. "No, I'm too tired to eat. But I'll stay up and make you something."

"Let's get you to bed. You've been up for almost two days straight. We'll make breakfast together tomorrow. Does that sound good?"

"Okay, I would cook if you wanted something."

"I know, but I'm going to bed when you do. It's been a long day."

She nodded, and we went inside. Part of me hoped for the

storm of the century. Sometimes, it felt like we were fighting our physical attraction to the point that it made us distance ourselves emotionally.

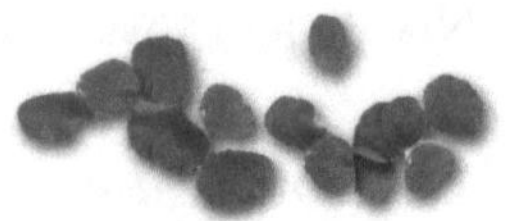

"Brandt, are you awake?" Her soft voice woke me.

I sat up and peered at the barely opened door. Her silhouette came into focus.

"Yeah, I'm awake. Is everything okay?" My voice was hoarse as I spoke.

"It's cold. I went to turn up the heat, but I think the power is out."

With the blankets now at my waist, I could feel the cold air. And the alarm clock on the nightstand wasn't showing the red numbers that would normally stare back at me. I checked the time on my phone—it was after two in the morning.

When my feet touched the cold wood floor, I cursed. "Shit, it's freezing."

Nikola's silhouette shook a little. "I know."

I walked toward her. It was still pitch black in the house and I couldn't see anything clearly. As I opened the door, she moved back a little.

"Let's get a fire going. We can sleep out in the living room next to the fireplace."

"O-o-okay."

Her teeth were chattering from the cold. I turned back and grabbed a pile of blankets and pillows from my bed. As I came back over to her, I handed her one.

"Use this to keep you warm until I can get the fire going."

"Th-th-thank-s."

We slowly made our way to the front of the house. I tossed the blankets and pillows on the floor and ignited the gas fireplace. Flames appeared and I turned it up on high. I set the remote back down on the mantel and turned. Nikola sat on the couch, barely visible with the covers wrapped around her. Only her eyes were showing. She was adorable.

"I'm going to close all the doors so the fireplace will get this area warmer quicker. Then I'll come out here and make us a place to sleep. With all the windows, the fireplace is going to have a hard time keeping up."

All I got was a nod that made me laugh. As I headed down the hallway, I heard her call, "It's not funny. I'm turning into an icicle in here."

I didn't respond as I went around and closed all the doors. It seemed like fate was working for me tonight. She was going to be cold, which meant my chances of sleeping next to her had increased significantly. I needed to play it cool.

An idea formed, and I grabbed the sleeping bag out of the hallway closet. In addition, I got a mattress pad to lay on the floor. I went back into the room where Nikola sat shivering on the floor right in front of the gas fireplace. I laid out the mattress pad and put a quilt from my bed on top, followed by the sleeping bag for two and another blanket.

"The bed is ready."

Nikola stood at my words and froze. "Are we sleeping together?"

Her eyes shot down to my chest. I'd forgotten I was shirtless and wearing only boxers. I moved into our makeshift bed as she watched me, still wrapped in the blanket.

"Do you want me freezing on the couch? I don't have another sleeping bag."

Since I only had the one sleeping bag, it was technically true. Nikola and I had bought it for a weekend camping trip. The part I left out was there were still enough blankets in the house to make a second bed. But maybe this would work.

The sound of the flames and the ticking of the mantel clock was all I could hear. She cleared her throat. Just in case she was on the edge, I added, "This is the sleeping bag we bought together. Remember how warm it is?"

"Yes, I do remember. I don't want either of us to be cold."

She dropped the blanket and without thinking I said, "Fuck me."

Nikola stopped and looked down at her outfit. She giggled. "Looks like we were both ill-prepared for this. I left my robe in the hotel in Memphis, and I only brought my nighties to sleep in."

Her black silk nighty had a deep V-neck lining, and it only came down to her mid-thigh. Her tits were front and center. She only hesitated for a moment before she slipped under the covers. Her little icy feet touched my legs as she sought heat.

"Shit, Nikola. You're freezing."

She was flush up against me. "I know. You're warm. This reminds me of Stone Mountain."

I brought her closer to me. She smelled like cherry blossoms. "Me, too. That was an amazing night."

"One of the best nights of my life."

Squeezing her a little firmer against me, I felt as if we were progressing. I knew being together would help things fall into place. This worked out better than I could have ever hoped. I tried to warm us up as her fingers wrapped around my middle. I kissed the top of her head, and she looked up at me. The flames danced about, casting shadows on her features.

Only the two of us existed in this moment. I could feel her breathing increasing and wasn't sure what to do. Fear of rejection and pushing her too far kept me from trying to kiss her. To have her in my arms all night was better than a few seconds of kissing.

Nikola scooted herself up slightly. "The only reason I didn't kiss you outside the club is because I didn't want secrets between us."

"And how do you feel now about me kissing you?"

Nikola answered my question with her lips descending on mine. Our mouths opened to each other as one hand went to her back and the other on her neck. Our tongues intertwined, getting reacquainted. She pulled back, and we continued giving each other small kisses. She tasted better than I'd remembered. I longed for more.

"Brandt, I'd be lying if I said I wasn't glad this ice storm pushed us to the next step. I was terrified to take it, and I think I've been keeping you at arm's length because of that fear. The moment you brought me into your arms, I knew I was ready to kiss you."

Music to my ears. I kissed her, afraid I was going to wake from this dream.

"You're mine, Nikola. Always have been and always will be."

And she surprised me again when she said, "I'm yours."

Those were the words she used to whisper every night before we went to sleep.

She settled back into my arms, and I pulled the blankets around us. Sleepily, she said, "This sleeping bag brings back good memories."

We'd laid in the moonlight, making love, and whispering our dreams on that trip.

"Hey, Brandt?" Her voice wavered, low.

"Yeah?"

She shifted her face down, and I couldn't see it when she spoke. "I know you promised not to seduce me for a month...but what if I wanted to seduce you?"

I thought for a moment. My dick had been hard most of the night. It jumped at the thought of not waiting sixteen days to be inside her. I tried to stay rational.

"I'd say sleep on it, and we can discuss it in the morning. I won't do anything that gives you any doubts. I love you too much for that."

"Okay, we'll talk about it in the morning."

I was silently cursing myself for starting that damn timer. Though, if it meant we'd have forever together, it was worth it. After a while, exhaustion and a happiness in my heart lulled me to sleep.

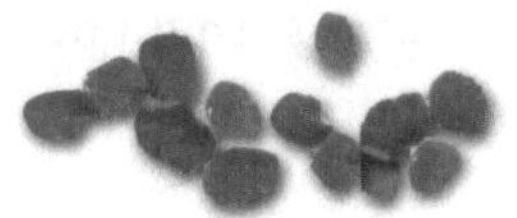

Nikola's hand caressed my dick and it hardened in response. *Best fucking dream I'd had in a while.* Feeling her touch me was heaven. The strokes became harder as she kissed my neck. My hands moved to her to breasts and pinched her nipples. She moaned and bit me in response. Her lips moved to mine as we kissed. My fingers trailed to her pussy and pressed her clit. I felt her body try to move on top of mine as her leg came across me and her hips moved over my abdomen.

My eyes popped opened and I realized I wasn't dreaming. *Shit.* Nikola had been about to sleep-fuck me. She used to do it from time to time when we'd been together. Normally, it happened when she was exhausted and we hadn't seen each other for a few days. She'd pounce on me in the middle of a deep sleep. I'd let it happen and wake her right before she would orgasm. She loved it that way.

I shot up as panic raced through my brain. *This is not how our first time is supposed to be together.* I stilled her, keeping her from progressing on top of me.

Loudly I said, "Nikola, baby, wake up."

Her eyes popped open, startled as she shook off sleep.

Nikola

BRANDT'S VOICE WOKE me, and I took in my surroundings. His hand rested on my hip. I'd thrown one of my legs over his body. *Oh no* I knew what I'd done.

I buried my face in his neck. "I tried to sleep-fuck you didn't I?"

Anytime I'd been hornier than normal, I'd basically attack Brandt in my sleep. He'd wake me right as I was about to come. I loved waking to that euphoric feeling.

He rubbed my back. "Yeah, I thought I was dreaming, but I stopped it when I realized what was happening."

The moment I'd touched Brandt in the sleeping bag tonight, I'd known I didn't want to wait the rest of the sixteen days. The sexual tension almost seemed to get in the way of us progressing emotionally.

Brandt continued rubbing my back. "Are you okay?"

I raised my head. "Yes, I'm okay." Putting my head back on his bare chest, I listened to his heartbeat. "I don't want to wait anymore."

His chest rose a little quicker and his heart pounded harder. The flames from the gas fire danced. The house was warmer but still had a slight chill to it.

"Nikola, we need to make sure. I want nothing more than to be inside you, but there is no way in hell I'm risking us. There's too much at stake for me—for us."

I looked Brandt straight in the eyes. "I know. I wouldn't jeopardize us, and I wouldn't say it if I wasn't sure."

Brandt's eyes searched mine. He was hesitant. But I knew this was right.

"Brandt, I wanted to make sure it wasn't based on sex when we got back together. I wanted to make sure we were still compatible emotionally. As I've been traveling and we've been talking, things are familiar but different— in a good way. We know each other, Brandt. My heart belongs to you, and I trust you with its safe-keeping."

He swallowed hard. "You want this?"

"Only if you do."

"Nikola, I've always wanted it. We've been on shaky ground since we got back together. I need you to trust me."

I sat up and looked at Brandt with all the love that I felt for him. My barriers were down. "I *do* trust you. Part of me is still scared that my heart is going to get shattered because you have so much power over me, but I'm tired of living in fear. I want to give all of myself to you, but we can wait if you want. I know I've been all over the place."

"I wanted to make it special for you." He brushed my cheek with his thumb.

"Then make it special. Make it our kind of special."

I gave him a light kiss then rolled off of him while pulling off my nightie. I was now naked with the top of the sleeping bag hitting me at the waist. I looked to him, and his eyes were on my perky breasts. Brandt's jaw worked hard.

He stroked the area around my left nipple, making me arch my back. His other hand trailed down my stomach to tease the slick folds of my pussy. His fingers barely dipped in me, dancing across my skin, building anticipation. His mouth found my other nipple, sucking it as his fingers finally plunged deep into me. I was alive with sensation.

I fisted my hands into his hair. I moaned as my toes curled. "Brandt—"

He bit down on my breast and pushed my clit. I tried to hold the orgasm back, but it came anyway. My head fell back as I reveled in his touch. The memories hadn't done this feeling justice. My legs were pushed open as Brandt positioned himself, naked, between my thighs. His tip barely brushed against me.

"Do you want me to get a condom? I will, but I swear I'm clean."

"No. I still take my monthly shot. We're fine." My voice was confident. Brandt wouldn't put me in harm's way. I knew he loved me too much to do that.

He brought his mouth to mine as he kissed me sweet and slow, with the slightest hunger. I wrapped my legs around Brandt as he pushed in at an excruciatingly slow pace.

I grunted as I tried to pull him fully inside me quicker. He stilled.

"Nikola, I'm going to savor this. I've been dreaming of being able to do this again. I told myself that if I did ever get lucky enough to have you wrapped around me, I'd memorize every second of being with you again."

Rubbing my legs over his, I relished the feeling of him being inside me. He was right. This deserved to be seared in our minds as we reunited our bodies and souls as one. Once all the way in, Brandt stilled. We kissed again as I wrapped my arms around him. Brandt made long strokes in and out of me. Our hands caressed each other's bodies. On the next upward thrust, Brandt hit the magical spot.

"Keep going. I missed this."

Our bodies knew each other, craved each other, and were ready to devour each other.

He put his mouth on my neck, and he whispered against my skin, "It's a dream come true, baby."

At his words, my sex clenched as the orgasm took over, numbing all my senses. Brandt's lips came back down to mine as he came inside me. We were one.

Brandt pulled out of me. I wrapped my legs around him, holding him. "I finally feel like I'm where I belong, where I'm meant to be."

He took a deep breath. "I love you, Nikola. I will forever love you."

"I love you, too." I hugged him closer to me and heard him exhale, long and slow. My heart had never stopped loving him. Fear had kept my heart caged, afraid of fracture.

"Say it again."

"I love you, Brandt. I never stopped. If I lost you again, my heart wouldn't survive it." I knew the statistics and the probability of a relapse was higher than I wanted to believe. Our love, knowing what we had lost, would help us stay the course.

Brandt pulled the sleeping bag around us, and I snuggled in deeper. "I'm never letting you go."

"I'm yours to keep."

I felt calmer and the fear lessened as I lay in his arms. Barriers crumbled as another piece of us fell into place. I tried to keep my eyes open to extend this perfect moment, but they became heavy and I drifted into a deep peaceful slumber.

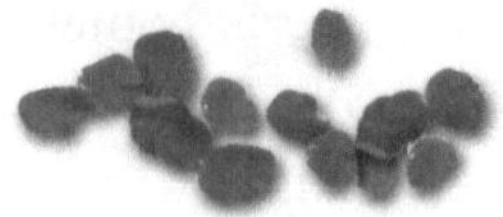

Light came in from the kitchen window as I peeked my eyes open.

"Morning, beautiful."

I stretched into Brandt. "Morning, handsome. I slept better than I have in a long time, even on this hard floor."

"So, no regrets?"

Brandt smiled, but there was worry in his eyes. The tribal tattoos on his upper arms were finally visible in the morning light.

I hugged him closer. "None. I feel whole again. I should have known my body wasn't going to let me go a month without you."

He chuckled. "I'm a huge fan of sleep-fucking. I always have been. Feel free to start on a nightly basis."

"I'll keep that in mind." I lightly slapped his stomach and snuggled farther into him when I felt something very hard. "Oh, someone is wide awake this morning."

Brandt had me on my back with my arms held above my head. I arched up and my stomach felt the tip of his dick.

"He's ready to conquer a land that's close by."

"Oh, yeah?"

He released one of my wrists, and I reached down to

touch the tip then ran my hand down the shaft. Brandt's head dipped down to my nipple. The stubble on his face and his hair tickled my skin.

"Yeah, he is. He's cocked and ready to go."

"What land is he going to?" The end of my sentence came out high as he sucked my nipple into his mouth.

His muscular torso moved down my body. "I'm going to explore the Land of Nikki. It's a magical place."

I giggled, but stopped, adjusting to his size as he pushed in. There wasn't a more complete feeling than having him in me.

"I love you, Nikola."

"I love you, too."

It was mid-afternoon and we lay curled up on the couch together, passing away the time under the blankets. The power had come on about thirty minutes ago, but the house was still freezing as the heater worked to catch up. We couldn't get enough of each other as the old wounds closed and healed. Brandt had been texting Adam. They'd decided to close the club tomorrow. The roads were getting mildly better, but were still relatively horrible. At least we had power now.

He looked up from his phone. "Adam's getting a little stir-crazy. He wanted to know if we were up for some company from him and Ainsley."

"Sounds like fun. Tell them to come over."

Adam lived about three streets over. Brandt typed a text and then put away his phone and ran his fingers through his hair. He had lent me a sweatshirt and boxers to wear, which were huge on me, but they were warmer than my nighties.

Brandt got that look in his eyes. "No way. Adam is on his way."

I stood and backed away playfully. Brandt stood and took his shirt and sweats off, letting his length spring free. "Nikola, come back here."

I continued to walk backward toward the kitchen. "I am not having Adam and Ainsley walk in on us."

Brandt prowled toward me as he stroked himself. "The door is locked. I'm going to catch you, baby. You know I will."

I took off toward the island and Brandt chased me, scooping me up and throwing me over his shoulder. I squealed in delight. Brandt turned and headed to a room off his kitchen.

"Where are we going?"

"You'll see." He pulled the boxers down my legs. "Kick them off."

I did, and anticipation pooled in my belly. Brandt flicked on the light and there was a washing machine. "Are you going to take me for a spin?"

He chuckled. "Something like that. It's not going to be the delicate cycle."

The room smelled of lavender. Brandt still used the same detergent we had when we'd lived together. For some reason, the thought had me squirming off his shoulder and taking off the sweatshirt.

Brandt was on me as we kissed. He backed me up until the cold metal hit my naked ass and I gasped in his mouth. I felt one of his hands leave me and reach backward, but I wasn't able to focus on what he was doing. Brandt could always kiss me into oblivion and make the outside world disappear.

A low vibration started on my back while he touched me. My legs spread open.

"You're still wet."

I nipped his lip. "You seem to keep me in that state."

We grinned against each other's lips.

"I like keeping you in that state. Turn around."

I turned and he pushed me down to lay on the top of the washing machine. The vibrations felt good against my nipples and I ground myself farther into the feeling. The cold air cooled my heated body. Brandt's feet pushed my legs farther apart and he aligned himself at my entrance.

"I forgot how good the spin cycle—"

Brandt entered me without warning and swiveled his hips, hitting every wall of my core before pulling back out. My body wanted to push against him but it didn't want to leave the magical vibrations of the washing machine. I was at the mercy of Brandt's pace. His hands held me flush against the machine and my insides absorbed it.

My need for friction took over as I pushed back on to him, making the penetration deep and glorious. The doorbell rang.

"Hurry, Brandt. Hurry."

Knowing someone was at the front door spurred us into a frantic action. The vibrations of the machine, the sound of our bodies slapping together with the bang of metal echoing our movements was erotic. We were fucking like wild animals in heat.

"I'm coming, Brandt."

"I'm right there with you, baby."

The orgasm exploded as Brandt hissed through his teeth. The doorbell rang again. The haze taking over my body left me uncaring as to what happened outside this room.

Brandt steadied. “I’ll be right back.”

He took off toward the front door where he’d left his clothes. I scurried to pick mine up from the laundry room floor as I processed that people, potentially Adam and Ainsley, were outside waiting to come in. When I made it back to the living room, Brandt held a bowl of something.

He shrugged. “My elderly neighbor made soup and wanted to make sure I had something healthy to eat. She’s always sharing food. She made the soup last night and heated it when the power came on.”

“Do you think she heard?” I was mortified that an elderly woman could have heard us.

Brandt chuckled as he set the bowl down on the counter. “She asked if everything was okay. I told her I was catching up on laundry.”

He had a mischievous grin on his face. My mouth dropped open as I curled back up on the couch.

“I’d say you finished your load.”

We laughed as Brandt tackled me. *This is happiness.*

My phone dinged, and I reached over my head to grab it.

I opened it when I saw the subject.

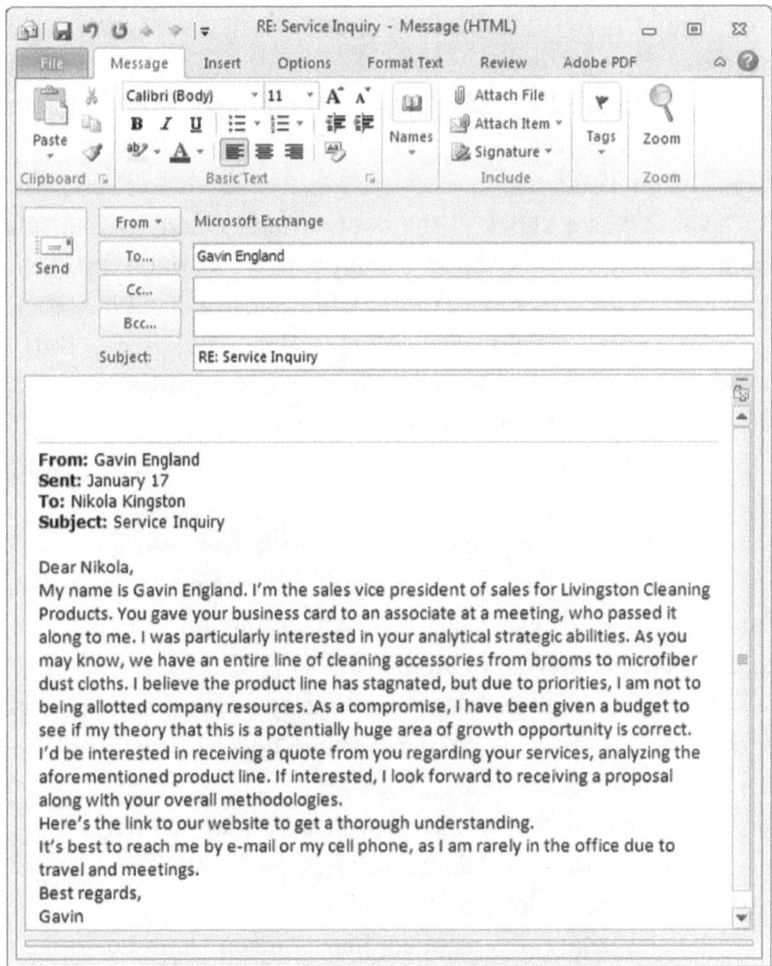
RE: Service Inquiry - Message (HTML)

From: Microsoft Exchange
To... Gavin England
Cc...
Bcc...
Subject: RE: Service Inquiry

From: Gavin England
Sent: January 17
To: Nikola Kingston
Subject: Service Inquiry

Dear Nikola,
My name is Gavin England. I'm the sales vice president of sales for Livingston Cleaning Products. You gave your business card to an associate at a meeting, who passed it along to me. I was particularly interested in your analytical strategic abilities. As you may know, we have an entire line of cleaning accessories from brooms to microfiber dust cloths. I believe the product line has stagnated, but due to priorities, I am not to being allotted company resources. As a compromise, I have been given a budget to see if my theory that this is a potentially huge area of growth opportunity is correct. I'd be interested in receiving a quote from you regarding your services, analyzing the aforementioned product line. If interested, I look forward to receiving a proposal along with your overall methodologies.
Here's the link to our website to get a thorough understanding.
It's best to reach me by e-mail or my cell phone, as I am rarely in the office due to travel and meetings.
Best regards,
Gavin

I squealed as I read the e-mail. "Brandt, Livingston Cleaning Products potentially might want to hire me to analyze their product line! This could be *huge* for me. I've never landed a company this big before."

Clicking on the link, I was taken to the website and found Gavin England's profile. I knew the company from business meetings. I remember giving my business card to a representative from Livingston Cleaning Products at a conference I'd been too.

Brandt pulled me onto his lap. "You're going to do great. I'm so proud of you."

"Thank you."

There was a knock at the door. Brandt untangled himself from me and went to open the brown, wood door. In came Ainsley, looking like the Abominable Snowman. She had on several scarves in multiple colors and a dark green, fluffy North Face jacket. Adam wore a knit hat and a leather coat.

"Fuck me, it's cold. I hate all this ice."

Adam and Ainsley were starting to take off a few of their layers.

Brandt chuckled. "Did you guys walk over here?"

Ainsley had undressed enough to uncover her face. "His car might as well be a sled. My car is at the club since Adam didn't want me driving in all the ice."

I got up and gave Adam and Ainsley a hug. They came in and sat across from us on the L-shape couch. Brandt put his hand on my knee.

Adam asked, "What have you two been up to today?"

I bit my lip, and Adam raised an eyebrow. "You turned off your blue balls timer early. Lucky bastard."

Ainsley playfully slapped his stomach, and he looked down at his fiancé with an adoring smile. "What? I like giving him a hard time. He's been giving me shit about singing that unicorn song."

Ainsley gave him a kiss on the cheek. "You do such a good job when you sing it for Emilyn." Ainsley turned to me. "Emilyn is Nora's little sister. Nora bartends on the other side. Emilyn adores Adam, and he sings the Prince Lir parts for her every time."

Adam gave Ainsley an incredulous look as Brandt and I laughed.

"You're supposed to be on my side. Hey wait, didn't you give him a nickname?"

"I'm always on your side, baby. I'm sure Brandt doesn't want you to have to share your nickname." She gave him an adoring smile as he hugged her to him.

Brandt got his two-cents in quickly. "Damn straight. Suits Adam perfectly."

Adam kissed the top of Ainsley's head while he mouthed to Brandt, *You're an asshole.*

I giggled as I asked, "Have you guys set a date and place for the wedding?"

"Yes, we are getting married on June seventeenth. It's going to be a destination wedding. We're trying to decide on where." Ainsley's voice was excited as she touched her engagement ring, which glistened in the light coming in from the window.

Brandt put his arm around me and hugged me to him. I hoped to be married one day. To have that person you would spend the rest of your life with, grow old with, and give everything to was something I had always wanted.

Responding to Ainsley, I said, "That sounds wonderful."

I wanted to know Ainsley more. She seemed like a kindred spirit. "Are you interning with anyone this semester?"

She shook her head. A few pieces of hair came down from the side. "No, I couldn't last semester because of my mom and most are year-long internships. The only one I found was two hours away, which was too far. Hopefully, it won't set me back too far as I start my career, but we'll see."

"My company is small, and I'm a one-person operation, but I potentially may land a bigger account and could use the help. If I land the deal, I'll give you a percentage amount so it would be a paid internship. I'm having to research an entire product line, put together some suggestions on where I would start, and bid for the project. You'd be involved from the ground up, which would be what internships accomplish in a year. Let me know if this even interests you." Hopefully she took me up on my offer. Brandt squeezed my shoulder.

Ainsley pale-blue eyes lit up. "Are you serious? Yes, I would love to do that."

"Perfect. I'll tell Livingston Cleaning Products that we'll need three days to put together a proposal."

Ainsley was all smiles. "Thank you. You don't know how much I appreciate it."

"You're welcome. I'm excited. You don't know how much *I* appreciate the help."

Adam mouthed, *thank you.* It warmed my heart knowing I was helping the person he loved.

Adam leaned forward. "Should we play cards?"

Ainsley stood. "Boys will have to play. Nikola and I have a project to start—if she's good with starting now."

I liked her attitude. We were definitely going to get along. As I got up to head back to the bedroom I'd been staying in, I looked at Brandt. He had that dopey-eyed-in-love look that thrilled me. I bent down and gave him a quick peck on the lips. Before I could catch my balance, Brandt pulled me down across his lap and kissed the life from me.

For a second, I remembered someone was in the room with us. But when our tongues met, it was only Brandt and me. He pulled back. "Have fun. Adam and I will figure out dinner."

"I will."

I had butterflies in my stomach. The remaining pieces of

ice around my heart melted. He gave me a smile before giving me one last hard kiss.

Ainsley tried not to laugh. I looked toward her. "Are you ready?"

"Yes. I can't wait."

We were walking to the back of the house when I heard Adam tell Brandt, "Welcome to the pussy-whipped club. It's a great place to be."

"Hell yeah, it is. I've missed it." Brandt sounded proud.

Ainsley and I looked at each other and laughed as we said, "Men."

Brandt

IT WAS FEBRUARY second. Today would have been the day, per the Blue Balls Timer, I would have been allowed to start seducing Nikola if we hadn't had sex yet. Thank fuck we hadn't waited. We'd agreed that not having sex put us more on edge. In the end, we wanted the same thing—each other.

Quentin had asked if I wanted to meet to catch up, and I did. A lot had happened since I'd left the diner to get Nikola back after our alcohol argument. I felt centered now, even though I was spread a bit thin between the long hours at the club and spending so much time with Nikola. That was what had driven me to try cocaine before. But this time, the fear of losing what I loved would keep me from going back to drugs. I'd find a healthy balance. Nikola had been traveling. She'd stay some with me and some with Anne. I wanted her with me all the time, but that would come eventually.

I was on my way to Anne's. She'd invited Nikola and me over for dinner. Nikola had gone over there earlier to spend some time with her. After landing the Livingston Cleaning Products account, life had been busy. She and Ainsley would work at Anne's a few times a week together. Nikola kept saying that she didn't know what she would have done without Ainsley. The girls were a good fit and were becoming closer.

Parking in the driveway, I shut off my vehicle. Through the dining room window, I could see Anne and Nikola cooking. Nikola talked animatedly while wearing a blue-and-white-checked apron. Anne stirred something as steam rose from a pot on the stove. I got out of the car and headed to the door off the carport. I was family again and it felt fucking great.

Opening the door, I walked in. "Honey, I'm home!"

Anne turned and winked. "I think you're a little young for me. Don't they call that a cougar or a lion or something?"

The aroma of dinner cooking assaulted my senses. Ham sizzled in the frying pan.

I gave Anne a kiss on the cheek while she continued to stir. "You'll never be too old for me."

Nikola called from behind. "Hey, what about me?"

I picked Nikola up and twirled her around. Little sounds of joy emitted from her as her green eyes sparkled with happiness. Nothing would ever sound better to me than Nikola's happiness. Stopping before I became too dizzy, I let her slide down body.

"You're my ultimate. I missed you."

She stilled as I bent down and gave her a sweet kiss. Nikola whispered against me, "I missed you, too. Supper is almost ready. Go wash up."

"It smells incredible. I'll be right back."

Being back here, like this, was perfect. It let me leave the pressures of life behind me.

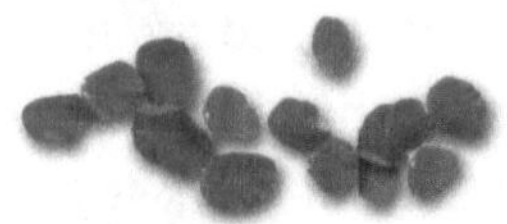

Full from dinner, I pushed back my chair. "Anne, I missed your fried okra and cornbread."

"Well, keep coming by and you'll keep getting it." She gave me a pat on the back as she made her way to the kitchen. I followed with my plate and the platter of ham. "Nikola says you guys are going to your mom's house next week."

I put the ham on the counter as I responded. "We are. Mum's on a cruise with her friends for two weeks. We're going over the day after she gets back."

Anne stored the leftover food in the fridge. "That'll be nice. I know Nikola has always loved your mom."

"My mum feels the same way about her." Nikola was the daughter that my mum had never had.

Nikola called from the dining room, "I'll be right back."

I loaded the dishwasher with dishes from the sink.

Anne deposited more dishes in the sink. "You and Nikola seem happy."

Stopping, I gave Anne my full attention. "We are. It finally feels like things are how they should have been all along if I hadn't fu—I mean messed it up."

Anne smiled with her warm blue eyes. "Brandt, sometimes it takes losing what's important to put it in perspective. You will always know what it feels like to not have each other. For many people, that knowledge happens too late, and their life turns into a list of regrets. It's through regret that we find our true north to guide us through storms."

"Thank you." I hugged Anne tightly to me.

Nikola came into the room and caught my eye. She was my air. I needed her in my arms to know I wasn't dreaming. Over the last year, there'd been many nights I'd dreamed we were together, only to wake to the harsh truth of losing her. I brought her to me and hugged her. She must have felt the need to connect, too, as I felt her fingers dig into my shirt. There was no way I'd ever let her go again. Anne quietly excused herself.

Nikola pulled back. "Are we still going to the club tonight?"

So far, Nikola and I hadn't visited the sex club side of Club Envy. We'd only been to the bar side. The raw passion between the two of us was ready to ignite. When Nikola had suggested us going to the club, I'd made all the arrangements. I wasn't sure how this would go, or if the club scene was still us. We'd changed a lot, but something still hummed between us.

"Yes. Whenever you're ready, we can head that way." I gave her a quick kiss.

"Grandmama asked if we'd be up for a round of Rook tonight. I said yes. Let's play one game, then we can be on our way— if that's okay."

Rook was a game we used to play with Nikola's grandfather. After he passed, we created a version for three players. I'd never played before meeting Nikola. Anne was a hell of a player— she'd wipe the board clean almost every time.

I grazed Nikola's nose with mine. "Sounds good. How about we make a bet?"

Her eyes lit up. "What are the terms?"

"If I beat you, I want you to do a striptease for me tonight." I raised an eyebrow.

A spark ignited in her eyes. Nikola loved a challenge. "If I beat you, you have to use my Magic 8 Ball for one question of my choosing."

I hated that damn thing. We stared at each other, contemplating the bet. Nikola held out her hand and cocked her head. Her auburn hair was piled up on her head.

We shook and both said, "Deal."

I stood tall as she called, "Grandmama, are you ready to play? I have a bet to win." She turned to me. "You don't intimidate me with that look. Sexy, but ineffective."

I slapped her ass, and she yelped.

Anne called from the other room, "Oh dear, not this again. I'll get the cards."

Spinning Nikola around, I cornered her against the wall and gave her another kiss. "Start preparing your routine, baby. I want it hot. I seem to recall you lost our last bet."

She nipped my lip. "I hope you're not a sore loser. I can feel the cards are going to be in my favor."

Anne hummed in the other room, and Nikola giggled, ducking under my arms to get to the card table in the far corner of the living room. We sat as Anne coughed. I knew Nikola was concerned about her. Whenever Anne was sick, Nikola would worry.

Nikola got a glass of water from the kitchen. "Grandmama, we're going back to the doctor next week. I thought this was supposed to be cleared up?"

Anne took a sip and got the coughing under control. "I get this bronchitis every winter, and you're always concerned. It takes it a while to go away. Remember?"

"Yes, but I always make you go back to the doctor." Nikola gave Anne a kiss on the cheek before sitting at the table.

Anne masterfully dealt the cards. "I'll make another appointment."

Nikola picked up her cards with a smile on her face. Anne always indulged Nikola with these types of things.

Turning over the top card, Anne said, "What's your bid, Brandt? I wonder who's going to have that bird."

Looking at my hand, I hoped my luck turned or else the damn 8 Ball and I were about to be reacquainted.

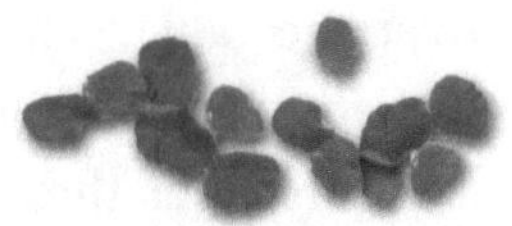

Nikola sat in the passenger seat of her car with her lips pressed together. The Spice Girls played low on the radio. They'd been one of her favorite bands for years. I glanced over at her again, and when I saw her bare legs, I had to resist taking her back home and stripping her naked. She had on a white and silver strapless top with no bra. Her skirt was more like a bandana, as little skin that it covered. It matched the silver in her shirt. Her killer fuck-me heels were about to send me over the edge.

We'd left Anne's and gone back to my place to get ready and take one car to the club. Nikola bounced in the seat. "Go ahead. I know you're dying to brag."

She squirmed, exclaiming, "I won! I won! I won!" Her auburn hair was all over the place as she wiggled around. "Should we go ahead and ask the question?"

I knew it was a rhetorical question, so I stayed silent. She reached into her purse and brought out her miniature version of the ball. The lights from the dashboard created a faint glow on

Nikola. She was gorgeous.

"Let's give this a trial run. This does not count. I want to know if the Magic 8 Ball is going to love you or hate you tonight."

Please. Please. Please, Magic 8 Ball, love me tonight. I'd never admit I'd mentally pleaded with that idiotic toy.

"Let's see."

She held the ball. "Magic 8 Ball, should I take my top down so Brandt can look at me until we get to the club?"

Please. Please. Please, Magic 8 Ball, love me tonight. Nikola slowly turned over the ball. "The 8 Ball has spoken. The answer is—" She looked over and giggled. *Please, 8 Ball, love me tonight.* Nikola cleared her throat. "The answer is—yes definitely."

"Hell yeah! Me and the 8 Ball are getting along great tonight. Take down your shirt, baby."

My windows were tinted dark, so no one could see in, but I was about to get one hell of a show.

Nikola leaned back in her seat. With hardly any effort, she pulled down her top, exposing her perky tits with their pink tips. I sped up, trying to get to the club quicker.

"Are you in a hurry?" The teasing tone had me getting harder.

"Touch your right nipple. Roll it between your fingers."

She complied without even questioning. Her back arched slightly. My hand crept to the breast closest to me. With my index finger, I lightly traced the curve. She was getting herself worked up. A wild abandonment consumed Nikola when she let her guard down, trusting me completely. Knowing I had her trust back made my heart grow huge.

Turning her head my way, Nikola licked her lips and asked, "Are we going to use a room tonight at the club?"

The club sign came into view, so Nikola adjusted her top and sat back up. Her leg bounced. Clearly, nerves were beginning to take over as Nikola looked at the club. Club Envy had six private rooms in total, and two additional rooms—one communal and one for exhibitionism. I liked sex in public places, but I'd never wanted anyone else to see Nikola in the thralls of an orgasm. We hadn't talked about using a room, but I'd had our private one cleaned just in case. Nikola and I had our own room off of my office. Since our breakup, I'd hardly used the office and hadn't been back to that room. This seemed like a big step for us, like coming here tonight would complete the circle. We'd be free from the pressures of our past and able to navigate our future anew.

When Adam fell for Ainsley, he'd converted the room off of his office into a special room, like I had for Nikola. Adam and I never spoke of mine and Nikola's room or my abandoned office, and I hadn't reminded him. I'd thought it 'might spook him' since he'd been wrapped up in all his boundaries and rules.

I wanted to surprise her tonight since we'd been back together for a month. "I do have us a room, if we want to use it."

"I do."

I glanced over and she nodded. If there was any hesitation on her part, we'd leave. I pulled up to the club. It was around eleven.

Every corner of this club had a piece of Nikola and me, it seemed. It's what made working there while we were apart bittersweet. I got out and met her on the passenger side. Leaning down, I kissed her sweet lips.

My hair came forward and brushed her cheeks. I tasted her mouth, barely. She looked me in the eyes. "Brandt, I want to be honest. I'm nervous. I want to go in there. I keep thinking about how we used to be, and I feel like we have to be that way tonight. What if we aren't the same?"

Night traffic sounds pierced the air. Tires screeching sounded off in the distance. I put my forehead to hers. "A few minutes ago, in the car, did that feel like us?"

"Yes."

"We have to let go of the past and accept who we are now. If we get in there and we aren't ready, we'll leave. No pressure. Adam and Ainsley should be here. Let's go see them, and we'll see how things go. If the club scene isn't for us anymore, then it's not, and that's okay. But, so far, everything we've done is better—for me at least."

I'd learned from Quentin that I had to live in the now and look to the future. The past wouldn't lead me anywhere good. That terrified me, and I refused to look back.

"It is better. Thank you. I love you, Brandt."

"I love you, too. As long as we have each other, that's all I care about. Nikola, there are things that are different about us now. We don't drink, we aren't living together, you work more hours, and I meet with a sponsor. But there are many things that are the same—like our love for each other. We can leave now if you want to."

She looked around. Across the street, a crowd came around the corner, whooping and hollering. "Thank you for being understanding. I know sometimes I seem like a swinging pendulum, but I want to go in the club."

I took her hand. "We're in this together. Are you ready?"

"Yes." She walked, and I followed.

We came to the side entrance of the red brick club. Trigger was at the door. The girls liked him with his messy blond hair. He always wanted me to tag along when he went to the bars. I'd go for a few hours, have a beer, then leave—like on

New Year's Eve. Trigger hadn't worked here when Nikola and I first dated.

"Hey, Brandt. All's good. Matt has everything under control. Adam and Ainsley are at the bar." He reached into his pocket. "Adam said you'd need these."

Trigger handed me two white bracelets. It was our way of identifying people at the club. There were two colors: black and white. Black was for nonmembers who'd been granted a visitor's pass. They weren't allowed to engage in sexual activity. White bands were for members who had exclusive partners. If someone wore either color, they were not to be approached. No bracelet was fair game. Adam was strict on the rules, and I supported it.

Nikola knew what the bracelets meant as I handed her one to put on. "Thanks, Trigger. This is Nikola, by the way."

They shook hands and Trigger gave her a friendly smile. He respected the rules of the club. Hell, he wanted nothing to do with exclusivity or dating. One day, someone was going to knock him off kilter and fix that thinking.

Nikola and I walked through the club. Low, erotic pulsing infiltrated our bodies. Normally, it did nothing for me, but my dick was at full attention tonight. Nikola was beautiful, her long, auburn hair cascading down her back in big curls. The sex club side had a retro style with frosted glass tables of all sizes surrounded by odd-shaped chairs. Multi-colored lights illuminated the room and the bar area with a sexy glow.

We spotted Adam and Ainsley at the bar. For now, I'd give Nikola a little space to see how she felt about being here. She didn't need pressure. If she wanted to stay, then I'd take her to our room. Adam and Ainsley were talking to Nora. Nora changed her hair color frequently and this week she had coal-black hair with bright blue streaks in it. Nora loved pranks, and her discovering my blue balls timer had meant endless torture. Blue cattle balls that usually hung from trucks kept appearing in random places. I had a feeling that Adam had been behind it because everyone else—other than Nora—would give me weird looks when I happened across a set before tossing them in the garbage.

Ainsley saw us out of the corner of her eye and she turned to Nikola. Ainsley wore some sort of itty-bitty halter dress that I'm sure had Adam ready to pound the shit out of anyone who looked her way.

"Yay, you're here! Adam said you were coming. How was dinner at Anne's?" Ainsley gave Nikola a hug.

Nikola grinned. "It was great. We played Rook after dinner, and Brandt lost a bet."

Nora sat my standard bottle of beer on the bar. It was out of habit, even though I'd told her I didn't drink anymore. Nora chimed as she hit the countertop. "Here's to the timer almost being up. Hopefully those balls aren't too blue." Nora turned to Nikola. "Make him suffer."

Nikola winked. "Oh, I will."

As Nora walked to the next customer, she called to Ainsley, "I like her. We need a girls' night."

The bar was getting crowded with a sudden influx of thirsty members. I glanced at the beer and felt no desire to drink it. I knew Nikola saw Nora set the beer down, but she continued her conversation with Ainsley, not even glancing to see what I was doing. I liked that. Nikola was beginning to trust me. I pushed the beer toward Nora. She made eye contact and mouthed the word, *Sorry*. Panic set in as Nora hurried to take the beer. I winked to let her know it was okay as I turned toward Adam and put my hand on Nikola's back. She leaned into my touch. I fucking loved it.

I asked Adam, "You guys going home or staying here tonight?"

Adam took a swig of Guinness. He ordered the beer special for the bottle. I thought it was better from the tap, but to each his own. "Nah, we'll be at home tonight. Ainsley has class in the morning, and those cock-blocker books apparently need her attention."

He looked around me at Ainsley and winked. She giggled. Adam turned back to me. "Have you given any more thought to hiring a manager?"

Adam thought we should hire someone to come in and manage Club Envy. I'd asked for a few days to think about it. There were additional liabilities we could incur by not being as involved. Plus, I'd run some numbers to see if the finances added up. The club was doing extremely well, but we still had to make sure our return on investment was there. Hiring someone else was a big step for me to take. The club was my security blanket in a sense. But Quentin gave me some perspective. I remembered his words, *It's okay to take a step back. Not being able to do everything doesn't make you a failure.* The club required an immense amount of attention and it was time to enjoy life a little more.

"I think we need two managers so we're covered," I told Adam. "One can be designated for the bar side and one the sex club side. It'll help keep Trigger and Snake from bouncing back and forth. The club can support the extra personnel and has probably needed it for a while. We'll oversee everything and cut back our hours significantly."

I ran my hands through my hair and pushed my sleeves up to my elbows. In the end, I was relieved and knew I had made the right decision.

Adam raised his beer. "I'll get Hampton to start looking

for candidates."

Hampton was our guy who helped with background checks and investigations. Last year, some guy had been taking photographs inside the club. Cameras were prohibited, but an employee had snuck the guy in. Hampton found the two guys and handled it.

I nodded. "Tell Hampton we want people with at least five years of experience."

"Sounds like a plan. I'm going to give my girl some attention." Adam set his beer on the iridescent bar top. "I'm going to out-maneuver the cock-blockers."

"I heard that," Ainsley called.

We laughed, and I said, "I'll see you guys later. Good luck."

Adam picked up Ainsley, throwing her over his shoulder as she slapped his ass. He slapped hers back and said, "Oh, luck has nothing to do with it."

No, luck had nothing to do with being with the person you were meant to be with. Fate. Fate had everything to do with it.

Nikola

ADAM AND AINSLEY disappeared into the crowd. Brandt turned to me and came into my space, pushing me against the bar. I put my elbows on the bar top, which lifted my breasts. The moment we'd walked into the club, memory after memory had assaulted me like a freight train. When we'd pulled into the parking lot, the fear of not being what we had been felt all-consuming. But having a few minutes to talk to Ainsley had helped as I eased back into the club and felt Brandt's hand on my back. I knew Brandt thought it was good that I was different now, but this step was still intimidating for me.

The place was alive with sex. Members had to be clothed in the main area, but touching and groping and practically anything else was okay.

Brandt looked into my eyes as I watched him. We were both figuring out the next step. I tipped my head back in invitation, and Brandt accepted as his warm lips touched the base of my neck and worked their way up. Couples around us were engaged in their own fun. No one cared what we were doing.

He murmured against my skin, "Nikola…"

Goose bumps prickled my flesh as his hand wandered up and cupped my breasts. His leg came between my legs and Brandt's mouth found mine. The kiss intensified, and I wrapped my hands around Brandt's neck, knotting my fingers into his hair. He kissed my ear and brought the lobe into his mouth.

His breath tickled my ear. "Do you want see our room?"

I nodded and Brandt picked me up, cradling me in his arms so we could continue tasting each other as we walked. The music wrapped around us, building the desire. I lost track of where we were, until I heard a door open and close. I looked around the room.

"Brandt, this is our room…" I never thought he'd have kept this room. It was our special place at the club. I had assumed our room was gone. My head turned back to Brandt, who watched me closely. "You kept our room?"

We searched each other's eyes, not sure what to say to each other.

Finally, Brandt spoke. "I did keep it. Tonight marks one month since you agreed to give us a shot. I thought we could be together somewhere that was special to us."

He put me down. I imagined so many of the times we were together as I looked at every piece of furniture. The Tantra Chair, the bench, the sex swing, and the bed all had beautiful memories of us. Brandt put his hands on my hips. His fingers flexed. He seemed unsure of what he was supposed to do next. I was unsure, too. The bed had black satin sheets. The walls were painted a dark silver-gray. Mirrors hung on the ceiling.

My nerves shot up. I didn't want to mess this up. I wanted it to be perfect like it had been before. I shifted my purse and remembered my Magic 8 Ball. I turned and stepped back. As I handed Brandt the 8 Ball, he furrowed his brow, taking it, bewildered.

"You want me to fulfill my bet now?" He chuckled.

I nodded. "I do."

"Okay."

I know it seemed way off-base, but this was the only way I knew to lower our barriers. Brandt was unsure on where I stood, and I was afraid to ask for what I wanted.

Running my tongue across my lips, I said, "Ask the Magic 8 Ball if you should fuck me hard."

Brandt nearly dropped the ball and took a step forward. I took a step back and took my top off, leaving me naked from the waist up in my tiny silver skirt and heels.

As Brandt spoke, I shimmied out of my skirt, kicked it off, and left my heels on. "Magic 8 Ball, does Nikki want me to fuck her hard?"

Using the nickname he only used during hard sex had me squirming with anticipation. *My Magic 8 Ball better be on my side tonight.* Brandt shook the 8 Ball and closed his eyes. When he looked down, I held my breath waiting for the answer.

"That glorious blue triangle has spoken. *It is certain* that you should be fucked tonight."

Brandt prowled toward me, discarding the 8 Ball on a nearby chair, as he pulled his thermal shirt over his head. "Leave your heels on," he commanded.

He unbuttoned and unzipped his jeans. I could see the base of his dick—Brandt was commando. Next, off came his boots. Then I was the hunted again. I stood firm as he approached without slowing. In an instant, I was thrown over his shoulder. A finger trailed down my spine, toward my ass. As he passed lightly over my back entrance, my muscles flexed involuntarily. There was more pressure as he passed over my other opening, making a trail of wet desire to my clit and then back to my core. I squirmed, wanting him to enter me. Brandt had taken control, and I gladly gave it to him.

"Grab the straps, Nikki."

As he pulled me off his shoulder, I saw the black straps of the sex swing. I held the straps as he positioned them: one below my ass and the other to support my back. When those were in place, I let go and let the other swing straps hold me. My legs were threaded through the holders to support them. I was on display as I leaned back and looked at myself in the mirror on the ceiling. My body was slightly tanned and my hair cascaded behind me. My eyes were wide and my breathing had accelerated slightly as I watched the rosy pink tips of my breasts rise and fall.

"You're beautiful, Nikki." Brandt appeared in the mirrors as he trailed his finger tip from between my breasts to my navel. A flip-flopping feeling came over me as he passed over my lower stomach. I was still looking up at the mirror as Brandt came to stand between my legs and his fingers felt my opening again. The tatted tops of his arms and messy hair were all I could see.

I glanced at his face. His jaw was set and his muscles taught. "Keep your eyes on the mirror. I want you to watch yourself come undone. Don't shut your eyes."

"I won't."

My eyes focused back up to the mirror, and Brandt lowered to his knees. He pushed my body out on the swing, then brought it back in. When my sex touched his lips, Brandt sucked my clit into his mouth before releasing it, allowing my body to relax again. On the next motion inward, his tongue entered me and swirled about and noises of pleasure escaped my mouth. He repeated the motion, alternating between my clit and core. The moans were becoming desperate as he kept me out of reach of my orgasm. It was heaven and hell simultaneously. Desire and need were at the surface, waiting to escape.

I was close to begging, which I knew would only prolong the agony. I clamped my mouth shut and kept staring at the ceiling, where the mirrors were, watching Brandt devour me. The noises in my throat turned to whimpers. My body couldn't take any more. I was on the verge of cracking. Brandt's name was on the tip of my lips when he brought me back swiftly to him and flicked his tongue on my clit in that way that made me scream incoherently as a mountain of an orgasm exploded like a volcano that had been waiting to erupt. At the peak of euphoria, my back arched from the onslaught of feeling.

As the orgasm ebbed, my body went limp in the swing and Brandt let me go, allowing the swing to sway. I closed my eyes.

"Feeling better, Nikki?"

The rough sound of his voice had desire building within me again.

"Yes. Much better. But I'd feel better with you inside me."

"Open your eyes." They shifted open. Brandt still had on his jeans, but they were pulled down enough for his cock to be free. It pulsed with lust. He swung me a little more. "I love watching you hang here with those fuck-me heels on. They're about to get what they want."

"I hope so."

The swing moved enough now that I was getting close to being able to touch Brandt. On the next move toward him, his dick touched my entrance but didn't penetrate, even though I tried to keep the swing from swinging back. Brandt knew how to build up my body and take it to the edge of no return.

He smiled at me. "We're going to watch each other in the mirror as I fuck you."

"I'm ready to feel you in me."

On the next swing in, Brandt grabbed the strap to hold me in place and minimize the swinging motion. He slammed into me and I hissed at the stretching sensation. Pain mixed with pleasure was one of the headiest combinations I could ever want.

Brandt became a machine as I watched him move in and out of me in the mirror. His cock would nearly leave my body before ramming back in. The inner pool of desire rose, waiting to break and release again.

He came into me faster, harder, and deeper. I was at the edge and I couldn't hold back as I called his name.

Brandt called out, "Nikki!" And we reached bliss simultaneously.

I was exhausted and covered with sweat. Brandt hoisted me out of the swing, then laid me on the bed. He unbuckled my shoes and they disappeared from my feet. The lights dimmed and a low, classical melody replaced the silence. Brandt slid next to me and pulled the sheet on top of our bodies. Our legs entwined and our faces were mere inches from each other, making our breaths mingle. The smell of sex filled the air.

"I'd say we are still quite compatible in the club fucking department," Brandt declared, grinning like he'd won the lottery.

I matched his expression. "I'd have to agree. I don't know why I was nervous."

"I think we're both scared to lose the only things we want in life— love and happiness." He stroked my bottom lip with his thumb.

"I agree. I'm glad we found this side to us again." Our noses grazed each other as we talked.

An unwanted thought came into my mind. I bit my cheek.

Brandt looked at me for a second. "What's on your mind?"

Brandt was one of the few people who noticed my nervous habit. A lump formed in my throat and I closed my eyes. I knew Brandt had been with one other person while we were apart.

Just above a whisper, I asked, "Did you sleep with her in here? In our room?"

Silence came and I squeezed my eyes tighter, afraid of what he was going to say.

"Nikola—" I waited. "Nikola, look at me."

My eyes slowly opened. Brandt watched me, concerned. He shook his head. "The last time I was in this room was with you. I told you, I took over the security office. It was because the reminder of you, that close, was hard. But I couldn't bear to get rid of anything. It made it feel too final, and I wasn't ready to give up on us."

I breathed a shaky sigh of relief and kissed him. "I'm glad you didn't give up."

"I'll never give up on us as long as I'm alive. We're forever."

I believed him. Brandt was my happily ever after. I had all I'd ever wanted in my life. Tonight, another piece of the puzzle had fallen into place for us. We were piecing us back together. I was excited to see what the puzzle would look like when we were done.

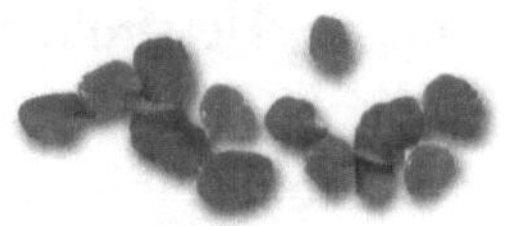

A week had passed, and I was at the doctor's office with Grandmama. The doctor had decided to take some precautionary chest x-rays, even though they still believed it was bronchitis. I'd spoken to my parents this morning. They'd signed on for another three years in China for my dad's work. I missed them, but it felt like I was a stranger to them.

Grandmama sat on the red, plaid chair as I walked around, looking at all the certificates Dr. Grieger had received. His list of accomplishments was extraordinary. He was a pulmonary specialist and we'd been lucky to get in so quickly when I called in to make the appointment. I wanted to become more proactive with Grandmama's bronchitis. Hopefully, we could become proactive with the yearly battle of bronchitis Grandmama seemed to face.

"Did Brandt tell you what he's planned tonight after dinner at his mom's house?"

I turned and smiled big. "No, I can't get it out of him. All he says is that it's my early Valentine's Day surprise and to be ready by six."

Brandt's mom, Faith, had returned from the Bahamas, and I was going to see her for the first time since the breakup. I'd missed her. Faith had been like a mom to me and it had been devastating when I'd lost her too. Part of me had still wanted to keep talking to her, but I knew it wouldn't have been fair to Brandt. He needed his mom.

Glancing at my watch, I saw it was after four. Ainsley was working on a broom analysis I'd left her with. Gavin had challenged our initial findings regarding his lack of diversification in broom styles. We'd talked a few times, but the majority of the time, all communication with Gavin happened via e-mail.

We'd been waiting for a while. "If you need to leave, Nikola, you can."

"No, I'm waiting on a report from Ainsley. She's handling the broom piece of the Livingston account. She's doing extremely well."

Grandmama crossed her legs the other direction. "Do you think you'll hire her on at the end of this? She seems to help you, and I like her. Ainsley has a good heart."

"I'm hoping to, but we'll see if I'm able to compete with the other offers she'll probably receive."

The door cracked open and Dr. Grieger came into the office carrying a large envelope. His face was blank, which was how he'd been during the entire examination. "Sorry to keep you guys waiting so long. Can I get you anything?"

We both answered, "No, thank you."

The board the x-rays were on lit up. It was a picture of Grandmama's lungs. A massive white ball on each side covered more than a quarter of the lung.

"Oh man, Grandmama. Your bronchitis is bad. I'm glad we came so we can get you fixed right up."

I smiled at her, and she gave me a small smile in return. The doctor looked at me as I waited to hear what we needed to do to get her better.

He cleared his throat. "After examining the x-rays closely, it appears you have either Stage Three or Stage Four lung cancer."

I stood. "What?" Panic rose in my voice.

"Until we do a biopsy, we won't know the type of cancer, but it is definitely advanced." The doctor's voice was calm and steady.

"Lung cancer? Are you sure? This has to be a mistake. She can't have lung cancer. She can't. She has bronchitis. Please, check again. The first doctor we went to never mentioned lung cancer."

Tears were beginning to stream down my face as I let the emotion take control of me, knowing Grandmama needed me strong, but not being able to push it down. My chest rose in jagged breaths. I felt like a knife was being dragged through my gut. I went to sit next to Grandmama and grabbed her hands. Tears were in the corners of her eyes. The look of sadness on her face tore me to shreds.

The doctor continued as tears created a haze over my vision. The lung x-ray looked like one big blob. "Yes, this is undoubtedly lung cancer. We'll first need to do an MRI to see if the cancer has spread elsewhere. If it hasn't, then we may be able to operate and remove it."

My brain was on fire. "How long do you think she's had it?"

Dr. Grieger sat in the chair opposite us. "It's hard to say. We won't know until we get the results of the biopsy."

"When do we start treatment?" Tears continued to race down my cheeks.

I squeezed Grandmama's hand, and she returned the pressure. Her hand shook.

The doctor put some papers he'd been holding on the table. "If you guys can make an eight a.m. appointment, we'll do an MRI. Then, we'll discuss the next step. All the information is in these papers. The appointment is in this building. Afterward, we'll meet here to talk about all our options."

"Okay." My voice was shaky, and I turned to Grandmama. "We're going to get through this. Everything is going to be okay."

Her blue eyes looked back at me, and I wanted to start crying again. Grandmama tried to be strong as her lower lip slightly trembled. "Yes, we are. We're going to get through this."

I let out a deep sigh of relief. As long as we had hope, that's what mattered.

Hope.

That was the word I was going to tether myself to.

Brandt

WE WERE AT the hospital waiting room while Anne was getting her MRI. Nikola sat beside me with a blank look on her face. I'd canceled all our plans last night, and we'd slept over at Anne's house instead—or attempted to. Nikola had cried all night, and I'd done the only thing I could to help— I held her.

"Can I get you anything, baby?"

She shook her head. "No, I couldn't eat or drink anything even if I wanted to."

I stretched my legs as I held Nikola. We'd been sitting here for about two hours. The antiseptic smell of the hospital always reminded me of when I'd broken my leg as a kid. I'd fallen out of the tree house that I'd built with my brother and my dad.

My phone vibrated, and it was my mum. We were supposed visit her house last night for dinner. Afterward, I'd planned to take Nikola away for the weekend, up to the cabin we'd stayed in at Stone Mountain. Nikola had called me in tears, and I'd rushed to the doctor's office instead.

Mum: I wanted to check on Nikola and you. I'm glad you're there for her. She's going to need you. Hopefully, the results will come back and you'll find out they can operate. Tell Nikola I love her.

Me: She's as good as can be expected. I'll tell her and keep you posted. She's it for me. I'll do whatever I need to help her through this.

I pulled Nikola closer and kissed the top of her head. She wrapped herself around me, holding me close. "Mum, says she loves you."

"Tell her I love her, too. I hate that we had to miss dinner last night." Nikola's voice cracked.

I rubbed her arm, trying to soothe her. "Don't worry about it. We'll figure out another time."

"Okay, that sounds good."

From the doorway, two familiar faces came into view holding a cardboard tray full of coffee cups. Adam had texted earlier, asking if we needed anything. Even though I'd said we were fine, I knew they'd stop by to support us. Ainsley sat next to Nikola. Everyone looked tired. Late last night, I'd texted Adam with the news. He knew Anne, and he loved Nikola like a sister.

I took my coffee and said, "Thanks, guys."

Nikola murmured her thanks and set her coffee on the table.

Ainsley hugged Nikola. "My mom and I are going to bring you guys some dinner tonight if that sounds okay,"

Ainsley sat back up and Nikola adjusted herself slightly so she wasn't buried in my chest. "Thank you."

Ainsley had been through a lot with her father. He'd beaten her mom for years before leaving her. The years of abuse had led to Ainsley's mom having a breakdown. Luckily, she'd ended up getting help at a domestic abuse center. Unfortunately, shortly after, the deadbeat had shown up and nearly killed Ainsley's mom. Fortunately, that fucker would rot in jail for the rest of his life.

Adam crouched in front of Nikola. He scrubbed a hand down his face and adjusted his leather jacket as he touched Nikola's knee. "Let me know if you need anything. Ainsley and I are here for you."

Ainsley chimed in, "I have Livingston completely covered. I'll look over my email and make those additional changes we discussed."

A cart rolled down the hall in front of the doorway. The sound of the wheels hitting the floor filled the quiet hospital.

Leaning her head against Ainsley, Nikola said, "You go ahead and send that email to Gavin. Give him a short message about my grandmother. Just be sure to include the seasonality lifts for spring cleaning in your numbers to justify the brighter color scheme we're suggesting."

I watched the exchange closely. Ainsley's eyes lit up. "Really? Okay, I promise I won't let you down."

Nikola gave Ainsley a tired smile. "You've earned it, and you know this project as well as I do."

The nurse came into the room. "Miss Kingston, would you please follow me? The doctor is ready to go over the results of the MRI."

Nikola stood, and I followed. "Yes." She gave Adam and Ainsley a quick hug. "Thanks you, guys. We'll keep you updated."

They nodded as we left the room, following the nurse. I had my arm around Nikola's waist as she leaned into me. The only sound that filled the hallways was the rubber of the nurses' shoes squeaking against the floor. This was the worst part about learning the results—the ominous march to the doors, knowing the doctor knew the answer. We didn't say a word, but I knew we wanted to ask what the prognosis was. *Please, let her be okay*, I prayed *Please. Nikola needs Anne.*

We made it to the large doors and entered an exam room. Anne was dressed and sitting in a chair along the wall. The hospital bed sat untouched in the middle of the room with several machines that weren't plugged in. For some reason, it felt like bad news hanging over us.

Dr. Grieger, whom I had met yesterday when I'd rushed to the hospital, sat on a roller stool a few feet away from Anne. Their expressions were unreadable, and I wasn't sure what to expect. Nikola smiled, took a seat next to Anne, and grabbed her hands. When I sat next to Nikola, I got an uneasy feeling. Anne had a look of knowing about her, the way she sat back in her chair, watching Nikola closely rather than the doctor. I glanced at the doctor and all the attention was on Nikola. My first instinct was to stand and stop whatever was about to happen. It wasn't good.

My heart pounded hard against my tightening chest. This was how I'd felt when I lost my dad. *Please, let me be wrong. Please*, I prayed. I glanced up at Anne and her blue eyes met mine. There was sadness in them. *Shit.* I nodded as I tightened my arm around Nikola's shoulders. Anne cleared her throat.

She spoke in a soothing voice, and I closed my eyes, hoping I'd wake from this terrible nightmare.

"Nikola, I asked Dr. Grieger to go over the results with me first," Anne explained.

My eyes opened. Nikola started to speak, but Anne touched her cheek as the corner of her eyes filled with tears.

"The MRI shows the cancer has spread to my lymph nodes, spine, brain, and pretty much throughout my body," Anne said.

I squeezed Nikola's shoulders.

Nikola addressed the doctor. "But there's chemo, right? We can use different therapies to go after the different cancers. I read about this last night. We'll need to find which is worst and go after it first."

The doctor gave Nikola a sad smile. Anne continued speaking. This had been rehearsed, I was sure of it.

"Nikola, I have decided to not undergo any type of treatment."

Nikola shook her head. "No! No! No! We can fight this. We don't want to give up." She turned to the doctor, desperate. "Please, say you have an experimental drug to use. Something. We can't give up."

The doctor gave a sympathetic look as Anne started to speak, "Nikola—,"

Nikola kept staring at the doctor and my heart broke. Anne waited for Nikola to turn back to her. A tear slid down Anne's cheek as she watched the granddaughter she loved fall apart.

Nikola turned to me. "Brandt, please. Please, talk to them. I'm begging. Help me."

Tears were falling down her face. I spoke to her as my thumb caressed her cheek. "Baby, your Grandmama has something else to say. Let's hear her out, okay? Let's listen to what she's thinking."

The one person I would walk through fire for was hurting, and there was nothing I could do to take away the pain. Nikola turned back to Anne and leaned into me.

The doctor stood. "I'm going to give you guys a few minutes. I'll be back." He left without another word and quietly closed the door behind him.

Anne spoke after taking a breath. She touched a small, gold heart on a delicate, gold chain. She wore it all the time. It had been a gift from her husband years before.

Anne's voice was soft. "Nikola, the cancer has spread everywhere. I asked what the treatments would be like, and the doctor said it would be eight hours, several days a week, sitting in a chair getting chemotherapy. Plus, there would be radiation and mounds of drugs and monitoring for white blood cells and other various things. With the aggressive chemo I'd probably need, it would have side effects a mile long."

"H-h-how l-l-long are t-they s-saying?"

Anne took a deep breath. "No one knows, but it is aggressive with how much it has spread." Nikola protested and Anne held up her hand. "Sweetheart, this is hard for me, too. However, I would rather spend the rest of my days living my life to the fullest rather than hooked up to machines. I want quality, not quantity. Can you understand that? I know what I'm doing may seem selfish, but I don't want you to remember me sick and miserable. I want you to remember me happy. They don't know how long, but let's make the most of what we've got."

My heart broke. There wasn't a silver lining in this situation. There was heartache and loss on the road ahead, with nothing I could do about it. Nikola's hands were cradling her face as she sobbed. She was one of the strongest people I knew, but this was a devastating blow.

Anne looked at me and mouthed, *She's going to need you.*

I nodded and mouthed back, "I'll be there for her."

Nikola sat up and hugged Anne. "I love you, Grandmama. I'll support you in your decision."

Anne hugged her back. "I love you, too, sweetie. More than words can say."

We consoled Nikola as she continued to sob. Tears fell down Anne's face as we tried to come to terms with the hand life had dealt us.

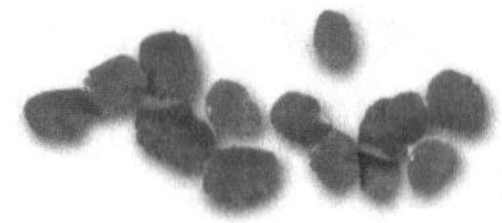

I lay awake and stared at the ceiling as Nikola slept in the crook of my arm. Last night had been a shift of emotions, from one extreme to another. We'd stayed at Anne's, and one minute, Nikola was angry, the next sad, and the next a blank slate. I'd been there for her but was at a loss. There was nothing I could do. I wasn't sure what she needed.

Everything I thought of felt hopeless and I wanted to tune it out long enough to get my thoughts together. I heard some pots and pans shuffling in the kitchen. Nikola turned, and I brought the bedspread up to cover her. I slipped out, put on my sweatpants, and pulled a long-sleeved tee over my head.

As I went to the kitchen to talk to Anne, Nikola's words from last night haunted me between sobs.

"Brandt, she'll never be part of my life or know where I end up. See me married and happy. She'll never know if I have kids or if I'm a good mother. She'll never know. Who will I go to when I need help? Who will I go to when I don't know what

to do? Grandmama won't be there. My heart is breaking, Brandt. My heart is breaking."

I gently closed the bedroom door and padded toward the kitchen. Anne had flour, shortening, butter, and milk on the counter. She was making biscuits and was already dressed for the day in jeans and a pale pink sweater.

She turned my way. "Good morning. How's Nikola?"

I went to the coffeepot and poured myself a cup of black coffee. The more caffeine, the better at this point. Taking a spot next to Anne at the bar, I leaned against the counter and took a sip. This was the first time we'd been alone since finding out about the cancer.

"It's difficult to come to grips with a truth we don't want to accept or believe. Nikola is a fighter, and it's hard for her to sit back and not try."

Anne mixed up the ingredients, like she had a million times before. "I know. Going through this and accepting what's to come…well, it's easier knowing she has you again. Nikola is tough, but she needs to be loved." Anne paused and pressed her lips together before she continued speaking. "I wish I was going to be there to be part of all those special moments in her life. That's the hardest thing about all this—knowing I won't be there with her."

We stood in silence as more pressure built in my mind.

"Brandt, I don't think I'll be here by the time summer comes."

I was stunned, nearly dropping my coffee cup. Finally, I said, "I'm going to hope for the best, Anne. I'm going to hope for the best."

For some reason, I'd imagined at least a year—not a few months. My mind was going in a million directions and I needed to get control over it, think everything through.

"Do you think I made the right decision or that I'm being selfish?"

Anne's question floored me. I tried to put myself in her position. *What would I do?* It didn't take long. "Anne, I think people make the right decisions for themselves. There wasn't a good decision in all this. There's only the decision you think is right."

A sleepy voice from the doorway spoke. "I think you made the right choice, even though I want to fight. But if it means suffering, I don't want that for you, either."

Anne went to hug Nikola at the doorway and they held on to each other tight. I knew Nikola hadn't heard the comment about Anne not being here come summer. If she had, she wouldn't be as together as she was now. I tried to remain calm, but I was a jittery mess on the inside. I needed to talk to Quentin right away.

Nikola

IT WAS MID-MORNING, and Brandt had gone into town to see Quentin. He seemed on edge. At some point, I hoped I could meet his sponsor. Eventually, I'd ask. There was so much going on now, and it didn't feel like a good time. I also thought it was important for Brandt to have his safe place to vent when he needed to talk. People had talked in group about how some addicts liked their sponsor to be a safe place, separate from loved ones. As long as Brandt was doing well, that's all that mattered.

I was alone with Grandmama in her sewing room as she worked on the red vests. The comforting sound of the sewing machine gave me a temporary peace. Grandmama stopped and swiveled her chair to face me.

"Do you want to talk about it?"

My jaw tightened as I tried to keep my emotions in check. I needed to be strong. "Are you scared?"

Grandmama got up, adjusting her pale-pink sweater, and sat on the edge of the daybed. A slight drizzle began outside.

"I'm scared of the unknown and of leaving you. But death is a part of life. I'm grateful for being blessed with a wonderful marriage with your grandfather. I'm grateful for my son and that he brought me you. You and I have always been connected in a way people don't understand, even when you were a baby. I'm grateful we can prepare ourselves and treasure the time we *do* have. Do you remember when your dad moved you to Arkansas on business?"

I nodded.

"When my time comes, it'll be like I've moved. We'll have our dreams. We'll have the sunsets and the sunrises we'll both be able to see. We'll always be connected."

Blinking a few times, I kept the tears at bay. "I love you."

"I love you, too, sweetie. There's something else I want to talk about."

I hesitantly responded, "Okay."

Grandmama patted my leg and picked off a piece of fuzz that had stuck to my sock. "I don't want you to stop living your life, Nikola. I want you to come around, but don't put you and Brandt on hold for me. You two are both still finding your way, and it's important that you guys don't put that on the back burner."

"I'll try, but it's hard to not want to stop everything and be here every second." The thought of leaving this house was hard when all I wanted to do was stay.

She patted my leg. "I know, Nikola, but you can't. I plan on living life the same until I have to change what I'm doing. There will be plenty of time for you to take care of me. Please, reschedule dinner with Brandt's mom. Don't put that off. She was like a mother to you. Also, I want you sleep at Brandt's place tonight to spend some time with him, alone. Promise me."

"I promise." I grabbed my phone from my pocket and she smiled. "Do you think it's bad Brandt and I have gotten back together so fast?"

She thought about it, taking her seat at the chair. "When it's meant to be, it's meant to be. I don't think you can put a timer on it. Despite the time apart, you and Brandt have a strong history that's full of love. I think what you've gone through has only strengthened what you have."

"I feel the same way."

Grandmama swiveled back to face the wall. The sewing machine started again.

I texted Brandt.

Me: Hey, I still want to do lunch or dinner with your mom this week. I'd also like sleep at your place tonight if that's okay.

Brandt: Okay, I'll text Mum. She'll love that. Only if you're sure about coming to my place. I'll pick you up in a few hours if that sounds good. As long as I'm with you, I don't care where we are.

Me: I want to. I can't wait to see her again.

"I'm going to make a sandwich. Do you want anything, Grandmama?"

She continued to sew, saying, "No, I'm good."

I made my way down the hallway. Her words made me feel better, and the horrible situation didn't feel as dismal as it was. Pulling out the bread, ham, lettuce, tomato, and mayo, I made my lunch as my phone rang.

I answered without looking, "Hello, this is Nikola."

A warm voice came on the other end. "Hello, Nikola. It's Gavin England. I received Ainsley's e-mail, and I wanted to let you know how sorry I was to hear about your grandmother."

"Thank you, Gavin. I appreciate it. It won't affect the deadlines or my work, I wanted to assure you of that." I discarded my lunch-making efforts and tried to focus, not knowing if the account was in trouble.

"Nikola, I know that. I've seen your work, and you're brilliant. Once we get through this project, we're going to have to celebrate. A night on me. You and Ainsley can bring your significant others and I'll bring my girlfriend. I believe we're going to make a difference, and I'll have you to thank for that."

Gavin was a gentleman and had been on every call. He was one of the most polished businessmen I'd dealt with in business.

"Thank you, Gavin. That sounds great."

"Wonderful, Nikola. I'll review the e-mail and get back to you on changes."

"Perfect. Have a great day."

I knew there were going to be more challenges. Gavin was tough.

"You too."

After I made my sandwich, I put everything away before sitting at the bar. I was going to survive.

I kept repeating it, hoping the words would begin to make it true for the long battle we were about to face.

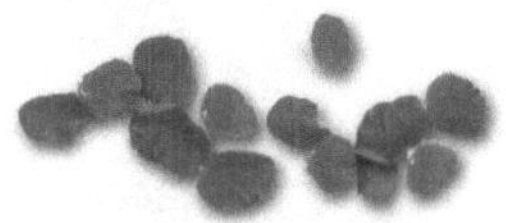

A few days had passed since the Grandmama's news. It was the day after Valentine's Day. With everything going on, I'd asked for a quiet night indoors where Brandt made us dinner and we laid next to the fire, holding each other. It had been exactly what I'd needed. We were going to Brandt's mom house for dinner tonight. As we pulled up to Faith's house, I was excited and nervous. It had been a while since I'd seen her. Part of me was ashamed of how I had vacated everyone's life overnight without so much as a good-bye when it came to Brandt's family.

"Don't be nervous." Brandt's voice reassured me.

I looked at the house, longing to have Faith hold me like a mother would.

My mom wasn't affectionate. Everything felt clinical with her, but I think she did the best she could with showing she did love me. I guess it worked for my dad's excessive working hours, but I wanted more in my life than what they had. I wanted the fairytales Faith and Grandmama told me about. Sometimes, I wondered how in the world my dad was raised by my grandmother. I loved my dad, but he seemed disconnected. As a child, anytime I'd ask them if they loved me. My parents would say, "Of course, we do." I'd asked Grandmama about why she thought my parents were like that and her response had been, "We don't always follow how we were raised. Look at you. You aren't a replica of your parents. As long as we're true to ourselves, that's what matters."

She was right. Brandt hadn't been raised in a family that did drugs, but he had turned to them. But, he hadn't gone back to them.

The opening of Brandt's door sent a rush of cold air into the car. I followed suit before he had a chance to come get me on the passenger side. He grabbed my hand, and we walked toward the front door that had a twig wreath with hearts on it. Brandt's mom loved wreaths and had one for almost every holiday. Before we made it to the door, it opened and Faith came out. She was in jeans and a red sweater. Her brown hair was up in a French twist.

"Nikola, oh my sweet darling, you're here. It's so good to see you."

I didn't have a chance to respond as Faith pulled me into a tight hug and I wrapped my arms around her, feeling the comfort of her motherly embrace.

"It's good to see you, too, Mom. I mean Faith." I fumbled my words. I'd called her Mom before, but wasn't sure if I still could. Brandt had always called her Mum. It was something special between them. He called anyone else's mother Mom.

She pulled back. "There's no pressure, but I still consider you my kiddo. If you want, you can still call me Mom."

Tears welled in my eyes. "Thank you. I'd love to."

Faith moved to Brandt and gave him a hug and kiss on the cheek. His hair was pulled back tonight, and he was wearing one of his signature thermal shirts. "Hey, Mum. It's good to see you. It's a bit cold, you mind if we take this reunion inside."

"Yes, yes, of course."

We moseyed to the door with Faith in between us. As soon as we crossed the threshold, I smelled one of the most divine smells. "Did you make Ruebens?"

"Yes, sweetie, I did. I knew they were one of your favorites." Faith gave me a squeeze.

I took in the surroundings, and they were as I'd remembered. The fireplace was the focal point of the living room that sat off the kitchen. The wooden mantel was covered with family pictures. The blue plaid couch sat at the same angle as the fireplace. There wasn't a television in the living room. Faith had wanted family time to be actual conversations, rather than everyone staring at a screen. I loved the concept.

We went to the breakfast nook and sat. Rueben sandwiches were piled high. "There's plenty to eat, and I'll send some home with you."

"This looks delicious. And I know that all the leftovers are mine, not Brandt's."

We chuckled. Faith replied, "They're all yours. Let's dig in."

We grabbed sandwiches and ate. I was mid-bite when Faith cleared her throat. As I glanced up, I was met with warm, chocolate eyes.

"I'm glad you guys got back together. You two belong together, and I can't wait for your wedding." Her eyes shot to Brandt, then added, "Someday."

"Mum, *please*." Brandt was semi-censoring, and I'd never heard him talk to his mother like that.

She looked down for a second. I didn't know what to say. Brandt looked uncomfortable as he stared down at his Rueben. I wore a fake smile as I swallowed another bite and tried to force it down. This had turned awkward quicker than I'd thought possible. I wanted to marry Brandt, but I wasn't sure he was even ready to broach that subject. The look on his face confirmed my suspicions. In time, we'd both want to be there. For now, I would enjoy us.

Faith rebounded and talked like the awkwardness hadn't happened. "So how's the business going? Brandt says you landed a big account."

I responded, but couldn't keep my eyes off Brandt, who wouldn't look at me a lot through the rest of dinner. He did all the things I was used to— putting his hand on my knee, sneaking kisses—but he was slightly withdrawn. Not enough for anyone to notice, but the difference was there.

A difference I had experienced before.

I trusted him.

I was stressed from everything with Grandmama.

I trusted him.

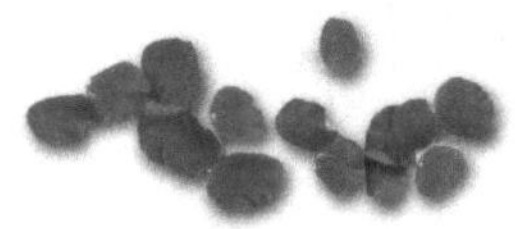

We were lying in Brandt's bed after getting home from Faith's. Our legs were entwined, naked from our last bit of lovemaking. I'd needed Brandt inside me. Making love helped me realize that there were still things in this world that were beautiful, despite what I faced with my grandmother.

Brandt's hand idly stroked my hip. His bedroom was the most decorated space in the house. He had a metal bed that filled the center of the room. The rest of the furniture— side tables, dressers, and chest— were all black. He had a green velvet comforter that felt heavenly on your skin when mixed with the satin sheets. Black-and-white art hung on the wall over the bed.

"Is there something bothering you, Brandt? You've seen withdrawn since diner over at your mom's."

He turned to me and said, "I'm perfect. I have you."

Fingers grazed the underside of my breast. Clearly, he needed a distraction, and I was happy to oblige until he was ready to talk. My thumb grazed my nipple. Brandt watched me closely as my hand made its way down to my clit.

"Fuck me, are you about to touch yourself?"

He got his answer when he wrenched the sheets from my body and my fingers had already made contact. My hips were beginning to pump on their own accord, and I could feel the wetness from my core increasing. Brandt flipped his body and hovered above me. His head was right at my pussy.

"Ah hell, Nikki, your pussy is swollen. Rub it baby, finger-fuck yourself."

I stroked myself faster, but at a pace that kept the internal build slow. Brandt's dick was hard and throbbing above my face in a dark red state. His purple vein bulged. I ran my tongue down his shaft. His dick jumped at the touch.

Brandt looked at me from below. I opened my mouth and angled my head so his dick could go in all the way. The tip entered my mouth and I created a suction around it as it continually slid in, filling my throat. My throat opened and I breathed through my nose to keep my gag reflex at bay.

"You have me in all the way. Oh, fuck. This feels good."

I kept touching myself and hummed around Brandt's length. He moved in and out of my mouth as he kept a steady pace. I entered myself deeper and moved my fingers in a scissor motion.

As I was about to reach the edge, Brandt removed my fingers and sucked my clit into his mouth. I screamed and he pumped faster at the noise of my ecstasy. Hot liquid spurted to the back of my throat.

My mouth fell open as I came down from my high. Brandt flipped around, sliding on top of me, capturing my mouth, mixing our bodily fluids. Salty combined with the sweet cream tastes, and it was sexy as hell as our tongues battled each other. Pulling back, his blue eyes locked with mine.

"You're mine, forever and always."

"I'm yours."

We laid in each other's arms, content and happy. This was what I'd needed, and Brandt had been there for me. My eyes were about to close when my cell phone vibrated on the black, wooden nightstand.

Brandt nuzzled my ear. "Let it go to voicemail."

I was still reaching for the phone. "It could be Grandma-ma, she might need me." He squeezed my waist in response.

Feeling for the plastic case I had around my phone, I grabbed it and answered,

"Hello?"

"Ni-Nik-Nikola."

I sat straight up, dread filling my head as Wesley's broken voice came through on the other end. "Wesley, what's wrong?"

He sobbed, and I clutched the phone tighter to my ear, hoping I didn't miss what he said. "S-sh-she's d-dead. Di-Diane is dead."

"Wait. What? Diane is dead?"

Brandt sat up beside me as he wrapped his arm around my shoulders.

"S-she over-overdosed. She's de-dead. It's a-all my f-fault."

I got out of bed and hunted for my clothes. "Wesley, where are you? I'm coming to you."

Brandt got dressed, too. My lip quivered at Brandt's nev-er-ending support. He had a long day of interviews tomorrow for the new Club Manager positions, but he was going out with me in the middle of the night.

"I'm a-at m-my pl-place."

"Okay, Wesley. I'm on my way. Don't do anything. I'll be there right away."

He sounded lost. Wesley had been there for me through so much. It didn't seem fair I was getting my happy ending and he wasn't. If something had happened to Brandt, I knew I'd be in the same shape. He was my beginning and my end.

"T-t-thank y-you, Ni-Nikola."

"Of course. Hang tight."

I hung up the phone, and Brandt stood at the door as I finished putting on my T-shirt. As I got closer, I went into his arms. "Thank you for getting better. Thank you for coming back for me. Thank you for fighting for your sobriety. I love you."

Brandt's hands came down to the side of my face, and I looked up into his eyes. "I will never stop fighting for us, and I'm never leaving you now that I have you. Let's go help Wesley. I'm sorry this happened to him."

"Me, too. I had hoped they were going to get their happily ever after. They deserved a happily ever after."

Brandt

NIKOLA AND I were in a church, sitting in the third row with Wesley. At the front of the church sat a cream-colored, closed coffin. The pastor spoke about seeking help before it was too late. The words rattled in my head as I tried to make sense of everything.

Why me? Why had I been given a second chance at life? I glanced over at Wesley, who stared blankly ahead as Nikola held his hand. My arm was draped around her shoulder, hoping to be the pillar of strength she needed to help her friend through this horrific time. The choir sang a song that sounded angelic as my mind drifted.

Two days ago had been sobering when Nikola and I went to see Wesley.

We were pulling into a neighborhood with cookie-cutter houses lining the streets. Nikola had put his address in the GPS as we drove there.

"If it makes you uncomfortable to come in, I understand." Nikola's eyes were sad as she looked at me.

"I want to be there for you and your friend. Maybe I can help."

She nodded as a few tears fell down her cheek.

A female voice sounded. "You have arrived at your destination on the right."

I pulled into the driveway, and Nikola was out of the SUV and running up the sidewalk before I had a chance to put the car it in park. Quickly, I got out and followed her up the short pathway as she knocked on the door.

A voice called, "It's open," from the other side of the door. Without hesitating, Nikola opened the door and walked into Wesley's home. I followed and took in my surroundings.

The place was warm and had a feminine touch. Pictures of Wesley and a woman, whom I assumed was Diane, were everywhere. Wesley sat on the brown suede couch with his head in hands. He had on sweats and an old T-shirt. Nikola sat on his right side. I stayed back at the entrance to give them a minute.

"Wesley, I'm here. I'm so sorry, but I'm here."

He turned and wrapped his arms around Nikola and sobbed into her shoulder. Nikola's eyes connected with mine. Normally, I was possessive and didn't like people close to my woman. Nikola knew this, and I'm sure she was nervous. But this was an exception. Wesley had lost the love of his life, and I couldn't fathom what the emptiness would be like. I gave Nikola a reassuring smile, and she nodded.

She consoled Wesley. "Let it out. I know it hurts. Let it

out."

Wesley grabbed her shoulders until his knuckles turned white. "Why wasn't our love enough? Why didn't she beat the statistics? Why did she have to lean on the drugs and not me? Why? I loved her, Nikola. I loved her with every fiber of my being."

Wesley was a broken man. If I hadn't chosen to get clean, I pictured what this would have done to Nikola. I'd never put her through that. Never. I'd do everything in my power to keep doubt from ever entering her mind. There was a picture right beside me on a sofa table. Diane and Wesley were gazing at each other. It was a stolen smile, captured on film. The emotion came through the photograph. In the right hand corner, a date appeared. It was from this past Christmas, when Diane had been clean.

Things can turn upside down and inside out before you know it.

Nikola continued to console Wesley. It was obvious she'd attended group sessions as she prompted him to feel and express his emotions. Wesley grasped onto Nikola as if she were the only thing keeping him here.

"All I wanted was to have her in my life and love her. I never needed a baby. I only needed her, and now she's gone. Diane is gone."

I was speechless as I saw firsthand what addiction does to the ones we love. The guilt hit me like a fresh punch imagining her sobbing and heartbroken when I'd been so messed up. I was beyond fortunate I'd been given a second chance to make things right.

The song ended, and the pastor preached. Light shone through the stained-glass windows. Nikola's free hand came down on my knee and squeezed it. I placed my hand on top of hers. Diane had left the rehab facility and scored some drugs. From there, it appeared she went on a mind-numbing binge that resulted in taking her life. There were no words to console someone in this instance.

The service ended and we went through the line to greet the family. Wesley had joined them in the family line and was now standing next to Diane's mother and sister. They were dressed in black with tearful faces. Nikola gave them each a hug, and I followed. When I got to Wesley, he pulled me in close.

"Nikola deserves to never have to face what I'm going through. Promise me you won't go down that road again." His voice pleaded.

I whispered back, "I promise."

He released me, and I walked over to meet Nikola. We got into my vehicle to follow the procession to the burial site. Wesley was going to ride with the family there. He'd wanted Nikola to ride with him, but there wasn't room. The hearse was parked in front of the church steps. It was like a curse that rang throughout the area for everyone who looked upon it. There were so many reminders of death; I needed a way to show that I chose life. The noise in my head became louder as I tried to sift through it, telling myself I made the right decision with what I had planned for our future.

Nikola's voice broke through my inner ramblings. "Thanks for being here with me through all this. I've needed you."

I looked over at her sad, green eyes. Nikola looked like she had the weight of the world on her shoulders. She looked frail.

"I'll always be there for you. Never doubt it. Nikola, I

will be the man you need even with my last breath."

Nikola's eyes watched Wesley, holding Diane's mother as they walked to the car behind the hearse. He consoled her.

Nikola continued to look in their direction as she spoke. "I beg you never to go back to drugs, Brandt. Don't let this become our ending. I want the life we imagined together. I want to grow old with you as we watch our kids play outside. I trust you, but seeing what Wesley is going through scares me." Her lip trembled. "I'm scared of losing the only man I've ever loved and will ever love."

Tears fell down her face. "Nikola." She kept staring forward. "Nikola." My tone was firmer, and she turned my way. "I'm never going back to drugs. I promise you. We are going to get the life we planned together. I love you. Never doubt my love for you."

"Why were you distant the other night at your mom's house?"

Shit. With all the things I was trying to sort through, I'd hoped Nikola wouldn't have picked up on the near slip at my mum's house.

People were all getting in their cars and starting them as the hearse pulled away from the curb. We had a few minutes before it was our turn to slide in to the long line. "Mum mentioned things we hadn't discussed yet. That's a decision for you and me to make. I didn't want it to be awkward for you, which it did anyways."

Nikola nodded and bit her lip. "You're right. Someday, we'll be ready for that." I knew she was holding something back.

I knitted my brow. I put the vehicle in drive and pulled forward. "Yes. Someday."

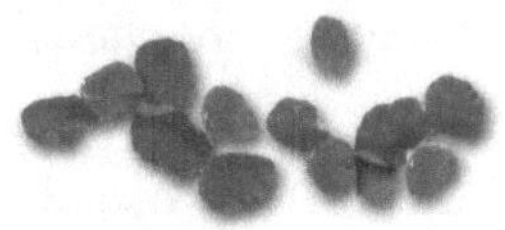

A couple of weeks had passed since the funeral. It was the beginning of March and the weather warmed. We were leaving Anne's house, where we'd watched a movie together. Anne's condition didn't seem worse. I was thankful. Between making sure we went to Anne's regularly, helping Wesley daily, work, and Club Envy, we were both exhausted.

Nikola massaged her temples. I was going to try to leave her alone tonight and keep my dick tamed. She needed the rest.

"You tired, baby?"

She looked my way. "Yeah, but I still want you to make love to me. If you don't, I may end up sleep-fucking you."

"Now, that would be fun." I wiggled my eyebrows.

She playfully slapped my arm. "Of course, you *would* think that."

Sirens blared from behind me. I pulled over to let the fire truck pass. The lights illuminated Nikola's car in red and white. Soon we were bathed in black again. I merged back onto the highway as Nikola's phone rang.

She sighed. "It's Wesley."

Fuck. He was going to want her to come over. I wanted to help, but anything Nikola or I suggested, Wesley would turn down. He was stuck and wasn't attempting to get up. It made me sound like a cold-hearted bastard but, as an addict, I wasn't able to stay down like that. I had to get up and keep pressing forward. It felt like he was trying to drag my girl down with him, and that wasn't going to happen. I wouldn't allow it.

I knew Nikola was at her wits' end. Wesley was a wreck and slipping further and further into despair. She answered, and I could hear him talking before she said anything.

"Hey, Wesley. I know it's tough. Yeah, I can swing by for a bit. I know. You're one of my best friends, too. You'd be there for me. Okay, I'll see you soon."

She hung up. "Brandt, I don't feel like I'm helping him. I feel like I'm creating a co-dependent relationship like they talk about in the groups I've attended. I don't know how to break it. I feel like I'm losing my mind."

Nikola was stressed. I didn't like her having all these additional pressures on top of Anne's cancer. She had too much on her plate. "Do you want me to see if Quentin is available to come? He might be able to hook Wesley up with someone who could help him."

"I'll try anything at this point. If Quentin wouldn't mind, that would be great. I'd get to meet him, too."

That caught my attention. "Have you wanted to meet him?"

Nikola looked down and pulled some imaginary lint off her pants. "You see him a lot. It'd be nice to meet someone you hold in such high regard."

"If you ever want to meet anyone in my life, all you have to do is ask."

She kept picking. "I didn't want to pry. Sometimes it's good to have that safe place you can go to that I'm not a part of."

The stoplight turned red and I pulled out my cell phone and gave Nikola a wink.

Me: The buddy of Nikola's whose girlfriend died of an overdose needs help. Are you up for a house call? He's become dependent on Nikola and she doesn't know what to do.

Quentin: Of course, send me the address and I'll head on

over.

Me: Thanks. I'll send right over.

Quentin: See you there.

I sent the contact to Quentin, then focused on what Nikola had said when the light turned green. A sleek sports car sped off beside us, making the tires squeal. Nikola looked out the window then looked back in my direction.

"First, you pry all you want. I'm an open book for you. We have to be open with each other. And, second, Quentin is on his way to see if he can help. Just so you know, he'll probably ask us to leave so they can talk about everything. It helps the person to share what's on their mind."

Nikola nodded. "I'm good with that. I know Wesley will never forget Diane and he'll always love her. I can't imagine how you move on, but he's sleeping in a pile of her clothes. He calls her cell phone forty times a day to listen to her voicemail message. Wesley won't turn off her credit cards, because he doesn't want to stop getting mail with her name on it. At some point, it can't be good to be drowned in the memory."

"No, it's not. Let's see if Quentin can help and we'll go from there."

We drove in silence. Once I'd been worried about Wesley liking Nikola as more than a friend, but when Diane died, I saw the brotherly-sisterly love they shared. Nikola and Wesley had been united by having loved ones turn into addicts. Now with Wesley regressing, I'd been watching him to make sure he didn't overstep his bounds because of loneliness or fear. Those two emotions could get strange reactions out of anyone.

We pulled up to the house and Quentin's red pickup was parked a few houses down. Quentin got out and adjusted his cap. He had on his trademark flannel shirt.

Quentin patted me on the back. "Hey, man. Thanks for calling me to help."

Nikola stood next to me, and I introduced her when Quentin stepped in. "You must be the lucky lady I hear so many wonderful things about."

Nikola extended her delicate hand. I knew Quentin sized her up, but the warm smile on his face told me he approved. "It's nice to meet you, Quentin. I've heard many wonderful things about you, too. I'm sorry we're meeting under such horrible circumstances, but I appreciate that you're trying to help Wesley."

"It's wonderful to meet you, too. Hopefully I can help."

Quentin turned to me, and I knew what was coming. I nodded and spoke first. "I'll wait in the car while you guys talk to him. I'll be right out here if you need anything."

Nikola gave me a quick peck on the lips and whispered against them. "Thank you for being so wonderful."

"You're welcome. Thanks for being mine."

We smiled at each other, exhausted, before she turned and headed to the door. I got in my vehicle and turned on the heat as I sat and waited.

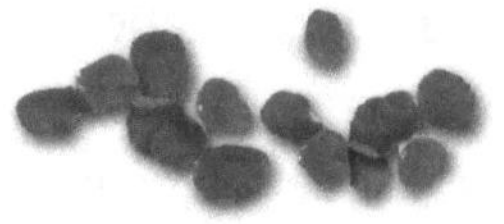

An hour later, Nikola came walking out of the house with a small smile on her face. In case Wesley watched from the windows, I remained in the car. There was no need for us to talk out on the street, and I needed to get her home.

She opened the car door and got in. Her back sagged against the seat.

"How'd it go?"

"Hard." She put her seatbelt on before continuing. "He was in denial to begin with and begged me not to leave him. Quentin kept talking, and finally Wesley was ready. Now they're talking, and I left. I'm relieved, and I hope he listens to the advice Quentin gives him. Your sponsor is patient and kind. He lets the person come to the conclusion on their own but acts like a guide. I like him. He's a keeper."

It was important to me that Nikola liked Quentin. "He's a good man and will do what he can for Wesley. Let's get you home. I took tomorrow off. Is there any way you can take tomorrow off, too?"

"Let me check something." Nikola dug through her purse and pulled out her phone. After a few minutes, she leaned back and closed her eyes. "Yes. Gavin accepted and agreed on all product lines we've submitted so far. This is huge. I was prepared for rework tomorrow, but now I can definitely take the day off. Let me text Ainsley."

We were going to lock ourselves away from the world tomorrow and focus on some much-needed *us* time.

Nikola

I WAS IN Brandt's kitchen making coffee while he got ready for work. I looked at the envelope I'd placed on the counter after checking my mail. My rental agreement was coming due in two months, and I needed to find another place. *Lance.* His name came to mind as I tried to recall the last time I'd heard from him. There had been no communication since the night Brandt had called to demand he leave me alone. On occasion, his car had been parked in his driveway when Brandt and I would swing by my place. Looked like Brandt's threats to Lance had worked—or maybe now that I was off the market, the chase wasn't as fun. Whatever the reason, I was glad it was over. I'd expected Lance to be harder to shake, but I was glad I'd been wrong.

Yesterday had been incredible as we'd locked ourselves

away from the world and spent time together. I felt confident that our relationship wasn't based on sex—what I'd worried about initially. It didn't take much to ignite our bodies when we were close, but we talked a lot, too. Brandt had been supportive as I continued to vocalize my fears about Grandmama and, now, Wesley. As the days passed, our relationship only grew stronger and my insecurities faded.

My hair was wet and hanging as it drip-dried. I was naked under my white silk robe as I poured coffee into Brandt's thermal mug. He had an early-morning meeting, and his shenanigans with me in the shower were making him late. I was headed to Grandmama's this morning to work. Once Ainsley was done with class, she was going to meet me there to start on the last cleaning product line for Livingston: buckets and mops. Technically, it was two, but the company grouped them together since they believed they were synonymous with each other. I disagreed. Ainsley and I were going to pull together our findings to present to Gavin to prove our hypothesis. The payment agreement was four installments. I'd received the second wire yesterday, and today Ainsley was going to get her first check. She'd stepped up beyond expectations lately, so I upped her commission on the project.

I tightened the lid on the black thermal mug and set it back on the counter as a hand grazed my lower belly, under my robe. Brandt's other hand undid the belt, exposing me. Turning into his embrace, I put my arms around his neck, making my silk robe slip off even more—now it only covered my nipples. His blue eyes glanced down.

"Didn't you have enough of me in the shower this morning?"

Brandt nipped my lip. "I'll never get enough."

His long hair was almost dry, and he was freshly shaved.

He was dressed up today in his khakis and button-up shirt.

"You'll be late."

He hoisted me onto the edge of the counter. "I don't give a fuck." My legs spread as Brandt's fingers circled my nipples. "You might as well be wearing nothing. Your wet hair has turned this robe see-through. There's no way I can leave this house with this image in my mind without taking you. No way."

His hands were gliding down the fabric as Brandt's gaze took me in. My hands went to his shoulders, and Brandt unzipped his pants enough to release his dick. I licked my lips. Brandt's hands came to my ass, scooting me to the end of the counter.

We looked down as he lined up at my entrance. My core squeezed in anticipation, and my hips rocked to gain friction. The tip of his length touched my clit, and he pushed as I tried to rub against it.

Brandt restricted my movement with his hands. "You're always ready for me, Nikki. So responsive to me."

"I need you."

He moved his hard length to my entrance, and we both watched as the tip breached me. I gasped, watching a piece of Brandt disappear inside my body. More of him continued to disappear. Having him in me was perfect. In that instant, we were one.

When Brandt was buried in me, he looked up. His thumbs moved to my breasts and stroked my nipples. Our eyes connected. I squeezed him with my inner walls.

"There's nothing better than the moment I enter you. It's perfection. But now, I'm going to fuck you. Hold on tight."

"Please."

I bit down hard as I prepared for impact. Brandt pulled

out excruciatingly slow. The moment I saw his throbbing head, Brandt plunged in deep and hard in one thrust.

"Ahh…" The moan escaped at the raw sensation.

Brandt kept up the speed as he squeezed my breasts. We watched him disappear within my body. The visual along with the physical made my insides quiver.

"Let go, Nikki."

Two more pumps and we were both screaming as my legs wrapped around Brandt. On his last stroke, he stilled as I held him to me. He put his forehead to mine.

"You're mine."

"I'm yours, forever and always."

Brandt's lips came down to kiss me. He pulled away slightly. "I have to go. I wish we could stay wrapped up in each other all day like we did yesterday, talking. The next few nights are going to be late. We're training the two new managers."

"I can go stay with Grandmama, so you don't have to worry."

He cleared his throat then looked at me while he was still buried within. "I don't care where you stay, but I want us in the same bed at night. I know this isn't the most romantic way to ask you, but I do want us to live together again. Your lease is coming up and we could move you in here, or find another place for both of us."

Swallowing hard, I tried to calm my beating heart. I was ready for more with Brandt. I was ready for so much more. "Are you sure?"

"I've never been more sure in my life."

We were still connected. I thought about what I wanted, what was best for us, and what my heart was saying. As I'd initially thought, everything said the same thing. I responded,

"Yes, I'll move in with you."

He pressed his lips to mine as he picked me up and moved us against the wall on the opposite side of the kitchen. We were hungry for each other as Brandt moved into me. My hips ground into him. The textured wall rubbed through the thin material of my robe, adding to the overwhelming sensations all over my body.

Brandt's voice rumbled in his chest as he moved within me. "Nikki. I. Love. You. So. Fucking. Much."

"Love. You. Too."

Our words were broken as we raced to the finish. There was nothing long or drawn out about this release. Brandt yelled, "Fuuuuck!"

His raw power spurred me into orgasm. I threw my head back against the wall.

Brandt nuzzled me and held me tighter. "I've got to go. We'll get you packed. Or, hell, I'll hire movers to get you packed sooner."

I giggled. "Are you that anxious to get me over here? I've been staying with you every night for a while."

"I want it permanent."

His words did so many things to me. Brandt pulled out and set me on the floor and didn't release me until I was steady. The wood floors were cold against my feet.

Brandt looked at his pants. "Ah, shit. I need to change. I've got cum all over me."

He gave me a chaste kiss before he dashed back to the bedroom. I was still standing against the wall, trying to catch my breath when Brandt walked back in, grabbed his coffee cup, and turned my way.

"You look sexy, leaning on the wall, your breasts showing through that sheer robe, and fully satiated." He stopped and adjusted himself. “Hell, I want you again.” I gave him a shy smile as his phone rang. Brandt answered gruffly, “Hello. I know. I’m on my way. Well, they can fucking wait. It’s us paying them and not the other way around. Okay, I’ll be there in a few.”

Brandt came over and kissed me hard. His tongue sought entry and tasted my mouth fully. “I have to go, or Adam is going to kill me. I’ll miss you and I love you.”

“I’ll miss you and love you, too. Hurry home.”

Brandt smiled, gave me one last kiss, and was out the door again. I leaned back against the wall, thankful that this part of my life was headed in the right direction.

I’m living with Brandt again. I was practically skipping as I made my way back to his—*our*—bedroom.

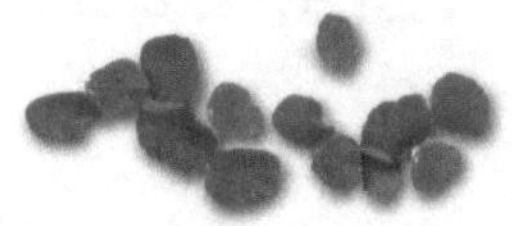

A week had passed since I’d agreed to move in with Brandt. I hadn’t seen him except at night when he’d crawl in late after I had been asleep for hours. Adam and Brandt were having to work a lot. Late-night club visits had been out for both Ainsley and myself. Brandt and I loved the club, and the few times we’d been there were great, but our relationship seemed to have grown outside the walls of Club Envy. We spent less time there than before, which was different, but it suited the new us. Deep down, I knew they were training the new managers at Club Envy, but the familiarity was hard to ignore. When Brandt had been high, he’d been gone like this. I glanced at the note he’d left this morning. I believed him when he said that being together was more important than drugs.

I miss you, Baby.

Sorry it's been so hectic lately. Another late night planned. I'll call you. Tonight should be the last one—hopefully.

Then it's me and you.

Love

Brant

I sighed as I packed a bag to head to Grandmama's to work. She had a doctor's appointment this afternoon. It was the first checkup since we'd found out her diagnosis, and I was nervous, wondering if the cancer had stayed the same or gotten worse. At the last minute, I packed some clothes to stay the night. It was pointless for me to stay here by myself while Brandt was gone.

The sky was a dark gray. At any moment, it looked like the heavens were going to open and pour buckets on us. Getting in the car, my phone rang. It was Gavin.

"This is Nikola."

"Hey, Nikola. Gavin here. I received the last of your proposals, and they look good. I think we are cleared to proceed to the next phase of this. Can you prepare executive summaries for everything? I'll schedule a meeting with my boss within the next week or so. I'd like graphic representations of everything. I'll have them printed on boards."

I pulled out of the driveway. "Ainsley and I already have the executive summaries prepared. I'll be going through them today and will e-mail them to you. The graphic representations of the data won't take long to create."

Squeezing the phone between my ear and my shoulder, I shifted my car into drive and used my other hand to turn the wheel as Gavin spoke. "Perfect. I knew I hired the right person. Oh, look at the time. I'm meeting my girlfriend for coffee in ten minutes. I've been working long hours lately. I'll talk to you later. Thanks, again."

"Thanks, Gavin."

I hung up the phone, and Gavin's comment gave me an idea. I'd get Brandt coffee and surprise him at the club. Part of me needed to see him during the day so I could squelch the uneasy feeling I had that something was up. Part of me wanted to call Wesley for his advice, but he'd gone to his parents' place in the mountains for a few days. His mom had been over at his place putting all Diane's things in storage. Hopefully if he wasn't surrounded in the constant reminders of what was lost, Wesley would be able to begin functioning again. I'd offered my help, but Wesley wanted his mom. I understood. Wesley texted daily to keep me informed of how he was doing.

Stopping at a coffee shop on the way, I got Brandt a black coffee and a caramel macchiato for myself. It smelled heavenly as the freshly brewed aroma wafted through the car. Pulling up to Club Envy, I noticed that Brandt's vehicle wasn't in the lot, which piqued my curiosity. I parked right next to the red-bricked building and made my way to the side entrance. Adam had a doorbell installed that rang through to their devices if someone was inside and not at the door. Brandt had said that last year, Ainsley had come to the club and no one was at the door. Some guys had scared her, and Adam wanted to keep it from happening again. I walked up to the ringer and pressed the button. Within two minutes, Adam opened the door.

He looked shocked. "Hey there, what are you doing here?"

I held up the cups of coffee as the steam evaporated into the semi-cold air. "I brought Brandt a coffee. I hoped I could steal him away for a few minutes. He's hardly been home."

Adam opened the door, and I stepped in. He scrubbed a hand down his face. "Umm—Brandt had a meeting across town and isn't here. I think he'll be back later this afternoon." Alarms went off in my head. I was sure he said he'd be spending the day training the new employees. He continued. "If you want to stay here for a bit, you know you're welcome."

Suddenly, my stomach was all knots, and I handed Adam the coffee. "Here's some coffee to enjoy since Brandt isn't here. I'm going to head on out. It was good seeing you."

I plastered on a fake smile. I needed to call Brandt before I voiced my concerns. He deserved the benefit of the doubt.

"Good seeing you, too." I quickly made my way toward the door when Adam called after me, "Nikola, is everything okay?"

Looking back over my shoulder, I said, "Yes. I'm missing Brandt and hoped to get a few stolen minutes. Better luck next time, huh?"

Adam adjusted the coffee cups in his hand and watched me closely. Trigger walked over and gave me a small nod. Something seemed off with Adam, too. Normally, he was a balls-to-the-wall kind of guy, but he was hiding something.

"Yeah, we should be done with the training soon. It's going to mean a lot fewer hours for both of us." Adam looked down at his phone as it rang.

This was the perfect time for me to make my exit. I chuckled and said, "I'll be ready for that. I'm headed to Grandmama's. I'll see you later."

"See ya, Nikola. Thanks for the coffee. Tell Anne I said hey."

Smiling once more before I left I said, "You bet."

I pushed open the large metal door. A light drizzle had begun, only adding to the dreariness of the day—and my mood. I felt alone with no one to turn to. Everyone had so much on their plates, and it felt trivial for me to add to the worry with unfounded theories.

After getting on the road to Grandmama's, I decided to call Brandt. It was better to face it head on than ignore the situation. Connecting my Bluetooth, I dialed Brandt through the car's interface. A slight crackling came over the speakers as the line connected. People ran along the sidewalk as the rain came down harder. The phone rang.

Ring.

Pause.

Ring.

Pause.

Ring.

"Hey, baby. Are you headed to Anne's?"

I took a deep breath, relieved to hear his soothing, normal-sounding voice. "I just left the club," I said. "I brought you coffee, but Adam said you were at a meeting across town and wouldn't be back until this afternoon. I thought you'd be training all day."

I sounded a tad accusatory, which made me feel guilty, but not enough to retract it. With my nerves standing on edge, the need to know won. Lately, any little thing seemed to magnify ten times.

I heard Brandt take a deeper than normal breath. He'd definitely picked up on my tone. "Something came up, and I was needed across town. Is there something else going on here? Just say it, Nikola. Don't start accusing me without a reason."

My anger flashed as I thought about his response and what I had been through. "You've been gone a lot. I'm getting very vague explanations. Of course, one of the first things I'm going to wonder about is drugs."

"I can't fucking believe this. This is not what you think."

Those words were close to what he always said to me before and I recoiled in my car as if they were covered in acid as they absorbed into my ears. I stayed silent.

"Nikola?"

"Yes." My voice was pointed.

More silence followed. "Do you think I'm doing drugs?" I paused for a second too long. "Wow, I thought we'd moved past this. I've got to go. I'll talk to you later."

"Brandt, don't hang up."

The line was dead. I'd royally messed up, and a lump formed in my throat. Tears streamed down my face. Hitting

Redial, I prayed he'd pick up for me. It went to voicemail. I tried again. Voicemail. And again. Voicemail. Panic rose in me.

He wasn't doing drugs, and I didn't know why I'd accused him of it. Part of me felt off-balance, waiting for the other shoe to drop at any minute. Everything in my personal life hung by a thread, and I'd cut the only secure lifeline I had. I'd hurt the only man I'd ever loved.

Maybe if I text him. I pulled over and swiped at my eyes.

I texted Brandt.

Me: I'm so sorry. I deserved that. I don't think you're doing drugs. It was wrong of me to jump to conclusions. Please talk to me.

Brandt: I need a few minutes. Let me grab some coffee. I'll call in a bit.

Coffee. I knew where Brandt potentially was. I turned my car around and drove as fast as I could through all the traffic, weaving in and out as quickly as possible. *Please, let him be there. Please.* If Brandt was within a reasonable distance, he always went to our coffee shop. He loved Kennedy's Coffee. The place was special for us, since we'd had both of our first dates there. I was within two minutes of the place as my heart raced. I increased my windshield wiper speed.

Pulling in, I parked in one of the last spots. I scanned the parking lot for Brandt's truck. Thunder rumbled in the distance. My heart soared when I saw his SUV parked off to the side at the alley entrance. I hopped out of the car and ran toward it. I looked at everyone who came out of the coffee shop doors. The rain became harder and it soaked through my clothes. I didn't care. A familiar body walked out, and my throat was dry as he ducked his head down and ran for his vehicle.

I called out, "Brandt!" but the thunder and lightning drowned me out.

Pushing my feet faster, I tried to catch up. He was in his car and about to start it when I practically slammed my body into the side of the vehicle and tapped on the window. Brandt jumped at the sound and had a shocked look on his face.

"Nikola—"

More thunder rolled through and I couldn't hear what he said.

I yelled, "I'm so sorry. I'm so sorry."

Brandt opened the door and stepped out onto the sidewalk. "What are you doing here?"

"I couldn't let that stand as it was. I'm so sorry. I didn't mean it. I don't think you're on drugs. Everything seems upside-down, and you're the only thing that hasn't fallen apart on me. I'm waiting for you to be taken from me, too." My lip trembled as I spoke and the drops of rain mixed with my tears.

Brandt's strong arms brought me to him. "I'm never leaving you, Nikola. I know you have a lot going on with Anne and Wesley, who were there for you when I was in rehab, getting my shit together. But I'm here now, and I'm not leaving. Fuck. I shouldn't have made my work week so busy. You've needed me, and I haven't been there. I'm sorry, baby."

I hugged him closer, needing his heat as the cold water soaked through me. "You didn't deserve that, Brandt. I'm so sorry. I love you."

Brandt held me tight. "I love you, too."

After a few minutes of holding each other, Brandt pulled back. As we looked into each other's eyes, it felt like we were encapsulated in our own world.

Without warning, his lips descended on mine and our tongues intertwined. We walked backward and all I cared about was being in Brandt's arms.

He's was my forever and I was his. It didn't matter where he was taking me as long as I was with him.

Brandt

NIKOLA CAME FOR me. She'd chased after me. Her doubting me cut me to the core. I know I'll always be an addict, but I expected to be judged fairly, not accused. I shouldn't have taken on all the extra work training a manger *plus* trying to get Nikola's surprise ready. Deep down, I felt like I was running out of time, so I'd pushed forward, knowing this week would be hard for us.

Her tight body pressed against mine as the rain pelted our exposed skin. The sky had darkened around us and there was a faint roll of thunder in the background. Our mouths devoured each other as our tongues collided.

I needed Nikola.

I wanted her.

I had to have her now.

When our mouths connected, instinct took over as I walked us backward into the alley past my vehicle. Nikola's eyes were closed. I made sure no one was out here with us as we kept kissing. My hands roamed and I found the smooth skin under her shirt. The shirt was tight, restricting my access to her tits. I guided us to a place between some crates back in the corner of the alley. Stepping back, I looked at Nikola. She wore the look that told me she wanted me as much as I wanted her. I was about to give her exactly what we needed.

Her teeth grazed her lower lip as the rain came down harder. I couldn't handle it anymore. I needed to see her. Grabbing the bottom of her shirt, I ripped the buttons off and they flew in every direction, soon lost in all the water. Nikola wore pale-pink bra. Her dark-pink nipples stood out behind the lace. My left hand went to the clasp of her bra while the other crept under her loose skirt.

I grazed her clit through the silky fabric of her panties and pushed.

A moan emitted from Nikola's throat. "Rip them off, Brandt. I need more."

The front clasp of the bra came undone; her luscious breasts spilled out. The rain found them and water beaded on her skin. Quickly, I tore the panties from Nikola's body. My lips tasted her cherry-ripe points. They were firm and ready to be played with. My other hand dipped within Nikola's warm pussy as she wrapped a leg around my waist, moving her hips, trying to get my fingers inside her, deeper. Keeping my touch on the edge of teasing, I heard a frustrated sound from Nikola.

I released her breasts and got down on my knees, putting her hiked up leg over my shoulder. Water streamed down my face. The thunder grew louder as my lips made contact with her clit. Her wet warmth tasted like honey as Nikola ground on my face.

"Brandt, give me my release."

Her demanding tone made me lighten the pressure. My hands went up to her hips as she tried to move closer to my tongue while I traced the rim of her sensitive bud.

"Brandt, please. Please, ahh—"

With her plea, I pushed in against her harder, tasting all of her.

"Yes, Brandt! Yes!"

I released Nikola's hips, and she pushed against my tongue as her hips gyrated.

Nikola was close as I pushed a finger inside her. My dick ached to be within her. As I felt her come, I moved my mouth to the opening of her pussy to lap up everything she gave me. I wasn't able to hear any sounds from the storm that intensified around us. As I stood, I unzipped my pants to free my dick. Nikola leaned against the wall as her eyes fluttered shut. Her tits were half-covered by her torn shirt. I grabbed her ass and hoisted her to let my dick breach her entrance.

I yelled, "You're it for me, Nikola. Never doubt my love for you. I fucking love you with all that I am."

Her eyes snapped open at my words. It was similar to what I'd said last time we fucked in the alley. I remembered every part of each time we made love. They were the memories I treasured at night when I didn't have Nikola with me. Those memories were what made spending time away from each other bearable.

"Brandt, I remember, too. You have every part of me."

I entered her as our teeth collided in a heated kiss. The need to expel myself in her, to mark her as mine, reached an all-time high as we went crazy for each other. My cock throbbed on every upstroke, preparing for the explosion. My balls drew up, tight. Nikola's inner walls quivered. It wasn't going to be long. We were both burning for each other. My flesh felt like it was on fire, even though the cold rain saturated my clothing.

Nikola bit my lip, and the pleasure-pain that coursed through me kept my dick rock hard and deep within her. From her gasps, I could tell I'd hit the spot that drove her wild; Nikola starting coming. We released ourselves. I loved knowing I was part of Nikola, that she had a piece of me inside her. We held each other. Lightning struck across the sky right over our heads.

"Shit, I need to get you in my car. The weather is getting bad." I pulled back. We were still alone in the alley. Nikola's shirt was a wreck.

Nikola drew her torn shirt together. "I have clothes in my car."

We were drenched. I yanked my shirt over my head and handed it to my girl. "Put this on. Give me your keys, and I'll get your bag. I'll meet you in my SUV."

"You were a little rough with my shirt." Nikola giggled as she tugged on my T-shirt. At least she was covered. She handed me her keys from the pocket in her skirt. I shot her a cocky grin and winked.

I grabbed her hand and jogged toward the passenger side. I opened the car door and she got in. I kissed her. "You should have worn something that zipped up the front. It might have fared better."

The last time we'd been here, Nikola wore a dress that zipped down the front. Damn, I loved that dress. I shut the door and jogged down the sidewalk. Pressing the clicker for Nikola's car, I saw the lights flash, giving away the location where she'd parked it. There was some whooping and hollering coming from the coffee shop window as someone banged on it. I turned to a group of women standing at the glass window, saying all sorts of stuff as they clapped and pointed. I glanced down and remembered I was shirtless. I chuckled and shook my head as I continued to the passenger side of the car. There was the black duffle bag Nikola used.

Why is this packed?

I grabbed it and jogged back to the car. The women were still at the window watching, so I gave a friendly wave, which resulted in more screaming behind the window. *I will never understand females.* Making it to my car, I unlocked it and got in.

Nikola rubbed her hands over her arms as I cranked the car. "Shit, I should have cranked the car. Sorry."

"It's okay." She let out another giggle—one of the most wonderful sounds in the world. "I saw you had an entourage watching you. I'm one lucky lady."

I grinned, putting the car in drive to head to Anne's. "I'm glad you think so."

Nikola rummaged through the bag.

"Why'd you have that packed?"

She stopped rummaging. "I … umm … I was going to stay at Grandmama's tonight. I figured since I hadn't spent any time with you this week and you were having another late night, I'd spend time with her and see you tomorrow."

That hurt. Nikola had no idea everything I had been up to, so I couldn't blame her. We'd hardly seen each other.

"As I said, I want you in bed, with me, at night, Nikola. If you go to Anne's, that's where I'll be. I don't want to spend the night without you."

After Anne had gotten sick, Nikola canceled her out of town trips and was doing everything via phone calls. This arrangement suited me just fine. I didn't like when she traveled.

"Brandt—"

"Nikola, I want us in bed together at night. If you go to Anne's to stay, pack me clothes, too. Unless we're in different towns, it's important we're together at night." My voice was sincere but firm.

A shirt and some yoga pants came out of the bag. "Why is this so important to you? It didn't used to be as much as it is now."

I looked straight ahead as the wipers cleared a path from the rain. "When I wake with my heart beating frantically, and I can smell and feel your body, it's then I know it was a nightmare and I can go back to sleep."

"Nightmare?"

I didn't look her way as I stared ahead at the rain coming down in sheets. The sound of the wipers echoed until I spoke. "That you're gone. I never got you back."

That was one of my worst fears—not having Nikola in the future I'd imagined. A slender hand with pink nail polish landed on my knee.

"I'm all yours. I never stopped being yours in my heart. I want to be in your bed every night, too."

I took a deep breath before my hand landed on top of hers. Somberly, I spoke. "Talk to me when you start doubting things. I'll always be an addict. That will never change. But we have to trust each other if this is going to work. I can't wonder if you're doubting me all the time. We have to be open with each other."

There was an intake of breath from across the vehicle. I glanced over, and Nikola had a sad smile on her face. "I know." She closed her eyes. "I promise I will. I promise." Nikola opened her emerald eyes and glanced my way. "Promise to talk to me, too."

"I promise."

By the time we got to Anne's, Nikola was changed and I had on a dry T-shirt. I'd change my pants when I got to the restaurant to start all the preparations. Anne's red Cadillac sat to the left as I steered the SUV partially under the carport so Nikola wouldn't get wet. Nikola leaned over and gave me a kiss. Her skin was soft.

"See if Anne wants to come to dinner with us tonight. I'm going to clear my work schedule. The club managers are almost trained, and we need some time together. Does that sound good?"

Nikola kissed me harder, and I fought the urge to take the kiss from appropriate to inappropriate.

"I'd love that. I'll get the rest of the proposals off to Gavin. Text me with the details and we'll come. Even if Grandmama can't come, I still want to go."

"Well, that was a given, baby. I'll make reservations and see you in a bit. Work hard so we can take a couple days off together, if that sounds good."

Nikola's face lit up, and I couldn't wait for this evening. "That sounds fantastic."

She kissed me once more before going into the house. Right before the door closed, Nikola turned and gave me an air-kiss goodbye. Now it was time to finish all the arrangements for a moment that would change my life forever.

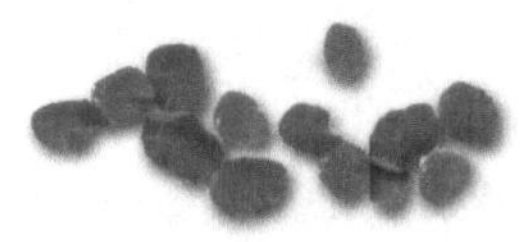

I checked everything again as I looked at the clock. I'd rented the private dining room of one of the nicest restaurants in Atlanta. Ainsley and Nora had handled getting everything set up. Nikola still didn't know Nora well, but they were becoming friends through Ainsley. They all seemed to get along. The tables were set, the lights were turned low, classical music played softly in the background, and a massively tall flower arrangement sat on the large, round table.

This was either going to be a great idea or an epic failure. Today, when Nikola had accused me of doing drugs, I'd wondered if I'd made the right decision. But after what Nikola and I shared in the alley, knowing she came for me—not the other way around—I knew I made the right decision. Hopefully, Nikola felt the same way.

Logan came up to me. "If she says no, I cleared a path through the back for you."

I looked at him incredulously; he tried not to laugh. I felt sick.

Logan's face dropped. "Oh, shit, I'm sorry. You are nervous. You know there's no way she'll say no. That girl loves you more than anything in this world."

"I hope so. Hell, I hope so." My heart felt like it was beating a hole in my chest.

"She will. Here comes Adam. I know he probably wants to talk to you, too. Dad would be proud of you. Hell, I'm proud of you for fighting for what you wanted."

That meant a lot. "I think he would be, too."

We nodded. Thinking of my dad was sometimes hard, but he would have loved Nikola. All he'd ever wanted was for his boys to be happy. Logan walked to where my mum stood as Adam came over. He slapped me on the back. My nerves were starting to get the better of me and I rubbed my hands up and down my legs.

"How you holding up?"

"I'm a wreck. I know this is what I want, but what if Nikola doesn't think we're ready? What if she thinks I'm doing it for the wrong reasons?" My pulse was at an all-time high.

Adam stepped back and looked at me seriously. Ainsley was at the back of the room talking to Nikola's parents, who had flown in from China. They'd arrived last night.

"You know Ainsley, in the beginning, thought I wanted to keep her around as only a fuck buddy. Even though I didn't know this at the time, I loved Ainsley, and that's why I kept pursuing her. My love was showing through, even though I wasn't aware. This may make me sound like a puss, but it's the truth. You and Nikola are meant to be; it just took you guys a bit to get there."

"Thanks, man. I appreciate it."

Adam slapped me on the back again and walked back toward Ainsley. I watched Nikola's parents with everyone and thought back to my phone call with them. Nikola was a mixture of them. Her dad, Richard, was tall and slim with dark hair and dark eyes. Her mom, Melanie, was medium height and slim with blonde hair and green eyes.

I had left a mid-morning meeting with Quentin. We'd found out about Anne's serious condition yesterday, and I needed a bit to get my thoughts straight on what I wanted to do. Nikola had said something that struck me deep through the night: "Brandt, she'll never be part of my life or know where I end up. See me married and happy. She'll never know if I have kids and if I'm a good mother. She'll never know. Who will I go to when I need help? Who will I go to when I don't know what to do? Grandmama won't be there. My heart is breaking,

Brandt. My heart is breaking."

Through the night, I'd known I wanted to give Nikola as much as I could when I reflected on what she said.

Now, I was on my way to my mum's before going to Club Envy to make plans for proposing to Nikola. I thought about my talk with Quentin at our diner, regarding my decision to ask Nikola to marry me. Any major changes in my life, I liked to talk to Quentin. He sometimes helped me see what I wasn't able to in order to clear the fog or prepare me in general for what was to come. Quentin's only words of advice were: "If she's not ready to take this step, don't push or be disappointed. It's a big step for anyone to take. It takes two to be ready, and it's not rejection if Nikola says she's not ready. Don't look at it as a sign of not trusting you."

Quentin's words had made me nervous that there was a possibility Nikola would say no. Before talking to him, I had only imagined her saying yes. Even if Nikola wasn't ready, I was ready to put myself out there. If she wanted to wait, I'd wait. As long as we had each other, that's all that mattered. Pulling into my mother's driveway, I got my phone out to call Nikola's parents. They were nice, just different. My family was warm and loving. Nikola's mom loved her but was unemotional in showing it. Anne gave Nikola the motherly love I knew she craved. In some ways, Anne was like her mother.

I'd only met them once when they were in town for a couple of days before heading back to China. Hoping I'd be able to catch her dad at dinner, I called them.

After three rings, a smooth voice picked up on the other end. "This is Richard."

"Hi, Richard. This is Brandt Mattox, Nikola's boyfriend. Do you have a second?"

There was background noise that sounded like he was at

a party. Cheers erupted in a toast. "Give me a second. Melanie and I are at a function. I'll step out for a minute."

"Thanks, Richard."

The sound of a door closing came through the phone, then the party noises were muffled. "How's Nikola? Is everything okay?"

My palms sweated. I was about to ask the father of the woman I loved for her hand in marriage. We'd only met once, and I'd talked to him a handful of times. "Yes, she is. She's over at Anne's house now while I'm running some errands. I wanted to talk to you about something."

"Okay, go ahead." His voice sounded hesitant.

I cleared my throat. "I want to ask for your permission to marry Nikola. I know we've had our ups and downs, but I'll love her and always provide for her the best I can. She'll always be my first priority."

Richard chuckled. "I've been waiting for this day. You guys have been together for a while. I figured it was getting close to time. Of course, you have mine and Melanie's blessing."

The response threw me. Had Nikola not told them about the drugs and our breakup? I knew she didn't tell them a lot, but figured this would have made it into at least one conversation. Knowing how unconnected they were from Nikola's life saddened me. "Thank you, Richard. I plan on asking her in a few weeks. If possible, I'd love for you guys to be a part of that moment for Nikola."

"Let me check our schedule and we'll see. My office will be in touch if we can make it. Is this a good number for them to reach you at if we're able to come?"

Again, Richard's response gave me pause. His daughter's engagement was getting pushed off to his office personnel.

"This is a good number. Thanks again."

The doors must have opened, because the sounds of the party came over the phone. "No problem. Have a good day. Talk to you later."

The phone disconnected before I had a chance to respond. I opened my door and was greeted by the crisp air. I'd only texted my mum about an hour ago to see if I could swing by. I knew my mum's response was going to be night-and-day-different from Richard's.

My mum gave me a hug, breaking me from my thoughts. She was glowing and excited, as I'd expected. She'd almost slipped the night I'd taken Nikola over there for dinner after Valentine's Day.

As she hugged me close, she said, "Your dad would be so proud. I cannot tell you how happy I am you've found your soul mate. It's a mother's dream for her babies to find true love and happiness. I see the same love your father and I shared. Thanks for letting me be part of this special moment. Don't be nervous."

She pulled back, and I nervously chortled. "Easier said than done. She hasn't said yes yet."

My mum patted the side of my face like she has throughout my childhood. "She will. I know Quentin prepared you in case she said no, which is good, but she loves you. That night I almost slipped, I saw her eyes light up at the thought of marrying you."

"I hope so."

"I know so."

My phone vibrated. It was Anne.

Anne: We are about ten minutes away. Nikola is going to drop me off at the door, then park the car. Thank you for giving me this memory.

Me: It's a memory I want us all to have. Thank you for giving me permission to marry her.

Anne: I love you like a son, Brandt. Always have and always will. Putting my phone away before my precious granddaughter gets nosy.

Me: Love you, too—like a mother.

Anne had cancelled her doctor's appointment today and told Nikola when she went over there to work. Nikola had already helped her schedule another appointment next week. I'd noticed Anne's cough getting worse, and she tired more easily. I think she'd known the prognosis wouldn't be good and didn't want to overshadow what happened tonight. I still prayed for a miracle.

I put my phone away and announced to the room: "Nikola is about ten minutes away. She's going to drop Anne off at the door, then park the car."

Everyone Nikola and I loved was in the room: Adam and Ainsley, Nikola's parents, my mum and Logan, Nora and her boyfriend, Jude, and Wesley. It had been an internal debate on whether to invite Wesley, with what he had been dealing with, but he deserved the choice. One of the worst things for me was not being giving the option to decide for myself. Wesley was doing well. The time away had done wonders for him. Wesley told me he wanted to come, without hesitating.

He approached me. "I appreciate the invite. I'm happy things are working out for you guys. It's good to know happy endings do happen for people who have been through what we have."

"Thanks, man. I'm glad you could make it. I know it'll mean the world to Nikola to see you here. I appreciate that you were there for her when I wasn't."

Wesley gave me a genuine smile as he headed to stand with Nikola's parents. He and I were going to be good friends as time passed.

A few minutes later Anne walked in, wearing a pale pink suit. Anne gave everyone an update. "She's parking the car. I told her I was going to the restroom and I'd meet her at the table."

Anne gave me a kiss on the cheek before going to stand by her son, daughter-in-law, and my mum. I'd wanted them off to the side, to be part of this as much as possible.

"Thanks, Anne."

I focused on the entrance. My present, my future, my everything was about to walk through those doors. My palms were sweating and my heart was running the Kentucky Derby as I waited to see what would happen. I kept telling myself, *It's okay if she says no. It's okay. We'll still have each other.*

The door creaked open, I heard the hostess talking, and then the door closed. I held my breath as it opened again slightly, then closed. This prolonged the agony unnecessarily. The door then cracked open and I heard the hostess answer a question. "I would definitely recommend the chicken cordon bleu. It's one of my favorites."

Oh hell, Nikola chatted someone up.

My brother chuckled behind me and said, "Well, this is comical, watching Brandt nearly pass out from anticipation. I'm buying my future sis something special for this."

I turned around, wanting to flip him off, but refrained with everyone here. My brother tried not to laugh as the hostess and Nikola kept talking about menu options outside the door. Everyone tried to stay quiet.

The door opened wider and the room hushed. The hostess said, "Someone will be right in to get your drinks."

Nikola's sweet voice sounded from the other side, "Thank you."

The door finally pushed open and Nikola came walking in wearing a black lace dress with tan lining. Her hair was curled. She was breathtaking. She stopped when she saw everyone standing around then looked at me in question.

Here we go.

I got down on one knee, and Nikola's mouth dropped open.

Nikola

BRANDT KNEELED BEFORE me in slacks and a black, button-up shirt. My heart dared to hope, but I was scared I was wrong. My mom and dad were here. I'd had no idea they'd left China. Everyone I thought of as family was here in this room. A large, round table sat in the back with a huge flower arrangement. My one true love knelt before me. My feet shuffled as we smiled at each other. The room was silent except for the quiet, classical music.

Brandt reached up and took my hand in his. This was the moment I'd dreamed about since meeting Brandt all those years ago.

I spoke up, "Hey."

He smiled. "Hey. I'm glad you decided to finally come through those doors."

I giggled as I thought about asking the hostess a million questions about the menu. She had seemed as though she was trying to get me into the dining area, but I'd pressed on. "You know me. I like to keep you guessing."

That earned a low laugh from everyone.

"That you do. It's one of the many things I love about you." He squeezed my hand. "I have something important to ask you."

My smile was larger than life, and Brandt let out a long breath. In front of all our family, Brandt exposed himself, which he didn't do often.

"I'm listening. You've piqued my interest, with everyone gathered here and your fancy shirt." I couldn't stop smiling as my reply garnered more laughter from the guests.

Logan said, "I love Nikola. She makes my bro work for it."

Brandt turned toward Logan then back to me. Logan smiled back at Brandt. Tears formed in my eyes as Brandt gave me a tender look. The moment of laughter had passed; now it was time to say yes to the man of my dreams.

Our eyes searched each other. Brandt was strong, dependable, and mine. His hair was down and he ran his hair through it once as he cleared his throat.

"Nikola, we've had our ups and downs, and we've weathered the storms and come out stronger in the end. I know what it's like to lose you, and I never want that feeling again. You've been my future since the first moment I laid eyes on you at that concert. It's why I chased you in the parking lot and flirted with you until you gave me your number. In front of all our family, and those we love, I want to ask you something important. I want you to be my wife, my soul mate, and my best friend—forever. I want to someday have kids and give a piece of the love we share to them. I want us to be each other's one and only through all life's trials. Nikola Kingston, I'm down on one knee, humbly asking you to do me the honor of uniting with me forever. Will you marry me?"

Tears fell freely down my cheeks as Brandt looked up at me, vulnerable. I sank to my knees, bringing us eye level.

"I never could have imagined that going to that concert would result in us finding each other. Growing up, all I ever wanted was to share my heart with someone who'd take care of it. I found that with you. Despite our ups and downs, we've loved each other even in our time a part. Yes, I'll marry you."

Brandt brought me to him and kissed me. Cheers erupted around us. This was a perfect moment. We stood as everyone came and congratulated us. I could hardly see through the tears. Ainsley and Nora were next as they hugged me.

Nora spoke. "Girl, let me see the ring."

I looked down at my hand and realized I didn't have a ring. Not knowing what to do, I looked to Brandt. "Oh shit, I forgot the ring."

He let go of my hand and searched his pockets. Everyone chortled. Brandt pulled out a gray velvet box. Everyone gathered as he popped the lid open. My hand shook. Brandt took the ring out and took my hand.

As he slipped it on, he said, "The solitaire diamond in the center is us. The diamonds that surround the ring are from my mother, your mother, and your Grandmama's wedding rings. There's two from each representing their blessed marriages of love and happiness."

The ring shone like a thousand brilliant stars as the light danced off it. I jumped into Brandt's arms as he twirled me around slowly. In my ear, for only me to hear, he said, "Our forever is finally happening."

I nodded, too choked up for words. He set me down and kissed me once more before saying, "Are you ready to sit and eat?"

I nodded. Brandt brought us to the table. He squeezed my hand over and over. Everyone followed, staring at us. I wasn't sure why there was an awkward silence all of a sudden.

Brandt spoke up, "The food should be out any minute. They placed everyone's orders when we got here." He turned to me. "I ordered you the chicken cordon bleu. They said it's phenomenal."

"Perfect. It's what I was asking the hostess about."

He laughed. "I know. It was giving me a coronary, waiting for you."

I glanced around nervously as everyone continued watching us intently. Adam gave Brandt an expectant look. Brandt seemed clueless as he picked up my hand and kissed it. My ring looked perfect on my finger, where it would stay forever. Thinking back on this morning, and what I'd almost jeopardized due to insecurities, firmed up my resolution to always talk to Brandt if I ever had doubts. I glanced back around—everyone was still watching. Brandt had caught on, it seemed, as he looked around.

Brandt spoke up, "Did I miss something?"

All our family and friends were staring back in disbelief. Finally, Brandt's brother, who was a replica of Brandt but with short, blond hair, spoke up.

"Umm, wasn't there something about a wedding happening in the next day?"

My head snapped to Brandt. He closed his eyes. "Shit." Then, he looked at Grandmama. "Sorry." He looked toward me. "Once you said yes, I forgot the ring and next big part."

Everyone chuckled, and I was at a loss as I stared at

Brandt in wonder.

Anne laughed. "I guess he forgot everything when he got the girl of his dreams."

"That I did." He turned to me. "Nikola, what would you think about getting married tomorrow evening. I wanted—"

I put my fingers to his lips. "I think tomorrow night sounds like the perfect day to become your wife. Do you think the justice of the peace will have an opening?"

He kissed my lips. "They do. Ainsley helped me with the planning. She's been getting details from you covertly over the last week."

Ainsley had been asking me questions lately about my opinion on her wedding. It made sense now.

"Just tell me where to be and I'll be there."

My heart was happy. Brandt was making so many of my dreams come true. The ones I loved would get to see me marry the person I was meant to be with forever.

He kissed my hand again. "I'll be waiting for you at the end of the aisle."

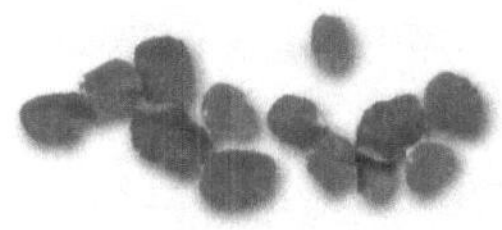

We were at the bridal shop with my mom, Faith, and Grandmama. Brandt, with Ainsley's help, had found a place and set up the appointment. Currently, they were serving mimosas. I abstained. The amount of work he'd put in to making this so magical was unbelievable. I felt guilty for being agitated at him for being gone so much when that time had been spent training the new managers *and* arranging our wedding.

The shopkeeper had a selection of gowns to choose from

in my size. She was a petite thing with dark hair and eyes. A dress that caught my eye from the rack was what I wanted to try on first. The older salesclerk helped me slip into the down. As she zipped up the back, my heart beat faster at the thought that this could be the dress.

My eyes were closed, wanting to wait to see what the dress looked like after it was completely on.

"Open your eyes. It's beautiful."

I gasped. The sleeveless dress hugged my body to my waist, then gently flowed out. Fabric gathered at the waist, like a belt. I looked like a Greek princess. The back had a gathered train that extended from my lower back. A smattering of sequins sparkled in any light that I was in. It was beautiful.

I went out to stand on the pedestal in the viewing area. My loved ones stopped drinking and looked at me from the cream-colored sofa. I looked toward Grandmama first as she stood.

"You look beautiful, Nikola. Absolutely stunning. I think you may have found the one."

"Me, too."

I was practically jumping in place. Looking over at my mom, Faith, and Ainsley, they all had tears in their eyes.

My mom spoke as she wiped away her solitary tear. "It's beautiful, Nikola."

This was the most emotion I'd ever seen from my mom. Since arriving we'd only spoken a few times. I stepped off the podium and went to give her a hug. She stood.

"Thanks, mom. I'm glad you could be here."

Her hand hesitated on my back, but I kept holding her for a few more seconds before I released her. I knew showing emotions was hard for her.

Brandt's mom was next. "You look beautiful. Brandt's

going to pass out when he sees you. You're better than I could have ever imagined for my boy."

"Thank you."

Ainsley, my maid of honor, came and gave me a hug. "He's going to love it."

"I hope so." My voice got thicker as I realized how much more real this was becoming by the second.

As I walked back toward the raised platform, Faith said, "I'm going to be especially excited when I get a grandbaby out of this deal."

"Now, that may cause me to pass out," I said, laughing.

My heart hoped Grandmama would still be here for that moment. Brandt and I were ready to be married, but I knew he'd put this all together to give me the memories with my grandmother. Grandmama sat by my mom and held her hand. My mom looked genuinely happy as she relaxed.

I cried. "Thank you for all being here. I couldn't have imagined this day without each and every one of you."

My words had us all crying and hugging. Among sniffles, I said, "I'm going to take this off and let them know this is the one. What's next on the agenda?"

Ainsley looked at the itinerary. "Massages. We are all getting massages. Brandt has it arranged."

"I love him."

As smiles emerged on everyone's faces, I headed back to the changing room. The shopkeeper helped me out of the gown and had taken it out of the dressing room. I was bent over getting my regular undergarments when familiar hands came up behind me. I stood and Brandt's hand came over my mouth.

"Shh, if they know I'm here they'll kick me out. I had to see you."

I kissed him when his hand uncovered my lips and I could

turn into Brandt's embrace. His hands slid down my waist.

Brandt pulled back. "Fuck. I want you so bad."

"I want you, too. Hurry."

I helped Brandt get out of his pants. We were fumbling with each other in the mad rush. His length fell out when a voice on the other end of the curtain came through. It was Brandt's mom. "Hey, Ainsley got the massage appointments moved up. We have to be there in ten minutes. Do you need any help?"

Panic struck both our faces as Brandt and I looked at each other. I went to the curtain and barely moved it back so my head would pop through. "I'm getting changed. I'll be right out. I'll meet you in the car."

Faith flicked her wrist. "It's okay. Ainsley's getting your dress. I'll wait here."

"Okay."

I turned back to Brandt. We were both in a desperate state. He mouthed, *We can still do this.*

Shaking my head, I mouthed, *No way. Your mom is right outside that curtain.*

I got ready and Brandt looked pained.

"Oh, Nikola! Ainsley has your dress. Are you ready?" Faith called from the other side of the curtain.

"Coming."

I went up to Brandt and whispered in his ear, "I love you. You should have to abide by at least one tradition."

"I want you," He whispered back.

I grabbed my purse and kissed him quietly. "You're about to have me forever."

With my parting words, I dashed out the curtain to head out to get my massage with the girls. Brandt could rely on his trusty five if he got too desperate.

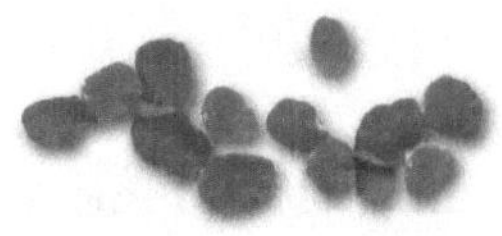

I stood off to the side of the chapel doors, waiting to go inside and meet Brandt. The chapel was solid glass and lit up as twilight approached, casting a glow from the chapel. It was meant for small parties of thirty people or less. We'd gone with simple green ferns to decorate the already beautiful chapel. All I needed was Brandt. Strangely enough, all I'd ever wanted was a simple wedding.

Ainsley stood beside me in a teal dress. The doors to the chapel opened. My Mom and Grandmama came out from inside the glass structure.

My mom spoke. "Anne and I wanted to give you something to remember this day, always." She pulled out a slender box and opened it. It was a beautiful bracelet made of white gold, diamonds, and sapphires. The bracelet looked like several flowers, connected with diamonds in the center.

"It's beautiful."

My mom continued, her green eyes moistening, "The diamonds are your something old. They came from a bracelet your Grandaddy gave Anne. The sapphires are your something blue, a gift from your dad and me. The bracelet is your something new. On the inside is a passage inscribed from Brandt's parents' wedding. Faith wanted you guys to borrow the words on your special day to have as your passage."

I tried to keep the tears at bay as I blinked rapidly. "I love it. Thank you."

My mom gave me a hug. I had never hugged her this much in my life.

Grandmama smiled as she watched the exchange.

"I'm so proud of the woman you've become, Nikola. So proud."

I nodded as Grandmama said and gave me a hug, "I've always dreamed of being part of this special day with you. I'm glad you found the happiness that everyone deserves. We're going to head inside now. We'll leave the doors open. When you hear the music, come on in and see your forever after."

My dad walked up beside her dressed in his business tux. He had auburn hair, like me. Instead of green, he had chocolate brown eyes. "I think we're about ready if everyone wants to head on in,"

Mom, Grandmama, and Ainsley all made their way inside. We'd decided, due to the small wedding, that there wouldn't be a processional. It was only my dad and me left outside. I honestly couldn't remember the last time we'd been alone.

"I know your mom and I haven't always voiced how we feel, like my mom does, but I do want you to know we love you, Nikola. Your mom and I are proud of the woman you've become. Brandt's a lucky man to have someone who loves him like you do. Not all of us can show and express love like you're able to." He adjusted his bowtie, obviously rattled by his declaration.

My emotions took over and I hugged him hard. Dad hugged me back. This day couldn't be any more perfect. "Thanks, Dad. I needed that."

He pulled back as the music played. "Are you ready to get married?"

"I am, Daddy."

We walked and any nerves residing in me left as we turned the corner and I saw Brandt standing at the altar with Adam to his right, the preacher in the center, and Ainsley to the left. Our eyes connected, and my feet felt light as they drifted toward Brandt. He was dashing in his black tux. His hair was down. We were both grinning. A day I never thought would come was *happening*.

Time stilled as I stood in front of Brandt. The pastor in front of us asked, “Who gives this woman away in marriage?”

My dad squeezed my arm softly and said, “Her mother and I do.”

Dad let go of my hand and Brandt took it, leading me to the altar. He mouthed, *You’re beautiful.*

I blushed and smiled as the preacher commenced the ceremony. The ceremony was a blur as I focused on trying to remember every feature of Brandt’s face as we said our vows. They were said as not only a promise, but a declaration.

As the preacher concluded the ceremony, Brandt jumped the gun and kissed me.

In the background I heard, “You may now kiss the bride.”

Brandt pulled away. “I couldn’t wait.”

A few people chuckled. “I could tell. You’re stuck with me.”

“I couldn’t think of anyone I’d rather be stuck with.”

We turned as everyone cheered. Brandt leaned in. “After the cake, the dance, and whatever else Ainsley is mandating, I’m taking you away from here and we’re going on our honeymoon.”

“Honeymoon?” I hadn’t known we were going on a honeymoon.

He wiggled his eyebrows. “I hear it’s the best part of a wedding. Of *course* we’re having a honeymoon.”

I giggled as we walked out of the church to the small reception hall. This was our new beginning, and I was truly happy.

Brandt

WE WERE DRIVING to our destination for the next two days. This weekend there was a huge benefit going on in Atlanta, so all the decent limos had been rented. I knew neither of us cared about a fancy car, but it would've been fun to have some foreplay on the way to our honeymoon location. Nikola and I were the same when it came to these types of things. We liked our lives simple.

The road was winding and the headlights from the car illuminated the trees on the sides of the road. A deer stood off to the right, eyes glowing. I slowed to make sure the animal didn't dart out in front of me.

Nikola had fallen asleep in the passenger seat. She'd tried to stay awake, but when I turned on the classical radio station, I knew she'd be gone. We'd both slept like shit last night, as she stayed with her parents at Anne's house to follow tradition, which I thought was total bullshit. Nikola's parents, I think, had wanted to spend some time in her presence, even though they didn't say as much.

I glanced over at my Sleeping Beauty. *My wife.* I would've never imagined that only four months after our New Year's run-in at Coyote Ugly we'd be married. Part of me wished we could freeze this moment forever, relive it day after day, and not have to fight life as it led us into the unknown. The fear of the unknown haunted me. I knew I was stronger than addiction, but I wanted to always control what was happening.

The only thing left on Nikola's wish list was for Anne to be a part of us having a baby. But we weren't ready. I wanted to enjoy Nikola, to learn each other in new ways.

The cabin came into view. The last time we'd been to Stone Mountain was when Nikola got stuck here on a business trip. I'd forged ahead before the roads had closed to join her.

This was a special place to both of us. Those two days away from the world had been magical, and hopefully the magic remained. Ainsley had come up yesterday and gotten the keys for me so I wouldn't have to check in. Nikola sighed in her sleep, and I quietly got out of the car and went to her side.

My brother had dropped off our bags, so we wouldn't have to deal with any of it. When I opened Nikola's door, the wind blew a gentle, cool breeze and her eyes fluttered open. She gave me a sleepy smile.

"I'm sorry I fell asleep. I didn't mean to. I'm a snoozefest on our wedding night."

She stretched, arching her back, making her breasts plump slightly in the white satin. I needed to feel her.

"I plan to keep you up all night."

"I like the sound of that." Nikola went to get out of the car when I picked her up. "How proper of you, Mr. Mattox."

I kissed her on the lips before saying, "Trust me, baby, there's not much that's proper about what I'm thinking. But I want this official. No loopholes."

She leaned her head on my shoulder. "This has all been perfect. I'm glad we didn't have a long engagement. Though I wish we could have had longer in the dressing room at the shop."

I kissed her pouty lips. They were addictive. Kissing and being with Nikola were two of the few vices I allowed myself. I climbed the four steps that led to our escape. I slid the key card and walked through as our tongues danced with each other.

Lust raged through my veins. I kept telling myself to savor this moment. Having her for the first time as my wife was only going to happen once. I knew Nikola hadn't realized where we were as I broke the kiss. The lighting was set low. The cabin had a pine scent to it. A fire crackled in the fireplace and a bottle of sparkling grape juice chilled on the table. In front of the fire was a fur blanket and pillows. The bed, located in the back of the room, had white linens with red rose petals sprinkled on.

Nikola walked toward the fire. We'd made love in front of this fireplace all weekend, last time. Thinking on it, at my place, it was the cold that had reunited us, leading to our expressing our love again in front of my fireplace. Her fingers reached out, feeling the warmth of the flame. The fire cast a light on the sequins of her dress. She looked like a goddess. I walked up behind her.

"Do you like it?" I nuzzled her ear.

She turned in my embrace. Her eyes were huge with amazement. "It's perfect. This is where we stayed at during the storm. It's where you first told me you loved me."

"It is. And where you first told me you loved me."

My hands crept to the back of her dress as I pulled down the zipper. Nikola's head drifted back and a stray curl graced her neck. I moved it to the side as I kissed down her jawline, bringing her zipper down farther, wanting to prolong this moment for as long as we could stand. I planned on telling her I loved her at the exact moment I had when we were here before.

I kissed down her neck and let go of her dress as it sank to the floor. Nikola stepped out of it and kicked it to the side. I nearly stumbled at the site of her. She wore a light gray strapless bra etched in pink. Her tan stomach was completely visible. Her panties were sheer with the same color scheme. Nikola's legs were bare and at the end were fuck-me heels that made her legs go on forever. She was gorgeous.

"You're beautiful. So beautiful. I can't believe I'm looking at my wife now."

Nikola walked toward me and pulled off my jacket. Her fingers went to my tie to undo it before going to my shirt buttons. As she made it halfway down, she glanced back up at me.

"I've been waiting since the moment you first took me ice-skating on our second date to be your wife. You've made all my dreams come true."

I pulled off my shirt as Nikola ran her hands along my abs. "Go lie down on the rug. I want to watch the light of the fire bathe your body while I finish undressing you."

Nikola walked over and lay down. One leg was bent and her shoes sparkled in the light. I removed the rest of my clothes, trying to be smooth and not rush it. Obviously, I was failing as Nikola smirked. She knew what I was trying to do. *Fuck this shit, I want to feel my wife.* I'd take it slow once I could feel her in my arms. Yanking the rest of my clothes off, I came and lay beside her. I dragged my finger from the top of her panty line to the bottom of her bra.

A little moan escaped her sweet lips, and my inner beast raged, wanting to mark her as mine. "You're taking things slow."

She gave me a look of lust as she wet her lips. I couldn't keep my eyes off her as I said, "I want to savor our first time together as husband and wife."

My hand made its way back down, dipping into her panties, needing to feel more of Nikola. When I made contact with her clit, the sexy noises that escaped as she let the feelings move through her were nearly my undoing. I moved between her legs and took off her panties, sliding them down her legs, revealing the pink heaven I was going to bury myself in. Nikola had unfastened her bra and her breasts came into view.

"I get to have this body for the rest of my life."

She smiled at me. "And I get yours. It's a comforting thought."

"It is." I knelt between her legs and tasted her before trailing feather light kisses up her abdomen. My guy was raring to go; he kept jumping, thinking he was about to make entry. Finally, I made contact with her entrance.

Nikola's fingers came around to my back as she held onto me. We were searching each other's eyes as she urged me inside her. As my tip breached her entrance, I repeated what I'd said the last time, "I love you, Nikola."

A happy sob escaped. "I love you, too, Brandt. Don't let this be a dream."

I kept pushing in as her walls wrapped around me. "This

is our reality, baby. No one is going to take that away from us."

"Kiss me."

My lips went to hers. We kissed, slowly making love in front of the crackling fire.

I memorized every movement, never wanting it to end. Our bodies climbed, beads of perspiration formed on our skin, and when we couldn't hold back anymore, we came simultaneously. I rolled Nikola on top of me, still buried in her.

She sighed contentedly. "Thank you for giving me the special memories you did today. I'll treasure them forever. I know you were thinking of my wishes from that night."

I rubbed my hand down her back. "We were both ready but there's one wish I don't think we are ready for."

"A baby." Nikola had put it out there without hesitation. My breath caught, wondering if she were going to want one right away. We'd talk it out, but I wasn't ready. "You can start breathing again. I'm not ready either."

I chuckled beneath her. "I didn't stop breathing."

"Yes, you did." She kissed my chest. "Someday, in the future, when we're ready, we can have a little Brandt running around the house. I still want to enjoy our time together while it's only us. We have plenty of time for a family. It's not something that should be rushed." Nikola traced light circles on my chest as she spoke.

I continued to run my hands down her back. "I agree. We'll work through all our ups and downs together. My mum told me the downs are what make a strong marriage. I'd say we have a good strong foundation to build our life on."

Nikola nodded. "I couldn't agree more."

We basked in the afterglow of our love-making and our feelings for each other.

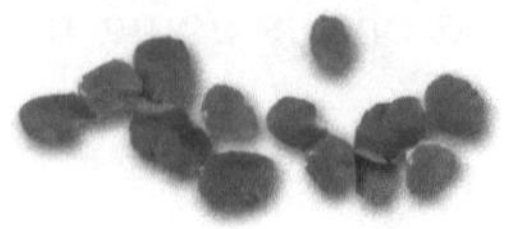

We were over at Anne's, having lunch before heading home from our honeymoon. Nikola's parents had gone to Tybee Island after the wedding. I didn't understand them. They were here from halfway across the world but still wanted isolation. I'd stepped outside to call to Adam. He'd sent a text asking me to call him when I had a moment.

The hum of the traffic sounded in the distance. A bird chirped a late afternoon song. My world seemed as close to perfect as it could be at the moment.

Adam picked up on the second ring. "Hey, man. How was the honeymoon?"

"It was the best part of the entire wedding."

Adam chuckled.

I reaffirmed my earlier statement. "You'll see. You've got a wedding coming up."

Someone spoke from a distance. It sounded like Trigger. Adam responded, "Yeah, let Karen handle it. She's the manager now; it'll be a good learning experience for her." Trigger's voice answered Adam, but it was muffled. "Brandt, are you there?"

"Yeah."

Adam took a deep breath and my anxiety went up. "A member is trying to get in early. We'll see how Karen handles it. The reason I wanted to talk is that I received a phone call the other day. We have an offer for a buyout of the club. It's a good offer."

"What?" My voice sounded in disbelief.

"We got the offer the morning of your wedding. I didn't

want to talk about it then, but someone wants to buy the club and franchise it. We need to discuss. It's a serious offer, Brandt."

I couldn't believe Adam was actually contemplating selling the club. "Adam, I don't know. I don't know if I want to do this."

"Okay." He paused. Adam sounded shocked that I wouldn't jump on this. Did he think marriage would make me want to give up my entire life? He continued. "Will you at least look at the proposal?"

"Sure. I need to get back inside. But you need to be prepared I may not want to sell." I knew I sounded frustrated. I *was* frustrated.

He took a big breath. "We'll talk about it later. Tell Nikola I said hey."

"Will do."

I hung up and jammed the phone in my pocket. I pinched the bridge of my nose while I tried to quell my temper. Why was he wanting to change things? I needed to hear his side of the story. In some ways, the club had become a burden as it required constant supervision. It was getting hard to manage with everything else I wanted to do. But I refused to think that way. The club was a huge part of our lives. I pushed the thought of selling the club to the far recesses of my mind. I'd deal with that later. Now, I was going to focus on my bride.

After a few minutes, I went inside. As I approached the kitchen, I heard Nikola and Anne talking as they ate chocolate pie.

"How does it feel to be a married woman?" Anne asked.

"I never imagined it would feel like this. There's this peace I feel, knowing how committed we are to each other. I love the feeling of belonging to Brandt."

I pushed up my sleeves, casually walked into the kitchen, and leaned against the counter. Nikola raised an eyebrow at me. She sat at the bar.

I knew Nikola sensed something was bothering me from the way she looked at me. Anne walked over and set down a plate with a piece of pie on it.

"Here's your piece. It's still warm. Are you up for another game of Rook? Have you paid your debt to Nikola?"

I shot Nikola a sultry look as Anne turned her back to grab a container out of the cabinet. Nikola giggled as I said, "I've paid my debt. I'm up for another game." I looked at Nikola. "Shall we have the same stakes?"

I picked up my plate and took a big bite. Warm chocolate goodness filled my mouth. Anne made a mean chocolate pie.

Anne put her hand up as she walked out. "I don't want to know what you guys are betting about. I'll get the cards."

Nikola and I continued smirking at each other. There was coughing down the hallway, then a door closed to muffle the sound out. Anne's cough had significantly worsened. She seemed slower and more tired. We had a doctor's appointment in five days. At dinner, Nikola had tried to talk Anne into an earlier appointment, without success.

After she climbed off her wooden barstool, Nikola moseyed over to me. "Are you ready to be defeated again? And to put your fate into the hands of the Magic 8 Ball?"

I bit her lip then ran my tongue over the bite. "Are you ready for that striptease?"

"If you lose, I'll give you a striptease with a little extra something I bought."

Nikola swayed her hips as we walked out into the living room. I walked right behind her, whispering in her ear, "What'd you buy?"

"Win and you'll find out. Lose and it'll stay my dirty little secret."

We made it to the card table. Anne was sitting there with a glass of water. She must have brought it from the back of the house. I watched her closely as she dealt the cards. The gravity of Anne's illness sunk in. For now, I'd enjoy this moment.

Grabbing my cards, I prepared for battle. Whatever my wife had purchased on the sly was going to be a hell of a surprise. I had to win.

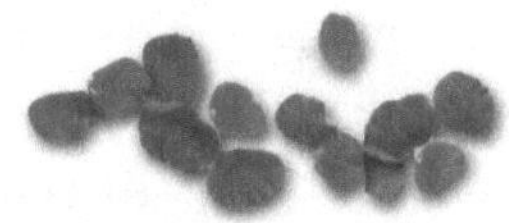

We pulled onto the highway as we made our way home from Anne's. The sun was setting as the dusky sky turned a brilliant orange. As I went around a truck, Nikola asked, "What was bothering you when you first came back in from calling Adam?"

Remembering what Adam had brought up about the club had me flustered again. I wondered what Nikola would think. I hadn't even thought about whether she'd want me to sell the club and get into something else. "Umm—we got an offer on Club Envy. It's supposedly a good offer that Adam wants to entertain, but I don't know if I do. I don't know why, but I never thought of us selling the club."

Nikola laid her hand on top of mine, resting on the console. "That would be hard," she said. "The club was there for you this last year as you buried yourself in security."

Exactly.

"What do you think I should do?"

She took a deep breath. I saw Nikola's chest rise from the

corner of my vision. "I think it wouldn't hurt to at least hear the offer, but you have to be the one who decides. I'll support you regardless of what you choose."

This was why we were meant to be together. I should have known Nikola would support me in whatever I decided.

We continued driving as we reminisced about our wedding. As we were pulling into the neighborhood, Nikola's tone changed as she tried to hide her laughter. "Hey, Brandt, can I tell you something?"

I glanced to her as she sat, relaxed in her seat. "Sure, you know you can tell me anything."

Nikola held up her index finger and middle finger in a V. "Boy oh boy. I can't wait to have all five of these babies up when I keep pummeling you at Rook."

The garage door went up as I hit the button on the visor in the car. I'd given Nikola the spot next to my Corvette. I'd park in the driveway until we decided what we wanted to do about a house.

Chuckling, I responded, "I figured you were going to say you still want to do your wifely duties and striptease for me."

She countered, "Or maybe the Magic 8 Ball will want you to do a striptease for me while I play 'It's Raining Men.' But, it has to be the Geri Halliwell version. I think that would be great." Nikola nodded, as if it was the perfect plan.

I pulled the vehicle into the garage, trying to play it cool. "The Weather Girls know their stuff."

Nikola withdrew that dreaded, black, round sphere of doom. The last time the fortune had gone my way, which meant that that horrid thing was bound to turn on me.

She handed the ball to me. "Want to give it a go and see how cool they are to dance to?"

To stall, I hit the button to close the garage door. The

moment the door hit the floor, I felt like I was being sentenced. Nikola faced me, trying to suppress a laugh. She spoke again.

"I'll sweeten the pot. You can choose to ask one of two questions to the 8 Ball. The first choice is to ask the 8 Ball if you should do a striptease to the song. The second choice is to ask if I should be the one to do the striptease in your place. If you ask the sacred 8 Ball if you should do the striptease and it says no, that means I have to do it and vice versa. So one of us will be stripping tonight regardless."

I turned to face her. "You're giving me the choice on what I ask the 8 Ball?"

She nodded and giggled.

I held out my hand. "Give me that damn ball."

There was still a faint light in the garage from the light hanging from the ceiling, so I could still see everything. Nikola handed me the Magic 8 Ball, and I stared down at it.

Are we going to be friends still? I hope so. I don't want to make threats, but if you make me dance to that fucking song, it's not going to be a pleasant end for you. Shit, I'm talking to you like you're not some toy. Just be kind and we'll get along great.

I looked up at Nikola to make sure I hadn't slipped and said something out loud. She was barely holding in her amusement, but I hadn't. *Whew.*

Holding the 8 Ball out, I still didn't know which question I was going to ask. This was either going to go extremely well or terribly bad. I closed my eyes as I wished with all my might. "Magic 8 Ball, should I get my dance moves on and strip for my wife?"

Shaking the damn ball, I turned it over and waited for that blue triangle to float up to the top. Nikola leaned over, waiting to see what our fate was going to be. When I saw the words,

My reply is no, I cheered in the car.

"Boo-yah, Magic 8 Ball. Boo-yah! The tides have turned. This little beauty is now my BFF, and not yours. Yes! Yes! Yes! Baby, get your stripper shoes on, you're getting naked for me tonight!"

I stopped when Nikola laughed. "You've come to the dark side of the power of the Magic 8 Ball."

"Fuck that stupid Magic 8 Ball."

Nikola got out of the car. "Be careful. It may pay you back next time you have a question if you don't love the Magic 8 Ball."

I'm sorry, Magic 8 Ball. It wasn't personal. I promise.

I got out of the vehicle after mentally apologizing to the Magic 8 Ball. "Go get on something good. I'll be waiting in the living room for you." I met Nikola at the front of the car and swatted her ass. "Make sure to bring that special gift, too."

Nikola opened the door that led into the house as she pulled her sweatshirt over her head. I didn't say a word as I enjoyed her backside. This was going to be a good time to-night. I made my way to the couch and positioned the coffee table across the room to give her room to dance right in front of me. I stripped out of my clothes, ready to fuck her brains out until I couldn't stand anymore.

A few minutes passed and what sounded like music from the club played through the speakers. My docking station at the back of the room was wired throughout the house. The low, erotic pulse sounded throughout the room.

I stroked my dick as I waited for Nikola to come stand in front of me. A velvet pouch came over my left shoulder and dangled in front of my face. Warm lips came to my right ear. "There's a vibrator in my underwear, positioned in front of my clit. This is the remote to control the strength of those vibrations as I dance for you."

"Holy shit." I stopped stroking myself, afraid I was going to come on the spot.

Her tongue traced the rim of my ear. "I thought you'd like that."

I took the pouch and opened it to find a small, rectangular remote. On it were ten numbers. Nikola came to stand in front of me, wearing black sheer panties and a matching bra. There was a matching robe of the same material over top.

"Nikki, you're fucking gorgeous. Whatever I did to deserve you, I'll never know."

She twirled. "I take it you like."

"Oh, baby, I like."

Nikola swayed her hips as she undid the tie to her robe. I hit the One on the remote and her eyes closed for a second before letting the garment slide off her arms. Nikola continued to walk my way before turning and bending, leaving her pussy mere inches from my reach. I went to touch her, but she stood, swaying and touching herself in the sexiest way as her body moved to the beat. I pressed the five on the remote and got an audible gasp. She faltered, but continued.

I squeezed my dick harder as Nikola unsnapped her bra. Instead of letting me see those luscious tits, she covered them with her hands and massaged them. I hit the number six and was rewarded with her eyes closing, and her fingers went to the end of her nipples. She pinched them. Nikola didn't lose her rhythm this time.

Knowing I wasn't going to last, I pressed seven, and Nikola said, "That feels so good. I'm so wet. So wet. I wish you could feel how ready I am for you."

I pressed eight, and Nikola moved my way. She didn't touch me as she put her hands on the couch to the outside of my legs. Licking her lips, she leaned down and swirled her tongue around the tip of my cock.

"Shit, baby." I pressed ten, and Nikola dropped to her knees. We were both getting close. I got up, moving her hands temporarily, and positioned myself behind her. Getting on my knees, I lifted Nikola's hips to the perfect height to fuck her. The vibrator was still going as I pushed the fabric aside and plunged inside. She was wet, warm, and tight as I pounded into her.

"Brandt. Don't stop. Don't stop."

I grabbed her hips and rammed myself in, balls deep, starting the ripple effect of our orgasm. Pulses began in the center and continued to move outward, overtaking our entire bodies. We sagged onto the floor after I pulled out. I held Nikola to me. I reached for the remote and turned the vibrator off.

She looked over at me, the picture of a satiated woman. I brushed a piece of hair off her face. "I'm glad the Magic 8 Ball did not pick me to do that."

"Me, too. I think the vibrator was a hit."

I kissed her hard. "Oh, it's definitely going into the frequently-used pile."

We were touching each other and kissing. It wasn't going to be long before I was in Nikola again. We weren't going to get any sleep tonight if I had anything to do with it.

Nikola

THERE WAS A noise from the bathroom as I peeled my eyes open. Something crashed. I felt for Brandt, but his side of the bed was cold and empty. Throwing back the green duvet, I headed toward the bathroom. I could hear someone sniffing, as if they had a runny nose. Glancing back at the clock, I noticed it was a little after three a.m.

Is Brandt sick? Why didn't he wake me?

My voice tried to work, but it was dry from sleeping and only a croak came out when I tried to call out his name. Fear pooled in my gut as I tried to stay positive about what was going on behind the door. The time it took to close the distance seemed to last forever. It was as if I was stuck in tar, barely able to move.

I tried to speak again, but nothing came out. *What is*

wrong with me? My hand went to my throat as I tried to make any type of noise. Only a raspy sound came from my vocal cords. Finally, after what felt like hours, I made it to the door and cracked it open.

There was a mirror on the cabinet and two lines of white powder were evenly spaced on it. A hand appeared holding a rolled-up dollar bill. Brandt leaned over and snorted a line of coke. My heart broke as tears fell freely down my face.

My vocal cords broke free as I screamed, "You promised! You promised! You promised!" My world ended. I kept yelling, "You promised! You promised!"

"Nikola, wake up! Wake up, baby!"

My body jolted forward and my skin was damp from the perspiration. Breaths were heaving in and out of my lungs. Needing to see the bathroom, I ran in there and flipped on the lights. Everything was as I'd left it when I'd gotten ready for the striptease. I turned around and ran into Brandt's chest. His hands came out to steady me.

"Baby, what's wrong?" I cried and crushed my face into his chest. "Nikola, you're scaring the fuck out of me. Please, tell me what's wrong."

I sobbed harder. Brandt picked me up and cradled me in his arms as he walked back into the bedroom. He sat on the bed, and I clung to him.

"I'm trying to be patient, but I'm about to go out of my mind here, baby."

"I had a nightmare. A horrible dream. I don't want you to think I don't trust you. I do. I don't know why I dreamed it." My voice was choked up, barely understandable.

Brandt's arms were soothingly rubbing my back and he let out a big sigh of relief. "It's okay. I've got you. It was a dream. I know you trust me."

I pulled back, my lip trembling. "But, but, I dreamed you were using again."

He flipped on the lamp. Brandt's blue eyes looked at me seriously as he pulled a cream-colored throw from the end of the bed and draped it over me. "I told you why I like you to sleep with me every night regardless of where you're at."

I nodded. "To know I'm there and haven't left you again."

He continued, "I know you're not actually leaving me, but I like to have the reassurance. We know what it's like to lose each other. It's only natural to be scared of losing that love. Time will lessen the nightmares. It has with mine."

I held him closer as I breathed his scent, comforted by it. Brandt laid us back on the bed and discarded the throw before pulling up our green duvet to cover our bodies. His arms pulled me closer. I needed his touch and the comfort of his embrace.

"Do you think I'll have that dream again?"

Brandt kissed the top of my head. "You could. Or you might not. When I told you about mine, they lessened. I've only had two since then."

I hoped I never had that dream again. The gut-wrenching pain the dream caused me is something I hoped to never feel again. "I keep thinking something is going to take our happily ever after away."

"Nothing is going to do that. If anything tried, I'd kick its ass."

That caused a small giggle out of me as I took a few long deep, soothing breaths. "Thanks for not getting upset or thinking I didn't trust you."

Brandt positioned me in a way that we could look at each other, inches apart. "You married me. If you didn't trust me, you wouldn't have said yes, despite how much you loved me."

A couple more tears came down my face. His thumb brushed them away.

"I do love you. So much it scares me sometimes."

"Same here, baby. Same here."

I bit my lip. "Will you make love to me?"

Brandt rolled me under him. "There's no place I'd rather be than inside you."

He sealed his words with a kiss.

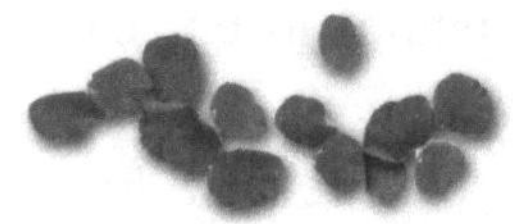

My head pounded as the phone vibrated on the night-stand. I heard pots and pans in the kitchen—Brandt had cooked breakfast. From the sound of it, he was putting things away. I loved breakfast with Brandt. Gavin's name flashed across the screen.

I cleared my throat before answering. "This is Nikola."

"Nikola? Gavin. I hear congratulations are in order if what Ainsley said is true."

"It's true. I got married." I looked down at my ring and wiggled my fingers.

A scooting noise sounded. "That was fast. I didn't know you were serious."

I was silent as I didn't know how to respond. Gavin and I had never had a personal conversation before. It had all been top line with no specifics. He finally spoke.

"I'm sorry. That was rude of me. My girlfriend is pressuring me to tie the knot, and I'm not sure what I want to do. Please, accept my apologies."

"Apology accepted. Marriage is a big step. My only piece of advice is to follow your heart."

Papers shuffled. "I think that's good advice. I'll probably reflect on that for a bit. I wanted to let you know all the boards with the graphs you made are printed and the Executive Summaries have been bound. A meeting is scheduled for next week. Thanks for all your hard work. The third wire should come to you today. If the board accepts the proposal, I'll get the fourth wire sent to you immediately."

"Thanks. I appreciate the update. Let me know if there's anything else you need."

"I will. Have a good day."

"You, too."

He hung up. I was glad commitment was not an issue Brandt and I had. When I'd been talking to Gavin, I hadn't wanted to say anything, but some questions he seemed to have were clear indicators that he wasn't ready for that next step. I wasn't his friend, so I'd kept my mouth shut.

As I was about to lay the phone back on the nightstand, it vibrated. Ainsley's name flashed across the screen. I opened the text.

Ainsley: Hey, Adam told me Brandt was coming to Club Envy this morning to talk. Are you up for Nora and me coming over for some girl time?

Me: I'd love that. Come on over whenever.

Ainsley: Okay, we'll be there in a bit.

Me: Sounds good.

I placed the phone back on the nightstand, stood, and grabbed my robe from the end of the bed. The stress from the nightmare ebbed. Brandt had taken it well and believed me that I still trusted him. The panic and loss I'd felt still resonated in me. It was going to be good to have some girl time. Most of my girlfriends had left me as Brandt and I got closer. As I buried myself in work, I drifted away from the rest of my friends. All they wanted to do was hook me up with someone which was the farthest thing I had wanted. In the end, I was better off not having fake friends. For the first time in a while, I felt I'd found a true friend in Ainsley, and I was getting to know Nora better.

I headed into the kitchen in my robe. On the table sat a plate of pancakes and a bowl of fruit. The aroma of cooked batter filled the air. Only one place was set.

I looked at Brandt. "You aren't joining me?"

Brandt was in jeans and a long-sleeved T-shirt. "Adam asked if I could come in early before the other employees got here for training. I was going to come in the bedroom and tell you but didn't want to wake you."

I puckered my lips, and Brandt walked over to kiss me. I pulled back and smiled against his lips. "Have a good day at work, honey. Ainsley and Nora are going to stop by for some girl time."

"I'll be back as soon as I can. Have fun with the girls. Don't get into too much trouble. Enjoy breakfast."

He kissed me quickly then started toward the door.

"Thank you. I love you."

"I love you, too. Wish me luck."

"Good luck."

The door opened, closed, and then I was left alone. Hopefully, Brandt and Adam could come to an agreement. I put some butter on my pancakes and drizzled the syrup over them. The first bite was heavenly. I kept thinking about the big decision ahead of the guys and wondered if they would end up selling Club Envy. Before Brandt had mentioned it in the car yesterday, I had never imagined them selling.

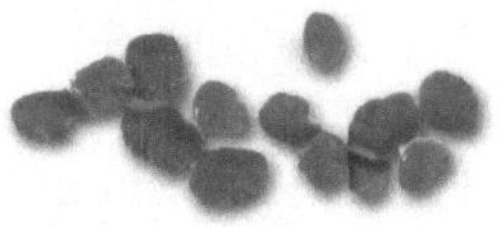

Ainsley, Nora, and I were all on the couch with our legs tucked under us. Nora's black hair had bright pink pieces sprinkled throughout. She wore torn jeans with a shirt that fell off one shoulder. Ainsley had on jeans and a fitted, pale purple sweater. Spring was tempting to shake these cooler temperatures but hadn't succeeded yet.

We were reading an article about the top ten ways a guy should seduce his girl. Every time we read a tip, we'd end up in a fit of laughter. My sides were hurting.

Nora grabbed the article from me as we were coming down from our last laugh. "Okay, I have to read the last one. I don't know where these people got their facts, but I can sure as hell say if a guy ever gave me a kitty growl, I'd turn and leave immediately."

That was number two in the top ten. We giggled, and Nora continued reading.

"The number one way to seduce your girl is, every chance you get, thrust your hips out to remind the woman there's machinery in those pants. The movement will draw attention and make the girl think of sex. That third leg is there for a reason. Use it, boys."

Nora was barely able to finish as we became hysterical again. "Tears, I have tears." I was barely able to get that out. Nora stood and tried to imitate what had been described. It only made us laugh more.

Ainsley was laid back, and she sputtered, "I can't breathe. I can't breathe."

This felt good. A few moments later, we were finally becoming coherent again. Ainsley asked Nora, "So, Jude never pulled any of those moves on you?"

"Oh, hell no, he didn't. They should have definitely used him as a source on what to do to seduce a girl." Nora sobered for a second. "Jude took me to dinner last night and told me he's got to head home for a bit to Australia."

Ainsley sat up. "Oh no, Nora. How are you doing?"

Nora shrugged. "We'll see. He says he's coming back for me, but I don't know. There's no way I could leave my mom and sister. I told him that."

I knew from Ainsley that Nora's mom was in remission from cancer. Ainsley watched Nora's sister, Emilyn, from time to time. Nora helped her mom a lot as they tried to recover from all the medical bills.

Ainsley gave her a hug. "Do you know how long he's going to be in Australia?"

Nora shook her head, then wiped a tear. "His dad is sick, and he has to go back and help him. I don't know. Jude's dad has always wanted him to take over the family business. Last night, Jude told me he loved me. I told him I loved him too. It was the first time I ever told a man that. And now he's leaving. I don't know what to do."

I scooted closer. Maybe what I'd been through would help. "Brandt and I, as you know, broke up for a time. Eventually, we found our way back to each other. Nora, if it's true love, you'll find your way if you stay true to your heart."

She nodded and worked on clearing her emotions. "I know. The phrase 'love will find a way' hopefully rings true this time around, despite how corny it sounds."

"I do believe it will. I'm so sorry you're having to go through this."

Ainsley squeezed her best friend as she said, "Maybe when you guys Skype, Jude can hip thrust you via camera to get you good and going."

All of us were holding each other as our laughter was all-consuming.

Nora added, "And growl like a kitty cat. Maybe a long distance relationship will work if he has moves like that." She stood then, as if something had come to her suddenly. "Do you mind if I skedaddle? I told him I didn't know if I could do the long distance relationship thing, but I need to tell him I want to."

Ainsley and I both said, "Go!"

Nora was out the door in a flash. I loved young, blossoming love. I had a feeling they would find their way back to each other. Somehow, they'd make it work.

My phone rang from the kitchen. "Let me get it. It might be Brandt."

I ran into the kitchen and picked it up, seeing the word *husband* flash across the screen on the black granite countertop. Brandt must have been messing with my phone. "Is this my *husband* by any chance?"

"Hey, baby. I see you saw the change I made."

Just hearing his deep voice caused things to happen within me. "I like the upgrade. How's it going?"

"Good. I was going to see if you and Ainsley wanted to meet us for lunch."

"Hold on, let me check with Ainsley." I called in to the living room where Ainsley sat on the couch looking at her phone. "Do you want to meet with Brandt and Adam for lunch?"

Ainsley laughed. "I was about to ask you the same thing. Adam texted me. Sounds good."

Our men were so much alike. I turned my attention back to the phone. "Yes, we want to do lunch. Want to meet at the Korner Kafé near the club?"

"Perfect. We'll see you there. Love you."

I would never tire of hearing those words from Brandt. "I love you, too."

We hung up, and I headed into the living room where Ainsley laid the throw on the back of the couch. Ainsley looked at me, "Nora brought me. Do you mind if I ride with you?"

Bumping her shoulder in a friendly way, I answered, "Absolutely not. Thanks for today. I needed this."

Ainsley linked her arm with mine as we left the living room. "I think we needed a laugh. I think we should start making it a monthly thing. We'll make our men go hang out while we have a girls' night."

"I think that sounds like a good idea."

As we left the house, I thought about how it was time for Brandt and me to make this a home. The house was still empty, with minimal furnishings. My place had been furnished with the necessities and a few extras. I think, subconsciously, we'd both been waiting to find each other again.

We finally had.

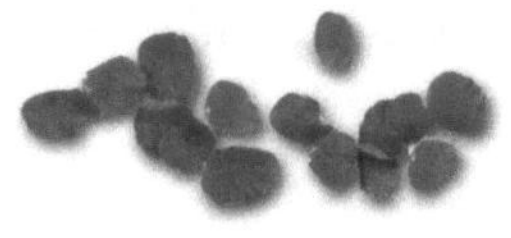

We were sitting at a wooden table at the Korner Kafé. The restaurant was eclectic. All the tables were different colors and shapes. None of the chairs matched, but it worked perfectly. Apple smells filled the air from the fresh baked pies that had been placed on the counter a few minutes ago.

Adam and Ainsley were telling us about the resort where their wedding was going to take place. They'd finalized the details shortly before our wedding but hadn't wanted to say anything to distract from our big day. Our mostly-eaten sandwiches were pushed to the side.

I looked at a resort in a brochure with palm trees in front of the ocean and the sun setting, creating magnificent colors. Running my fingers across the paper, I said, "This is beautiful. I'll book our tickets this week to go. I can't wait. Let me know if there's anything I can do to help."

Ainsley smiled. "I'd love for you to come with us to find my wedding dress."

Clapping girlishly, I said, "Oh, I'd love too. Let me know when."

"I will."

I was the matron of honor and Nora was the maid of honor. Brandt leaned back in his chair. He looked happy and at ease with himself. I felt his hand on my leg and placed mine on top. Adam and Ainsley launched into more details about the wedding. I glanced to Adam, he looked like Brandt did—at peace with himself.

The bell to the door chimed and Adam muttered, "Fuck."

I turned to see what Adam was looking at. It was the spitting image of Adam with dark hair and a tall, muscular build. The only difference was his brother, Jake, didn't have tattoos and had greasy, slicked-back hair. I glanced at Adam, and he looked fine.

I asked, "Do we need to leave?"

He shook his head. "Nah, not necessary. He's an asshole.

My sister told me he'd been caught cheating on Selena. It's a mess, but Ainsley and I are staying out of it. Then it came out Selena has been cheating on Jake, too. I feel bad for the baby, but I can't make them unselfish."

Selena was Adam's ex, who'd left him for his brother. The Adam I'd known a year or so ago had been a jaded man. Jake was a miserable person for going after his brother's girlfriend. Jake had always been jealous of Adam. I couldn't comprehend being that way. But, in the end, it had led Adam to Ainsley.

Brandt chimed in as he glanced back toward Jake. "Some people want to be miserable."

Adam picked up his glass before taking a sip. "Here. Here."

Jake got his drink to go, then left as he threw a slimy smile in our direction. Adam sighed. "I bet that fucker saw my car outside and stopped in here for the hell of it."

I stood. "Let me know if you need me to use my Kung Fu on him. I have a pretty mean crane karate move." I posed in a way that seemed martial arts-like. Then I straightened and put on a serious face. "I will return in a second."

They were all chuckling. As I turned to head to the bathroom, Brandt called, "Kung Fu and karate are not the same."

I slightly turned my body back as I continued on my way. "Don't focus on the details. Focus on the moves." Swiping my hand through the air made them all shake their heads.

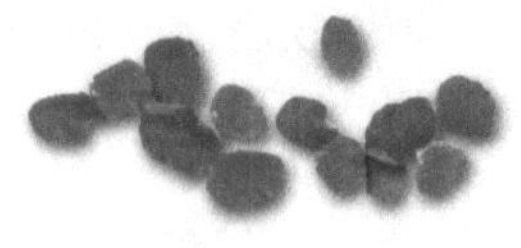

On my way back to the table, I looked at Brandt and something was wrong. Adam and Ainsley looked somber. I couldn't see Brandt's face since he was facing toward the restaurant window. A rock formed in my stomach, and the lunch I had eaten felt unwelcome. My steps slowed. Adam nodded his head toward Brandt. Ainsley was looking at me and biting her lip. The fingers of her right hand were messing with the light purple sleeve of the opposite arm.

Brandt looked, as if he was saying something, as he moved his head. Next, he stood and came toward me. "What's wrong, Brandt?"

His arm wrapped around my waste. "Let's go outside so we can talk."

I wasn't able to say anything but let him guide me out the door. My mind tried to come up with different scenarios that would cause a reaction like this. For whatever reason, I was coming up blank. Perspiration formed on my skin. As we pushed through the door, my face was greeted with a cool breeze I welcomed. It helped to focus on the cold sensation.

Brandt took me to the passenger side of his vehicle. "Nikola, we need to get to Northside Hospital. Anne has been admitted. It appears she had a seizure. Anne is stable, but they are running tests to see what happened. You were listed as an emergency contact. I picked up the phone while you were in the restroom."

My lip quivered. "Gr-gr-grandmama is in the hospital. She has to be okay, Brandt. I can't lose her. I'm not ready."

Brandt engulfed me in a hug. "I know, baby. I know. Let's get to the hospital and see what's going on."

Brandt opened the door helped me get into the SUV. I tried to be strong, but the tears broke free as I felt the cool streaks trail down my face. This had to be a dream. I prayed,

Please let this be a dream. Please let this be like last night. I can't lose her. I can't. I'm not ready.

Brandt

WE WERE ALMOST to Northside Hospital. Nikola looked out the window and tapped the door's arm rest. She'd asked me to repeat several times what the doctor had said, which I did without hesitating. We arrived at the hospital. Nikola got out of the SUV under the covered area before I had a chance to put it in park. I followed quickly and locked the vehicle.

I caught up to my love and wrapped my hand around her waist. People were everywhere. It was a busy day at the hospital.

"Brandt, you'll get towed." Even being stressed to the limit, Nikola was still thinking of me.

"I'm not letting you go in there alone. If I get towed, I get towed. Anne's on the second floor."

We had made it to the elevator as Nikola repeatedly hit the up button to summon one of the four lifts in the corridor. Pieces of her auburn hair fell into her face. The lights on the elevator read it was on the fourth floor.

I saw the stair sign to the right. "Let's take the stairs. It'll be faster."

Nikola was on autopilot as we made it through the large metal door. She took off in a sprint as we climbed. We were halfway up to the second floor when the loud clanking from the first-floor door echoed through the stairwell. Nikola pushed on and I was right behind her. We came out of the stairwell and onto the second floor. A dark-wooded nurses' station stood out against the stark white walls a few feet from the elevator doors.

Walking up, Nikola said, "We got a call that Anne Kingston had been admitted. She's my grandmother. I'm her emergency contact. My name is Nikola Mattox."

The young nurse gave her a sweet smile. "Hi, Nikola. Yes, Ms. Kingston is in her room. She's stable. Dr. Grieger will be right out to speak with you."

Nikola panicked. "Can I not go see my grandmother then speak to Dr. Grieger?"

Before the nurse responded, Dr. Grieger came through the doors.

Whatever he had to say, I figured it wasn't going to be good if he wanted to speak to us ahead of time. "Nikola, do you mind if we go into this office and speak? Your grandmother is sleeping now. She knows you're on your way."

"Okay. Can I see her, even if she's still sleeping, once we are done talking?"

Dr. Grieger walked toward a small room to the right of the stairwell. "Of course you can. When we're done, I'll take you back there."

We went in, and the doctor closed the door. There was a loveseat and two chairs. I can't imagine coming into this room meant anything good when you were with a doctor. If it had been good news, wouldn't he have told us out there?

Adjusting his white coat and then his stethoscope, Dr. Grieger talked.

"It appears your grandmother had a seizure. Once she was stabilized, we went through our routine checkups she was scheduled to have next week to see if the cancer had advanced. First off, Ms. Kingston has a fever that I believe triggered the seizure. Her breathing has significantly decreased to the point she is not getting the oxygen she needs. After reviewing the scans, the cancer is more aggressive than we'd originally thought. It's continuing to spread and has grown substantially. The lung cancer is constricting the bronchioles, which is making it difficult to breathe. In our last meeting, Anne refused to undergo treatments. Her only request was to stay comfortable. Has anything changed since our last meeting?"

"No, nothing has changed," I said. "I was with her yesterday, and she seemed okay. I mean, her breathing has gotten worse, but she wasn't this sick or else I would have made sure she came in."

I put my arm around Nikola and pulled her to me.

"Even as doctors, we don't understand all there is to know about cancer."

I couldn't imagine being a doctor and having to deliver this sort of news to people. My heart broke at what he was alluding to.

A sob erupted from Nikola. "How much time does she have?"

The doctor looked down. "I'm afraid not much. Her condition is deteriorating quickly. She's still cognizant, but I'm not sure for how long."

Nikola leaned into my shoulder and cried. I wrapped my arms around her, wanting to be everything she needed but not knowing what to do. Seeing the love of my life like this felt like a having branding iron slowly dragged over my skin.

The doctor continued, "Ms. Kingston is not aware yet as to the severity of her current condition, but you were cleared to receive all medical information. I didn't want to wake her to tell her the news, since family was on the way. Do you want me to tell her or would you like to? Sometimes the family wishes to be the one. I don't mind, but wanted you to have the choice since there's time."

What the hell? He was asking Nikola if she wanted to tell Anne she was dying. I had to try to shelter her from this pain. I knew Nikola would want to be the one.

"I-I-I will," she said. Her tearful sob was heart-wrenching.

Dr. Grieger stood. "I'll give you a few minutes. You can see Ms. Kingston whenever you are ready."

Without waiting, Nikola stood and tried to quiet the sobs racking her body. She continued to wipe the tears away as they fell. There was a tissue box on the table next to the blue couch. I grabbed a couple and handed them to Nikola. We stood and walked outside to meet the doctor.

Nikola addressed Dr. Grieger, "I'm ready. Can you please call my parents and let them know to come? Brandt will give you their numbers."

Pulling out a notepad and pen, Dr. Grieger handed it to me. I scribbled their numbers down. We walked toward Anne's room. The sounds of beeping were heard throughout. Nurses quietly worked at their stations. We walked through the door that led to Anne. Nikola held my hand in a death grip, which I knew was my answer—she wanted me here with her when she spoke to Anne. In the center of the room, on a hospital bed, Anne peacefully slept, though her breathing was substantially labored.

A blue pleather chair with dark wood sat off to the side of the bed. Nikola took a seat then grabbed Anne's hand. The smell of bleach wafted into my nose.

"Grandmama, are you awake?"

Anne's blue eyes fluttered open and focused for a bit on Nikola. "You're here. I knew you'd come."

"Of course I'm here. I came as soon as we found out." Nikola put her other hand on top of Anne's.

There was a cup to the side with a sponge on a stick. Anne said, "Water."

Nikola got the cup and sponge and put it to Anne's lips to wet them. After Nikola was finished, Anne said, "It's bad, isn't it? When I called nine-one-one for my head and chest hurting, I knew it was bad. Right after I spoke to the person, I passed out. I don't feel like I have much time." Anne's voice was weaker, not it's strong, vibrant self.

Nikola looked down. "It is worse. The cancer has grown and spread. The doctor is calling Mom and Dad."

A few tears fell down Anne's face, and she winced as pain hit her.

The doctor came in. "Ms. Kingston, I wanted to let you know that your son and daughter-in-law are on their way. They were outside Atlanta. I've prescribed a morphine drip for the pain to keep you comfortable. As the pain gets worse, we'll administer the morphine orally."

Anne coughed. "Will I be lucid?"

"We can set the drip to take the edge off, but you'll still

be cognizant. It'll ease the bronchial tubes' breathing for now."

"Okay, let's do that."

He nodded. "I'll let the nurses know. Let me know if you need anything else."

Our focus returned to Anne as we heard the door shut. Nikola dragged the seat closer to Anne and smoothed her sheets. There was another chair in the corner that I moved next to Nikola. I was at a loss as to what to do. Nikola chewed on her lips, trying to keep her emotions at bay. I grabbed her left hand while she held Anne's in the other. Nikola's hand shook.

"Grandmama, I don't know how to do this. I'm not ready."

Anne closed her eyes and a few tears trickled down her cheeks before she reopened them. Her voice was a tad shaky. "Nikola, we'll never be ready. But I do want you to know how proud I am of you. We'll always be in each other's hearts. Remember we can meet in each other's dreams. Every sunrise and sunset, we can gaze up together and know we are looking at the same sky."

Nikola sobbed. "I want to be strong, but I don't know what I'll do without you."

"You'll always have me. I've left you a surprise at my house. When I'm gone, go there with Brandt. It's for both of you."

Anne turned to me. I could tell she was getting more tired. "Take care of Nikola. She needs you like you need her. Treasure your love and never take it for granted. Going through all this has been easier, knowing she's got you. Be there for her, Brandt. I've loved you like a son and you have no idea how happy I was when you both found your way back to each other." Then, to both of us, she added, "In so many ways we're fortunate we can say goodbye to each other and tell each other everything that's in our hearts. When it gets tough, remember the good times, not the sad. Remember all the love and laughs we've shared."

"I promise. I'll be there for her forever. I promise I'll treasure her love forever and never take it for granted. I won't go back to drugs, Anne. I swear it. My commitment to Nikola is forever."

Nikola cried and squeezed my hand. She glanced at me with tear-filled eyes. I grazed her cheek with my thumb. "I love you, baby. Forever. I'm here for you."

"I love you, too, Brandt."

Anne had a smile on her face.

Nikola turned her attention back to Anne. "Grandma-ma…"

Anne turned to Nikola as she spoke with a shaky voice. It was killing my wife to be this strong, and the knife slowly went in deeper as I wasn't able to take control.

"I will treasure every conversation and moment we've ever had. You've taught me about love and life. You've guided me when I thought my compass was lost. I love you so much. I promise to make you proud. My kids will know you and what you mean to me."

Anne cried, too, as Nikola slid in the bed next to her. They cried as they held each other. I wanted to scream. Why would the world would do this to them? Life was tough as fuck sometimes; I didn't understand why we couldn't get a little peace.

The cries subsided as Anne whispered, "Let's not be sad. Let's treasure the time we've got to spend together. We've loved more in our time together than some people get to in a whole lifetime. You'll be okay. You've always been stronger than you knew."

"I'll remember each and every one of the good times, Grandmama."

"Me, too. Know I'll be looking down on you every second of the day."

Nikola and Anne continued to embrace each. They spoke in whispers about their memories. The door cracked open and Nikola's parents appeared in the doorway.

They looked shaken. Anne hadn't wanted to worry them with the cancer until after the wedding. Nikola and I had both respected her wishes, even though we'd disagreed. Imagining their shock was indescribable.

Nikola's dad spoke. "Mom, is it true?"

"It is, son. I didn't want to worry you."

Richard's normal demeanor cracked and emotions shone through like a bright light.

Anne spoke to Nikola, "Do you mind giving me some time with your parents?"

"Of course, Grandmama. I'll be right out in the hallway." She gave Anne a kiss on the cheek, and a loving smile graced her lips.

I followed Nikola. When we got to her parents, Nikola gave them a hug. Her dad embraced her. At first, her mom was a little stiff, but she softened, hugging her back.

I gave them whatever smile my face was capable of at the time, even though my heart was heavy. We stepped into the corridor, closing the door behind us. The curtains had already been drawn for privacy, so we weren't able to see anything. A few nurses were making their rounds.

Nikola turned to me and sobbed in my chest. "I'm not ready to let her go. I don't want to be strong. I want her to be okay. I want a miracle. I've been praying for a miracle. She's dying, Brandt. She's dying."

I stroked her back and walked us a little farther down the hallway to a more private alcove, from which I could still see Anne's door. Searching for soothing words, I said, "I'm not ready to let her go either, but she's in pain, baby. She's in so much pain."

"I know. I don't know if I'm strong enough to let her go. I want more time. I want to go back to yesterday when we were at our house. It felt like nothing was wrong. If I'd known that would have been our last day together, I'd have memorized it."

Sobs continued to rack her body as she clung to me. Her nails dug into my back.

"I know, baby. I know."

I held her close. Moments felt like hours. Time stood still.

The door to Anne's room creaked open and Nikola's dad stepped out with red-rimmed eyes. Richard nodded in my direction.

"Hey, baby, it's time to go back in there."

Nikola pulled away and walked toward her father. When we reached the doorway, he put his arm around Nikola and I let her go. She needed to feel this rare love from her father.

As we walked into the dimly lit room, Nikola's mother stood off to the side, wiping her tears away. Nikola went to the vacated seat she'd been in before. The pain was evident on Anne's face, and her breathing was still labored. Anne smiled at Nikola. The monitors continued to beep at regular intervals.

Nikola took a deep breath as the nurse came in and went to the bedside. The nurse was young with brown hair in a ponytail. She checked the monitors. "How's the pain, Ms. Kingston?"

Anne looked to Nikola and was about to speak when Nikola pleaded, "Don't stay in pain, Grandmama. Please, don't stay in pain. Don't worry about me. Be comfortable."

The nurse looked toward Anne, waiting for a response. Anne sighed in relief. "The pain is growing."

"Let's increase the morphine drip. You're going to get sleepy, but it'll help your breathing. You'll be in and out. When the pain starts to increase again, let us know and we'll continue to increase the dosages."

The nurse pushed some buttons. As the nurse left, Nikola talked to Anne, doing what she'd asked earlier, remembering the good times.

"Do you remember when it rained, how Grandaddy and I always sing our made-up song, 'It's waining all over da world?' You'd correct our pronunciation every time!"

"I do. You guys would stare out of the door, singing it over and over. That is a good memory. Tell me another one you have."

Nikola smiled at the memory. "Do you remember Grandaddy would always have me put the paper towels on the holder backward to aggravate you when I was younger?"

Anne's eyes got heavy as she chuckled. "I love that memory, too. He loved you, and he lived to aggravate me. Keep remembering things and telling me about them."

Nikola talked about all her joyful memories as Anne drifted in and out of sleep.

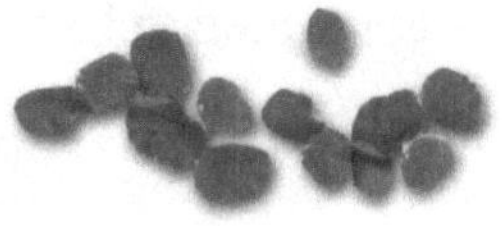

I glanced at the clock; it was after four in the morning. Everyone had joined in and shared memories all night. At times, Anne had been alert, and at others she'd lain in the bed, peacefully asleep, as we talked to each other, surrounding her with memories of our life together. The nurses had brought us all coffee as we stayed awake, talking. In some ways, it was therapeutic.

An hour ago, the nurses administered the morphine orally. Anne hadn't said much besides "I love you" throughout the night. The whimpers in Anne's sleep had spurred the doctors to recommend the more aggressive morphine doses. I'd been watching the heart monitor, and it had been slowly dropping. It was going to be anytime now, as the breaths came further apart. A rattle from the fluid that accumulated in Anne's chest in the night worsened.

The nurse checked the monitors again. "We'll be monitoring outside, but I'll give you some family time. Ms. Kingston's vitals are dropping rapidly."

Nikola got wide-eyed.

Richard spoke to Anne first, "Mom, I love you. It's okay to let go."

"Anne, thank you for loving me for who I was. It's okay to let go," Nikola's mother, Melanie, spoke softly.

I leaned over and touched Anne's hand. "You've impacted my life more than you'll ever know. I love you with my whole heart, Anne. It's okay to let go."

Next was Nikola. She said, "Grandmama, I'll remember you in every sunrise and every sunset. I'll remember you in every breeze and will meet up with you in my dreams to tell you what's happening in my life. I'm going to be okay. I love you. I love you so much. It's okay to let go. It's okay. I'm going to be okay. I don't want you to hurt anymore. I promise to remember the good. I promise."

All our eyes were wet as Nikola spoke. The monitor faded quicker. Nikola cried silently as she leaned her head down, listening to the beeps get further apart. Within a minute, Anne breathed her last breath and left us standing in the hospital. As she exhaled the last time, the world seemed a little dimmer.

We lost a piece of ourselves in that final moment.

Nikola

THE NOISE OF everyone talking around me was deafening. I needed silence. Since Grandmama's passing two days ago, I hadn't had a moment to myself. We were at the potluck in the fellowship hall that followed the burial. *I have buried my Grandmama.* The words still seemed foreign as they ran through my head. It didn't seem possible. It was like my life had been on fast-forward, unable to slow down.

There were constant reminders of Grandmama on the white paneled walls from different events she'd attended throughout the years. The picture right in front of me was of all the people who'd helped repaint the wood panels in this room. I was in the picture, covered in paint, hugging Grandmama. She didn't have a drop on her. That had been a good day, full of laughter.

Wesley had come for the funeral, but it had been hard on him, with the memories of Diane still fresh. Shortly after the funeral, he had to leave and was headed to talk to Quentin—he introduced Wesley to a guy who'd been through the same thing. Wesley had felt horrible for leaving, but I'd insisted. A funeral was the last place he needed to be, but it meant so much that he'd come. Faith and Logan were talking to my parents. I loved being part of Brandt's family. Faith made me feel like a daughter, and Logan made me feel like a sister—but I still felt like a piece of me was missing.

"Nikola, dear, did you hear me?" I blinked twice to see one of Grandmama's longtime friends, Janice, in front of me.

"I'm sorry, could you repeat what you said?" My manners kicked in. All I wanted was to be left alone. Everyone wanted to talk to me. I only wanted silence.

On a normal day, the food smells would have been delightful. Today, they made me sick. Grandmama would have delighted in the outpouring of love, but it was hard to find any silver lining today. Brandt sat beside me and placed a drink in front of me. It looked like ginger ale. I didn't want anything, but he'd insisted. He hadn't left my side the entire time except a few minutes ago. Brandt had been doing the majority of the talking for me.

"Oh, sweetie." Janice's wrinkled hand touched my shoulders.

My body wanted to flinch, but I stayed put. Janice's hair was white, and she had a frumpy middle. Janice was kind and had been there for Grandmama over the years. I'd always loved listening to stories between Grandmama and Janice.

"Your grandmother adored you. She loved you like a daughter. I know this is tough, but all her friends are here for you."

Another knife in the heart. That's what all her friends had said in some way or another. Each time was equally painful. I cleared my throat. "Thanks, Janice. I loved her, too."

She gave me another pat then left. I felt like my nerves stood on edge, waiting for the next person to approach and say the same thing, forcing reality on me again as if it weren't already a fresh cut in my heart.

Brandt scooted the glass closer to me. "Drink a little. The ginger ale will help." I was about to refuse when he pleaded, "For me. Drink a little for me."

I took a tentative sip. The cold liquid felt like an acid at first then calmed the knot in my stomach.

"Thanks, baby. Drink a little more." His encouraging tone got me to drink more.

I took another sip as someone to my right spoke.

"What should we do this weekend? Let's do something fun as a family."

I knew the world shouldn't stand still because my grandmother died, but listening to people be happy was more than I could take.

"Brandt, can you take me home? I need to go home." My voice was on the brink of breaking as I stood.

Following my lead, Brandt stood. "Yes, let's go. Do you want me to tell your parents?"

I glanced toward parents. They had three people surrounding them, which would mean a lot more talking for me. "No, text them. Tell your mom and brother, too. I don't want to talk to anyone else."

"Okay, let's go."

Someone else approached, and I was afraid I was going to be sick if anyone else told me how much Grandmama loved me. Brandt intercepted, "Hey, Mary. I'm going to take Nikola home. She's exhausted. It was good seeing you."

Mary gave a sweet smile. "I understand. You guys rest. I'll bring by some food this week."

"Thanks, Mary." Brandt always got people to warm to him.

I smiled weakly. Mary had ash gray hair and light brown eyes. She was thin and frail. "Anytime. I'll bring the food by tomorrow if that sounds good. I know how much Anne loved you, Nikola. You meant the world to her."

And there it was, the joust in the gut. Again. I knew my grandmother's friends meant well, but it was too much when I was still trying to process the fact that I'd never see her again. I didn't respond. I was drained to the core.

Brandt guided me out to my vehicle, and I got into the passenger side of the car. He got in on the driver's side, cranked the car, and drove. In the outside world, life was in full bloom as the trees revealed their green coat for the summer. The sun set. I looked at the sun, remembering Grandmama's words, *Every sunrise and sunset, we can gaze up together and know we are looking at the same sky.* I closed my eyes, then reopened them to see the brilliant colors.

I remember you, Grandmama. I remember.

More tears fell as I silently cried. Brandt's hand took mine, consoling me with his touch. I don't know what I'd have done if I hadn't had him through all this. The hurt would lessen with time, but the loss would be there forever.

As we drove, I watched the sun dip lower into the sky.

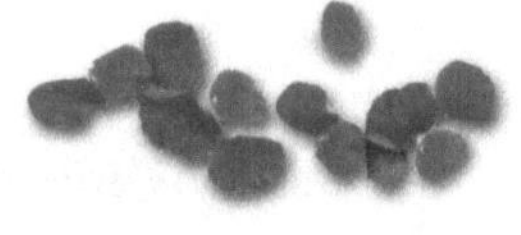

Four days had passed since Grandmama's death. I had to force myself to get out of bed every morning and live my life. It was difficult when all I wanted to do was stay buried under the mountain of blankets and pretend her death hadn't happened. I felt like a robot as I got through each moment. I knew this behavior wasn't healthy, but I was afraid to keep living. If I allowed myself a moment of happiness, part of me felt like I was forgetting Grandmama, even though that was irrational. Brandt held a cup of warm coffee in front of me as I sat on the couch, staring off into space.

"Here you go. Is there anything I can get you?"

Brandt was constantly worrying over me. He'd hardly been to work, and when he did have to leave, Ainsley would stop by from a few streets over to keep me company. Honestly, she was the one who did all the talking—I responded as minimally as I could. I hated being such a bitch, but I was being sucked into a black-tarred abyss. Trigger had been sick, and Jethro was out on scheduled vacation. Even Ainsley worked some at the club. When they were all working, Faith would come over. I liked being in her calming presence, but I was still not the best of company. I felt horrible that I was as useless as I was. Whatever had a hold of me was trying to suck me in, even though I tried to fight it.

I was at a fork in the road. I needed to decide to go down the right path versus staying in mental purgatory. I prayed something would spur me into action.

"Nikola?"

I snapped out of my never-ending thought process and remembered Brandt's question. I looked up into in his concerned eyes. "I'm good. Thanks for the coffee."

He nodded. "I have to work for a couple of hours. Wesley should be here in a minute."

"Okay."

Brandt sighed and kissed my forehead. "We're going to make it through this. Do you want me to stay?"

I looked into his eyes. "I promise it's okay for you to go. They need you at the club, Brandt. I need a little time to deal with all the sadness."

The doorbell rang, and Brandt looked torn as to what to do. I couldn't blame him. If I could tell him what to do to lessen the pain, I would. Brandt walked toward the door, and I absentmindedly sipped my coffee. I heard low voices—it sounded like Wesley.

A few minutes later, Wesley came in. He looked like he'd aged since Diane's passing. I wondered if the weight of the sadness would do this to me. His hair had grown out some, and his chocolate eyes were filled with sympathy. Brandt stood at the doorway, watching. I was sure he was trying to see how Wesley would be with me. I knew Brandt was nervous that, with the death of Diane, Wesley would start to feel more than friendship for me. But he wouldn't. We'd only been meant to be friends.

I set my coffee mug on the table as Wesley came over and gave me a quick hug. "How are you doing?"

I shrugged. "I'm here. Trying to survive, but it's tough."

Wesley sat on the opposite side of the couch. Brandt gave me a hug and a kiss, whispering in my ear, "If you need anything, call me. I love you."

"Love you, too."

He pulled back, and we smiled at each other. Brandt standing by me as he did only strengthened our love. Brandt was here for me in the good times and the bad. Nodding at Wesley, Brandt headed out the door. I sank farther into the couch with my coffee. For the first time, I was at a loss for what to say to my dear friend. My insides were hollow.

Wesley set his leg over his knee and played with the fray of his jeans. He finally spoke. "At first, I felt guilty that I was alive and able to enjoy life. Diane deserved a better ending, but that's not what the cards had in store for her. I'm coming to accept it. I'm accepting that I couldn't have done anything else to make her choose me over using. After talks with Quentin, I now believe Diane would want me to be happy and live my life. There will always be a missing piece, but I'm going to fill that piece with memories and try to move on."

We sat in silence for a while. My lower lip trembled. "I feel like I lost a mom. I keep thinking I need to call Grandmama and ask her something. Every morning, I wake up and, for an instant, everything seems okay, and then I'm forced to face the truth again. Last night, I dreamed she was alive and we were all playing Rook."

My shoulders shook. Wesley crouched in front of me, then he plucked the coffee cup out of my hand. I'd tried to be strong for the last few days, but I should have known keeping it in was the worst thing I to do.

"I understand what you're saying. Anne and Diane wouldn't want us to live in torment like this."

I nodded my head yes and tried to start believing those words. It was hard. Wesley stood. He pulled a DVD out of his back waistband. "Why don't we watch some Seinfeld? Funniest damn show ever."

Giving a small chuckle, I nodded as Wesley made his way to the television. This was what I needed. Hopefully, I'd keep progressing and not regress.

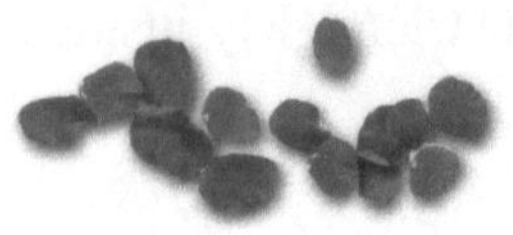

A couple more days passed. I was doing better, but there was still something off. There were times I wanted to fall back into the pit of sadness, but I fought like hell to stay where I was or to gain a little ground. We'd finished breakfast, and I'd helped clear the dishes. Moving back to the couch with a cup of coffee, I took a deep breath. Brandt was walking through the front room, holding the paper. Wesley had helped me tremendously, but I needed my soul mate.

I hoped Brandt would recognize my cry for help as I said, "Brandt, thank you for being so understanding. I'm trying to get out of this funk, but I don't know how."

This was the closest I'd come to expressing myself.

Brandt turned toward me and sat next to me. I kept looking down at my coffee, watching the liquid dance in the cup. I heard him crack his neck. He leaned his shoulder against mine.

"No one can tell you how long your mourning period should be, baby. Each person is different. It's not a betrayal of someone's memory you love because you keep living your life. They're a part of who you are, in everything you do. They want the best for you. They want you to live. Anne said when she died, to focus on the happy memories when you're sad. Think about how much time you did have together."

Brandt had heard my plea for help. He had heard me. The thick fog holding me captive dissipated as his words made sense. Grandmama would be sad I wasn't living my life. She wouldn't want me wasting away thinking about all the loss. We had one life to make the most out of it.

The doorbell rang.

Brandt chuckled and ran a hand down his face. "If it's another casserole, I honestly don't know where we're going to put it."

Our fridge and freezer was full of food. In fact, we'd given food to Ainsley and Adam. Some humor slipped into my mind, and I felt myself come back. I called after him, "Well, my wifely duties have been taken care of for a while. You won't have to ask, 'What's for dinner, honey?'"

We were both smiling as Brandt stood and went to the door. It felt good to banter with him. It felt good to see a glimmer of myself. I forced the negative thoughts from my mind and focusing on the positives. Brandt opened the door and spoke. The wooden door opened wider, making a slight creaking noise. A frumpy man in a dark-blue suit and tie came in.

Brandt was still in his sweatpants and T-shirt. His feet were bare and something stirred within me that hadn't for days. I involuntarily licked my lips. To the casual observer, it was a normal gesture, but Brandt saw it and knew what I thought. He stood behind the suited man, giving me a sexy smirk.

"Nikola, this is Andrew Liars. He was Anne's attorney."

I stood and shook the lawyer's slightly sweaty hand. "Nice to meet you, Mr. Liars. What can I do for you? Please, have a seat."

He sat and laid his well-used, leather briefcase beside his feet.

"Thank you, Mrs. Mattox. If you have a few minutes, I want to read Anne's Will for you. I went by your grandmother's place and found your parents. They were cleaning out the refrigerator, and I read the part that affected them. I know I should have made an appointment, but I was in the area and wanted to introduce myself. If now is not a good time, we can reschedule. Your father said he thought it would be okay."

"Sure, go ahead."

I was a little anxious, as I'd never discussed the Will with Grandmama. I'd assumed that my parents would get everything and wondered why I needed to be included in the discussion. Snaps clicked as he opened the briefcase.

Mr. Liars handed me a thick document in a black binder. "Here's a copy of the Will. Shall I read it to you?"

The idea of reading all this today was daunting. I was now finding myself, and I didn't want to be sucked back into the dark pool of whatever I'd been going through. I needed a few days to get my bearings to be able handle something like this.

"Can you summarize it? We can schedule a time to go through the specifics."

He retrieved another copy and laid it on his legs. "Yes, yes, of course. This is an informal visit, and we can talk in-depth in my office next week, as there will be several things to do. In summary, Ms. Kingston left all her financials and home to you. Your father was given full ownership of the piece of land that they owned jointly."

She'd left me practically everything? I was speechless and worried that my dad might be hurt.

Mr. Liars continued, "She wanted me to give you this letter. In the packet I gave you is a summary of the financials as of two days ago. We'll go through everything in-depth next week. If you have any questions between now and then, let me know."

The lawyer handed me a pale-pink envelope as he stood. "Thanks again, Mrs. Mattox. I appreciate your time. I'm sorry for your loss. Ms. Kingston was a dear friend and client. She will be missed."

I matched his movement. "Yes, she will be missed. Thank you for coming to my house to personally do this."

"Anytime, ma'am."

Brandt escorted Mr. Liars out as he tucked his leather briefcase under his arm.

Sinking back down to the couch, I looked at the outside of the pale-pink envelope. My name was on it in Grandmama's handwriting.

My sweet Nikola

I ran my fingers along the writing, imagining her sitting at her desk in the living room writing this letter. I recognized the envelope as being one from the stash she kept in her desk. I felt the couch dip, followed by the heat of Brandt's body.

"Are you going to read it?"

"Yes. I need a minute."

I continued staring at the envelope, wondering what words were on the inside. There was only one way to find out.

Turning the letter over, I opened the envelope delicately. The letter was on pale-pink matching paper.

I unfolded the letter and read.

My Dearest Nikola,

I know you're probably wondering if your dad is okay with me willing the majority of my estate to you. I called him a year or so ago to talk to him about it. He agreed it should go to you. Your parents love you dearly, Nikola, even though I know they are not the best at expressing themselves.

I estimate my cash estate to come in right around a million dollars. I hope this helps you and Brandt have an easier future—one where you can see the world and be with each other. That was a dream your Grandaddy and I always had. Hopefully, our hard work will make your lives easier.

Keep living your life, Nikola. Don't feel guilty for being happy. Knowing you are living your life to the fullest brings me joy. When you first moved to Arkansas with your parents all those years ago, I was saddened and sometimes would go days without getting dressed. Your grandfather came home one night and said, "Nikola would be sad to see you upset. She wants you to be happy." I want the same for you. I will miss our talks and our time together, but hopefully I've given you a piece of me that will keep us connected throughout your life.

Brandt is the exact person I would have picked for you if I had to choose a lifelong mate for you. Lean on him, he will be there for you.

I love you, Nikola. I'll be gazing upon the sunrises and sunsets like we promised.

Grandmama

I handed the letter to Brandt as happy tears accumulated in my eyes. These tears purged all the darkness I'd felt over this past week. It had nothing to do with the money, even though I was still shocked at the amount she'd left me.

Brandt finished reading. "Wow."

"I know. I'm going to be okay."

Brandt pulled me to him. "I never had a doubt. What do you want to do now?"

"I want you to make love to me. I've missed you." The need to be united with him overwhelmed me.

Brandt stood and picked me up. "I've missed you, too. I'll always be here for you."

Wrapping my arms around his neck, I pulled his face down to mine for a kiss as he walked. Our tongues reunited, and I felt our love coursing through my veins. Brandt's strong frame brought us to our bed, where he'd show me how much he truly loved me.

Brandt

I BECAME COGNIZANT as I felt a hand drifting toward my cock. Nikola had devoured me after I'd made love to her. I knew she'd needed time to know it was okay to still feel joy and live, but I'd missed her intimately.

I tried to assess whether she was awake or sleep-fucking me. My guess was sleep-fucking, since it normally happened after not having sex for a while and then starting again. In the past, it was because travel separated us. I hoped she was sleep-fucking me. I loved watching her wake in the thralls of passion. Nikola's naked breasts pressed against my chest as her fingers made contact with the tip of my cock. He was at full attention. She kissed my shoulder.

Lowly, I whispered, "Nikola?"

Nothing. *Hell to the yeah.* She was about to have her dirty way with me, and I couldn't wait. Nikola was bare as she mounted me. I felt my dick touch her clit, and she grinded on me, feeding her need. Her nipples dangled in front of my face like candy. Lifting my head slightly, I licked one perky, beaded tip while I lightly rolled the other one between my fingers. Her back arched at the contact, and a little moan escaped her lips. Nikola's eyes were closed as I lay back down to enjoy the view.

Her wetness found my dick and pushed down as it breached her entrance. The feeling of her without barriers had been incredible from the first time. She started the sexual slide, burying me in her. I still reveled in the feeling every time we were together. Her lips found mine as she increased her pace. She sucked my lip, almost painfully.

It was time to wake her. I pinched her nipples hard while I said, "Nikki, keep fucking me. Don't stop."

Nikola's eyes opened on the down stroke and she paused. A sultry grin appeared as she picked up the pace again. The sound of slapping skin filled the room. Her hands were on my chest, helping to propel her body faster. As she came down, I'd thrust into her, making the impact harder.

"Keep going, Nikki. Your walls are beginning to quiver."

We were fucking like wild animals, and we'd nearly lost all self-control. I needed her to come as I tried to keep myself from letting go. I wanted us to come together. I pressed my finger to her clit, and like the magic button it was, she screamed. Stilling her hips, I poured myself into her. We looked into each other's eyes as the orgasm pulsated throughout our bodies. Nikola collapsed on my chest and heaved out a contented sigh.

"Is your little guy getting worn out? We may need to get him new batteries."

That comment got her a slap in the ass, and she giggled.

"My guy, for one, is not little. He's manly, big, and can fuck your brains out for hours. Second, his batteries are at one hundred percent."

I twitched him inside her to demonstrate my point.

"Maybe we should name him?" There was a hint of playfulness to her tone.

"What were you thinking? He's beastly enough to have a name."

Nikola shook silently with laughter. *Oh, hell no. She is not going to give it a girly name.* "You will not be in charge of naming him. I revoke all your naming rights."

Nikola lifted her head. The moonlight gave enough light to bathe her body, making all her curves glow. "I think, as your wife, I'm entitled to naming rights."

"Fuck no. His masculinity will stay intact."

I slapped her ass again. In response, she ground down on me and my ultra-super-manly guy stirred. Nikola went to move off me, but I stilled her.

"Where do you think you're going?" I asked.

Matter-of-factly, she looked back at me. "To get the Magic 8 Ball so we can decide if I have naming rights. It's never wrong."

"Oh, no, no, no, no! The Magic 8 Ball and I are on good terms, but there is no way on this green Earth that I am leaving the naming rights of my dick to that thing. I'll end up with a name like Princess Squirt or some shit like that."

I love you, Magic 8 Ball, and you've been there for me recently, but I can't. If you had two balls and a stick, you'd understand. I promise.

Nikola was having a hard time controlling herself, and I looked at her sternly, but playfully. "So what would *you* like to name your 'beast,' as you call him?"

"Are you challenging my claim?" I bit her bottom lip, loving that we were getting back to our normal selves. She shook her head. "Well, I'd call him The Terminator."

"The Terminator?" she asked.

I smiled. "Yeah, when he gets near your pussy, he terminates it into oblivion."

She slapped my chest. "You're terrible. That does not sound pleasant at all."

"Oh, it's pleasant."

In a flash, I got on top of her. I pushed her hands above her head and brought "The Terminator" back to life. The room smelled like sex. Nikola's mouth went slack as I worked her into a blissful release.

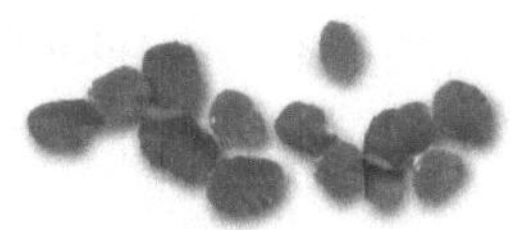

A few days had passed since the lawyer had visited. We were due to meet him the day after tomorrow. Nikola was returning to her old self. There were still times she broke down, but I was there for her. Nikola's parents had returned to China. They were opening up more, and they'd hugged her tightly before leaving. I think feeling love from them helped fill the void of Anne's love.

Currently, we were in a furniture store, getting pieces for our house. Nikola had said it was time to make our place a home, and I couldn't have agreed more. Nikola didn't want to move into Anne's house, which was her choice. I didn't know what she was going to do with the place, but she'd figure it out when she was ready. We'd spent the morning going through the storage building where we'd put Nikola's furniture. We hadn't had time to go through Nikola's boxes when we'd moved in together, and then time had gotten away from us when Anne got sick.

The furniture store was an eclectic place that had a bit of everything in it. Bright colors were everywhere. I was afraid to move with all the fragile shit spread about.

I got the text from Adam I had been waiting on.

Adam: The house on my street is for sure going to sell. It's selling under market value for the price I told you. If you want it, you'll have to act fast. I talked to her. If you're willing to pay asking price, she'll sell it to you before it lists.

Me: Give me five minutes.

Nikola asked about the pricing on a couple of lamps. The saleslady said, "Let me see what my manager can do. I'll be right back."

As the saleslady walked off, I wrapped my hands around Nikola's waist from behind.

"Hey, do you remember that house I showed you two days ago on Adam's street? The one with the pool?"

The house was more than thirty-five hundred square feet and would be perfect.

"Yes, the gorgeous red-bricked one with the three-car garage? What about it?"

Nikola played with some fringe on a black, metallic pillow. She picked it up.

I moved to stand in front of her. "It's for sale, way below market value. The lady is moving in with her daughter and needs to sell ASAP. If we want it, it's ours."

Nikola's eyes lit up. "How much?"

"It's going for three-fifty, but it's worth close to four. Adam was out working in his yard when the owner told him. She's already had an inspection done and everything. It's a good house."

I hoped Nikola wouldn't be upset that I'd looked at everything before. But there was no reason to get her hopes up if it wasn't going to pan out.

"Are you sure? I'm fine with living in your house. I don't need a bigger place."

I put my hands on her hips. "I know, but I want us to start our lives together in a place that we've only ever lived in together."

Nikola jumped into my arms as I spun her. "Where do we sign?"

"Don't you want to see the inside first?"

We were both making a scene. I didn't care if it meant Nikola was happy.

"I've already been inside. Ainsley took some cookies to the neighbor yesterday while I was with her. The owner, Mrs. Owens, gave me a tour. It's beautiful. I love it."

I kissed her hard. Grinning, I responded, "Let me make the call, and it's ours."

The sales lady approached. "We can take fifty percent off the lamps."

"We'll take them!" we exclaimed. Nikola was still in my arms with her legs wrapped around my waist.

We were finding our way after a bad storm. Even though the storm had left us changed forever, we were making the best of it and appreciating what we had.

I set Nikola down and said, "Let me call Adam. We'll get the ball rolling while you check out."

As my wife made her way to the mirrored counter, there

was a bounce in her step. I pulled out my phone and called Adam. He picked up on the first ring.

"Hey, man. What'd she say?"

"We're about to be neighbors. I'm going to call Mrs. Owens and let her know we'll take it. Oh, and Adam, I'd like to meet at the club tomorrow to talk about the offer we got. It's time for us to decide. I appreciate you not pushing me this last week, after Anne's death."

He paused for a second. "Have you made up your mind?"

"I think I have, but I want to talk in person. Do you want to meet at nine?"

He paused. I knew he wanted to know what I'd decided, but this wasn't the time to talk about it. "Sounds good. I'll see you then. Congrats on your new home, neighbor."

"Thanks, neighbor!"

Just minutes ago, when I spun Nikola around, I'd determined what I wanted to do with the club. First, I wanted to tell Nikola, and then see if Quentin could meet this evening. I liked sharing my thoughts with him. If I was jeopardizing my sobriety in any life changing decisions, he'd tell me. Not that I didn't trust my wife and best friend, but it's different when you're a recovering addict and can understand that one decision can have a domino effect on your life.

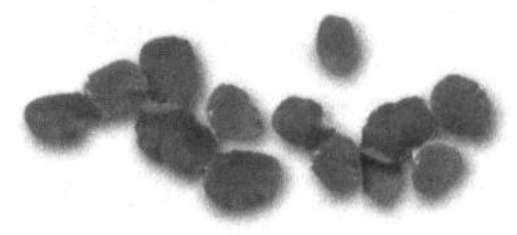

I pulled up to Club Envy and saw Chris from The Thrillhammers talking to Adam in the parking lot. The sun burned off the residual morning fog. Chris had texted Adam last night, asking if we could meet before the club opened. I had a feeling that The Thrillhammers were about to move on. It felt like a season of change. After getting out of my car, I walked over to see what was going on. Chris had on a Thrillhammers T-shirt.

Chris put his hand out. “Hey, man, what’s happening? I’m sorry to hear about your wife’s grandmother.”

“Thanks, I appreciate it. I heard you guys brought the house down two nights ago.”

He laughed as he rubbed his goatee. “We did. It was a good show. That’s part of the reason I’m here. I’ll cut right to the chase, a record label happened to be at the club and they’ve offered us a deal. It’s going to be nonstop touring for a few months at least. We haven’t signed, since I wanted to talk to you guys first. Club Envy got us recognition. The producers think our sound is unique. It was a hard decision for Wayne, Greg, Shannon, and me.”

Adam and I said, “Congrats.”

I nodded for Adam to speak first. He’d been the one to bring the band to the club.

“Congrats, Chris. You guys deserve it more than anyone I know. Just remember us little guys when you’re famous. Will you guys play one last time, to celebrate?”

Chris responded, “Hell yeah, we will. Let me talk with the boys, and we’ll come up with a date. Thanks for understanding. In the meantime, the Divas are making a name for themselves. They’ll take good care of Club Envy. They’re going places, too. Thanks for everything. We appreciate it.”

The Divas had become a substitution band we’d used regularly last year when The Thrillhammers’ schedule filled up.

I shook Chris’s hand. “Congrats again, you guys deserve it.”

Chris backed up toward his car. “Thanks, guys. I’ll be in touch about a farewell bash.”

I looked at Adam. He looked at me like he did when he tried to figure out what was on someone's mind.

"Do you want to talk in your office?"

"Yeah, but before we do, I need you to know something." Adam scrubbed a hand down his face, a nervous gesture he had picked up over the years.

"Okay—go ahead."

I worked on putting my neutral face on, in case I didn't like what he said. I'd let him know how I felt, but I didn't want to start this discussion on the wrong foot.

"Brandt, we started this together, and if we decide to sell, it'll be because we want to. I don't want there to be talks of buyouts or any of that other bullshit. Let's hear each other out. If we don't want to sell, we keep the club and figure out a way."

This made my decision even easier as I walked toward the side entrance. I didn't like being forced into things. "I agree. Let's talk this out and see where the cards land."

No one was at the club this early, and I took it all in. This place had been my safe haven, my security blanket, a place to hide out while I recovered. Nikola supported my decision, since it was what I wanted. We went into Adam's office. I still rarely used mine, except on the few occasions Nikola and I came here. It seemed we'd had outgrown the club in some ways. We still had awesome sex here, but it was somehow different.

The first time we'd had sex at the club after getting back together, it had been amazing. We'd still connected on that erotic level. But the club wasn't a focal point, like it had been in the past. We used to be here almost every night.

Adam hadn't said a word as we walked to his office. He was probably organizing his thoughts. We sat in the two chairs in front of Adam's glass desk.

"So, do you want to start?" Adam gestured to me.

Adam wanted to sell. He'd made it apparent in our last meeting. Part of me felt like I was cutting off a best friend by selling the club, even though the decision felt right.

"I think we should sell. But, I've gone over the contract in detail. The franchise option they gave for royalty payments is shit, and they need to up the amount. The non-compete clause needs to be changed from five years to one year. I get not wanting us to open a new club the week after we sell, but on the off chance we want to stay in this business, I want the option. The only other addition is for the employees. I want to add a clause to make sure they keep all employees for a minimum of ninety days. Anyone the new owners let go will receive a minimum of a thirty days' notice. We have good people here. They've been loyal to us. I want to make sure we return the favor."

Adam was stunned. It took him a few minutes to say anything. "You want to sell?"

Putting my arm across the back of the chair, I chuckled. "Yeah, if you still do. As you said in the parking lot, if we aren't both in, then we don't sell."

"Why the change of heart?"

I ran my hand along the stubble on my chin as I organized my thoughts. "There are several reasons. Even with the managers we've hired, this club still requires an obscene amount of time from us. If one of us has a crisis, it puts stress on the other guy. I don't want to be away from Nikola at all hours. When we have a family, I want to be there for my kids. Second, it feels like I've outgrown the place. When I come to work, the main thing on my mind is 'When I can go home?' The club deserves better. And, by the way, Nikola was neither for nor against this. She wanted me to decide."

The reasons I stated were similar to Adam's. In the end, it was time to move on. Adam looked around. There were memories in these walls. It was odd, realizing that this place might not be ours anymore.

We sat in reflective silence until Adam spoke. "I guess we'll call our lawyers to draw up a counter offer. What the hell are we going to do when we're unemployed?"

"I have no idea man, but I'm sure we'll think of some sort of business venture."

As we stood, I pointed out, "Well, if we miss the place too much, we could always apply for membership or even a job!"

We laughed as we stood and left the office. Adam pulled out his phone. "Let's see if the girls want some lunch."

And, like that, another chapter in our lives was about to close. It was a chapter filled with love, success, and hope. Adam had fallen in love in this place. I'd healed myself here. It was my home away from home.

Nikola

"HEY, DAD. I just left Mr. Liars's office." I was driving back to our current house. I'd had forgotten the extra key for the realtor, since Mrs. Owens had accepted our offer, and we were listing our current place. May flowers were budding—I loved this time of year.

I heard a door closing loudly over the phone. I imagined he and Mom were at a dinner party. "Good. Did he walk you through the probate process? Do you have any questions?"

I was momentarily stunned. Normally, it felt like Dad was always trying to get me off the phone as quickly as possible.

"Umm—yeah, he's going to take care of it and walk me through anything I need to do. He seems like a pretty nice guy. His name makes me laugh, when paired with his profession." I chuckled, thinking about all the liar lawyer jokes that would swim through my head when Mr. Liars talked.

Dad chuckled, too. "It is quite the pairing. I got your email saying that you were selling your house and had bought a new one. Congratulations. I meant to write you back, but knew you were calling me today."

My dad was actually talking to me, like *really* talking to me. Generally when I sent an email, his secretary responded, conveying words from my father. I grinned like a fool. The noise on the other end of the phone became louder, which probably meant that someone had come in. There was a voice, but it wasn't loud enough for me to hear. Sadly, I knew my time was ending, and my little happy balloon deflated. *At least I got a few minutes.*

Dad's voice was authoritative. "Please, tell Mr. Chow to wait five minutes. I'm speaking to my daughter in America. He should understand, since he was five minutes late from watching his son play soccer. Yes, thank you. I'll be out shortly."

His voice returned to normal as he spoke to me. "Sorry about that. I'll need to go soon, but I wanted to take a second to catch up. Your mother asked if we could all talk tomorrow. We don't have any plans and would love to Skype with you and Brandt, if that sounds good."

This was all surreal. It felt like a dream—I never wanted to wake. "That sounds great, Dad. I'd love that."

"Good. Have you been to your grandmother's house since the funeral?"

My spirits deflated some. I was doing better, but it was still hard. "Thanks for getting everything cleaned out of the fridge. I haven't gone yet. I'm afraid to. I think it's going to be hard. It'll feel like she's going to pop around the corner at any minute and ask me to bake with her or play a hand of Rook."

I blinked rapidly and took in quiet, deep breaths to fight the tide of tears trying to push their way through.

"Nikola, I think you'd find something there that would help you through all this. Nothing will ever replace your Grandmama, but I think this would help. Well, I think you should go find out for yourself. Take Brandt."

Memories from the hospital replayed in my head. How had I forgotten? Grandmama had said that she had something for me at her house. "I'll go with Brandt later when he gets back from the club. He and Adam have decided to sell, and they're going over the paperwork with their lawyer today to submit."

"Good for them. If they need any help, don't hesitate to ask."

My dad was taking an interest in my life. I wanted to scream with excitement. The noise came back into the room. I wasn't sad our time was ending since my parents wanted to talk tomorrow. We normally only talked once a month at best.

"Nikola, I probably need to go, but know I love you. Your mother and I love you. Your mom wanted me to wait, so don't tell her, but we're coming back to America after this year. I'm buying out the rest of my contract."

The dam in my eyes broke as he said those words. Feeling the love from my dad, even after the funeral, felt like we may be changing our comfortable paths we'd become accustomed to.

"You've made my day. I can't wait to tell Brandt. I'll act surprised when Mom tells me. Thanks, Dad. I love you, too. I'll talk to you and Mom tomorrow."

"Can't wait. Night."

"Night."

I pulled into the parking lot to wipe my eyes and decided

to text Brandt.

Me: My dad told me he loves me and wants to talk again tomorrow. They're moving back to America!

Brandt: I'm glad, baby. He's always loved you. Should I come home?

Me: No, I'll be there in an hour or so. Don't cancel the meeting with the lawyer.

Brandt: Perfect. May need to make use of our room before it's gone.

Me: Deal! Also, would you go with me to Grandmama's house later? Dad reminded me that she left something special for me. I remember Grandmama talking about it in the hospital.

Brandt: Of course. We'll go whenever you're ready.

Me: Thanks. Love you!

Brandt: Love you, too.

Brandt helped keep me centered and balanced. I guess we did that for each other in many ways. I started back for the house and my phone rang. It was Gavin.

"This is Nikola."

"Hey, Nikola. This is Gavin. Have I caught you at a bad time?"

The last thing I wanted to do was work, but he was the client. "No, I'm on my way to the house while Brandt handles some business in town. What can I do for you?"

His voice was still smooth as velvet. "I wanted to tell you how sorry I am for your loss. Ainsley updated me."

"Thank you. I appreciate it." I was ready for him to get to the point of the conversation. My emotions were a little raw after talking with my dad, and I wanted some time to process.

The last thing I needed was to cry on the phone with a client.

I heard a vehicle door open and close. "Well, I'm sure you're wondering what the point of my call is about since I'm not a man for idle chat. My girlfriend and I will be in Atlanta for a function tomorrow, and I wondered if maybe you and your husband would be up for lunch. Ainsley and her significant other would be welcome, too."

"Thanks. Let me check with Brandt, and I'll get back to you in a bit. We're meeting in about an hour. Does that work?"

"Perfect. See you soon."

I hung up. Gavin was an odd equation. He seemed personable, but he also seemed fake. I wasn't sure how to categorize him. The meeting with the board wasn't for another three days. However, it seemed normal, with the sum he was paying me, that he'd want to meet eventually, since they might hire us for the other Livingston Cleaning Products. For now, I was going to blame all these weird thoughts on all the stress I'd been under.

I pulled into the driveway, hit the button to open the garage, and got out. The neighborhood was quiet. I stopped right outside the garage when something caught my eye. It was a bird soaring in the sky. For whatever reason, I felt peace as I watched it glide through the air to wherever it was headed. As I was about to start moving again, a sharp pain tore through my body, starting with my head. I tried to stay upright, but my legs became jelly as the world faded from color to gray to black. The last thing I heard were tires screeching and then—

I felt cold.

I saw only black.

I heard nothing.

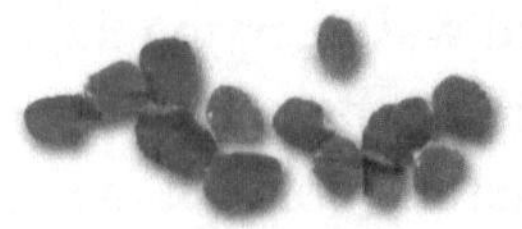

"Why is it taking so long? Is she going to be okay?"

Brandt. He sounded so concerned. My body felt like lead. My veins felt like sludge pumped through them, weighing me down. My eyelids felt taped down.

There was so much sound in the outside world. It hurt my head. I was lying on concrete. *Am I dead?* I felt the wind blow against my arms. *I don't think I'm dead.* I tried to speak, but my muscles wouldn't cooperate.

Fingers touched my jaw. "Sir, your wife is stable. Her heart rate is increasing. How long was she out?"

"I pulled up right as that motherfucker hit her on the back and she went down. That was twenty minutes ago." It was Brandt's voice answering.

"Was there any point at which you noticed that she wasn't breathing?"

I wasn't able to place the person asking the questions.

"No," Brandt said.

My mind loosened, trying to free itself.

Someone spat from the distance: "She's nothing but a teasing whore. I hope she dies."

Where do I know that voice from? It sounds so familiar. Lance. Is that Lance? It sounds like Lance. Why is Lance here? Why is he calling me a teasing whore?

There were sounds of commotion all around me. I couldn't make sense of all the noise, but it sounded like fighting. My heartbeat drummed in my ears as I tried to piece the scene together.

Brandt. I need Brandt. I willed my voice to work.

"Brandt. I need Brandt."

"Sir, your wife is waking," said the voice that had been asking the questions.

Next, I felt familiar hands on my face as my eyes fluttered open. Brandt's concerned, deep-blue eyes were looking down at me. He had a cut on his face. "Baby, you're awake. How do you feel? Thank God you're awake."

I tried to sit, but the world spun as the paramedic spoke. "Mrs. Mattox, let's stay lying down. We want to check you out at the hospital. How do you feel?"

I nodded as I lay back down with Brandt's help.

"My head hurts. What happened? Was that Lance? Were you fighting?"

The paramedic with sunglasses on top of his head had crystal-green eyes, like mine, and messy blond hair. He motioned in the air. I heard wheels rolling on the concrete. I turned my head slightly and saw a gurney being lowered. Part of me wanted to rebel, but my head was still spinning.

Two additional paramedics came into view. On the count of three, they lifted me and we were off to the ambulance. They were all speaking about my condition, but it was fast and hard to process. I wanted answers. They lifted me into the back of the ambulance, the big doors closed, and then we were on our way. The blond paramedic checked my vitals again. The inside of the ambulance smelled like a hospital. There were lots of doors and cabinets, and there wasn't much working room. In a real crisis, I imagined things could get pretty crazy in here. Brandt's eyes searched me over. His shirt had spattered blood on it.

"What happened?"

The paramedics sat back after they finished with me.

Brandt scrubbed his hands down his pants before grabbing my hand. "I was a few minutes behind you. The meeting was canceled, and I wanted to surprise you. I hurried through town to make it to the house before you left. When we were texting, I was already in the car. As I came into the neighborhood, I saw Lance running from his car to you. He hit you on the back of your neck with a bat and you collapsed right as I pulled into the driveway. He ran, and I chased that motherfucker down. The cops came and Lance is in custody."

Brandt trembled as he tried to control his rage. His hair was pushed back. I knew he'd probably beaten Lance's ass. Not knowing how serious it was, I didn't ask any other questions. From the amount of blood spatter, I guessed Lance looked worse.

"Thank you for being there. Are you okay?"

Brandt leaned forward and kissed my hand. "You're okay. That's all that matters. I'm fine. I thought I'd lost you. You're my beginning, end, and everything in between. I will always be there for you. Thank God the lawyer canceled because of his car wreck otherwise I wouldn't have…"

He didn't finish the sentence, and ice shot through my veins. It was a scary thought—how different things could have been. There truly was a domino effect to life, one event altering others in ways we couldn't understand until all the dominos had fallen.

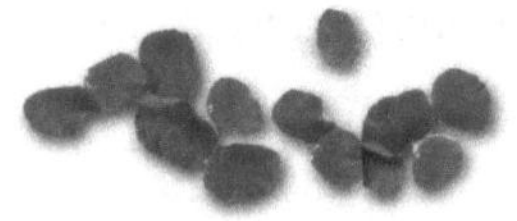

"Are you sure you're up to going to the precinct? We can go another time. I want to take you home and hold you."

I'd been released from the hospital after several hours.

They'd diagnosed me with a mild concussion. My head throbbed, but the aspirin helped. We were almost at the police station. The police had come by and asked us to come to the precinct as soon as possible. Brandt had wanted them to talk to us at the hospital, but it was important that we come down to the station. I'd agreed before Brandt could turn the police down.

The concern and love Brandt had for me was what fairytale ever afters were made of. In the hospital, Brandt had fussed over me, making sure every part of me was okay.

"I promise. I want to get this out of the way. See what options we have. I don't understand why Lance would come into the picture after all this time. I haven't spoken to him at all."

I was still trying to make sense of everything. It had all happened so fast that I wasn't sure how I felt. Part of me felt as though I should be terrified, but the cops had Lance. Brandt was with me. Maybe if I'd been conscious through the ordeal, I'd feel different. But, besides the headache, everything felt the same.

For the millionth time, Brandt asked, "Are you sure you're okay?"

"I am. I promise."

We parked the car and Brandt leaned over the console to rummage in his bag he kept in the back. He came back up with a Thrillhammers T-shirt he used to work out in. He pulled his bloodstained dress shirt over his head after unbuttoning the first couple of buttons. Brandt's tribal tattoos showed on his ripped arms. His abs were flexed as he pulled his tee over his head.

"Do you think they're going to press charges against you for attacking Lance?"

Brandt looked at me. "I don't think so. And if they do,

we'll get the best-damned lawyer there is. I'm not worried."

"Okay." We were both trying to read each other. I cleared my throat. "I don't want you to think I'm hiding my feelings from you. I'm scared for you, and I'm not sure how I feel about what happened to me."

He let out a breath. "I'm still shaken by what I saw today. I don't know why he came, and I want answers."

"Me, too. Thanks for being open with me."

Brandt took my hand, and gave it a kiss. "Let's go inside."

I nodded. We got out of the SUV and headed inside, hand in hand, ready to face whatever was to come our way—together.

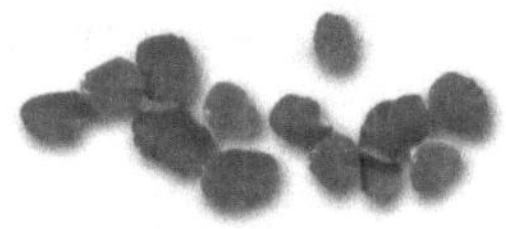

Brandt had given his statement exactly as he had recounted to me. There weren't going to be any charges pressed, which was a huge relief. Afterward, the officer had asked if I could stay and answer some questions. I agreed to, as long as Brandt could be with me. I wasn't sure how I was going to help, since I couldn't remember anything. We were sitting in a conference room with bland, gray walls.

Running a hand through his hair, Brandt squeezed my other hand. "If you start getting tired, let me know."

"I will. I wonder what they want to talk to me about."

The door opened. Brandt sat up and whispered, "We're about to find out."

Two officers entered in their black uniforms. One was a slender female with a tight bun, probably in her late twenties.

The other was a man in excellent shape with a brown crew cut.

"Mrs. Mattox, I'm Officer Denton, and this is Officer Spear. How are you doing?" The man had a deep voice.

I took a sip of my water. "I'm okay. Why did you want to speak with me? I don't remember anything from the attack today."

"We're working on getting a little more information. Do you know a Gavin England?"

Gavin? What does Gavin have to do with this? I tried to make the connection.

"Yes, Gavin England is with Livingston Cleaning Products. He hired me to go through a product line and analyze it to see if there was any way to increase market shares of one of their lines. I spoke with Gavin this morning, and he wanted to know if we could meet him and his girlfriend tomorrow for lunch when he flew into Atlanta. Gavin was to present the overall presentation to the board in three days. I've been paid seventy-five percent of the agreed to amount. The rest was to come next week."

They were writing on their notepads. "What is your association with Lance Thomas?"

The officers weren't answering any questions, and something in the deep recesses of my mind told me that somehow Lance and Gavin were associated.

"We dated for about a month. I broke it off with him. For a while, he kept trying to get a hold of me. We lived in the same apartment complex. He would ask me things about why I hadn't been home lately and how much he missed me. One night, when Brandt I reconnected, Lance texted me. Brandt called him to ask him to leave me alone. I never heard from him again until today." I cleared my throat as they kept writing. "Can you please tell me specifically what is going on?"

The female officer, Officer Spear, looked to Officer Denton. She waited for him to speak. Officer Denton tapped a manila envelope.

"We searched Mr. Thomas's place and we found a shrine to you, Mrs. Mattox. He was obsessed. He planned to abduct you today and take you to a place in the mountains. The details were mapped out in a suitcase we found in his vehicle."

The blood drained from my face. Hearing all this made my stomach hurt. I'd tried to distance myself from what had happened, but this forced me to accept the truth.

Brandt cursed under his breath and said, "What does Gavin have to do with this?"

Officer Denton took another a deep breath. "Gavin England and Lance Thomas are one and the same. Or, at least, the version of Gavin England Mrs. Mattox talked to. We spoke to the real Mr. England today and he'd never heard of your firm. Mr. Thomas purchased voice changing software and pretended he was Mr. England from Livingston Cleaning Products. The emails you received had a hyphen between 'Livingston' and 'Cleaning' and 'Products.' The real Livingston Cleaning Products does not have the hyphen. We also discovered that Mr. Thomas inherited a large sum right after New Year's. This money was how he paid for your services and the other purchases, such as the cabin in the mountains."

"What? Are you sure? So Gavin was a lie all along?" My voice was barely audible as I tried to assimilate the information.

Gavin is Lance. Lance is Gavin. He was going to take me.

Officer Spear spoke. Her voice was calming. "We have all his e-mails and the phone conversations you thought you were having with Mr. England. He taped them. He will remain in custody and we'll work with the prosecutor to see what can be done."

I was in shock. Ainsley and I had both been talking to a predator. Piecing it together, I said, "That's how Lance knew where I'd be today. I talked to Gavin—I mean Lance—on the phone. He told me about flying here tomorrow with his girlfriend. I told him where Brandt was and where I was headed. I can't believe it."

The shock of the situation was still sinking in. *Gavin is Lance. Lance is Gavin.*

"That motherfucker." I looked over at Brandt, and his rage boiled over. His knuckles were white as he gripped the table. "Whatever you need from us. Whoever I need to hire. Let me know. I want this asshole locked up. No plea bargains."

"We'll do everything we can, Mr. Mattox. We'll keep you updated. We needed to verify with Mrs. Mattox, of course, to start the proceedings. We'll be in contact."

The officers stood, and I followed. Brandt wrapped his arm around me, and I felt numb. *What if he gets out? What if he comes for me again? What if he gets me this time?*

Brandt

*M**OTHERFUCKER.* I BROUGHT Nikola to me. Today could have gone much differently. The thought of losing her was unthinkable. I couldn't imagine being without her. She was my life. The pale yellow, aged walls of the precinct hallways felt like a prison closing in on me. Lance was in this building, and I needed to get Nikola out. I needed fresh air. I wrapped my hand around her waist and fought the urge to hold her too tightly.

This whole situation with Lance was one of my worst nightmares. We cleared the doors and walked up to our car's passenger door. The fresh air helped settle me—slightly. Taking slow, deep breaths, I tried to calm myself.

Nikola went for the door handle. Her hands were shaking. I wasn't able to let go of her yet. "Can I hold you for a second longer?"

She turned, and I saw that she was chewing on her cheek. I knew she was upset—we needed a few minutes to ourselves. There was anxiousness and fear in her eyes. Nikola nodded and buried her face in my chest. She sniffled, and I held her tighter to me.

Her voice was muffled. "Brandt, if you hadn't come…I just…I don't…what would have happened to me?"

I tried to soothe her, even though my imagination ran wild with all the alternate scenarios running through my head.

Rubbing her back, I tried to be reassuring. "Baby, he didn't get you. Let's not focus on what might have happened. We'll drive ourselves crazy. You're safe."

Sniffling, she said, "I know. I'm trying. But I've been talking to a predator this whole time. I let him in my life. I never called the headquarters main line. I researched him online and everything. It seemed legit, especially with the contracts I received. Gavin, I mean Lance, always said it was best to reach him by his cell. I'm so stupid."

"There's no way you could have known. There's no way. You're okay and in my arms and that's all that matters."

I tried to follow my advice, but I was failing miserably. We needed a distraction, something to take our mind off the foul thoughts that were only going to fray our nerves. Holding on to my other half, I remembered her wanting visit Anne's home.

"What would you think about going to Anne's to see what's there? It might be the perfect thing for us."

Nikola pulled back. Her emerald eyes were bloodshot. "I'd like that a lot. Can we go now? I don't want to stay here a second longer."

I put my hands on either side of her face and leaned down

to taste her sweet lips, needing to feel a connection with her. The kiss was gentle and soft. Extending the moment, I left my lips pressed to hers while saying a prayer of thanks that I still had Nikola. Pulling back slightly, I said, "Let's go."

We got in the car and held hands as we drove to Anne's house. The majority of the trip was quiet and reflective as I rubbed Nikola's thumb with mine. At some point, I hoped life would give us a break. Lately, it seemed to be throwing a hefty deck our way. The comforting part of all this was that I had no thoughts of using. I embraced the emotions, not letting them overtake me. I still visited the airport from time to time, to see the planes taking off and to gather my thoughts when life felt like it spun too fast. I wanted to go there now, but I wouldn't. For now, I'd settle for calling Quentin later. There was no way I'd leave Nikola's side after this.

We were getting close to Anne's place when Nikola said, "Do you have any idea what Grandmama left us?"

"No, I don't. I wouldn't keep that from you."

We pulled into the driveway. The house seemed lifeless, but the memories would linger. I looked at the sidewalk and thought about New Year's Day, when I'd come after Nikola, to fight for her, to fight for us. Thinking about our battles, I knew we'd won. We'd never given up.

I looked over, and Nikola smiled. "There are so many good memories here. So much happiness. I hope I leave a legacy like this someday."

"Me, too."

It was strange to think that one day our kids would be doing the same thing that we were. *Someday.* I stared at the empty house as I reflected on this.

Nikola rubbed my hand. "Are you ready to go inside?"

I'd expected Nikola to need some time before she went

into the house again. She answered my internal question before I had a chance to respond.

"I thought I would be sad when I came back, but seeing this place brings back happy memories. Though my time with Grandmama was shorter than I would have liked, we still had so many years compared to some. I'm grateful for what I was blessed with."

We opened our car doors and met at the front of the vehicle. Hand in hand, we walked to the front door. Unlocking the door, Nikola stepped inside, taking a deep breath. Everything was as it had been. I had no idea where the gift would be, but Nikola turned right and headed down the hallway.

"Where are you going?"

"To the sewing room."

The sewing room had always been a place for Nikola and Anne to sit and talk. Standing in the doorway, I could imagine Anne at the table as she worked her sewing machine, the quiet hum of the needle as it plunged up and down a million times. There was a box on the bed. Nikola ran her hands along the edge. Next, she pulled off the lid. There was a pale pink envelope on top. She was beautiful as she wiped a quick tear away.

I stayed at the door, giving Nikola this moment. If she needed me, I'd be there.

Nikola opened the envelope carefully, unfolded the letter, and read aloud.

"My dearest Nikola, This is the only way I could think of to be there for you through all the years and different stages of life. Once I found out I had cancer, I made videos of different things. There's sewing videos to teach you and my future great-grandkids how to sew, baking videos for us to bake some of our favorite dishes together, some arts and craft projects, videos of advice and many more. There are also things I've learned in life that you may face someday. There are over one hundred and fifty DVD's in here. I know your first urge is going to be to watch them all, but wait, if you can. That way it'll be like I'm there seeing all those wonderful things with you and Brandt as you go through life. I love you, Nikola, with my entire heart. There's a video in there for you to watch today with Brandt. I hope it helps, even though it's short. I hope I'm able to give this to you in person, but I wanted to write this note, just in case. I feel deep down that my time is coming. Hopefully, I'm wrong. Live your life to the fullest and love with your whole heart. Until the next sunrise or sunset, Grandmama."

I was touched as I sat next to Nikola on the daybed. She leaned into me. "Brandt, the letter is dated the night she went into the hospital. I miss her."

Life was unyielding at times.

Anne had done the only thing that could make this loss a little bearable. I looked down at the familiar writing as Nikola continued to re-read it. "Now you have a piece of her. She'll be with you through our whole life. Do you want to watch the video she left us now?"

"Yes, let me find it." Nikola looked at the DVD's and laughed. "She made one for when our kids go to college. It's comforting to know I'll have pieces of her for that far ahead." She continued to look through the DVD's. "Found it."

Nikola was off the bed and sprinting to the living room. I jogged after her. Grabbing the remotes, Nikola turned everything on. After everything was set, we sat on the blue leather sofa.

She smiled big as she looked my way. "Are you ready?"

"I am."

Nikola pressed play, and Anne appeared on the screen.

She wore what she'd been wearing that night of the last Rook game—jeans and a pink button-up shirt. She sat at the bar in the kitchen. "Hey, Nikola and Brandt. You guys just left after playing Rook. Brandt, honey, she whipped you good. I love watching you guys bet and play with each other. The love I see reminds me of what I had with Nikola's grandfather." Anne paused and laughed before taking a big, tired sigh. She didn't look like she felt well—she seemed exhausted. "Well, if you're watching this, then I've passed. Remember, this isn't goodbye. I refuse to think so. We're going to have so many adventures over the years. Remember to live your life to the fullest. Don't focus on what could have been, but what you have. Until we see each other again. I love you both more than you'll ever know."

She smiled lovingly and blew a kiss before picking up the remote control and turning off the camera. The screen went black. We sat in silence until Nikola spoke.

"That was perfect, and it came at the perfect time. She always knew what to say."

"Yes, she did."

I was going to try to take Anne's advice and not focus too much on what could have happened today. I'd focus on what we had—love and each other.

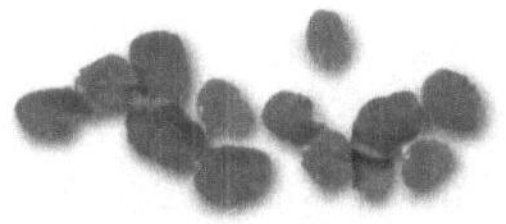

One Week Later

WE WERE AT Club Envy. The agreement had been signed last night and the sale of the club was announced today. When we'd sent a counter offer, the terms had been accepted and the sale was fast-tracked. There was never a doubt that we were doing the right thing for the club—and for us. There was still no update on Lance, and it was hard to let Nikola out of my sight, but I tried. I texted her regularly when we weren't together. Hopefully, the police would have news soon. They were still putting the case together. At least bail had been denied.

Tonight was our last night as the owners of Club Envy. It was bittersweet as I looked around the bar. All the people that had been there for us were here, and we were a family. I knew this was the path Adam and I were meant to be on, but leaving this chapter of my life was hard.

Adam and I still didn't have any idea what we were going to do at this point. We were contracted to help with the club for thirty days as the new management came in and learned the ropes. Ironically, tonight was the last night The Thrillhammers were playing before they went on the road. The place was in full swing as Adam and I leaned against the bar and took it in.

Adam took a swig of Guinness. "I'd say that, for two college dropouts, we didn't do too badly."

I tapped my bottle of water to Adam's beer. "I'd have to agree. Who would've thought that what started as a last ditch effort to make something of ourselves would have turned into this?"

The Thrillhammers took the stage and the crowd went wild. Nikola, Ainsley, and Nora were all a few feet in front of us, jumping. My girl had on tight leather pants and a green silk shirt that was begging to be removed. I couldn't wait to sink myself into her later. I was taking her back to our room for one last night at the club. Adam and Ainsley had been talking about staying in their room, too. In the final sale of the club,

Adam had negotiated for him to take the furniture from the bedroom off of his office. The movers were showing up in the morning. I didn't want to know where Adam and Ainsley were going to put it. Nikola and I had decided we didn't want anything from our room. We were starting fresh in this new chapter of life in all respects.

The Thrillhammers were about to start the show, and I wanted to give my present to Adam before they played. Payback was a bitch, and all the aggravating he had done while I had my Blue Balls Timer was going bite him in the ass. Nora had finally confessed that Adam had purchased those blue cattle balls for her to torment me with. Apparently, he'd bought more than twenty of those damn things to replace the ones I threw away.

Adam turned to order another beer. I leaned forward and tapped Nikola on the shoulder. "I'm about to give Adam my present."

She winked then turned to get Ainsley and Nora's attention, too. Jude, Nora's boyfriend, who was leaving in less than a week for Australia, came up and put his arms around Nora's waist. Nikola had filled me in on his dad's illness. At least Nora had agreed to give it a try.

"Hey, Jude." Jude had black hair and a lip ring. He and Nora fit together.

"Hey, mate. Sorry I'm late. The boys at work wanted to get a drink. Now, I'm done and get to be with my gal." He squeezed Nora and gave her a kiss on the neck.

She glowed with affection, leaning into him. Adam and I had approved for Nora to be off for the next week, paid, prior to selling the club. We didn't want to risk them rejecting her request.

Adam turned back around with his beer in hand as he said

hey to Jude. Nikola handed me the flat, square package from her purse.

Feeling the pre-victory of getting Adam good, I held up the wrapped gift and said, "I got you a little something as a thank you for always being there for me. I hope you're able to use this a lot while we're unemployed and looking for our next adventure."

I handed him the package, and Adam looked a little flustered. "Shit, I didn't know we were doing a gift thing. Hell, I would've gotten something for you, too, Brandt, even if it makes me feel like a pussy." Adam looked a little embarrassed, but we laughed.

Slapping him on the shoulder, I said, "Doesn't matter. It's nothing big. I didn't want you getting bored."

He chuckled. Everyone watched Adam as he unwrapped the gift. Nikola looked down with her lips mashed together. She and I avoided direct eye contact. The two of us couldn't stop laughing every time we thought about what I'd gotten him.

Adam threw the paper on the floor and turned it over. His eyes shot to mine. "You motherfucker."

I laughed and Nikola did, too. Nora plucked it from his hands and then bent over in hysterics.

Nora gasped for air. "Brandt, you're a genius. Now he can practice all his Prince Lir parts from *The Last Unicorn* for when he watches it with my sister."

She held up *The Last Unicorn* CD I'd bought when Adam had been giving me shit months ago. When Nikola packed, she'd found it in a drawer.

Ainsley, ever so sweetly, walked up to Adam. "We can have sing-alongs in the car when Emilyn rides with us now. She's going to be so excited!"

Adam brought Ainsley into a hug and shot daggers at me. "You're an asshole. You've caused me months of humiliation."

I glanced at Ainsley, and she shook with giggles. Deciding to lay it on thick, I used the name Ainsley had given him. "You're going to do great, manfriend."

Everyone laughed, even Adam. "I'm going to get you back. We're neighbors now."

"Bring it."

"Oh, I will."

Ainsley stood on her toes and said, "You're one sexy manfriend."

"Thanks, baby."

He gave her a kiss as I brought Nikola close.

Chris spoke over the microphone as the rest of the band waved to the crowd. Everyone turned toward the stage. "So as you know, we're going on tour and this will be our last night at Club Envy." Cheers erupted. "We've got a hell of a show planned, but first I wanted to thank Adam Ryker and Brandt Mattox for all the support they've shown The Thrillhammers. And, of course, we appreciate our fans, you guys have helped make our dreams into reality. We couldn't have done it without you." More cheers. "So let's get this party started!"

The Thrillhammers played one of my favorites, "Highway 369", and the crowd pushed forward. Nikola leaned into me as I absorbed it for the last time. Everyone moved and cheered, and I hoped this moment would be burned into my head forever as the band sang.

I'd been sitting in that barn since Nineteen fifty-three
Growing iron oxide like an acorn grows a tree
Never tasted blacktop, red dirt dust is all I breathed

Peering from the darkness you'd be surprised,
Just what I've seen

Well the man who held my title
From the Cadillac company
When they stole his right-of-way, he refused the D.O.T.
Vowed he'd never utilize that god-forsaken ground
The sacred wheels of progress
Might shut my motor down

Seems like just yesterday
I was rolling off the line
Now the dust hides the rust
And the paint that used to shine
Looking out through headlights
Frozen here in time
While I watch the world fly by on Highway 369

I was born in thirty-nine
A few years before the war
Dusty road to town amends,
Then right back to the store

Heard him cuss, raise a fuss
When they started laying tar
Once they'd paved that highway,
He parked me in the barn

He died in eighty-two alone
And nobody found a will
Guess they could look some more,
But they'd be looking still

Came before the auctioneer,
He brought that hammer down
Imagine that ten gallon hat said,
"Son you're Texas bound"

Hauled me out I-40, on a flatbed in a tarp
Pulled me off, shined me up
And got me lookin' sharp
They dug a hole, and bless my soul
My nose went in the sand
Sheltered from the world I lived,
But now I see firsthand

Seems like just yesterday
I was rolling off the line
Now the dust hides the rust
And the paint that used to shine
Looking out through headlights
Frozen here in time
While I watch the world fly by on Highway 369

The song ended and The Thrillhammers kept playing. They rocked the house, and I loved every second of it as I held the girl of my dreams, my wife, in my arms. This was our night. This was Club Envy's night.

Nikola

THE SUN BAKED my skin as I laid on a chaise longue in the Caribbean. It had been a month since our last night at Club Envy. My eyes were closed as I listened to the soft ocean waves. We were waiting for Ainsley and Adam, along with their family, to arrive this evening for their wedding two days from now. My hair was thrown on top of my head. It had been a crazy few months, and now it was time to relax. With Brandt's obligation to the club over and my decision to reduce my hours for the summer, we'd come down to Nassau in the Bahamas early to enjoy sometime to ourselves.

We were staying at an adults-only resort. The resort was fairly empty, which made us feel like we were on an island all to ourselves. Yesterday, I'd firmed everything up with Ainsley's wedding coordinator. This way, when she and Adam arrived, there wasn't anything for them to do other than enjoy themselves and get married. Only Adam's parents, Ainsley's mother, and Nora were coming down to join us. Adam's brother wasn't invited, due to their history. His sister, Jessica, was in Asia on a six-month internship. She'd offered to come, but Adam said he would send videos and pictures. The internship was a big deal, and he didn't want her to miss out on anything. I think it was good that she'd left. Jessica had always tried to fix problems with the family. Hopefully now she'd be able to find her own way in life.

The day after the wedding, everyone was heading home to give Ainsley and Adam privacy. The newlyweds were going to stay down here for an additional week.

Right before we had left the States, I'd received a phone call from our lawyer who assisted in the prosecution of Lance. During the night, Lance had hung himself in his cell. He'd attacked a female officer the day before, thinking it was me. The next morning, he was dead. No note. No explanation. We'd never know what truly happened to make him snap. It was a double-edged sword, thinking about someone's life ending, but I'd be lying if I said I didn't sleep better knowing Lance wouldn't ever come after me again.

Cold drops landed on my stomach, making it draw in. A smile graced my lips. Brandt had gone to the room to get sunscreen. "Hey there! I was beginning to wonder if you were lost."

"I've been watching my beautiful wife for a bit."

I loved the sound of his sex-riddled voice. It did things to me, even though we'd barely come up for air while we had been here.

Each couple could reserve a private space at the resort on the beach. Because we were staying in one of the suites, we'd automatically reserved one for the week. The structure was similar to a cabana—the back and two sidewalls were solid material that had a few slits in them to allow air circulation. The front wall had a curtain that could be drawn with your choice of sheer or solid material. The top was open.

"Do you like what you see?" I asked, keeping my eyes closed.

His warm voice purred close to me. "I do, but I don't want you getting burned. I've got more sunscreen for you."

"What about you?" I could hear the cap opening, then the squirting of liquid.

"I put on more up in the room."

I pouted. He chuckled. "Well, you can put some on me after I finish."

I grinned at his words.

"Feels fantastic. I think I could go to sleep," I said.

"Roll over and I'll get your back first."

I did as he asked, and Brandt came to straddle my ass without putting much weight on me. I felt him untie the tiny strings to my black bikini. His strong hands worked my back like magic as they added sunscreen. I was on the verge of dozing when his finger brushed the side of my breast and my body sprung to life. As the sunscreen was evenly spread, his fingers grazed a little farther twice more, coming within inches of my nipple. I squirmed as the need begin to build in my core.

"Flip over. Keep your eyes closed."

Brandt moved to the side, and I turned back over. I felt a pull on the side of my bikini bottoms. I liked where this was going. Brandt lifted my legs and sat on the lounge chair. He lowered my legs, scooting forward, draping a leg on each side of his hip. I could feel he was naked as his erection touched my entrance. I squirmed.

"Brandt…"

"We need to finish getting your sunscreen on."

He rubbed my lower abdomen and worked his way up to my belly button. My stomach did a flip as he caressed it. I relaxed and gave in to the pleasurable torture. When Brandt's hands reached the bottom of my breasts, he pushed into me unexpectedly and my eyes shot open.

Brandt's blue eyes burned with passion as he slid in farther. His fingers made it to my nipples, and my back arched. I could feel Brandt inside me. The thick ridge brushed against my walls. Moving his hands to my back, Brandt brought me into a sitting position, straddling him. The penetration was deeper; the pleasure was more intense.

My feet rested at the sides of the lounge chair. Brandt's mouth captured mine as I pushed off and slammed back down. We swallowed each other's cries of pleasure as we rode ourselves to ecstasy, knowing anyone walking by would hear us in the thralls of passion. My body warmed as the sensations worked their way through every inch of me.

Brandt nipped my lip as he fell back and I collapsed on top of him. We were both breathless. "I don't think I'll ever tire of being inside you, baby."

I kissed his chest. "I'll never tire of having you inside me. I love being yours."

"You'll always be mine."

The waves lulled us into a peaceful slumber.

We were sitting on a long pier as the sun set in the Caribbean. I loved sunsets. All the men were in khakis and cream linen shirts. Nora, Adam's mom, Ainsley's mom, and I all wore pale-lilac dresses in different styles. The groom and the bride stood under a trellis filled with light purple and white flowers. The scent of the flowers was heavenly when the wind changed directions and blew our way for a moment. Ainsley was in a simple white shift dress that waved gently in the Caribbean wind. Ainsley had a purple flower tucked behind her ear as she looked up at Adam. The bride and groom couldn't stop looking at each other as pure joy radiated from everyone in the group. This was love—I knew, because I had it.

The preacher announced, "You may now kiss your bride."

Adam bent down and took Ainsley's face in his hands and gave her a kiss.

As they sealed their vows, Brandt leaned in and whispered, "You're my forever."

I glanced at Brandt. "And you're mine."

We stood and gathered around the happy couple. Adam held Ainsley close to him.

Brandt went up and slapped him on the back. "Congrats, man. I'm happy for you."

"Thanks, man. Who would've thought a year ago we'd both be with the women we loved, happily married, *and* have sold the club." Adam shook his head as if he was lost in all the memories.

Brandt brought me to him as the coordinator walked up and discreetly said, "I have the cake and champagne set up, per your instruction, for whenever you're ready."

Ainsley and I both laughed. The coordinator had been given explicit instructions to keep the reception as short as possible. Adam and Ainsley were having a reception back home, so Adam had requested that this one last five minutes or less to get to the—as he put it—a-fan-fucking-tastic honeymoon. Ainsley had agreed, and now they were headed to the simple cake table.

Feeding each other cake, the couple interlocked their arms and sipped from each other's glasses. We clapped as they finished. This was what dreams were made of. Part of me hurt that Wesley wouldn't get his happily ever after, but he would heal and find himself again. Last week, he'd put his house up for sale to take a job in Florida. He told me he needed a fresh start. I'd miss him, but I understood. Things would be okay.

Adam cleared his throat. "Thank you everyone for coming. We've loved spending the last couple of days with you. Ainsley and I are fortunate to have such good friends, but now it's time for the honeymoon."

Ainsley playfully slapped him on the chest and everyone laughed. Adam gave her an innocent look and shrugged as if he couldn't help it. Earlier, I'd heard the coordinator tell Adam she'd found a Tantra Chair to add to the honeymoon suite. Brandt had high-fived Adam while Ainsley and I rolled our eyes. Thank goodness, the parents hadn't overheard that part of the conversation.

Adam picked Ainsley up, cradling her in his arms, and strolled off toward the resort. Everyone cheered. Ainsley looked back and waved happily swinging her feet.

Nora walked up to me and said, "Hey, I'm going to Skype with Jude. It's been hard to connect the last couple of weeks, so wish me luck."

"Sounds good. How's his dad?"

Nora had gone with solid black hair for Ainsley's wedding. She looked down. "No change. His dad talked him into learning the family business while he's sick. I don't know what to make of it. I miss him, and he misses me. Somehow we'll figure it out."

I gave her a hug. "Don't give up hope."

"I won't." Nora looked at her watch. "I should go."

Making a shooing motion, I said, "Go. Good luck."

She waved as she ran. "Thanks."

I said a silent prayer that they'd find their way back to each other. Knowing what it was like to be away from Brandt had me hoping that Nora would never know that pain.

Brandt brought me to him, and we walked out to the end of the pier. "What are you thinking about, baby?" he asked.

"How happy I am. How lucky we are. How one little misstep could have left us on totally different paths that didn't include each other."

Brandt held me as the sun disappeared behind the horizon. His blond hair was blowing as he stared out. "I never imagined I'd be this happy again, or that what we had could be topped if we were ever fortunate enough to find our way back to each other. But what we have now is more than I ever imagined. Being right here, right now, in this moment, makes all the pain worth it. All the tribulations we faced made us stronger. I love you, Nikola Mattox. You're it for me."

"I love you, too, Brandt Mattox. You're my everything."

So much had happened over the last year. I'd experienced heartache, loss, despair, joy, love, and happiness in all forms.

One small movement can impact the rest of your life, like a set of dominoes lined up one after another. It's only when you step back and see the big picture that you realize the damage you've done—it's in that moment that you can you right your course and return to the path you were meant to be on all along.

Brandt

THREE YEARS HAD passed since I'd married the woman of my dreams. I sat back in my office on a call with Adam. We'd hung up with a potential new client a few minutes ago, and now we were recapping everything needed to be done to secure the account. A couple of months after selling Club Envy, Adam and I were going stir crazy, so we started on a new adventure together—a security company. With all the practice we had at the club, monitoring and tracking, we could put together effective systems and sell them for a hell of a profit. Clubs were our largest clientele base. In three short years, the security business we'd started had become more profitable than Club Envy had been.

Club Envy was still going strong and had grown to ten clubs in ten different states in the last three years. None of us had been back since our last day there. I wanted to remember the club as it was when we owned it. That would always be Club Envy to me.

"Okay, Brandt. You have the notes. We can start on this next week. Ainsley wanted to know if you guys were still coming over at five." Adam's voice on the phone broke me from my thoughts.

I looked at my clock. It was three-thirty on a Saturday afternoon. "Yeah, we'll be there. How's Ainsley feeling? Nikola wanted you to know we could do it here if Ainsley is too tired."

Adam blew out a breath. "She's good, but I'm a fucking wreck, waiting for our baby boy to get here. She said Nikola had threatened to take away her laptop if she didn't stop working."

Ainsley was due with their first child any day now; Adam was beside himself with happiness. Nikola and Ainsley had become business partners about two years ago, after Ainsley had put in a year as an employee, seeing if this was the career she wanted. They were constantly turning away clients due to workload, but, for now, they wanted to keep it the two of them so they wouldn't have to manage employees. Maybe someday they'd expand, but the girls liked being in total control for now as well as being able to keep lighter schedules.

"You'll be fine. Adam, you're going to be a great dad. Did you get my package that arrived yesterday?"

"You're an asshole." I laughed a good hearty laugh. I'd found a T-shirt place that did custom orders. I'd sent Adam a T-shirt that said, *I pretend to be Prince Lir.* He was never going to live down singing the songs from *The Last Unicorn.*

I shut off my computer as I heard some stirring in the front of the house. "I know deep down you love it. You don't have to hide your excitement around me."

"I'm calling your wife next week to get dirt on you. Just wait."

Ainsley's voice came through the other line.

"I'm on my way, baby. I'll get it." Adam turned his attention back to me. "I've got to go help Ainsley. I'd sleep with one eye open if I was you."

"See ya in a bit. I'll be waiting for my payback."

Adam cursed as he hung up the phone. Pulling out my new T-shirt I'd ordered, I smiled. It was a surprise for Nikola. I walked toward the living room, where I could hear Nikola talking. Our home was full of pictures and warmth. Nikola and I had built a home that would have laughter and love reverberating through the walls—always.

I came to the doorway and watched Nikola speaking to our little girl, Anne. She was over a year old and looked so much like my love. When we'd found out we were having a little girl, we said the name at the same time. This morning, Anne had been with Nikola's parents. They'd moved back from Asia as planned. Since then, they'd been an active part of our lives. We had my family and Nikola's over often. Nikola loved that our little girl was surrounded by so much love.

Everything was as it should be.

Nikola talked to our daughter. "What book do we want to read after naptime today? Do you want to do *The Very Hungry Caterpillar*? You slept so hard. Did you have fun with Grandma and Grandpa today?"

Almost every day after naptime, Nikola and I would have story time with Anne. Her little pudgy arms waved in excitement as she squealed in delight, hearing her mom talk to her.

Nikola saw me, and her eyes shined as she spoke to Anne. "Hey there, your daddy's done working."

Anne looked my way and flailed her arms as she made spit bubbles in excitement. Her pink bib was already wet from all the drool she had produced since waking. I never understood how something so small could create so much mess. I loved her. Anne lit up my life in a way I never dreamed.

"Hey there, baby girl. Daddy missed you. Did you have good dreams?" I cooed.

I took Anne in my arms and kissed her cheek. I loved her baby smell. Anne slobbered on my chin as she tried to kiss me back.

Nikola laughed. "Oh my gosh, is that a shirt from the online store you found? The one you ordered Adam's from?" I grinned as she read what my shirt said out loud. "The Magic 8 Ball Loves Me." Nikola sat on the brown leather couch and said, "You have definitely come to the dark side."

Wiggling my eyebrows, I sat while she picked up the remote and whispered in her ear, "I think we should wager on a striptease again."

She kissed me. "Deal. After bedtime, prepare to face that blue triangle of truth."

Please, Magic 8 Ball, be my friend again. You've been there for me, buddy. I've got your back.

Anne made an impatient noise as she looked at the television. She knew what was coming. Nikola pressed a button on the remote control. Grandmama came on the screen. Grandmama had recorded several stories for every age on the videos she'd done prior to her passing. Seeing the familiar kitchen brought back so many memories. After we'd returned from the Caribbean, Nikola had decided to donate the house for Quentin to use for his work as a sponsor and as a halfway house. Grandmama would have been pleased that her home was being used to help people get their lives on track. I still met with

Quentin, but I knew I'd never use again, no matter what life threw my way. There was too much at stake to ever even think about going back to drugs.

Grandmama's familiar voice came on the television. She wore a white sweater, and her blonde hair was perfectly done. "Hey, little one, is it story time? What should we read today?" There was a pile of books on the counter that Grandmama sifted through before picking up the white cardboard book with the green caterpillar on it. Our daughter moved her limbs about excitedly when she saw the book on the screen while in my lap. Grandmama continued. "This is one of my favorites by Eric Carle. Let's see how hungry the caterpillar is. Are you ready?"

I glanced at Nikola, and she gave me a brilliant smile. I positioned our little girl half on my leg and half on Nikola's. Nikola leaned her head on me and let out a contented sigh. "This is everything I've ever wanted in life."

I kissed the top of her head. "This is everything I dared to hope for. I love you."

"I love you, too."

Everything in this room was my life.

My world.

My everything.

A Special Note to the Readers

CANCER IS A terrible disease that has affected so many lives. The never-ending effects of this disease are cruel and unyielding. My heart, thoughts, and prayers go out to anyone that has ever had to deal with cancer in any form

I lost my Grandmama and Grandaddy to lung cancer. There isn't a day that goes by that I don't think about them.

One day, I hope there is a cure. That is my dream.

Enjoy an excerpt from

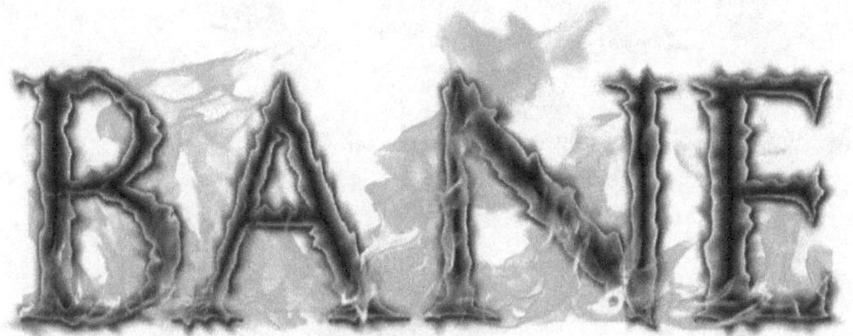

Stand alone Novel

CHAPTER 1

BANE

Six Years Ago

I WAS DONE. Finished. Out.

For the past seven years, I belonged to a division of the government that wasn't on the books. I operated alone. There was a mission: I either failed or succeeded. If I failed, that meant I was dead.

After all the shit I'd seen, done, caused—I had survived. It was a fucking miracle.

I was the best at what I did, but there were times I saw my life flash before my eyes. But when you're the government's covert assassin, what else was there to expect. If I was captured, I didn't exist. If I died, I didn't exist. If I succeeded, I was assigned my next mission.

The plane wheels screeched as I touched down in Alaska.

Finally, I was where I wanted to be.

At times, I wasn't sure I knew who I was anymore. My identity was erased from the system long ago. For the last three months, I'd been working on getting released from the program. It was a slow process with how deep I was in with Black Division.

Those suits knew I wouldn't share anything I'd done. Hell, half the time I wanted to forget. After three months of debriefing, the government let me out. Of course, there was an underlying threat.

If we so much as suspect you've betrayed this country, consider yourself dead, Mr. Bradley.

Yeah, nothing else was new. I wasn't an idiot. I knew I'd be monitored for years to come, but they wouldn't find anything.

In all the dark bullshit that swirled around me, there was one person who kept me grounded over the last two years … Jasmine. She saved my soul before it would have been lost completely to the animal beckoning to take over within me. Finally, I was going to spend the rest of my life with her.

The cabin of the plane dinged and the pilot came on to thank us for flying. Who the fuck cared? All the passengers wanted the same thing—to get off. The only thing I wanted was to see my girl.

Jasmine, the love of my life, waited for me at the front of the airport. I carried only a duffel bag. That was all I'd wanted from my previous life. Everything else I set fire to and tried to forget it. There was nothing good about my past besides her.

The last time I'd seen Jasmine had been a little over six months ago on my last furlough. I always flew her to different places to meet to maximize our time together, but the last time, I'd come here and fell in love with Alaska. Yeah, the winters were shitty, but it was isolated and away from the fuckedupness in the world. There was a true peace. Maybe I'd heal enough to be worthy of Jasmine.

Jasmine knew me as Bane Bradley. On the fly, I'd used it when we met at a local bar two years ago in New York. It stuck. And now, it would be my name for the rest of my life. I liked it.

The government hadn't even known about that name. All the names of my previous identities blended together, morphing into one. My mother called me *bastard* my entire childhood. That name was also fitting for the shit I'd done. Sometimes a person became a product of where they came from.

The cold air hit my face, and I debarked from the plane at the small airport. It was almost time to see my girl—Jasmine.

I was here. I was home. *Home.* The word lightened the load as I practically sprinted to the front of the airport. Over the phone yesterday, Jasmine said she had some news for me. Her voice shook minutely, which meant she was nervous. When I'd asked, *do you still want me to come?* The resounding *yes* was all I needed. We'd make it through anything else.

Until yesterday, when I'd been released, we hadn't talked since I'd last visited. But the moment I heard her sweet voice on the end of the line, I knew she still loved me. Jasmine knew I worked for a secret agency, although she thought about it more along the lines of James Bond type shit.

Nothing was further from the truth.

But, it kept her from asking questions and that was all that mattered, which, in turn kept Jasmine safe. As of that moment, all the other shit was in the past and didn't matter.

A secret smile formed as I thought what I had planned for us. Getting somewhere private was priority—another reason I insisted on Jasmine picking me up at the front versus coming in.

Outside the airport sat the love of my life in her old, tan four-wheel-drive SUV. Another bitter gust of wind hit me, but I made it to the vehicle in record time. As soon as I got in, her subtle vanilla scent greeted me. Oh how I missed that smell.

Jasmine leaned over. Our lips touched as she whispered against mine. "Hey, baby."

All the countless lie detector tests, questioning, and de-briefing were worth it in that moment. First, I had to taste her. As I cupped her face, her soft skin was a soothing balm against my callous palms.

Her lips formed to mine. My tongue sought entry in her mouth, and she opened to me, intensifying the kiss. That sweet little moan had my cock as hard as a rock. We needed to get out of here before I took her in the parking lot. As soon as we got somewhere, I was sinking deep within her—for hours on end.

A car honked behind us. Jasmine giggled and whispered against my lips, "Are you ready to go home?"

"Yeah, baby. Take me home."

Home. There was that word again.

I'd never had a home. Ever. There was no way the shithole I'd grown up in could be considered a home. As soon as I turned eighteen, I enlisted in the marines. Within two years, I was recruited to the Black Division. Life expectancy in the program was three years. I'd lasted seven fucking long years.

As Jasmine drove, I couldn't take my eyes off her honey-blonde hair and dark-chestnut eyes. She had a body made for worshiping that was hidden underneath her oversized thick coat. I was never going to have to let her go.

Glancing my way, she asked with a knowing smile,

"What are you looking at?"

"You. It's always you. I'm sorry it took me so fucking long to get home to you."

Her hand came out and held mine. "You made it. That's all that matters. And, you're here for good?"

"I am." A tinge of guilt raced through me. There had been several times through the last two years where I'd stood her up because I was on a mission in some hellhole. It was a miracle she'd stayed with me through it all.

While we were apart, I called as often as I could, but sometimes it was weeks before she heard from me. I craved to hear her voice like an addiction. Honestly, it was a miracle I got to date her. When you signed up to be an operative, there were no ties to the world. However, I'd disclosed our relationship as soon as it became one. After intensive monitoring and background checks, Black Division was satisfied and gave me the all clear to continue the relationship.

Driving to the small apartment complex in town, Jasmine parked. I'd only been here once, but with my photographic memory, I knew where we were. Jogging to Jasmine's side of the truck, I grabbed the keys out of the ignition and cradled her in my arms. The squeal of delight rang through me. I spun us around, earning peals of laughter. I had my girl in my arms, and I was going to spend the rest of my life cherishing her.

As we walked to the door, I kissed her slow. With my right hand, I managed to unlock the door while never taking my mouth from hers. I needed to know this was real and not a dream. Over the last year, I'd dreamed of being with Jasmine and having a child. Time would give me both.

I wanted it all—the white fence, the wife, the kids … everything. And for the first time in my life, I believed I deserved it.

The door closed with a loud thud as I kicked it. The atmosphere intensified as I plunged deeper into her mouth. A small moan of acceptance came from Jasmine as she held me firmly to her.

The next stop was the bedroom.

"Bane—"

Cutting her off, I murmured, "Later."

If she pushed me away, I'd stop. But right now, I needed her to know this wasn't a dream. Jasmine was here and pliant in my arms. It was tempting to fuck her hard in the living room, but the first time home, I was going to make love to her. Savor her. Adore her.

Sitting her down, I pushed the coat off her shoulders. Jasmine grabbed the hem of my shirt and together we took it off. A finger trailed down my abdomen eliciting a shiver.

"I missed this. I missed you." Jasmine's words fueled me as I reclaimed her mouth.

My cock ached to sink into that perfect pussy of hers. Going to her stomach to take off her shirt, I touched the soft skin. Jasmine's abdomen wasn't flat but had a bump to it. I took a step back. My eyes shot to hers.

Was she?

Both of her hands came up and caressed her stomach. "I wanted to talk to you first before we had sex. But then, we got in the moment." A beautiful flush crept on her cheeks. "Bane, I'm pregnant."

I nearly staggered back. Jasmine was pregnant. My girl was pregnant. With a baby. We hadn't been together for almost six months. Fuck, I wasn't sure how this worked. The baby had to be mine. Our baby.

She took a step closer. "Bane, it's yours. We're having a baby. I'm six months along. There was no way to contact you.

I wanted to tell you in person."

My hand shook as I touched her stomach. "We're having a baby."

The dream was becoming reality. A child. Jasmine as my wife. It was all real.

An unknowing feeling of love toward someone I'd never met flowed through me. I was connected to this little person already, and I'd known about her for less than a minute. It was a girl. I knew it.

Sinking to my knees, I kissed her stomach where *our* child grew. Instead of causing death, I'd helped create a life. If my soul was too damaged, I knew I'd never be given the responsibility to be a father. Maybe this was the world telling me I deserved to be happy.

Jasmine's hands came out and touched my shaved head. "Yes, the last time we saw each other. I found out about two and half months ago. It's a girl."

"We're having a baby girl." I swallowed hard as I remembered the little girl in pigtails on the swing from my dream. I couldn't stop giving little kisses to her stomach. My rough palms caressed as I whispered to our daughter, "I love you, little girl, with my whole heart. I will love you and protect you, little one. Always."

Glancing up to Jasmine, a tear came down her face.

What if she isn't ready to have a baby? What if she isn't happy about this?

Standing, I cupped her face. "Are you okay with this?"

She sniffled. "I love the thought of having your child. I was worried you would think I cheated on you. I've been so nervous."

"Never, baby. This is a miracle. Our miracle."

Bringing Jasmine to me, I felt her soft body meld to mine.

I smiled against her lips as the baby bump touched my stomach.

I was going to be a dad.

“I’m going to take you to bed and make love to the mother of my child.”

“I want you, Bane.” As she spoke her breathy reply, I walked her back to the mattress.

From this moment on, I’d never be the same.

2

BANE

ON THE BED, I watched Jasmine sleep with her hair fanned out around her face. Peace. That was an odd feeling for me, but I had it. Finally. Through all the mayhem and destruction I caused in nearly every country of the world, I'd found a form of forgiveness through the child growing in Jasmine's stomach. I couldn't stop touching her.

Almost everyone I'd killed was a motherfucker. Knowing that was the only thing that kept me from completely losing myself to the darkness that tried to drown me.

In all the years I'd been part of the Black Division, I ended the life of five innocent people on accident. They were called casualties of war. I called it murder. That burden would be on me forever. The faces of the innocent haunted me when I closed my eyes. The motto of the agency—their deaths had been a sacrifice to the greater good. Bullshit. Everyone deserved a chance at life.

Those innocents had been someone's child and the regret of what I'd done hit me harder than before.

I am so sorry. So very sorry for the sins of my past. I will spend every day for the rest of my life trying to make up for it.

Whoever I mentally spoke to, I hoped they heard my promise.

Thinking back to the night I'd met Jasmine, I'd been at a bar drowning my sins away with alcohol. I'd killed my fifth innocent person and was on leave. Who would have thought that night would change my life forever?

For the next three weeks, I was off until my next assignment for who-the-hell-knows how long to some forsaken shithole. All I planned to do was drink, fuck, and sleep. Simple.

The bartender approached and I slid my glass to him. "Another one."

Bourbon, of any kind, was my drink of choice. As long as it was amber and got me fucked up—I didn't care. Numb was numb and that's all that mattered.

New York was a good place to take a three-week hiatus. The city never slept and there was pussy galore. The stool next to me moved and I glanced that way. I always wanted to know everything that was going on around me. It was part of who I was now. Outside of the Black Division, I was a ghost.

A beautiful blonde that I could fuck into next week, if given the chance, sat alternating glances between her watch and the door to the bar.

She looked my way. "Excuse me. Is this the original Finnegan's everyone talks about? I'm meeting my girlfriend here and she's late."

For all that was holy, she had the voice of a goddess that would sound amazing screaming my name while I fucked her into oblivion.

The bartender sat my glass down and took an order from the girl. She liked girlie cocktails as she ordered a Cosmo. I brought my glass up in salute to the girl with the mile-long legs beside me. "The one and only original Finnegan's."

Fuck, I had no clue, but it sounded good if that meant she would stay.

"Oh, good." The gorgeous girl let her shoulders relax. "I'm from Alaska, so this big city is a bit intimating."

I took a small sip of the liquid heaven. "What brought you to New York?"

"I've always wanted to see the world. I've been saving up to come here for years. My friend from New Jersey is meeting me here to catch up while I'm in town."

Here was to hoping little Miss Alaska was at the wrong bar.

That first night we'd met there was no sex. Instead, I'd gotten her number and taken her on a proper date the following night. Shocked the hell out of me. I had to work five long days to get between her legs. The wait was worth it. The moment I sunk inside her for the first time, I was gone. Changed forever.

My life was perfect.

Sitting at the kitchen table, I sipped on my coffee while Jasmine finished eating the breakfast I'd cooked for her. I didn't care for breakfast. Maybe it was from all those years of waking up starving with my mom, only to be denied. I took another sip, letting the warmth of the liquid keep me from going to that dark, cold place called my childhood.

I loved seeing Jasmine's healthy appetite as she nourished our unborn child. Testing the waters, I threw a thought out there. "I thought we could look for a house today."

Watching her closely, she paused mid bite. "You want to buy a house together?"

It wasn't a no, and sounded hopeful. This was good. This was very good.

Not wanting to give her surprise away, I shrugged. "Yes. I figured it would be nice to have a place of our own, maybe get a dog."

Yeah, I was going for the whole fucking caboodle in this new life. I'd always wanted a dog. Jasmine's apartment was nice and felt homey, but I wanted us to have a home that stood by itself in its own yard. All my life I'd lived in apartments, hotels, or in some desolate place.

Thoughtfully, Jasmine rubbed her stomach. "You're not doing this because of the baby, are you?"

Scooting her chair out, I placed my hand on top of hers, touching her stomach while kneeling. She needed to hear and see my earnestness. "I promise. Baby or no baby, I wanted to get a house together. You'll see."

Quirking an eyebrow, I knew I slipped. Jasmine knew something was up, but I stood and gave her a quick kiss before taking my seat. To hide the slight curvature of my lips, I took another sip of coffee.

Biting her lower lip, she said, "I love the idea. It'll be nice to have a real home and family again."

Having Jasmine happy was all that matter. She'd lost her parents a few years back in a dog sledding accident. The dogs broke free when a bear came out of nowhere. The sled tumbled down the mountain with her parents still on it. They were found dead two days later. Up here in Alaska, it's beautiful but brutal. I knew how lonely she was, and it nearly killed her having to sell her parents' house. What was harder for Jasmine was seeing the new owners tear down the only place she thought of as home. Otherwise, I would have bought her parents' home for our place.

Taking her plate to the sink, Jasmine rinsed it and put it in the dishwasher. I couldn't take my eyes off her perfect body. I wanted her again and it hadn't been an hour. Fingers trailed along my shoulder. Jasmine leaned in and whispered, "I'm going to take a shower. I think there's room for two."

Seeing that ass sashay out of the room, I bounded out of my seat. Silently, I followed. My girl was as insatiable as I was. The shower curtain sounded as she got in. Quickly, I shucked my clothes and walked into the room as it steamed.

Pushing the shower curtain aside, Jasmine reached for the shampoo and glanced at me from over her shoulder, clearly pleased I'd followed her. "I thought you were going to stand me up."

I engulfed her in my arms. "I'll always be there for you."

After getting ready, we were in the car. Jasmine sat in the passenger seat, rubbing her stomach with her right hand while her left one settled on my leg. The early-afternoon sun was in the sky beginning its descent. Nights were long in Alaska during the winter months. The sign for *Fish Hook Road* was up ahead. I turned left and saw Jasmine look at me confused from the side. The driveway at the end of the street was where Jasmine's surprise awaited her.

"What are we doing here?" I didn't say a word as I parked in the driveway. Jasmine continued to talk. "Oh, Bane, I love this house. It's not for sale, though." There was longing in her voice as she looked at the two-story home. When I'd been here before I left Black Division, she showed me around town; Jasmine pointed out this house as one she'd always loved. There was no denying the dreamlike tone she'd spoken with.

Trying to stay nonchalant, I said, "I know, but thought we might look around to get some ideas."

"That's a good idea."

The snow crunched beneath our boots as we made our way up to the pale-yellow house. The smell of smoke filled the air from nearby fireplaces. Our breaths came out in little puffs. Jasmine danced about in front of me as she made her way to the front porch. I wanted to stop her, but figured being a crazed, overprotective guy this early was not smart. Jasmine had been fine for nearly six months. *Six months.* I'd missed over half of the pregnancy. When we had another kid, I vowed to be part of everything.

Touching one of the front poles, Jasmine said, "I saw them painting this a couple of months ago. I think it's my favorite shade of yellow."

I touched the door handle and turned the knob. "Bane, we can't trespass."

Opening the door anyway, I shrugged. "We're not going to harm anything. Let's take a look around."

Jasmine still protested, but I walked in. The living room was as I'd imagined it. Glancing back at the door, my girl stood at the threshold.

"Bane, it's wrong."

With a devilish grin on my face, I prowled toward her.

"Bane, no—" I ignored her and picked her up as she chortled. "You always get want you want, don't you?"

"Yes, because I got you." Jasmine gave me that soft look, filled with love, as her hand touched my cheek.

The builders followed the specs I provided perfectly. The

floor plan had been opened up. Bright colors were on the walls.

In my arms, Jasmine gasped when she looked from me to the sign on the wall.

WELCOME TO YOUR NEW HOME,
JASMINE!

"Bane, this is ours?" Her voice was unbelieving. "You bought us my favorite house and had it redone?"

I could tell she was beginning to get excited as the reality sunk in.

"I did. For you, me, and now our little girl. Do you like it?"

Glossy eyes looked at me, on the verge of tears. "It's incredible." She kissed me. "I love you. I love you so much. We're going to be so happy together."

This was all I needed. Ever. "Let me show you what they did in the bedroom."

Bane is available now
at your favorite online book retailer.

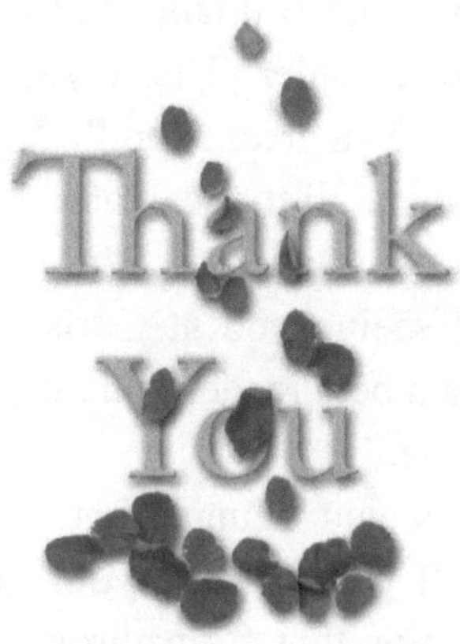

Paul – You are the love of my life. My happily ever after. Thank you for all your support in making my dreams a reality. I love you infinity factorial.

Makaela – I treasure each and every day we spend together telling stories, playing princesses, cuddling as we watch movies, and all the silly things we do throughout the day. Your love of stories makes my heart soar. I love you. I love you more. I love you the most.

Gehrig, Janet, Kathy, and Tim – Thank you all for all your unconditional love and support. I'm lucky to have four incredible parents.

Kelly – I'd be lost without you! I love our daily talks and all the giggles. Thank you for Here's to many more Special K adventures!

The Thrillhammers – Thank you all for letting me use your awesome lyrics in *Domino Effect*. You guys are a fantastic band. It was an honor putting you in The Effect Series.

Nikola – The Spice Girls Band was put in just for you! I'd think it's safe to surmise that #BrantIsNikola's. Love ya, girl! Thank you for being the last set of eyes.

April – You are one brilliant photographer and a super duper awesome Alpha reader. Thank you for all your honest feedback and being such a great friend!

Maren – I miss you all the way across the ocean blue, but can't wait to see you this June! Oh, I'm so impressed with my little rhyme. Loved seeing you at Christmas. Miss you tons! Thank you for being a beta reader and all your feedback. Truly means the world to me.

Brandy – Thank you being a beta reader for me. Love your feedback. Can't wait to read your next book! It's truly amazing the friendships that form through this journey! Mad love for you.

Kathy – Thank you for all that you do for me, Kathy! The profile pics are amazing! I love the random messages you send me when you have a thought.

3 K's and a J – Ladies, you guys mean the world to me. Thank you for all that you do and your daily support. I love you infinity factorial!

Kristin's Korner – Where's my spoon? I think I need to stir something up in the Korner today for sure. Each and every one of you guys means the world to me. Thank you for making the Korner such a special place day in and day out. And… thank you for grandfathering me in for multiple book boy-friends.

Damien's Darkside Divas – I need another Diva Pass STAT!!! Love visiting the group. Thank you for everything you guys do for me. Love you all gobs and gobs and gobs!

Readers – Thank you for all your support through this journey and allowing me to share a piece of me with you. Each and every one of you mean the world to me. Thank you from the bottom of my heart!

Available Now

The Trust Series

Trust Me
Love Me
Promise Me
Full-length novels in the TRUST series are also available in audio.

The Effect Series

Ripple Effect (Book 1 of the Effect Series)
Domino Effect (Book 2 of the Effect Series)

Stand Alone Novels

Dissipate
Bane

Joint Collaborations

Predestined Hearts

Coming Soon

Innocence

To join my newsletter to for up-to-date information:
http://tinyurl.com/mcppuhn

www.ingramcontent.com/pod-product-compliance
Lightning Source LLC
Chambersburg PA
CBHW032134190626
46814CB00005BA/1690
9780989991391